SHADOWS IN THE SMOKE

First published in 2012 by M P Publishing Limited
6 Petaluma Blvd. North, Suite B6, Petaluma, CA 94952
12 Strathallan Crescent, Douglas, Isle of Man IM2 4NR

1 3 5 7 9 10 8 6 4 2

Cover Design by Tony Broadbent
Book Design by Maria Clare Smith

    Broadbent, Tony.
      Shadows in the Smoke : a creeping narrative / by Tony Broadbent.
      p. cm.
      ISBN 978-1-84982-156-8

     1. Burglars--Fiction. 2. London (England)--Fiction.
     3. Detective and mystery stories. 4. Spy stories.
     5. Historical fiction.   I. Title.

     PS3602.R54S53 2012
     813'.6
             QBI12-600076

A CPI Catalogue for this title is also available from the British Library

SHADOWS IN THE SMOKE

Tony Broadbent

MP Publishing
WWW.MPPUBLISHINGUSA.COM

ALSO BY TONY BROADBENT

THE SMOKE

SPECTRES IN THE SMOKE

Visit: www.tonybroadbent.com

This one's for my brother, Seth.
And all my 'old chinas' – the world over
– they know who they are.
"Inspirations, still."

And in memory of dear departed friends:
Joe Nessler - a real pearl of a man
& 'Missy' Isgur - a lustrous pearl of a woman.

ACKNOWLEDGMENTS

Amidst all the unexpected tumult and turmoil there are always one or two bright lights to help you navigate through the fog. Heartfelt thanks to my wife, Christine, and my brother, Seth. Thanks to stalwarts: Kirk Russell; Barry and Mary Tomalin; Jacqueline Winspear; John Morell; Adrian Muller; Doug Lang; Chris Haigh.

Many thanks to my agent, Amy Rennert; a true North Star.

Thanks to Guy Intoci; editor and newly found 'old china.'

Thanks to D. P. Lyle, forensic guru.

I'd like to acknowledge my on-going debt to: the many works of James Morton, Robert Murphy, and Peter Hennessy; Donald Thomas for An Underworld at War and Villain's Paradise; David Kynaston for Austerity Britain; John Gosling for Ghost Squad.

A special thanks, too, to all those readers, booksellers, and librarians who ventured into The Smoke, without whom…

Thanks also to 'the Angel in the Hawaiian shirt' and 'James Grant' and 'Otto' and 'The Bee's Knees' for their generous support, without which…

CONTENTS

A QUIET WORD BEFORE THE CURTAIN GOES UP

Whoever it was that said "April is the cruellest month" must've had that September in mind. The cost of a loaf of bread went way up, the milk ration was cut to two pints per person per week, they devalued the pound by a third, and it was widely reported that the Soviets had just gone and tested an atomic bomb of their very own.

Reason enough for some people to think that rainy day so often talked about had arrived with a bang, despite the fact that much of Britain was still sweltering under a record ninety-degree summer heat wave. Even the thought of a nice Sunday drive to the seaside was out of the question though for all but the very wealthy or very well connected, as petrol was still very tightly rationed. And if that wasn't enough for Britain's austerity-weary great unwashed to contend with, soap was still on ration, as was fresh meat of any description. So it was a pound to a penny that anyone you came across who smelled nice or who looked a tiny bit plump had somehow managed to get their little black-market hands on more than their officially allotted share.

The only good thing you could say about that September was that it was the only month for months there hadn't been a dock strike, the threat of a dock strike, or the need for troops to be called in to help sort out the mess—yet again—at either the London or Liverpool docks; one unsavoury incident having caused more than the troops to feel a little mutinous when it became widely known that striking dockers had walked off the job and left over six thousand tons of Argentinean meat to rot in a ship's cargo hold.

Was it any wonder life's little luxuries, be it bed-sheets, women's nylons, tins of peaches, or bottles of Camp coffee—let alone bottles of Whisky or French perfume—had the scarcity value of the Crown Jewels? All of which meant that everyone was 'at it' one way or another. All that was needed was that "you knew a man who knew a man that knew a man" who could get hold of whatever it was you wanted, no coupons necessary, no questions asked; all for a price, of course. So crime couldn't help but pay and pay very well, too.

But that was London for you. 'The Smoke' was still pockmarked with broken abandoned buildings and bombsites and was as drab and as grim and as grey as ever it'd been in Victorian times. It was a world fueled by coal and driven by steam, where market vendors, rag-and-bone men, milkmen and coalmen still trundled the streets in horses and carts. And even Mr. Charles Dickens —dead nigh on a hundred years—would've still recognised much of what he himself had helped immortalise.

I don't want to paint too dark a picture though, as there had been one or two cheery events in Britain's post-war New Jerusalem. For starters, after eight long threadbare years of government-mandated "Make Do and Mend," clothing had finally come off rationing midway through March. (They had to do something to help pacify the ladies or there'd be more than hell to pay.) And even April had had its bright spot when the neon lights of Piccadilly Circus were switched back on after more than ten years of darkness—an event soon followed by miles of glittering lights along the 'sea-fronts' down in Brighton and up in Blackpool.

In the wider world, April had also seen the birth of the North Atlantic Treaty Organisation—NATO, for short—a military alliance signed into being by the United States, Canada, and thirteen European nations proclaiming that an armed attack against one or more of them would be considered an attack against all of them. An event that no doubt did a lot to bring the · Berlin Airlift to a close in the second week of May, the Russians finally lifting their blockade after three hundred and twenty-two days of non-stop relief flights by the Western powers. Mind you, as was mentioned earlier, the Soviet's newfound ability to grow mushroom clouds soon overshadowed any idea that a brave new world was on the horizon.

And all that before me even mentioning the troubles that beset me— humble London cat burglar that I am—towards the arse-end of that year. Troubles, which not in single spies but in battalions came marching, with each and every bastard one looking to put the boot in right up to the knee, a never-ending cascade of horrible people and events that all but proved the death of me. And, yea, though verily, I did indeed walk through the backstreets and alleyways of the shadow of death, there were—thank God—just enough staunch souls willing to hold out a helping hand, despite the awful danger to themselves. And if there is a definition of good fortune, surely the right person stepping into your life at the exact moment you need them to is it.

The hard truth is you're born into the world all alone and you exit it all alone and if anyone gives 'a tuppence for you' as you march along life's highway, then you can count yourself very lucky, very lucky indeed. For if, as is so often said, a trouble shared is a trouble halved, then a whole boatload of troubles shared is…well I'm sure you get my drift.

That's what this caper's all about, anyway: 'Who and what doesn't kill you, only makes your will to live and let die all the stronger.'

BUTCHER'S HOOK

So there I was, almost at the end of my rope, hanging like a prized leg of mutton stuck up on a butcher's hook, hardly daring to breathe lest it steam in the cold night air, my eyes two big round saucers pooling any and all available light from the darkness that encloaked me.

I'd heard him a split second before his shadow had emerged from out of the murky gloom below and faster than thought I'd turned into stone. Then I'd watched him climb the main stack-pipe with all the nimbleness of a steeplejack; a slow, slow, quick, quick, slow waltz of a movement that barely disturbed the soot on the stack-pipe's brackets. The easy, fluid motions of someone atop their game.

The mystery 'midnight plumber' made for a bend in the pipe that angled up towards the main bathroom window and unclipped his climbing belt with all the aplomb of someone removing an old cardigan. He pulled himself up onto the tiny sliver of ledge and anchored himself by jamming his body against three sides of the metal-framed window. His glasscutter already to hand, he stopped dead when he noticed the tiny top window was partially ajar, just as I'd done not fifteen minutes earlier. And, no, I hadn't believed my luck either, but you'd be amazed how lax people can be when they live higher than the third floor. The tiny window had been open but a fraction, but that's all any burglar ever needs and, for neatness sake, I'd left everything just as I'd found it. It was then as easy as pie for the bloke to open the large bathroom window. And seeing the shadow fold in through the opening with all the grace of an acrobat, it was as if I was watching an understudy play the role I'd very much made my own.

"Hard luck, sunshine," I whispered. "It's the early cat that catches the tom." It did set me wondering, though, how I could've missed someone else scoping out the place. I'd been my usual very thorough self. I'd sketched my way around the area and produced a few nice pen and ink drawings and one or two acceptable watercolours. I'd done a Harrods wrong-parcel delivery so I could check out the foyer manned by a commissionaire in full uniform by day and an ex-copper in a jacket and tie by night. I'd even returned in the guise of a plumber so I could get a close look at the tradesman's entrance at the rear. On top of which, I'd kept an eye on the building from nearby rooftops every night for over a week. Then, eyes firmly on the prize, I'd bided my time and waited for the very posh event that would have the very posh couple that owned the flat all dressed up to the nines and out on the town.

It was one of those ultra modern buildings that went up round London in the Thirties. In this particular case, an all-white stuccoed apartment block in South Kensington that resembled nothing so much, according to a copy of *Architects Journal* I'd eyeballed in Marylebone Public Library, as the superstructure of an ocean-going liner. Run neon lights up the front of it and it could've been mistaken for an Odeon picture house; which is to say, it was too flat-fronted and austere for my taste, there was nothing you could really get a grip on. The handkerchief-sized squares of green lawn, concrete paving, and brutally sculptured hedging that lined the front and two sides of the building only added to the cold aloofness of it all. I was very pleased though that the architect had thought to tuck the stairwells, lift shaft, kitchens, bathrooms, and all attendant pipes and paraphernalia round the back so as not to spoil the overall look and had then painted the whole lot a dull grey so that everything disappeared, as it were. Even the ramp down to the garage in the basement and the ramp that led to the service yard at the rear were hidden away behind high white-painted concrete walls. Stage design, it's called in some circles.

But it wasn't the architecture that'd pulled me to Meridian Mansions; it was a magnificent suite of jewellery. True, all the pieces in question were contemporary settings of the sort a Sotheby's catalogue would describe as "being in the Modern style" and, again, not exactly my cup of tea, but they were arguably some of Cartier's finest work. The centrepiece was an exquisite necklace consisting of a number of large brilliant-cut and table-cut diamonds set off by a pear-shaped emerald pendant worth a maharaja's fleet of gold-plated Rolls-Royces if it was worth a penny, and that *was* very much to my liking. When I'd first caught sight of the sparklers in a photo-spread in *The Lady*, then again in *The Sketch*, I'd feasted my eyes on the blessed things as hungrily as someone with an empty belly might eye a butcher's tray loaded with black-market cuts of meat.

Not that I needed the money, but being by trade cat burglar and jewel thief to London's idle rich I had to see if I still had the bottle to pull off a really top-floor creeping job or not. And the plain, unvarnished truth was I'd been out of the game, proper, for a good year or more, due to events entirely beyond my control. When, not to put too fine a point on it, a certain someone had my family jewels trapped between a giant pair of nutcrackers—blackmail is such an ugly word—and had forced me into dangerous deeds I wouldn't have been caught dead doing under normal circumstances. Then, having survived it all only by the tiniest hair of my chinny-chin-chin I, of course, wanted to put the whole sorry story behind me as quickly and as firmly as possible. Which is why, as soon as I got myself back on the right side of the looking-glass, as it were, I immediately set up a nice little caper to try get my life back into some proper balance.

Still, it wasn't often I stumbled across another creeper on a job. I was always very careful about avoiding such occurrences. It did happen, of course, as there's always competition at all levels of the burglary business, but that's why I spent so much time planning a caper and never ever went in for the obvious—certainly never anywhere fools might rush in. Me, I'd learned to wait in the wings with the angels, much the safer course. Error only ever landed you in the dock down at the Old Bailey, and I can face a lot of things—and have done—but not incarceration.

I've always hated being walled-in. As a kid, I found London to be nothing but a cold, dank, grim, grey prison. And I'm no steamer—I'll take clear blue open skies or crisp clear star-filled nights over prison bars, real or imaginary, any day of the week. Was it any wonder I got myself out of the Smoke and off and away to sea at the very first opportunity? The very thought of endless horizons and countless new worlds to plunder had me fizzed up and fit to burst, a cork ready to be shot from the bottle.

The soft squeak of the bathroom window being pulled-shut rose up from below like a feint wisp of smoke and I blinked myself into motion and quickly climbed hand over hand back up to the roof. I peered down over the edge again and carefully retrieved my black silk rope before raising my head and sniffing the cold night air. I smiled and gave my black canvas jewel satchel a reassuring little pat. "High time we were safe off home, my lovelies," I whispered.

Then I became as a shadow, faded back into the night, and was gone.

SOILED LINENS

Shaved to perfection and raring to go, I took the stairs two at a time back up to street level and stood there eyeing the traffic and rubbing my fingers over my chin. And very nice and smooth it felt, too. Breakfast done, after a successful night's caper, there's nothing beats a late morning visit to the barbershop down Edgware Road Underground station. A hot towel and a close shave, followed, if possible, by a long leisurely visit to the local Turkish baths for a steam and a massage, and I tell you anyone this side of ninety-nine would feel like a new man again.

"*StarnewStandard*. Read all about it. Get yer *Star, News, Standard*, here." Binnsy, who had the pitch on the corner, sounded more agitated than was normal for the arrival of the midday editions of London's three evening papers, and I turned to see what all the palaver was about. Even so, I had to look twice at the headlines inked on the news-boards leaning up against the ox-blood red-tiled walls of the Tube station. 'MP DEAD IN FALL.'

I snatched up copies of all three papers and gave each front-page a quick butcher's. The news was no cause for sweat, but it certainly had all thoughts of Harrow Road Turkish baths washed right out of mind, along with any thoughts the Meridian Mansions caper was over and done with. "Buggeration," I said to myself.

"Hat-trick of aper-pays, Jeffro? Classifieds, is it?" Binnsy—so called by all the locals because of the half-inch-thick spectacles he wore—gave me a very squinty-eyed look. "After anything special, are yer? 'Cos if…"

"Nah, just putting a few extra coppers your way, seeing as how you won't take charity." I gave him a threepenny-bit.

"Gertcher!" he said, his mouth twisted into a half-smile, half-scowl.

He nodded, I nodded, but it'd been enough to deflect an ever-inquisitive nose. Thing was, whatever 'a face'—past, present or up and coming—did or said or showed any interest in, anywhere in the Smoke, was always news to someone's ears, and I needed somewhere where I could sit and think without being spied upon. "Dunno about you, but I could murder a cuppa," I said. "See you, Binnsy."

"Not if I sees yer first, Jeffro," he called after me, but I was already across Edgware Road, headed for an out-of-the-way cafe not a truncheon's throw from Paddington Green police station.

Bishop's Bridge cafe catered to the general public on their way to or from Paddington railway station, but as it was also the unofficial canteen for the local CID, it was also the only place within spitting distance where all the usual wall-to-wall eyes and ears weren't always noting down your every move. Coppers' narks wouldn't go near the place, as it'd all too easily mark them out for what they really were. So 'the Bridge,' as it was known locally, suited my needs perfectly.

Apart from two plainclothes detective constables, who I knew only by sight, sitting at separate tables, their heads stuck in their newspapers, and a middle-aged couple and a young soldier in khaki reading the menu on the wall, there were four blokes chin-deep in conversation. Even with the railways now nationalised, three of the four men still had brown-striped Great Western Railway waistcoats on under their jackets— waiters from off the 'Pullman' restaurant cars, by the look of them, and each one as oily as they come. I wondered whether the bloke in dark suit and tie sitting with them was Transport Police. But I just kept my eyes to myself, ordered some tea and a bacon sandwich and, tea mug in hand, took a table at the back.

I sat down, pulled out a packet of fags and lit up, letting the blue smoke curl around me until I disappeared into the grease-stained walls. Then I started in on the *Evening Standard*, did the *News*, then *The Star*. There weren't too many details as it turned out, just eight or nine different ways of saying that an unnamed Member of Parliament had died from an apparent accidental fall from off the balcony of his apartment. It seemed the authorities were withholding further details until the dead man's next of kin could be informed, but all three newspapers had skirted legalities, if not niceties, by showing a photograph of the street on which a very modern-looking, all-white building stood out from its neighbours like a new Dior dress in a shop window full of drab utility fashions.

Odd thing, there was no mention anywhere that a fortune in jewellery had gone missing from the dead man's flat. That was food for thought. Just maybe it was someone else who'd died—a different bloke, a different balcony, a different flat; head bashed-in from a fall like that, it'd be hard to say. Maybe it was all just a nasty coincidence.

I sipped my tea.

No, it was odds on that the bloke who'd died and the man whose flat I'd burgled were one and the same. If I'd been able to find out without too much trouble that the late Nigel Fox MP had resided at Meridian Mansions when "up in town," then so could any newspaper reporter with half a brain.

The woman behind the counter yelled "bacon sandwich!" and I stubbed out my fag and went up and got my food and a refill of tea, returned to the table and continued to chew things over. "Stupid sod," I said, my mouth full. Whether or not the tom I'd nicked had had anything to do with it or not, nothing's ever worth throwing yourself out a window for, not a king's ransom in diamonds, not even all the emeralds, rubies, and pearls in a maharaja's hat.

I lit up another fag and peered unseeing into the curls of blue smoke. The one question that wouldn't go away was why there'd been no mention at all of the missing jewellery. And the only answer I could come up with was that no one knew about it yet, which said the other burglar had been as neat as me in his dealings and had closed the wall safe again once he'd discovered there was no jewellery inside. I mean, he wouldn't have had any reason to think someone had nicked the stuff mere moments before; he'd have just put it down to faulty information. It happens. Or maybe the MP had closed the safe himself once he'd discovered his wife's jewellery had been pinched. People do that when confronted by disappointment or disaster; they just sweep the problem under the carpet and pretend it's not there until such time as they can come back and deal with it, if ever.

Maybe that was it. The wall-safe still held its empty secret. Only time would tell. I stubbed out the remains of my fag and watched the smoke disappear into thin air.

I polished off the bacon sandwich, crusts and all, got myself a third mug of tea, turned to the listings of dogs running at White City, pulled a stub of pencil from my pocket and started ticking off likely winners. It wasn't long though before I found myself scribbling ever-smaller spirals in the margins of the *Standard*. I tried to focus, but it wasn't a pack of greyhounds hurtling after a mechanical rabbit that I saw in my mind's eye— it was the body of a man of wealth and power, supposedly with everything to live for, falling to earth like a big sack of spuds.

"Stupid sod," I muttered into my empty tea mug. But it started me thinking again and I jotted down some figures in the margin of the page. The numbers wouldn't have meant much to anyone else, but as indicators of form they were as good as any of the statistics listed on the sports pages. I work to the clock during a caper. I put start and finish times, and filled in all the points in-between: getting inside the place, the business with the safe, me exiting, me hanging on for the other burglar to do his stuff, me up across the roof and back down again, me getting back to the lock-up.

I tapped my fingers up and down on the red chequered oilcloth. A death connected to any caper—especially burglary—was always a bit of a sod, as any missing jewellery was so marked and became that much more difficult to fence on or even to have re-cut and re-polished. Whatever the game, anything out of the ordinary always reduces the profit.

I folded the newspaper and stretched my arms. Only then did I happen to read the 'Stop Press' on the back-page. Seems a waiter on the Bristol to Paddington express had been found decapitated on the main lines just this side of Ealing Broadway early that very morning. Enquiries into the tragic accident were still in the early stages, and once again the name of the deceased would be released when his next of kin had been informed.

I looked up. The two CID constables had finished and gone, their tables already cleared and cleaned, as had the table of Pullman waiters who were no doubt being interviewed about the very same incident by a London Transport Police detective. The young soldier was still there though, his mum silently crying, his dad staring at the half-empty plates on the table.

Goodbyes and departures are never easy.

I was suddenly struck by a particularly nasty thought. Had someone tried to mix it? Seen me setting up the caper, recognised me and then queered the pitch to make me the fall guy for another job? I blinked. No, I'd have sensed me being watched, I was sure of that. Next question. Had I done anything in the flat that could implicate me? Left anything behind? I blinked again. No. I'd worn turtles from start to finish, so there were definitely no fingerprints anywhere. There were no missing buttons on my creeping kit, no rips or snags or tears. I'd already gotten rid of my crepe-soled plimsolls as they were bound to have left tread-patterns, however feint, on the roof and window ledge and inside the flat. My old Austin taxi had false number-plates on, as well as a false cab license number.

I'd got back to the lock-up in Paddington Basin well before my self-imposed 2:00 am deadline for having the cab off the streets. On paper it'd all gone like clockwork and, apart from the bloke who'd died and the now blood-tainted jewellery, it was as clean a creep as ever I'd done.

"You stupid, stupid sod," I muttered. "Why on earth did you have to go and cock everything up by throwing yourself off the bloody balcony?"

I can't honestly say that's when I first started looking for answers, but I think I must've sat there and continued scribbling ever-decreasing spirals all over the back page of the *Evening Standard* for a good ten minutes or more.

NEWS ON THE WIRELESS

I was in the middle of having a wash and brush up and almost missed it for all the noise I was making towelling myself dry. It was the first item on the Six O'Clock News on the BBC Home Service. The authorities had just released the name of the MP who'd fallen to his death in the early hours of that morning. There was no doubt about it anymore. As the official Government statement said, "*It was a needless and tragic event that had profoundly shocked everyone in Westminster and Whitehall.*" The newscaster added that the MP's untimely death had already drawn forth an outpouring of messages of sympathy from all levels of society and that the late MP's wife was still in deep shock and in seclusion in the country. The kicker, though, was that the Metropolitan Police were eager to interview anyone that'd been in the vicinity of the dead man's flat between the hours of 8:00 pm the previous night and 6:00 am that morning so people could be eliminated from their enquiries. I stood there, lost in thought. The statement by Scotland Yard meant only one thing: The police had finally discovered that a magnificent suite of jewellery worth a prince's ransom had also gone missing from the flat. Had to be.

I stared out across the rooftops into the darkening night and got a sudden case of the itches. In the end, I shrugged it off and put it down to the increasing chill in the night air. Even so, I went and closed all the curtains in the flat, as if to shut out all thoughts of the dead MP. Daft, I know, as bad things happen on the best of creeps. I threw my clothes on, grabbed hold of an hat and coat, tucked a little plywood box under my arm, slipped down the stairs, and headed round to Ray Karmin's house.

Quick word about Ray Karmin, as it touches upon a lot of what follows. Ray was my very best china and my one and only fence, and I trusted him as I trusted no one else. It was to him and only him that I took whatever tom I'd half-inched and it'd worked that way, seamlessly, since well before the War, when under his ever-watchful eye I'd become one of the very best cat burglars in the business. I was a cocky young tearaway with ideas well above my station when I first met him. I'd been doing all right for myself, but truth be told the odds were I was well on the way to a stint of Borstal, followed by a life of increasingly lengthy prison terms. But Ray being Ray, he'd looked beyond that and extended a big, firm hand down into the gutter, knocked some sense into my skull and shown me the ways of the world, including how to keep out of the reach of the long arm of the law and, as the saying goes, I'd never looked back.

To his immediate neighbours, Raymond L. Karmin, Esq. was, as he appeared, a quietly spoken, scholarly Jewish gentleman known to frequent the Reading Room down the British Museum. Word round the local pub was that he was an author compiling a history of the Hatton Garden diamond trade, which not only helped explain the bespoke cut of his clothes, but the cut of some of the people that were sometimes seen to visit him. How the rumour had got started was anybody's guess, though I put it down to a briefcase full of typewritten notes Ray had left in the saloon bar accidentally on purpose. As Ray always said, it's best to let people find things out for themselves; they're far more likely to believe them. In similar fashion, his neighbours had long since put down my weekly visits to his drum to a flyblown hand-written postcard still on display in a nearby newsagent's window. It said, simply: 'Keen chess player looking to find same.' A torn bit of lined paper with the words 'Game in Progress' scrawled on it had been pinned to the card almost from the day it'd gone up, so no one else had ever bothered to respond to it. The art of dis-information, it's called in certain circles. And very handy, too, as going round Ray's house for a game of chess was the perfect cover for me to fence off whatever jewellery I'd acquired.

Thing was, Ray took the art of deception further than anyone could've ever imagined. Monday through Thursday, Ray was all-things Ray. But on Fridays, Saturdays and Sundays, he turned into a different bloke altogether, the infamous "Buggy" Billy, a Cockney costermonger of fearsome voice and reputation—*The Undisputed King of Bug Powder, from Church Street to Petticoat Lane and the Kingsland Waste.* And while Raymond L. Karmin lived in a house on one street, "Buggy" Billy lived in the adjoining house the next street over. And whereas Mr Karmin was always all things bespoke, Mr "Buggy" Billy was never ever seen out of his scraggy fur-collared long black coat, spotted silk scarf, and bowler hat. Stand the two characters back-to-back, like their houses, and you'd have been hard pressed to see any similarity at all. As far as I know, no one round Edgware Road and Lisson Grove ever twigged the two were one and the same person. And hard-eyed Londoners as all were round those parts, there wasn't much you could ever put over any of them.

It was from Ray I first got the idea of living a double life. Hiding in plain sight, he called it. Under his expert tutelage I'd learned how to pass unnoticed and unseen by day and by night, and gone on to improve my creeping skills in leaps and bounds. "A proper education properly applied can take you anywhere," he told me. "It's only a lack of imagination or self-doubt that'll ever stop you." And with that inwardly digested, it wasn't long before I'd managed to put enough aside to pay for a berth at the Seamen's College in Southampton, where I'd buckled down like a good 'un and soon made good my dream of getting out of the Smoke and off to sea.

Who'd ever suspect a young Cunard deck-officer of being a cat burglar? No one ever caught on in any of the ports I'd sailed into, that's for sure. And with the new me, all suitably polished and poised, I did very nicely for a few years, pinching diamonds from New York to Hong Kong.

Until, that was, the War started up in earnest.

Afterwards, having survived everything Adolf Hitler and his gang could throw at me and the ships I was on, I told everyone around town I'd given up the creeping lark and taken up as a jobbing stage-hand round London's theatres and music halls instead. People just shook their heads and put it down to me having lost my nerve. It was well known I'd had a couple of convoy ships sunk from under me, so no one thought I was soft or anything, simply that I'd lost my bottle for the more demanding aspects of the creeping business. Truth was, though, all the work on the theatre fly-floor with ropes and pulleys and counterweights kept me fit and my eye in for going up and down walls in inventive ways. Of course, being able to watch actors like John Gielgud, Laurence Olivier, and Ralph Richardson doing the business down on stage, night after night, helped no end whenever I had occasion to act like someone else. In a country where a person's always defined by the details of his clothes, his voice, and manners, there were no better teachers.

The only other significant thing I need tell you, is that whereas "Buggy" and me were known to be as thick as thieves, other than for our Monday night chess games, Ray and me tried never to be seen out together unless we were in disguise. There was no reason for me to push our luck, but it being a Monday, there I was standing outside Mr Raymond L. Karmin's house in my overcoat and hat, holding a plywood box with a picture of a chess-piece on its lid.

The front door opened within seconds of me knocking.

"I reckoned you'd be early," Ray said as he closed and re-bolted the door. He stood there shaking his head in the half-light of the hallway. "I had a funny feeling it was him."

"You heard, then?"

"Six O'Clock News," he said, "but I got wind of it earlier, front page of *The Star*." He glanced at the little plywood box, then back at me. "For God's sake, don't tell me you did his place last night."

I nodded. "Saturday night was a complete wash-out, Ray. They stayed at the Savoy, never even went near the Mansions. Then Sunday morning, she took the train back up to the Midlands and he went on to the flat. I kept an eye on the place during the day, saw me chance, and did the caper last night."

Ray turned back down the hallway. "You better come on through to the kitchen. The untold delights of me thrashing you at chess will have to wait. I'll put the kettle on. This calls for a family conference. God's holy trousers, the stupid sod throwing himself off the balcony like that, what was he thinking?"

"Yes," I said, "that's what I said, when I heard."

He filled the kettle, lit the gas, and busied himself with the tea caddy, sugar bowl, and teacups. I stayed stumm. He glanced over his shoulder. "The Yard already wanting to interview anyone who was in the vicinity last night, says something's up. See anything out the ordinary?"

"Not if you don't count me seeing another burglar coming up the main stack-pipe just as I was making good my exit."

Ray's eyes narrowed just as the kettle started whistling. He pursed his lips, in thought, turned, and took the kettle off the stove and did the business with the teapot. "Don't believe in coincidences, Jethro," he said, over his shoulder. "Was it a mix, do you think?"

"I had the same nasty thought; somebody spots me setting up the caper, takes the opportunity to put me in the frame for something worse. Only question then, Ray, is who'd want to fit me up? I'm a nobody as far as most people are concerned, just another 'face' from the past, all my bottle gone. And, believe you me, seeing as it was my first time back on the lids by my own hand for seems like years, I was doubly cautious about everything. I'd have sensed anything out of the ordinary, I know I would."

"Let's hope you're right, Jethro, for both our sakes." Ray scoured his throat and bent forward and spat into the sink, then made a warding gesture with two fingers of his right hand. "That's to help ward off any evil eye." He turned and leaned back against the sink. "So tell me about this other climber you said you saw."

"Bloke used a steeplejack's harness. Sort of reminded me of our old chum. I knew it couldn't possibly be him though, as he's still in prison, but it was as good as ever I've seen it done, poetry in motion."

Ray nodded and ran his tongue back and forth across his teeth. He nodded again as he poured the tea, then the milk, and placed both cups on the kitchen table. Then he heaped so much sugar into his cup I thought he'd forgotten what he was doing. "It helps my brain think," he said as he stirred the teaspoon round and round his cup with overly precise movements. Then he tapped off the drops and placed the spoon down in the saucer with a deliberate snap. He took a long swig of tea and peered at me from over the rim of his cup. "You better go over exactly what happened, Jethro, just as it happened, and don't leave out any details, not a single one."

So I took a sip of tea, cast my mind back to the Saturday just past and gave him chapter and verse on the Meridian Mansions caper.

'PLAN B'

And what I told Ray was this:

"As planned, I took out the old Austin 'growler', a steamer trunk strapped in the luggage compartment, flag down to show me and the cab were unavailable. And I was outside Euston Station early Saturday afternoon when Fox's silver-blue Alvis drophead coupe drove up. He waited at the ticket barrier for his wife's train to arrive, a bunch or red roses in one hand and a lady's brown leather hatbox in the other, and they greeted one another with all the usual displays of affection. A porter loaded her two matching brown crocodile leather suitcases into the boot of the Alvis and I tailed them all the way down to the Savoy Hotel.

"I'd expected they'd go straight to Meridian Mansions, just like they'd done the two previous occasions she'd come up to town for the weekend. Difference being, Saturday night, he was guest speaker at the Police Federation dinner at the Guildhall. And what with the Home Secretary and all the other 'big-wigs' being there, I might've known the two of them would do the night in style, especially after all the brouhaha in the linens about him and the speech he was expected to make.

"Come evening, there they were outside the Savoy just stepping into the back of a Daimler; she, looking lovely in posh fur, gown and exquisite diamonds; him, in full black-tie. I followed them to the dinner, waited, and then followed them back to the Savoy. Half the reporters from Fleet Street were camped outside, so I knocked it on the head for the night. But I was back on the Strand come morning—different get-up, different set of cases in the luggage compartment. I waited until the Alvis appeared and followed them. My one concern was they'd drive to their place up North so he could fulfil his constituency duties on the Monday, but he made for Euston Station. I followed them inside, watched her train leave, and saw him walk back down the platform carrying her leather hatbox. So I reckoned the caper was on again and beetled back to the cab, sharpish."

Ray nodded in agreement.

Thing is, you see, Saturday and Sunday nights were champion for a cat burglar. Most society women had learned the hard way it was far safer to keep their better jewellery in the vaults of a nearby bank. The lady in question then retrieved her trinkets from the bank the day of or the day before whatever 'big do' it was she was attending. Only problem then was that the only protection immediately to hand for her precious jewellery until Monday morning was the humble in-home in-wall safe. It was the sole reason all the bigger jewel robberies—stuff nicked from houses and flats as opposed to stones half-inched from jewellers' shop—were determined by the calendar of major social events; the timetables of which were pored over as avidly by the Smoke's better burglars, as they were by Society's better hostesses.

"The way I reckoned it, Ray, the Cartier jewellery was inside the brown crocodile hatbox and destined for the wall-safe back at their flat, in which case it was already as good as mine. So I followed the Alvis to Meridian Mansions and saw it disappear down the ramp to the building's belowground garage. I waited until dark and then nipped back to the lock-up for a quick wash and brush up, a sandwich, and a change of clothes.

"I returned to the Mansions and saw the lights were still on in his flat. Then I noticed a big black motorcar waiting outside.

So I drove past and parked. A few minutes later the motor purred on by, with Fox sitting in the back. Lights in the flats above and below his stayed on until just gone eleven.

"I knew the layout, as the week before I pretended to be a plumber called there on an urgent job. The building manager gave me a right bollocking for having the gall to come in through the front door, but after I'd apologised profusely for my mistake, he calmed down enough to show me the proper tradesman's entrance, which just happened to be the rear service door and fire exit. So of course I accidently managed to drop my entire bag of tools all over the floor. And by the time I'd finished apologising again and picking everything up, even sweeping the floor, I had a dirt plug and metal plate inserted into the jamb to prevent the rear push-door's vertical bolt from fully-pushing home. Later, I went back in the dead of night, did a proper job of it, and wired the door alarm so I could short it out whenever I needed to.

"Rear door to the service stairs got me in and up, but other than blowing it off its hinges there was no way to open the inner push-door to the seventh floor, so I went out a window and up and onto the roof, down the back of the building and in through a bathroom window. Wall safe was key not combination and I picked it clean and bagged the jewellery. Then I was back out the window, back up to the roof and gone. So apart from those few minutes, hanging round while the other creeper climbed up the soil-pipe and got in through the bathroom window, I was in and out of the place in around fifteen minutes flat and back down and in the cab and off up the street in another ten. And apart from some nutcase in an ambulance almost smashing into the cab, it was pretty much a doddle. The rest you know."

When I'd finished, Ray just nodded, got up, and disappeared into the front parlour. He came back with a bottle of The Glenlivet and a couple of lead-cut crystal glasses. He poured us each a generous measure, poured water into his to open up the precious single malt, and then offered the little jug to me. But I shook my head. I had a sudden hankering to take everything neat.

He took a sip, nodded appreciatively, then unfolded a small square of black velvet. "Right," he said, "to business. Let's see what the cat's brought in this time."

I pushed the plywood box across the kitchen table and he slid back the top to reveal the chamois leather bag inside. "I haven't even had a peek since I slipped the lot into the bag at the Mansions," I said. "It's always nice to first see them again through your eyes. I tend to learn more that way."

"Nice weight," he said, his hand going in and out of the bag like someone playing 'Housey-Housey,' but it wasn't numbered wooden counters he produced each time, it was piece after piece of jewellery that even made me start swallowing again in anticipation. "So much better in the flesh," he said, carefully arranging each piece on the black-velvet square. He pulled out his loupe and examined each piece in turn. I, in turn, kept my peace; this was where Ray's expertise took Centre Stage. "Diamond necklace with emerald-cut pendant, double-strand bracelet, pair of drop-earrings, ring; all diamonds of the first water and all nicely matched and in very nice settings; about two hundred carats all told; and even though I know you don't appreciate anything too modern, lovely work through and through."

"I'm always open to new ideas if they lead to more money," I said.

"Yes, but Fox's death has thrown a huge bloody spanner in the works. Any death involving a VIP has got to be resolved and quickly, the powers-that-be daren't let it be otherwise, it throws too much light into places they'd rather keep good and dark. And the way the Yard has been playing it makes me want to be more than a mite cautious. For a start, there's been no mention anywhere of the missing jewellery and you can do the sums. Next, they want to interview someone seen in the vicinity prior to the suicide. Cause and effect are back to front. Which to my mind begs the question, was it suicide or wasn't it?" He paused and swirled the amber liquid round and around in his glass. "Made me go and dig out the Sunday papers again so I could read the speech Mr. Nigel Fox MP gave at the Guildhall. Seems he was the first public official to say what the rest of London witnesses every day: that the rise in crime since the end of the War has only been matched by the rise in police corruption. All the Sunday papers said the speech had put him in line for Shadow Home Secretary. Then, as you say, there he was: dead on the pavement come Monday morning." He took another sip of malt and looked at me over the rim of his glass. "And, as you well know, I don't believe in coincidences, as a matter of principle."

Ray put down his glass and slid the square of velvet to the centre of the table. The jewellery came alive with serried arrays of white, blue, and green fire. He picked up the diamond-studded emerald necklace. "Lovely jewellery. Really beautiful. I had plans to fence the whole lot off to a private collector in Chicago who'll pay top dollar for top-quality Art Deco, no questions asked. Even with them being such highly recognisable pieces, they could've gone out via Rotterdam, no problem." He put down the necklace. "Fox's suicide makes that all a bit too risky for now." He scratched his chin. "Acquiring tom to order is one thing, but blue blood on the loupe is quite another. It's as bad as killing a copper, stirs up a veritable hornet's nest, and we can't afford to have anything point back to us, not ever. You know what Hatton Garden's like. Anything outside an open-and-shut case that adversely affects the normal conducting of business is severely frowned upon and can get the causee of said disturbance shunned for life. It's the veritable kiss of death. And that's something we don't ever want happen."

Too true, Ray's word around Hatton Garden was *unquestioned* and that was priceless to us. It was the very cornerstone of our business arrangement, if not our entire world. "Whatever you say, Ray," I said.

"It'd be a pity to break up such a lovely suite of jewellery, but we will if we have to. We can hold off for now, but I reckon the safest bet is to have it disappear out of the Smoke as per the usual method. Agreed?"

I nodded. "Out of sight and deep down a mine."

DIRTY LINENS

Fleet Street started airing the dead MP's dirty washing in public on the Wednesday—three days being the usual allotted time for resurrection or immolation. The worst of the dirt being dug up just in time for the following Sunday's linens to have a field-day. Obsequies aside, it didn't do for the Tories' once "coming man" on Law and Order to have had any sort of questionable past, even though he'd been cold but a week and not yet buried. All of a sudden there was enough speculation swirling around the Smoke for pointed questions to be asked about everything he'd ever said or done and his motives challenged for any and every cause he'd ever championed. As a hatchet job it rivalled anything the underworld could've mustered in the flesh.

It was reported a suicide note had been found at the scene of the crime —suicide of course being a crime in England—the contents of which suggested moral turpitude and certain issues regarding "biographical leverage," or blackmail as it's more commonly called. Just a few lines typed on a piece of paper: *I would like to apologise for errors of judgement in personal behaviour and for the embarrassment it will undoubtedly cause, firstly to my wife and family, but also to my friends, my constituents, and my party.* Not much of a goodbye, but more than enough to suggest the MP had "taken his own life while the balance of his mind had been disturbed." How anyone outside Scotland Yard could've come by such details, no one bothered to ask.

Thing being, you can't libel the dead. You're free to pick over the bones until they're picked clean, especially when it comes to ascertaining motives for jumping from a seventh-storey balcony. So, naturally, speculation ran riot.

One story hinted that Fox was, secretly, a *name* unable to cover massive insurance losses at Lloyds in the City. Another, that he had huge gambling debts and that a shadowy underworld figure had both him and his markers in his pocket. One of the Sundays—you can guess which one—reported there was a secret mistress, possibly even a child, hidden away somewhere near Brighton. While one of the posher linens—its newsprint yellowing by the minute—hinted darkly at rumours that the MP had been unable to live with the shame of imminent exposure as a pederast. It didn't really matter if any of it was true or not. It never does. If enough mud gets slung, some of it's bound to stick. But so much mud was thrown into so many dark places so very quickly that even Ray was prompted to say that someone, somewhere, had to have orchestrated it.

I had a mad thought Colonel Walsingham, the gentleman from MI5 who'd had me under his thumb for most of the previous year, might be behind it all. I knew for a fact he possessed whole regiments of safes stacked full of blackmail-worthy material, any of which was more than enough to turn the blood of even the most eminent of men to water and their knees and principles to jelly. On reflection, though, I dismissed it out of hand. Not that for one minute I thought Walsingham incapable of doing anything that was called for in 'Defence of the Realm,' but as I'd learned from him first hand, the true power of blackmail was never having to use it. And muddying the water *post mortem*, so to speak, just didn't fit with what I knew of the man.

It wasn't until the following weekend's pile of ink-smudged Sunday linens that news of the missing suite of jewellery finally hit the headlines. A development Ray and I discussed over that Monday night's game of chess. We knew that news of the missing jewellery would come out eventually, but it was disconcerting that right out of the blue Scotland Yard was suddenly very interested in questioning a man who'd been seen in the area of Meridian Mansions. The description could've easily fitted at least half a dozen men in any pub in Soho.

Trouble was it also described me to a 'T'.

"All this 'man wanted for questioning' malarky gives me the itches, something chronic," I said.

Ray shook his head. "The inquest's still ongoing, so the law has to be seen to be doing something. Same with the Yard's all-points bulletin; it's all simply business as usual." To let some more air out of my worries, he suggested I go over events again in case I'd missed anything. And in between chess moves and sips of single malt, we tried to put a name to the other burglar I'd seen at Meridian Mansions, but neither of us could come up with one we could agree on.

That bloody itch of mine was always there, though, dying to be scratched. And it may've been the look on my face, but Ray gave me one of his looks and signalled for a break and poured us both another generous measure of The Glenlivet. "Funny how water poured from a nice little porcelain jug seems much purer than water straight from the tap," he said, chuckling. He trickled some water into his glass and sat there, eyeing the tiny swirls in the golden amber liquid. "It's this burglar with the harness that's in real trouble, Jethro, not you," he said. "Ever since yesterday's news about the missing jewellery, he's been turning the air blue, cursing whoever got to the wall-safe before he did. But that's about all he can do, curse you." I pulled a face, held up a pair of crossed-fingers to ward off evil, but didn't say anything. "And even then that's only if this mystery burglar set up the job himself. It's far more likely some big-cheese somewhere set it up and hired him to do the business. I'll bet a pound to a penny this Mr. Big now thinks he's been double-crossed and is looking to hand out some very serious retribution. Even so, that's no skin off your nose, you're well in the clear." He chuckled and leaned over and patted me on the shoulder. "So don't you worry, all we've got to do is just bide our time."

It's true, sometimes the best course of action is to sit back, do nothing, and see what develops. The whole 'man wanted for questioning' business was likely nothing more than a coincidence. So, what was my problem? What was my bloody problem?

Me and my bloody nose for trouble was the bloody problem. God gives you a sixth-sense and only a fool pays it no heed. Also, it wasn't at all like Ray to push 'itchy feelings' aside, his or mine. After all, it was from him I'd learned the old saw: '*Heedings left unheard, oft herald harm.*' I scratched my chin, pulled another face, and put away the rest of my Whisky.

Ray raised an eyebrow at my act of sacrilege but just smiled a tired smile and moved the bottle of The Glenlivet to my side of the table. "Best try that move again, eh?" he said warmly. "It's all probably nothing. Why don't you find yourself something to do? Go get yourself some work round the West End. Let everyone see you're just an honest, hard-working stage-hand and scene-shifter with nothing at all to hide except your good nature."

I thought for a moment. The clouds shifted. The itches departed. "Yes, that's the ticket. Go up West, fly a few flats, take my mind off things." I nodded and poured myself another large wee dram to dam up my worries. "As usual, Mr. Karmin, when you're right, you're bloody right. Cheers."

"Yes, cheers," he said. "Right then, my old cock, back to business. My move. Checkmate in three."

I groaned inwardly, but even with defeat staring me in the face, I still had to have a go at holding off his pieces. It's how I'm made.

So, come Tuesday lunchtime, I went up West, breaded the waters around Soho with a drink here and a packet of fags there, and I had an offer of a relief job by afternoon closing time. A bloke from Durham that I knew from the Palladium who now worked the fly-floor at The Globe needed to go arrange the funeral for his old mum who'd passed away over the weekend. Funny thing about that, it helped put my own worries into proper perspective, and I cheerfully attended to the mechanics of *The Lady's Not For Burning* for the rest of the week, marvelling again at John Gielgud's ability to render sense out of even the most convoluted of rhyme.

Ten minutes before 'first call' I picked up a late Friday edition of the *Evening Standard* that'd been left up on the fly-floor, then immediately wished to God I hadn't. The story on the front-page said that the pathologist's report on the late Nigel Fox MP, having been delayed once, was now not going to be made public because of the Coroner's eleventh-hour decision to adjourn the inquest. And that of course said only one thing to anyone with half a brain: the authorities suspected unlawful homicide and in due course criminal proceedings would be enacted against person or persons as yet unknown.

As with most official secrets of a certain sort, a day or two and a bundle of well-placed fivers was all it took for full details of the autopsy to leak-out from "people familiar with the situation." And thus the self-proclaimed '*Voice of the People*' scooped all the other Sundays and that morning's 72-point banner headline, 'MP DEAD BEFORE FALL!' was enough to catch most eyes. Of course, they went to town rehashing all the earlier rumours, but there was no mistaking the new facts as presented. The Coroner had appointed not one but two examining pathologists and both men had independently concluded that there was more than sufficient evidence to suggest the late MP had been dead for several hours before his fall from the balcony. Which is to say he'd been topped before he'd been dropped.

I'd planned to spend that Sunday over at the lock-up, lost in the mundane: servicing the taxicab, the van, my motorbike and sidecar. But with the immortal phrase "death caused by violent and unnatural means" suddenly fogging every thought and feeling, I desperately needed some fresh air and some room to think. And with the weather for once not too bad, and with a hat stuck on my head and a favourite paperback book stuffed in my pocket, I hopped a bus down the Edgware Road to Marble Arch. I crossed over to Hyde Park, tacked fully to starboard to give the crowds at Speaker's Corner a wide berth, and then walked over to the Serpentine. I found a bench, sat down, and lost myself in re-reading *The Thin Man*. Something, anything, to take my mind off unfolding events. I knew from my time at sea that there's nothing better sometimes than a wide-open space to hide you or your thoughts in.

I needed to talk to Ray Karmin, that was for sure, but with it being a Sunday, I knew his hands would be good and full with being "Buggy" Billy down Petticoat Lane. Selling tubs of his patented bug powder to London's vast herds of 'great unwashed' was a job he still took very seriously and I knew he'd be at it non-stop till dusk and beyond. Anyway, even on the best of Sundays, the Lane could be absolute murder, what with the never-ending crowds and everyone jostling each other like mad in case they missed a bargain the next stall over. Petticoat Lane was also the very worst place for a private chat of any kind; there were always more eyes and ears than there were people hunting for bargains. And though by then I was feeling that itchy about things I could've done with being doused with a half a dozen tubs of "Buggy" Billy's bug powder, I contented myself knowing I'd see Ray the following night for one of our regular Monday evening chess sessions.

I finished off Dashiell Hammett, grateful for the diversion, and started walking home, but the itchy feelings seemed to increase with my every step. I'm not saying I was flinching at shadows, but for reasons I couldn't fathom I felt more and more like a hunted man.

I remember stopping in some cafe and having a plate of something or other, then popping into a picture-house somewhere, but for the life of me I can't remember what it was I saw. Afterwards, still feeling at odds with the world, I landed up in The Green Man, next to the Tube station, and drank away the hours until closing time and it was gone eleven o'clock when I finally got back to Church Street.

There was no light on in the flat below mine and, knowing that my sister and her husband must already be abed, I tiptoed up the stairs to my own drum. I think I might've had another drink or three, I can't remember. I do know I woke up still in my clothes, though where my hat had disappeared to, I hadn't the foggiest idea. Killing time is such hard work sometimes.

MINE'S A DOUBLE

With the cat out of the Murder Bag, Scotland Yard could do little but confirm to the world at large that the incident at Meridian Mansions was now a full-scale criminal investigation. And come Monday noontime it seemed Binnsy and the rest of London's veritable Greek chorus of news-vendors were yelling, "MP murdered! Not suicide!" at the top of their lungs from every street corner, which of course did nothing at all for the mother and father of all hangovers I had. Binnsy rolled his eyes at the state of me and I rolled mine back at him. I dropped three coppers into his outstretched claw, carefully folded the copies of all three midday papers up under my arm, and trudged over to the Bridge Cafe for some peace and quiet.

I drank the Bridge's idea of coffee until I couldn't taste it anymore and read the linens until my eyes no longer seemed to be peering through red-lace curtains. The only trouble with being sober was realising Monday's itches were just as bad as Sunday's. This time, though, I had something very definite to scratch at. Both the *Standard* and *The Star* had big front-page articles on the increasing number of burglaries in London since the end of the War, each piece lengthy enough for it to spread over onto page 2, where it ran alongside a separate piece listing the capital's top dozen major jewel capers. It wasn't a full accounting by any means, as there must've been ten times as many equally lucrative gem jobs during the same period, but it sufficed.

Now I'm as fascinated by lists as the next man, and more so in this case as I'd done a couple of the jobs myself and had a fair idea of who'd pulled the others, but what got my antenna waving back and forth was that both papers had come up with the exact same list of unsolved burglaries. And that might not seem too significant to you, but jewel thieves keep as eagle an eye on each other's successful capers as ever any punter does the winning form of a boxer or football team. It's our stock in trade, you could say. So I put a name to each job and came up with a very short list of the very best creepers working the Smoke. Odd that a random list would've nailed them all so exactly considering the huge number of burglaries there'd been to choose from.

Let me put it another way. Imagine you were at a racetrack, horses or dogs makes no difference, and you saw a card of runners all of which you knew to be ringers (stand-ins, lookalikes, meant to run faster or slower as required) or dopers (runners, lucky if they can find their way out of the starting gate, let alone the first turn). You'd get the definite feeling that something was up; that 'the fix' was in. Same difference with the list of creeping jobs I was looking at. The point being that two different crime reporters, working for two different London evening newspapers, had both come up with the exact same list of top creepers working the Smoke. All of which begged the question, how in hell had they come by their information?

When I eventually got back to Church Street I found two messages pushed under my front door, both of them signed 'Mary.' Mary was the new 'little miss helpful' at the Victory cafe and I made a mental note to thank her for climbing the stairs up to my top-floor flat twice in one workday. The first message 'For Mr. Jethro' had been telephoned in just gone one o'clock and was from the bloke who headed the fly-team at the Prince of Wales. Was I interested in filling in for a couple of weeks? Was I? The second note read: *3:25 pm Message for Mr. Jethro. Mr. Moofty said, "6 to 1 on the eagle."*

I knew right away it was from Ray. The pub he'd selected was the real message. The Eagle was way off our usual stomping grounds and signalled that he thought one of us was in jeopardy of some sort. "Mufti" meant come in disguise.

I had a quick wash and brush up and hotfooted it over to the lock-up, wondering what in hell else had happened. I left my dark thoughts in an imaginary black box by the Judas door—there was no reason to take those inside with me—and I attended to the necessaries, donned the persona of old 'Albert' and motored over to the City Road in the old Austin Eight taxi.

I got to the pub around opening time and sat there, hand glued around a pint, eyes seemingly glued to the 'Final' editions of the *Evening Standard* and *The Star*, and waited. In my flat-cap, silk muffler, spectacles, weather-beaten puffy nose and cheeks, a brassard pinned on my coat sleeve, I was a London cabby to the life. True, I may have overdone the *Leichner* sallow skin-tone No. 6 grey-pencilled wrinkles and white wispy-haired Willy Clarkson wig, but I needed to disappear into the furniture and the ranks of London's elderly and poor have ever provided refuge for those seeking invisibility. And catching sight of myself in one of the pub's huge gilt mirrors, even I wouldn't have recognised me.

"Allo, Albert," said a raspy voice loud enough for anyone quietly listening to hear quite clearly. "Fancy seeing you in here. Still driving the old heap of yours? Thought both you and that old boneshaker of yours would've been on the scrap heap by now. Mine's a double, by the way."

I looked up into tired but still razor-sharp eyes and went straight into my patter: "Blimey, Moisha Fabrikant, you old sod. Sit down why don't you and give your mouth a rest. Alright then, a double it is."

There was no sign at all of the bespoke-suited Raymond Karmin or of 'Buggy' Billy's trademark bowler hat, spotted bow tie and long scraggy fur-collared overcoat. The middle-aged man now standing before me wore a battered old brown trilby, tartan scarf, oil-stained mackintosh, and scuffed shoes that looked like they'd seen the inside of a pawn shop one too many times. Even his voice was different, high-pitched and raspy. And a simple enough makeover, but one no less effective for that, and should the need to establish its veracity ever arise, Ray always carried a driving license, rent-book, and identity card in the name of said Moisha Fabrikant upon his person.

I got them in while Ray—I mean Moisha—lit up a cigarette from a crumpled packet of Woodbines he'd pulled from out a pocket of his mackintosh. He didn't offer me one; my character smoked roll-ups, as could be attested by the tobacco tin and packet of Rizla cigarette papers on the marble tabletop. Tiny details, maybe, but I'd long learned that anything and everything is grist for the mill when it comes to establishing a character, and that includes the choice of smokes. Ray nodded thanks, took a sip of Johnny Walker and a sip of beer. Then he coughed, scoured up some phlegm, spat the result into a red spotted handkerchief, and loudly blew his nose. A little performance that had everyone in the place inching their chairs away from the two of us. Ray's sure-fire way of clearing the stage. I moved in closer as he murmured in the direction of my right ear.

"Murder it is then. Read about it in the '*News of the Screws*' yesterday. Bad enough for the poor sod that died, but it couldn't be worse for us. News of it will be all round the world by week's end, which means that little pot of tom you brought home is now officially hotter than hell and will be for years to come. Even trying to have the sparklers re-cut could lead straight back to our door, and neither of us want that to happen."

I nodded in vigorous agreement as he took another sip of beer.

"First thing you should know is I had bloody itches about this thing right from the very start. And I know I told you different, but me piling my worries on top of yours would've been like throwing petrol onto a bonfire and given the way the winds were blowing it was best you remained unaware of the currents swirling around you. You running around beating the bushes would've only had the wrong people asking more questions, which is why ever since that first week following the break-in I've been out and about in the Smoke, nosing the wind and catching hold of anything on the breeze. That's also why we're meeting here in the Eagle and why, as of now, Monday night chess is out. Even you being seen on the same street as Raymond Karmin, Esq. might lead someone to put two and two together and earn themselves a fiver."

It was a lot to swallow and I all but blushed at having doubted Ray or his senses. I raised my beer glass in salute. "Thanks, me old china," I said. And the overture over, Ray raised the curtain on the First Act.

"A sketch of the person the police wish to interview in connection with the Meridian Mansions murder is being circulated tomorrow to all Met and City police stations, along with photos of the missing jewellery. The insurance company's also passing out the photos to every major diamond dealer in Hatton Garden." Questions hung in the air like smoke. He swivelled his eyes towards me. "Let's just say I know a man who knows a man who sweeps the floor in the printing shop at the Yard and you'd be surprised what he sometimes finds in the rubbish bins." He pulled something from out the pocket of his grubby mackintosh and pushed it towards me. I unfolded it very slowly. The creased face of the man staring back at me from out of the 'HAVE YOU SEEN THIS MAN? REQUIRED FOR INTERVIEW BY THE POLICE' poster could've been me if I was ten years older, had a broken nose, a scar and dark curly hair. As it was, there were two other blokes drinking in the Eagle that looked more like the bloke in the poster than I did.

"He looks a right villain, I must say," I said, feeling very relieved it didn't look too much like me. "It could be any one of a hundred blokes. The police sketch artist must've been wearing boxing gloves."

"A sprat to catch a mackerel," Ray said. "Not meant to look like anyone in particular, just meant to get people talking. And it will. This whole 'dead before he was murdered' business has tickled people's fancies something rotten and it's only going to get worse. It was the talk of the Lane all day Sunday. Names being bandied about like nobody's business, everyone betting on who they thought was up to the job. Haven't heard anything like it since the world and his brother went after the killers in the Alec de Antiquis affair." He paused to rub his chin, never a good sign. "Thought it was just the same old nonsense at first, but as the day wore on, the same half-dozen names kept on being mentioned over and over again, almost as if it was an officially sanctioned list of runners or something."

I loosened my silk muffler. "Er, this bunch of names, anyone I know?" Ray gave me one of his looks and rattled off a list of names. I knew them all. I'd compiled the exact same list back at the Bridge Cafe. "You said half-dozen names, but you only mentioned five."

It was then I realised Ray was still giving me the same funny look. "Yours is the other name," he said. "It's you everyone's put in trap No. 6."

"Me? You've got to be joking," I said, but even as I said it I knew I'd seen it coming; it was already starting to be all of a piece.

"I wish to God I was joking, old cock, but it's true."

"What the hell's going on?" I said, pushing the *Standard* towards him.

"Seen it," Ray said, "and *The Star*. Odd, isn't it, both newspapers coming up with the exact same list? Almost as if someone delivered the linotype-plate already etched and ready for the presses." I nodded and Ray leaned in and tapped the *Standard* with his packet of Woodbines. "I take it then you put names to each of the jobs?" Ray narrowed his eyes. "And everything put together and stitched up in less than twenty-four hours. And not by chance, that's for sure. Even the Methods

Index that the Yard's Criminal Records Office puts out after a major crime wouldn't be that exact."

"All the hallmarks of a stitch-up."

He nodded. "It's obvious now someone's gone way out their way to drop you and the other creepers in the cart. The million-dollar question of course is who's doing it and why?" He reached for another Woodbine and tapped it up and down on the packet. "And I might never have seen the answer if it wasn't for something else I heard yesterday."

I suddenly felt like I had a dead rabbit stuck in my throat and I could hardly get the words out. "What...what did you hear?"

Ray's whisper dropped to the level of a hand wiped across a sleeve and I leaned in close enough to him for our hat-brims to touch. "You remember I've always told you that if ever you really want to understand something, you should try looking at what the world would be like if that something was absent?" I nodded, hardly daring to breathe. "So I asked myself, which jewellery jobs are conspicuous by their absence and whose name would I put in the frame alongside them? Then not half-hour later, on my lunch-break, biting into some salt-beef on rye at Bloom's, I overheard a whisper. Seems Darby Messima became extremely interested in having a little chat with one Jimmy Mooney the exact same day news hit the streets that a large cache of finest-water jewellery had gone missing from Meridian Mansions. He offered some very serious money for a quick result, too."

"Jimmy Mooney?" I blurted out, earning myself a hefty kick under the table. "'Monkey' Jim?" I said, hardly able to contain myself. "But he's still inside on a three-stretch and not due out for another year yet. That's why you and I never even considered him being the midnight plumber."

"Shows how bloody wrong, we were," Ray muttered into his beer. "But I'd say it's even money it was him that you saw climbing up that soil-pipe."

"Blimey, Jimmy Mooney," I said, the years suddenly collapsing like the walls of a house hit by a Jerry bomb. Jimmy was the bloke Ray had sent me to way back when—the bloke who'd taught me everything there was to know about climbing and creeping. At the time, he was the best human-fly in the business and always in the top tier of creepers until he took to drink in a big way after his missus, his sister, and his two little girls all died in the Blitz. I always reckoned he'd have topped himself, too, afterwards, if it hadn't been for his brother taking him in. I shook my head. "'Monkey' Jim, right under my bloody nose. It's amazing what you can't see for looking sometimes."

"He got remission for good behaviour and has been out these last three months and more. But he's a changed man, apparently. The poor sod had the DT's, the lot. Word is he screamed and shouted himself hoarse trying to get himself sober and can barely whisper now."

"Well, he'd have soon got his voice back once Messima started skinning him alive," I said, my beer tasting of bile. "Poor old Jimmy Mooney."

Ray shook his head. "No, that's the thing. Messima's goons are still pulling the city apart looking for him."

I sat up, sharp, my beer suddenly tasting like beer again. "Yes, that figures. If Jimmy got wind Messima was after him, he'd have gone to ground. On a good day old 'Monkey' Jim could stand in front of you in the street and still not be noticed; up on the tiles, though, he's nigh on invisible. So if he's camped out on a rooftop somewhere, you can bet no one will find him."

Ray nodded. "He always reckoned you, you know. Wouldn't take a penny for your tutoring. Said you paid in full by watching and learning and showing the proper respect."

I smiled at that. It's funny the chickens that come home to roost. I scratched at something, my chin I think it was. "Doesn't add up though, does it, 'Monkey' Jim doing business with Messima?"

"He probably didn't have too much choice in the matter. After all he's been through these last years, he's hardly likely to have been in any position to pick and choose. His brother Harry will have done what he could for him, but Jimmy Mooney was always his own man. It's only in his nature to want to climb back up again. No different from you."

For one brief moment I thought of Jimmy Mooney's barrel of troubles rather than my own. I looked over at Ray—I mean Moisha—I mean Ray—and saw by the look on his face there was a second shoe yet to drop.

And by the look if it, another big one.

"The other whisper all round Petticoat Lane yesterday was that the Ghost Squad are already out everywhere, looking very hard for someone to put the finger on."

"The Ghost Squad? Jesus 'aitch Christ, that's all we needed," I said, suddenly scratching at myself like there was no tomorrow.

GHOSTS IN THE SHADOWS

Blimey. The Ghost Squad—or 'Shadow Mob' as they were referred to by almost every villain in the Smoke—were a secret even to themselves, let alone the rest of London's police forces. You'd never catch them wearing little trilby hats, belted raincoats and size twelve daisy roots. No, they raided props cupboards and wardrobes just like me, and for the very same reason: they wanted to disappear into plain sight, as well, the only difference being they wanted to be taken for villains. The idea was for them to sink deep into London's seedy underworld, pick up whispers about up-and-coming jobs and capers, and then tip off their mates in the dreaded Flying Squad. They were the witch-finders to the thief-takers. Sometimes, though, they even went so far as to join a gang and help set up the very job they then gave away, which was all very nasty as it meant the person swigging tea at the next cafe table or quietly sipping their beer next to you in a pub could well be one of the Shadow Mob. I'd even heard rumours about big drinks being offered around the Smoke—from both sides of the law—for any word as to who these ghostly individuals might be when they were at home. The general feeling being that anyone so employed deserved a damn good smacking, as did the Deputy Assistant Commissioner (Crime) who was reputed to have come up with the idea in the first place. Any London copper already 'on the take' got nasty chills at the very thought of the Ghost Squad.

And as for London's top villains, they didn't take too kindly to the idea the Yard would be so underhanded as to spy on them in their own clubs, pubs, and spielers. It wasn't how things were done. It certainly wasn't cricket; that was for sure.

Still scratching like mad from Ray's revelations, I all but staggered up to the bar to get the next round of drinks in and I think I must've been in a bit of a state as the barman had to ask me twice whether I wanted the same again or not. I coughed and nodded and made out I was a bit 'mutt and jeff' and dug round in my leather change purse for some coins, but the question I was really wrestling with was what on earth to do. If I was being set up, the smart thing was for me to get out of town and disappear up North somewhere, and quick. Or go sign on the first cargo ship leaving King Edward Docks for foreign parts. (I'd kept my National Union of Seamen card fully paid up. Or 'cards,' I should say, as I had a bunch of them in different names all tucked away for a rainy day.) What to do? What to do? I couldn't stay in disguise the rest of my life. I scratched at my chin again, enough to draw blood. It's surprising how very alone you can suddenly feel, even in the midst of a crowded London pub.

I carried the drinks back to the table, my throat so dry I all but sank my beer in one. I wiped my mouth on the back of my sleeve and let slip my thoughts. "I can see how my two capers made it onto the list in *The Star* and *Standard*, they were tasty enough to warrant mention, but everyone in the Smoke believes me long gone from the game and only you and me know I pulled off those jobs. So, question is, why drag my name back into the spotlight? Where's the profit in it? Doesn't add up."

"It does if you remember this Meridian Mansions business is the Yard's number-one priority and they'll be like a pack of slavering bloodhounds on any old nonsense that gets stuck under their noses. I'd bet a bent copper to a brass farthing that it's Messima's mob dropping the list of names into the ears of interested parties in every pub, club, dive, cafe, spieler, and penny arcade in the Smoke. Messima's breading the water with red herrings for the Ghost Squad to swallow whole, setting shadows to chase shadows, leaving him and his mob clear to hunt for the real quarry: 'Monkey' Jim."

"But why would Messima want to mess me up?"

"He stuck you in the frame before, Jethro, with that foreign bloke, von Bentink, for no other reason than that he could and you almost ended up dead that time. And whatever profits him once he'll do again; it's how's he's made. Of course, there's also the distinct possibility he heard you were in on Jack Spot's failed Heath Row caper. So this could be him serving up his revenge, double cold. He knows someone's neck has got to go into the hangman's noose, so this business is tailor-made for him to pay off old scores and wipe the board clean of everyone he thinks deserves it."

"And every creeper on the list, his own man, who'd rather take a long jump off a short roof than get roped in on one of Messima's dodgy capers."

"Thereby denying him payment of what he sees to be his rightful tribute for any jewellery jobs pulled on his manor. So there's your answer, Jethro. If he even gets one or two of you off the slates for the foreseeable, there's that much more top-drawer loot in town for him to get his share of. At little or no cost to himself, he's got all six of you trussed-up, ready to be picked up by Scotland Yard's finest as and when they so choose. That's why I've already started taking measures to get you a cast-iron alibi for the entire weekend of the Meridian Mansions business. And I mean rustproof. Photos of you down by the sea, ticket stubs, hotel bill, stamped postcards, the lot." He paused. "When all's said and done, Jimmy Mooney's probably the key to what went on that night at Meridian Mansions after you left. So, for both our sakes, if he's still in London, you better try and find him before Messima does."

I nodded. "I've been thinking the exact same thing. Is his brother Harry still working the corners in the Quarter?"

"Harry 'Rabbit'? Yes. Greek Street, corner of Bateman Street, last I heard, but he could be anywhere round Soho depending on who's paying the piper. Everyone knows, though, Harry would never grass up his brother even if they threatened to pull out all his fingernails with red-hot pliers."

I pulled a face and reached for the last of my beer. "All the same, Messima's mob will be being watching him like a cast of hungry hawks, as there's no surer way of finding 'Monkey' Jim than going through Harry."

"Yes, but finding 'Monkey' Jim before Messima does is only the start of it." My hand stilled and I looked at Ray, my beer turning sour on the back of my tongue again. "There's a risk Jimmy Mooney may still end up a dead end. The real task is to find out who murdered the late Nigel Fox MP and why. And the only sure way of doing that is for us to dig up whatever skeletons he had hidden away in his closet. Dig into his private life to see if he really was the feckless, immoral, adulterous bastard all the linens say he was. We've got to chase down all them rumours about him having dodgy dealings in the City or him being up to his neck in gambling debts. Find out if he had a serious taste for nancy-boys or had a secret mistress and child or both. And all of it, I might add, without calling any more attention to ourselves."

"Blimey O'Reilly," I said, rolling my eyes. "Is that all?"

Ray gave me another one of his looks. "Got no choice in the matter, old cock. Given everything that's happened, it's the only way of ensuring it's not your neck that ends up in the hangman's noose. It may just be a series of unfortunate coincidences, maybe not. What I do know for sure is there's a nasty little riddle wrapped up in a mystery surrounding a murder made double-deadly because Messima's mixed up in it." He scowled and reached for his Whisky. "I'll start the ball rolling on Fox by calling in some favours in the City. I'll also squeeze what I can from the crowd down the Reading Room. They're all very well connected and if anyone around St. James's clubland was known to be holding his markers, someone's bound to have heard something. I think you're best situated to do the rest."

I nodded. "Horses for courses? Sure. I'll get on it," I said. "First, I'll try see Harry 'Rabbit', see if he'll tip me the wink as to his brother's whereabouts. As for Fox, I was thinking I could give Sylvia a visit, then maybe pop in on Lil, then go see Glover."

Ray wiped a tired hand down a very tired face. "Yes, good thinking. As for me, I'll keep up appearances as both 'Buggy' Billy and Raymond Karmin, Esq., but either way you best keep your distance. I'll even put it around you and 'Buggy' have had a falling-out; it might help. Meanwhile, I'll bring old Moisha out of mothballs for as long as is necessary. It'd also be wise if you got yourself firmly berthed on some theatre fly-floor, somewhere, even if you have to pay someone to go lame for a couple of weeks. You've got to make it easy for people to keep their eyes on you. If you were to up and disappear, the powers that be on both sides of the law would take it as proof of guilt and hunt you down without mercy. So, for now, as hard as it may be, it's best you just act your usual cheeky, charming self and appear to one and all as if you don't have a single worry or care in the world."

"Funny you should say that," I said, trying hard not to scratch at a sudden itch that'd erupted underneath my scraggly wig. " Only, I've just had offer of another stage-hand job. Perfect timing you might say."

"Perfect timing is right," said Ray, waving his empty glass.

JEWEL OF MANY FACES

A word or two about Soho, as it's always been a bit of a world unto itself. Soho's that area bordered and bound by Regent Street, Oxford Street, Charing Cross Road, and Shaftesbury Avenue, and so was sometimes referred to as the Quarter. It was as famed for its writers' and artists' colonies and out-of-hours drinking clubs as it was its speciality shops, delicatessens and street markets. And if there was ever a hub to Britain's blackmarket, Soho was the undoubted jewel in the ring of crime. It was also the undisputed Mecca for theatres, restaurants and nightclubs, as well as the centre of the film biz, the rag trade, and anything and everything to do with the world of vice, whether in the flesh or photos. And each and every little world that made up Soho was subject to its own unspoken laws and unwritten rules.

The greatest of all being that any sort of news, anything at all out of the ordinary, was sent immediately and unerringly towards the centre. High or low, knowledge was currency and the sooner someone got to hear whatever it was that needed to be heard was a sure sign of their place on the totem pole. And with me having 'officially' taken myself out of the burglary business, I had to be trebly careful about asking questions outside my new occupation in London's theatreland. The theatre may have been my chosen castle, but it was my prison, too, because it bound both me and my actions. I could drop by a few stage-doors, slip into the odd hotel bar, pub, cafe or milk-bar, and sop up whatever gossip might've puddled there, but if I stuck my nose in anywhere I shouldn't or loitered anywhere for too long—even a street corner or a trader's barrow—questions would be asked about what exactly it was I was up to. And that would've been me just asking for trouble.

The following afternoon I met up with the guv'nor of the fly-team at the Prince of Wales and got myself squared away. He said as how he'd heard I pulled my weight and was pleasant with it, and the job was mine for as long as I needed it; which was all very nice of him. He also said he'd be grateful if I'd keep an eye on a young lad working his NATKE union ticket; his second cousin's son, from up North. "Happy to show him the ropes," I said, eager to demonstrate how I always pulled more than my weight. "Helping people's right up my street."

The Yank play that'd been on at the Prince of Wales since January was right up my street, too. It was called *Harvey* and starred Sid Field—famous to one and all for his take-off of a London 'Spiv'—as a man who talked to a six-foot-three-and-a-half-inch-tall, invisible rabbit. By which I mean to say he could see it, but others couldn't. The irony of which wasn't lost on me; "Monkey" Jim was a good foot shorter than *Harvey* the rabbit, but no less bloody invisible to the eye.

I walked out the stage-door with a smile on me face, though I did happen to notice a good few 'faces' giving me more than the usual butcher's as I walked back through Soho, which told me the rumour mill had already done its turn for the day. I'd expected as much, though, and as per Ray's suggestion I continued to comport myself as if I had not a care in the world and had even less to hide. Acting, it's called, in certain circles.

I kept my eyes peeled for Harry Mooney but didn't see hide or hair of him, but if he shared one thing with his brother, Jimmy, it was an uncanny ability to remain unseen and overlooked, even in broad daylight. Harry "Rabbit" was hands-down the best corner-man in the business. And a good corner-man was worth his weight in gold, as he helped provide the one thing that every villain always needed—time to get away. No one in London could read a street half as well as Harry. He had eyesight a gold eagle would've been proud of and a photographic memory of damn near every police officer serving at West End Central, if not the Yard, as well as of every 'face' and would-be 'face' in the Smoke. His job was to spot and sort any and every body that entered into a given stretch of Soho street and, when necessary, mutter an urgent warning to any interested parties standing close-by. His timely words of silent alarm had saved many a London villain from getting his collar felt, which is why everyone held Harry's ability 'to rabbit' in such high esteem and why his skills were always in such demand.

I wasn't unduly worried. I knew Harry Mooney was probably on one his recce missions, hidden in plain sight outside a police station or magistrates' court somewhere, clocking everybody going in or coming out, memorising everyone's faces. Beefing up his stock-in-trade, he called it. The real worry was what to do once I'd located him. I still had to find a way of getting close enough for us to talk without it piquing too much of the wrong sort of interest. And the only thing I could come up with was that I had to get myself accepted by the guild of Soho 'corner-men,' even if only for an afternoon. Not impossible, but not that easy. So as I do with any knotty problem, I just let it all percolate in the back of my mind until the answer presented itself. In the end, the spark of an idea came from a bit of lunchtime gossip I overheard in a pub.

I'd learned from Ray one of the very best ways of becoming invisible was to shine a very bright light on yourself. And that was why, the following afternoon, before going off to do my first matinee at the Prince of Wales, I visited Moroni's the newsagents, then popped next door to Patisserie Valerie and spent a good half-hour over a coffee and a bun, pouring over the latest copy of *The Stage* and ear-wigging the latest theatrical tittle-tattle. And by the end of my second cup I had my plan all worked out.

There was a new play about to get-in at the tiny Gateway theatre in Westbourne Grove that was without its scenery because the nominal owner of the painted flats and other necessary items of theatrical paraphernalia had been declared bankrupt, his stock impounded, and his place of business padlocked. The play was only set for a short run and would be off by the time all the requisite legal permission to use the 'flats' was obtained. Miles of red tape and official forms meant weeks and weeks of delay and, as the gossip had it, the whole production was in danger of closing even before it'd ever opened, putting a whole boatload of actors and stage-hands out of work.

Enter Jethro, Down Stage Left, eager as ever to lend a helping hand.

I got hold of a bunch of coppers and strolled over to the bank of telephone-boxes that stood just off Cambridge Circus, then with my copy of *The Stage* prominently propped up on the coin box and my pennies arrayed out in piles of two, I made the first of several local telephone calls. To any wandering passer-by or interested party watching in the shadows it looked like I was trying to drum up some more work. Truth was, I was using whatever pull I had to help untie someone else's knot in the hope it would help undo my own. And after a few whispered words in a few 'King Lears' the stage was set for the opening of the new play at the Gateway and for the unfolding of a little drama of my own devising.

GOING FLAT OUT

There was no matinee scheduled at the Prince of Wales the next day, yet there I was, off to work, strolling down the Edgware Road, raincoat slung over me shoulder, sans hat so people could clearly see it was me. I walked down as far as the Tube station, where I bought a midday-*Standard* from Binnsy. He gave me a nod; I nodded back. Then, his sheaf of papers tight tucked under his arm, he mimed someone pulling on a rope and asked whether it was true I still had some pull in the Smoke. I threw him a look that would've done Humphrey Bogart proud and hopped on a handy No. 15 double-decker bus going to Oxford Circus. I sat upstairs at the front and stuck my head in the newspaper, marvelling that however fresh the printer's ink, it was no competition at all for London's own jungle drums.

I stayed aboard until the bus turned down Regent Street, jumped off by Dickens & Jones, then cut through to Great Marlborough Street, the reverse of the route I'd taken home the previous day. I stopped by the London Palladium to drop off a packet of fags for Alf the stage-door keeper, an old mate. And a tiny thing, but you'd be surprised how well people will think of you if you don't always want something in return. We chatted for a bit about old times. I told Alf where I was filling in, but from the slight twitch of his moustache, he probably already knew. I bid him adieu and went back out into Great Marlborough Street and must've lost myself in memories of people and past times, because before I knew it I was deep in Soho and already standing on the corner of Bateman Street.

I glanced over at the boarded-up bombsite opposite where the old Royalty Theatre had once stood. I'd never worked there; it'd closed just before the War had started and then been blown to smithereens in the Blitz, a good five years before I'd been reborn as a stage-hand. Now here it was, its broken spectral shadow acting as a backdrop to my own little play, as was the narrow building just opposite that'd been the Royalty's scene-dock before it'd been turned into the business premises of the aforementioned recently bankrupted theatrical storage-company.

I blinked. Curtain up. And with the *Standard* folded open to the classifieds held out in front of me like a divining rod, I marched right up to the storage-company's tall green double doors and loudly knocked on the knocker. I effected not to notice the big padlock and chain snaked around the brass door handles, and bent down and peered in through the big brass letterbox, at which point my raincoat unaccountably slipped from off my shoulder all the way down my arm. I wrestled with it for a moment then pushed it back over my shoulder. I stood up, banged on the doors again and rattled the padlock, then stepped back to look up at the still shuttered windows in the floors above. I looked down at the classified ads as if mystified and then shook my head and the newspaper in a display of obvious annoyance before disappearing back around the corner into Dean Street, thus successfully bringing the curtain down on the end of Act One.

I sprinted up the street, tooled round into Soho Square, and sped down Greek Street. Then, adjusting my pace to a jaunty saunter of success, I approached the motley group of men standing on the corner of Bateman Street. All of the corner-men would've seen my recent performance at the far end of the street, given it marks out of ten, then dismissed both it and me from mind. One or two would've recognised me, though, as well as question my actions, and it was their suspicions I had to allay first, now that I'd reappeared from a different direction. As I got closer I heard the usual whispered hubbub subside.

"Eye-eye, if it isn't Jeffro." Harry Mooney filled the empty silence with his patter. "What you up to, then? Being on the knock was never your game. Thought you were supposed to be treading the boards. Anyway, them premises you were butchering are padlocked; a bankruptcy, so we heard."

"'Lo, Harry," I said. "Pardon me, gents. Hope you don't mind me cornering for a few minutes, just doing someone a favour." In the theatre it all comes down to proper timing, so I glanced down at my wristwatch even though I knew the exact time, as I'd been counting the seconds off in my head. "Helping half-inch some scenery to help keep a troupe of actors and a band of brother stage-hands in work," I said. I looked up again—taking all eyes with me—and nodded as a large green removals van appeared at the far end of the street. The driver trundled forward and stopped in front of the premises I'd stood outside of not five minutes earlier and flashed his lights on and off. I stepped to the edge of the pavement so I could be seen and, using my rolled-up newspaper as a baton, executed the all-clear sign. The driver and three men—all in overalls—exited the van and approached the tall green double doors and, with only the briefest of pauses, in they went, no trouble at all.

I reached into the pocket of my raincoat to forestall any further questions and pulled out the original padlock, now cupped safely in my hand. "Would you Adam-and-Eve it?" I sneered, "I could've picked this bloody thing with a fag-end."

It got a weak laugh, but it was enough to get me accepted, because Harry Mooney immediately picked up his patter and resumed his lookout. "Eye-eye, bint with the titfer, young bloke carrying a box. Nit the bint. Box-boy's gone into the grocer's—not the usual delivery boy—so eye, eye that one when he comes out. Eye-eye. Narkit. Two scruffs, duffle coats, long scarves. Nit those two—students at the art-college. Eye-eye. Box-boy again. Nit box-boy. Eye-eye the full-dress 'Hatty'." A young copper had just turned into Greek Street and as fast as any 'flat' had ever been flown onto any stage, the corner was suddenly a different world; people just disappeared into the brickwork or slouched into invisibility behind a newspaper. Harry picked up again from where he'd left off as soon as the policeman disappeared up to Soho Square and the corner reverted back to normal.

Harry Mooney's 'rabbiting' was as good as anything you could hear on the wireless or down the racetrack. His flow of speech dotted with pithy asides about any 'faces' he'd spotted, his mind as sharp as anyone you could ever hope to meet. There'd be a laugh here, a chuckle there, but never anything too malicious, and even his quiet glances up the street to see how my theatre-props removal friends were doing seemed good-natured. I played along with everybody, stiffening into alertness whenever Harry called out "eye-eye" and waving a 'downer' to signal 'beware the person now approaching' at the mere mention of a "narkit." I knew full well none of the removals men would've remotely understood what the hell I was doing, but it didn't matter—it was all just to help me blend in. I gave another 'all-clear' sign; only to realise I was using both hands as this bloke who'd asked to have a butcher's of my newspaper had disappeared with it. I tell you, the things people will half-inch from you if given half the chance.

Time passed quickly enough and so too did the large, green removals van. I'd made it abundantly clear to my partners-in-crime that they flash the headlights twice when they were done with loading the 'flats' and ready to depart, but otherwise to show no other sign of acknowledgement or recognition. And bless them, they'd been only too willing to play their parts as written and had even supplied the lorry, too, once I'd explained it wasn't so much a question of thieving as borrowing the scenery and paying the fine of no more than a couple of quid if caught.

And as I watched the van disappearing off down the street, I knew I'd fully passed muster when I was offered a fag by none other than Harry Mooney himself. "Not bad for an amateur," he said, as another one of the corner-men stepped in to light the cigarette. And that was when I risked all my winnings on one turn of pitch and toss and I nodded 'thanks' and said, "Blimey, the things you get called on to do for mates, but that's any close-knit brotherhood for you. If Romulus calls, Remus needs must come-a-running."

I took a quick drag on the cigarette and feigned difficulty in drawing sufficient smoke, which was hardly surprising, as I'd given the end of the fag a quick pinch, hopefully unobserved. This time it was Harry that offered a light. "True friendship runs evergreen from cradle to the grave," he muttered, his last syllable nothing more than the sound between breaths. But it was all I needed to hear. It was the very thing I'd come for.

"Ta, Harry," I said. "I needed this." I took a long, slow drag on the ciggie, then blew out a long stream of contented smoke as a precursor to my curtain speech. "Well, thanks, gents, one and all, for letting me join your happy throng. My good deed now done for the day I must away to the Prince of Wales to assist Sid Field be his actorly best as he rabbits on again this evening to an invisible six-foot rabbit." I shook a few hands, gave several bent-eyes to suggest that drinks might well be in the offing at some future date, and took my leave. There were some good-natured mumblings about how the theatre had obviously gone to my head and how past it I was. And that was it, done.

And off I went down Greek Street, making for Shaftesbury Avenue, Coventry Street and the Prince of Wales theatre. I didn't once look back, but then I never do.

FLYING COLOURS

The only thing I had against the Prince of Wales—the theatre, that is—is that from the outside it looked like one of those hideous Odeon picture-houses; a slab of concrete festooned with neon lights. It's hardly surprising, though, as the bloke that re-built the place just before the war had only ever designed cinemas previously. However, backstage got a big thumbs up from me as apart from all the mod-cons—such as electronically operated house tabs, safety curtain and a 22 foot revolving stage with 7 foot 6 inch centre revolve—it had hemp-lines and counter-weight laid alternately to give the very best of both worlds.

There were no rehearsals scheduled for *Harvey* that day, so I'd told the guv'nor I'd get in early to help show the new bloke the ropes. The backstage of any working theatre always looks like complete and utter chaos to the uninitiated, but there's method to the madness.

Bob, he said his name was. He was a little older than I thought he'd be and it was soon very apparent he knew his way around backstage, at least enough to know to always look which way he was going, so as not to come a cropper falling over an errant brace weight or misplaced sand-bag. But as I always find it's best never to take anything for granted, I began at the beginning. And I told him, always remember to watch your step and keep your sea legs about you as the stage is raked and slopes down towards the footlights. I pointed to the grid, way up in the roof, where all the scenery got pulled up to and was flown out of sight, the height and size of which is always a bit of a surprise to people, but he seemed familiar with all that, too. So then I asked him straight if he'd had any previous experience in the theatre.

"A little," he said, and left it at that.

I did notice he seemed far more fascinated with the 96-way dimmer board, one of London theatreland's largest, than with any of the paraphernalia that helped move scenery back and forth. So I suggested being a 'sparks' might be more up his alley, adding that anything and everything to do with electricity and wires personally gave me the heebie-jeebies, though I didn't go into why. He looked surprised I'd noticed his fascination with things electrical, but he chuckled good-naturedly and said as how he'd always had a bit of a hankering to be an electrical engineer, but times and tides had led him elsewhere. There was an almost wistful look on his face when he said that, but his guard went back up again as quickly as it'd come down.

"It's never too late," I said. "You should have a word with the guv'nor, see if he could get you placed with one of the lighting crew instead. That is if you think an Electrical Trades Union card is more in keeping with your talents than the illustrious National Association of Theatrical and Kine Employees." But he just smiled and shook his head and said that there were personal reasons that made NATKE just the ticket.

"Righto," I said, "the false proscenium is 38 feet wide, distance between side-walls is 60 feet and between fly-rails 51 feet. Height from stage to grid is 49 feet, height to take cloths up out of sight 23 feet, depth from under the Fly Platform to the stage is 19 feet, depth under stage is 11 feet 6 inches." I rattled off all the facts though I'd only just learned most of them myself. I threw him a length of No. 8 sash cord and had him tie me some knots, starting with the fly-man's friend, the bow-line. From there we went up onto the fly-floor itself and I took him through the process of 'deading' a flat and how to ensure the lines were always properly secured and tied-off at the cleats. And that's how we went on until show-time, when his first real test was to look and learn from all hands on deck without getting under anyone's feet, which he passed with flying colours.

Afterwards, he offered to buy me a drink for my time and trouble and we popped into The Elizabeth, a stage-crew pub behind His Majesty's. It wasn't long until last orders, but there was time enough for a drink or two. He told me his name was Bob Miller. He was a pleasant enough chap with an easy-going manner, which is to say he didn't laugh too much and he didn't laugh too little and, as he'd ably demonstrated, he had a good head on a strong pair of shoulders and was more than willing to pull his weight.

He reminded me a little of John Mills, the actor, only he was taller and a good twenty pounds heavier. And by the way he moved, I reckoned he must've gone a few rounds in the ring in his past, probably as a lightweight pushing welterweight. It was funny how with some people you noticed that the mark of the Forces never really left them; even something as small as the precise way they picked up or set down a glass gave it away. It denoted sergeants, usually, or officers who'd been up the sharp end with their men; they'd learned that life costs.

Bob asked me a few questions and I told him no lies, sticking to the truth as much as I could. I pushed again on why he'd settle for the life of a lowly stage-hand when people were crying out for electrical engineers. It came out in a rush. His family had originally hailed from Southampton and his dad was an ex-seaman who'd managed to work a union ticket at the Opera House up in Manchester, thanks to a former shipmate putting in a good word for him.

"I used to go watch him work every chance I got," Bob said. "I loved seeing all the goings-on backstage; it was like another world."

"That would explain it," I said. "Your dad still work there, does he?"

He went silent. "No," he said. "Come the war, he got called back into the Merchant Navy, the Atlantic convoys, and one night, February 1941, his ship was sunk by a U-boat. I joined up as soon as I was old enough, did my bit, got demobbed late '46, found it difficult to settle ever since."

"They were bad times," I said, "but it's for sure the country wouldn't have survived without their sacrifice." He gave me a quizzical look. "I was in the Merch," I said. "Got sunk a couple times, too. So I know how very lucky I was to have survived it all in one piece. Sorry to hear about your dad."

He nodded. "Funny, you having been in the Merch," he said.

"Not really," I said, "I have it on very good authority there's been whole boatloads of ex-seamen working London's fly-floors ever since Shakespeare's time. Also, if it's any consolation, I couldn't settle afterwards either. I certainly couldn't go back to what I'd been doing before the war. It's one of the reasons I took up as a stage-hand. At least, out there, on stage, every night, the world gets set to rights every time the curtain drops. And twice daily with Wednesday and Saturday matinees."

I'd hoped my remarks would lighten the mood a little, but it only seemed to set him off. "It makes me bloody sick," he said, wiping beer from the corner of his mouth. "You come back from the bloody War, when so many didn't, and everywhere you look it's chicanery and spivvery and the black market and blokes who managed to avoid the call-up pulling strings and controlling things. Throw in the constant shortages and all the rationing and it's steamers like me that end up having the hardest time of it, only you soon find out you can't fight it; it's bloody everywhere." He looked off into the distance—seeing in, not out—downed the rest of his beer, placed the empty glass down on the bar very carefully, and looked at me. "Sorry about that," he said. "Funny how deep it goes."

"Very understandable, considering," I said, waving at the barman for two more pints.

"Anyway, one day I got the idea I should try pulling the

only string I had, try and get myself into NATKE, like my dad, perhaps even get into Elstree or Pinewood film studios. So I wrote letters to a few people at the Opera House and, bingo, I got to meet the guv'nor of the fly-floor here at the Prince of Wales. So with a bit of luck this job could be my way in, Jethro."

"Why didn't you try working your ticket up in Manchester?" I asked. "Wouldn't that have been easier for you, your friends, your mum?"

"No, not really. There's more theatres down here, isn't there, and then of course just outside London is where all the films get made and, well, there's this girl I'm a bit soft on and she's from the Smoke and..."

"Say no more," I said. "It's a wise man that knows when it's time to follow the lady." And on an even keel now, we chatted on until they called 'Time gentlemen, please,' for the fourth and last time and slung everyone out.

Outside on the pavement, Bob stuck his hand out and said, "Thanks, Jethro, for taking the trouble this afternoon and again tonight. If I never pick up the hang of flying flats properly, it won't be because of you."

"Gertcher," I said, "you're a bloody natural. See you and *Harvey* the invisible rabbit up on the fly-floor tomorrow, and don't you worry none—you'll get your ticket, you mark my words."

I waved a goodnight and walked off in the direction of Regent Street, back up towards Piccadilly Circus, keeping an eye open for a No. 15 bus going my way. When I got back home, two messages had been pushed under the door of the flat. The first was a telephone message from a Mr Fabrikant, written in Mary's big, round handwriting on a scrap of paper. It said simply, *'Lessons abound, if ye will only seek wisdom from the Apostles. 12:12.'* The other was an envelope with no address, just my full name and the words 'DELIVERED BY HAND' across the top. A note pinned to the letter said a Mr T. Nutkins had left it for me, which meant it was likely it was from his boss,

Jack Spot. Although, what on earth Spottsy wanted with me, I had no idea. I went through into the kitchen, got a table-knife, and slit open the envelope. It seemed Spottsy wanted to talk to me at my earliest convenience, about what the letter didn't say, but then the letter didn't say much at all beyond, *'Jethro, be a good lad and find me and be quick about it we need to talk. Yours, Jack Spot.'*

APOSTLES OF IRON

The clock on the mantelpiece chimed the quarter hour and I pocketed a handful of pennies from an ashtray on the table by the door and headed out to a nearby telephone-box. I'd only taken a few steps down the stairs when the light-bulbs in the stairwell blazed on and standing in her dressing gown on the landing below, rows of metal hair curlers glinting in the glow, eyes flashing and glaring up at me as if her very gaze might well turn me into stone, was my sister, Joanie.

"Hello, Joanie, you're up late…er…what's up? 'Bubs' okay, is he? Nothing wrong is there?" I said. "Sorry if I disturbed you, just got to pop out. Won't be long, back in a tick." But my attempt at evasion went for nought.

"Don't you 'back in a tick' me, Jethro," she said. "I'm not entirely unaware of how your world turns."

I tried another diversionary tactic. "Got the messages, ta very much. That new girl Mary seems to be working out a treat."

"Don't you try coming the old soap with me, Jethro, just you hold your horses a minute. There's something I want to talk to you about."

It was the tone of her voice that did it, and even though I was on the clock to telephone Ray, I sat on the stairs and listened to what she had to say. "Okay, dear sister of mine, you've got my undivided attention. What's up?"

"That slimy sod DI Morton from Paddington Green is what's up. He was in lunchtime, lording it about. And when I served him up his dinner he said the next time I saw you I was to tell you it'd be a very good idea if you stopped by the station for a little chat and that soon wasn't soon enough."

Detective Inspector Dicky 'Deadeye' Morton was the fastest gun in West London when it came to spotting an earner, but he usually kept his distance from me and mine. "Did he say what it was about by any chance?"

"Oh yes, I'm in his full confidence, I am. Once he'd eaten and drunk his fill, the sod just walked out, bold as brass, never offered to pay for nothing, not even a penny tip for the girls. And if Dicky 'Deadeye' feels he can try that sort of nonsense on, knowing I'm your bloody sister, that tells me he thinks he can put the arm on you for something, too. And I don't know what the hell it's all about, Jethro, but you just better watch yourself, you hear me, or I'll bloody kill you myself. Now get on and do whatever business it is you're off doing at this time of night I'm sure I don't want to know, but that's it, I've said me piece, and so a very good night to you."

"Everything alright, Joanie?" It was Barry, her husband— or 'Bubs', as I called him—and still half-asleep by the sound of him. "You should come back to bed, girl. It's half past your beauty sleep. 'Allo, Jeffro, been up to your old tricks again? Go careful, old cock."

" 'Lo, 'Bubs', just trying to earn an honest crust, is all. Very sorry Dicky 'Deadeye' bent your ear, Joanie, but I have no earthly idea why he'd want to chat with me. He probably wants to see if I'll grass someone up, but I promise I'll go careful when I go see him. I'll even try and get the starting price on what he's up to before I set foot in Paddington Green Police Station. Okay?"

She nodded, but she didn't look at me, she just gathered her dressing gown all the tighter to herself and disappeared in a huff. You know how women are when they're worried that something bad might befall you.

My first thought was that DI Dicky Morton had got wind of my troubles and was looking to be among the first to put the boot in to see if he could come away with some money in his hand. It's funny though how one thought leads to another, then another that unravels a whole string of forgotten memories. And suddenly all I could see was a young PC Dick Morton, not that I knew it was him back then, it was just that the 'J' Division Number glinting on his collar was forever afterwards etched on the back of my eyelids. He was stepping out from a side door, having just enjoyed a free beer and a packet of fags from one of the many public houses along his beat at the exact moment Jimmy Mooney and I happened to pass by. He clocked us. We clocked him. No words were spoken. Nothing was said. But it was one of those moments that get filed away and never forgotten by either party. At the time, I was a known 'face' round Hackney, Dalston and Bethnal Green, so I could've been pointed out to him by any number of coppers. And I knew then, as sure as eggs is eggs, that what Dicky 'Deadeye' wanted was to press me very hard about the whereabouts of "Monkey" Jim.

There were four telephone-boxes that stood in a row like soldiers on parade outside the West London Stadium on Church Street, and in short order they'd become such necessary landmarks to business for the street's many itinerant market traders, they'd earned the nicknames 'Matthew', 'Mark', 'Luke' and 'John'. Any young tearaways that tried to mess with the coin-boxes were very quickly dealt with. It was all very well for someone to try and turn a dishonest penny, but the number-one rule was you never ever shit in your own backyard. So, G.P.O. engineers aside, the telephone-boxes were nearly always in good working order.

It was nigh on midnight, well within the designated 'twelve minutes to, twelve minutes after' time-period and, apart from the odd rat and cat scurrying about, Church Street looked pleasingly deserted. I approached the Stadium, nipped into

'Matthew' and dropped a couple of pennies in the slot, dialled a number, let it ring three times, then pressed button 'B' to get my money back. Before you could count to ten, a telephone in one of the other phone boxes started ringing and by the time I'd stepped out of 'Matthew' and into 'John' it'd gone silent. It'd been Ray starting to call each telephone-box in turn. The idea being the first number that returned a ringing tone told him that telephone-box was unoccupied, and that would be the one I'd then go and wait in. I looked at my wristwatch. It usually took him no more than five minutes to walk to one of the many telephone-boxes along the Marylebone Road.

If ever there was dire need, I could always call Ray and speak to him direct, as the official requirement of him having to share his telephone line with another household had long been solved via the disbursement of a couple of fivers into the right back-pockets. The net result of which was that Ray shared his 'party-line' with none other than his other self, "Buggy" Billy. Our public-phone-box-to-public-phone-box calls were simply an additional precaution whenever we were unable to discuss urgent business face-to-face.

'John' rang. I picked up the phone. "It's John," I said into the mouthpiece. "I want to be saved."

"And you need to be saved," Ray said. "We all do."

It wasn't a long call. Worsening news, like worsening weather, needs to be dealt with quickly.

"I had an unannounced visit from your mate, Squirrel Nutkins," Ray whispered. "Didn't recognise me, though, but then he doesn't know me as me, it's only 'Buggy' B he knows from around the markets."

Blimey, Tommy Nutkins, my old mate from off the boats, and now the number-one minder for Jack Spot, one of the Smoke's top villains. Tommy and me went back before the war and as fate had had it we'd both served together throughout much of the conflict, too, on both the Atlantic and Northern Run convoys. Yet even with all that, Tommy hadn't a clue about

Ray and me. No one but the two of us knew that, save for the aforementioned Colonel Walsingham of MI5 and his *aide de camp*, Simon Bosanquet of Special Branch.

"What did he want?"

"Very polite, no threats," Ray said, "but what it came down to was that his employer, Mr J Comer, wondered whether I'd be open to meeting him in regard to my knowledge of all things Hatton Garden."

"He said 'J Comer'? That's interesting."

"Isn't it?" said Ray. "Said his guv'nor had once been introduced to me by that name. So I asked him what sort of help was Mr Comer looking for: buying, selling, or appraising? Seems he wants me to help locate and then acquire some articles. So I explained that I only dealt with such business on Monday mornings and I arranged a meet with him next week."

That's when I told Ray I'd also got a message from Jacob Comer, alias Jack Spot, and that Tommy Nutkins had hand-delivered mine to the Victory Cafe in a sealed envelope. "Spottsy wants to see me, too, doesn't say what about, but again, no threats implied. What do you think he's after?"

"Word's been out on the street for years he can help secure the return of missing items for a price. So if he wants my help in re-acquiring a specific set of tom it'll no doubt be on behalf of a third party. It's a good little earner for him and does his reputation a world of good, as everyone ends up happy, especially the insurance company. It's also well known in certain circles that I have a certain amount of experience when it comes to knowing the various ins and outs of the diamond trade. The question of course is why Spottsy has chosen to call on me now, when he never has before."

"Maybe you and I weren't the only ones he visited," I offered.

"I can't speak to that, but the fact the message came from Comer and not Spot tells me it's probably due to my connections with London's Jewish community, not from my contacts down the Reading Room."

"I got a funny feeling I know which set of sparklers he's after."

"I have the very same feeling."

"Do you think Spottsy's also trying to find 'Monkey' Jim?"

"No, I don't see him going through me to fish for Jimmy Mooney. I suspect he's trying to move downstream so he can get a lure in the water and try catch the whole lot before it ends up at the breakers and re-cutters or leaves the country for good. Clever of Spottsy, really, given the current feeling around the Garden; no one's going to touch anything they think is to do with the Meridian Mansions haul with a ten-foot bargepole. That's why he's turned to the old Yamaka network. So I'll see him Monday—it'd be impolitic and impolite not to. Who knows, I may well learn something to our advantage."

"I wonder who Spottsy's working for. Given past form, I suppose the obvious person would be the deceased bloke's missus."

"Again, can't comment. Could be the insurance trying a back-door deal. I also wouldn't put it past Messima to play on Spottsy's vanity like a violin and set someone up as a supposed intermediary for the bereaved widow."

Blimey, that was a nasty thought, but he had a point; Darby Messima was as duplicitous as they come. "Talking of weasels," I said. "DI 'Deadeye' Morton stopped by the Victory earlier today and left word I should stop by Paddington Green Police Station at my earliest convenience. Given the size of the earner Messima's put up, I just know he's going to try and tap me about 'Monkey' Jim. Thing is, you see, I recalled an incident, before the war, when Morton was a young copper doing the rounds of his earners, and he just happened to see Jimmy and me coming out of a pub together. It's funny what sticks in your memory; it has for me, maybe it has for him, too."

"Now it's you who's putting two and two together and coming up with five. Believe you me, if DI Morton or any other of the local plainclothes wide-boys had anything concrete on you they'd have had you banged up already. They've got nothing to go on except the half-dozen names they've heard whispered round the streets and markets. Morton's just shaking the tree to see what falls, see if he can shorten the odds. Him filing away the fact he once saw you and Jimmy Mooney together, some dozen years ago, is stretching coincidence a bit far, even for me. Best you put it all in a box and put it on one side until you know what you're dealing with. You've got enough on your plate, as it is."

"True," I said. "It's probably nothing. Anything else on the wind?"

"Yes, there's heavy whisper Messima's upped the price on 'Monkey' Jim's head again. He's gone bonkers about finding him, apparently. On top of which, there's also word Messima's putting feelers out to all the other gang-leaders, north of the water. I don't know what in hell he's up to by doing that, but it makes this other business with Spottsy seem even more iffy."

"It gives my itches the itches just thinking about it," I said. "How do you think we should play it?"

"Play out our lines and see what we reel in. No other choice."

"Right," I said. "I'll go see Spottsy, as and when, then go see what 'Deadeye' wants. First, though, I'll try go and see a man about a missing monkey."

"Most important you do that," Ray said. "You go safe."

"I certainly will," I said. "Call you in a couple of days, same pack-drill. Bye, me old china." I put the telephone back down in its cradle, pushed my back against the door, and left 'John' and the rest of them to the night.

It'd started coming on to rain while I'd been in the telephone kiosk and I'd been that wrapped up in talking to Ray I hadn't even noticed. It wasn't that far back to the flat, but I was well soaked by the time I put the key in the door. That was just for starters, though, for with things as they now were, I had little choice but to be off out again to do those things that can only be done at night, and in a bloody cemetery, no less.

What's that they say about it never rains, but it pours bloody buckets?

ANGELS OF STONE

I slipped over to the lock-up on North Wharf Road, back of Paddington Station, changed into some dry clothes, and brewed some tea for my Thermos flask. I put on a slate-coloured bicycle cape and black knitted 'watch' cap, tucked my waxed-cotton wet weather balaclava and pair of Zeiss 7 x 50 binoculars into a satchel, and got on my bike. The Kriegsmarine night-glasses had cost a bloody fortune, but they were light and small and extremely waterproof and far better suited to what I had in mind than the big Afrika Korps binoculars I usually used whenever scoping out a place up on the tiles.

I was headed for Kensal Green. During daylight hours, I had choices aplenty—a No. 18 or No. 52 bus, a No. 662 trolley-bus, the Tube—but navigating London's highways and byways at night unnoticed and uncommented upon always demanded a certain measure of forethought. Night buses were out, as they were too few and far between, too well-lit, and with far too many nosy passengers minutely clocking your face and pondering why on earth you had to be abroad at such an ungodly hour. If driving the taxicab I could push it to 2:00 am, but when on foot or bicycle I always tried to be off the streets by 1:30 as then I could be taken for a waiter, a barman, or a bottle-washer on his weary way home. Anytime after 5:30 am and you were just another honest worker on his way to clock-on for the six o'clock, early shift. But if you were out on London's streets anytime in the witching hours of the night, you were just asking to be stopped and questioned and, as like as not, cautioned, arrested, and taken into police custody to assist with enquiries.

If I was stopped and found in possession of an expensive pair of binoculars, it'd provoke very pointed questions, so I carried a receipt of sorts, as well as a little sketchbook showing drawings of birds in the bicycle's saddlebag. Kensal Green Cemetery, the adjoining St Mary's Cemetery, and Scrubs Common were a well-known Mecca for bird-watchers, and across the length and breadth of Britain no one was less likely to arouse suspicion than a mad amateur ornithologist in pursuit of his passion.

Thanks to the incessant rain, any coppers out on the beat had all very sensibly found a shop-doorway in which to keep themselves dry, and I all but flew down the Harrow Road. I didn't mind all the peddling as it helped get the blood circulating. It also helped that my old Raleigh bicycle, even though it looked much the worse for wear, sported Sturmey-Archer 3-speed gears, one of mankind's better inventions. And with my feet going up and down like the clappers and the sound of my tyres in the rain repeatedly 'shushing' me to silence, it wasn't long before I found myself passing the cemetery's Main Gate. And, as I peddled on past, I switched off the headlamp and quickly faded into the darkness.

Six hundred yards up the road, just before the Upper Gate, was a spot obscured by a dense tangle of bushes where I could hide the bike and slip in through a break in the perimeter wall—the result of an errant bomb dropped by the Luftwaffe. And with that soon done, and me safe inside the grounds, I stood amidst the rustling waves of bushes and swaying stands of trees and waited for my eyes to adjust to the greater darkness in the night.

Kensal Green Cemetery, London's oldest public burial ground, is spread over seventy-plus acres and laid out more like a country park than a country of the dead. Apart from the owls and foxes abroad that night, I counted myself as being the only other living thing there, bar the person I'd come to find. And I pulled my waxed-cotton balaclava down over my head and became as a shadow and moved silently through the granite-edged stillness of tens of thousands of tombs, monuments, and mausoleums.

I drifted north by north-west towards Terrace Avenue then took a south-westerly course, avoiding the narrow avenue known as Inner Circle, until I came to the Anglican Chapel at the very heart of the cemetery. The huge Doric structure built of Portland stone, with its equally impressive porticoes and flanking colonnades, was just as imposing in the dark as in daylight, but I gave it no heed. And I certainly wasn't there to explore the catacombs below. I had a higher purpose.

The big double doors to the chapel were locked, as you'd expect, as was the little side door to the vestry, but that was easily dealt with and I was soon inside, padding up the stairs as silently as a draft seeps into a room.

I eased open the little maintenance hatch that led out onto the top of the colonnade and prayed that the bloke responsible for the upkeep of the place had oiled the hinges. From there it was an easy climb up onto the chapel roof. The cornices at each end masked my presence and the roof's gentle slant meant I could lie spread-eagled on the eastern slope of the roof and peer over the ridgeline without fear of sliding down the tiles and over the edge. And with my binoculars pointed in the direction of the West London Crematorium, the western boundary of the cemetery, I settled in to my task.

Over to my left were the motor factory and gas works. Straight ahead, beyond St Mary's Catholic Cemetery and the other side of Scrubs Lane, were the Hythe Road Goods Depot and Engine Shed. And between them all, at eleven o'clock, less than a mile away across the Grand Union Canal and Great Western Railway line, was Wormwood Scrubs, one of His Majesty's less salubrious prisons. The perimeter lights from the prison, the factories, the marshalling yard, together with the streetlights along Scrubs Lane and Harrow Road, threw a feint nimbus of light up into the night sky; just enough for me to discern shadow from shape once my eyes had fully adjusted, and hopefully more than enough for me to catch any movement outside the naturally ordained rhythm of things, thereafter.

The 'Scrubs' was significant in another way, as it was where Jimmy Mooney had been banged up and shouted himself back to sobriety and an early release back into society. He'd doted on his family and the killing of them during the Blitz had all but killed him, too, or at least everything in him that he'd considered worthwhile. It must've driven the poor sod potty knowing he was so near yet so far from the place where what few remains there'd been of his wife, two daughters, and sister had been cremated and lain to rest in a tiny plot in the cemetery's Gardens of Remembrance.

That's what Harry 'Rabbit' had meant when he'd whispered, "True friendship runs evergreen from cradle to the grave," back on that Soho street corner. He'd twigged immediately that if I knew 'Romulus' and 'Remus', the nicknames the brothers had used ever since their Romany mother had told them wild tales of her people having originally been succoured and protected by wolves, then I knew more than enough to be trusted; I'd certainly know about the fate of the Mooney women. That's why he'd pointed me towards Kensal Green Cemetery.

So there I was, in the dark of night, a creeper out to catch a creeper, and I must've spent a good three or four hours up on the chapel roof just staring out into the rain-swept darkness. And even though I saw neither hide nor hair of Jimmy that night, I got a strong sense he was out there somewhere.

I got a good sense of the cemetery, too. Like everyone else lying there in the dead of night, it didn't matter who or what you were or had been in life—son of a commoner or son of a king; gentile, Arab or Jew; dissenter or unbeliever—the blessed place gladly took all souls into its ample bosom.

Then, finding it harder and harder to stay awake, I knocked it in the head for the night and made my way back towards the perimeter wall. Where, with my back against a tree, I sat draped in dark wet shadows and supped hot tea from my Thermos flask until I felt life flow into me again. Even with there being no result, I was pleased I'd at last made a move on whatever chessboard it was Messima had set up in pursuit of even more wealth and power.

Tomorrow, I'd try and get more pieces on my side of the board, put together some sort of defence and perhaps even position myself to go on the attack. I finished off the tea, folded my arms, put my head down on my knees, and promptly fell asleep.

OLD FLAMES. NEW HEAT.

Later that morning, a little bleary-eyed but otherwise feeling very much like a new man again after a session at Harrow Road Turkish Baths, I was about to cross the Edgware Road to go for a shave at the barber's in the Tube station and of all people who did I have to bump into, crossing over from the other direction, but DI 'Deadeye' Morton. I jumped in feet first, holding my nose. "I was just coming to see you," I said brightly.

"That's good," he said, knowing full well Paddington Green Police Station was in the opposite direction. "Fancy a cup of tea?" he said, not waiting for an answer. "I want to keep this unofficial. See you in the Bridge in ten minutes. Don't be late."

Out the corner of my eye, I caught sight of Binnsy eyeballing the two of us stuck like lemons in the middle of the road, so when I reached the other side I marched straight up to his newspaper stand. "Morning, Binnsy. A *Mirror* and a *Mail*, please." I handed him a couple of coppers.

"Bump into all sorts round here," he wheezed, his mince pies looking as shifty as ever behind the bottle-like lenses of his National Health glasses.

"You're telling me," I said. "Seems everybody and his mother's son wants a bloody drink these days. It's worse than having to pay taxes." The mere thought of having to pay hard-earned money to the Inland Revenue was enough to dampen his curiosity for a split-second, so I threw in a, "I could murder a cup of tea," and an even quicker, "See you, Binnsy."

"Not if I sees you first," he yelled after me, but I'd already crossed back across the Edgware Road, heading for the Bridge, as by then I really did need a cuppa—always the ticket in an unexpected crisis.

"Just a word to the wise," 'Deadeye' said, stirring his tea. "Come into the station of your own accord and make an official statement that you were nowhere near Meridian Mansions. It'll help show you've got nothing to hide and might well help if you later got yourself arrested and formally charged."

I narrowed my eyes. "I don't get it," I said. "Why on God's green would you go out of your way to help me?"

"I could tell you it's because you're still trying to go straight with that theatre lark of yours, but the truth is this so-called list of Meridian Mansions creepers is a load of old bollocks. And me, I don't like people trying to lead me round and round in circles as if I've got a bloody ring through my nose. I'll do me own detective work, in my own way, thank you very much."

And that *was* interesting; it said he wasn't in on 'the list' or getting a back-hander for it. "I thought you were going to tap me for a drink," I said.

He looked at me straight. "If you were still in the game, I might well have done, only you're just another punter now, not a proper 'face' and I don't deal in pennies." He looked round. "I don't come in here too often. I prefer the grub down the Victory."

I looked at him, still not believing my ears or the flannel he was giving me, so I kept it non-committal. "Yeah, that's why I eat there, myself," I said.

He nodded. "Gets me out from under all my little playmates at Paddington Green nick; gives me room to think," he said. "Food's always good, too. That sister of yours obviously knows all the right people."

He was right, of course. But, again, I didn't offer anything.

"There is one other little thing," he said, very quietly.

"Eye, eye," I said to myself. "Watch it, here it comes."

He reached inside a pocket for a brown paper envelope. "Only, I was in there not too long ago and had to rush out as I saw Larry 'the Dip' lifting a bloke's wallet, right outside the window, so I dashed out to collar the bastard and left without paying. And what with one thing and another, I haven't been back down Church Street for a week or two. So I was wondering if you'd give her this. There's a couple of quid in there, tell her to put it on the slate for me."

Fuck me, if he wasn't handing me money, a very unexpected turn-up with a very definite downside. I looked round the cafe to see who was in and who was watching and wondered what the going rate for a copper's nark was these days. Five quid, a whisper? Ten quid for a racing cert?

"Er, I better not," I said. "The walls in here tend to have eyes as well as ears. Very nice of you to want to settle the account with Joanie, and I'll mention it to her, of course, but I'm sure she'd be very pleased if you gave her the money yourself next time you're in the Victory."

"Fair enough," he said, not batting an eyelid. "I understand." He stood up and dropped a two-bob piece on the table. "That's for the tea," he said. "Wouldn't want you thinking I was tapping you for a drink. Just remember to come into the station, sooner rather than later, and do yourself some good."

Then he was gone and my thoughts dashed in asking nasty questions. Was I being set up, again? And if so, and if it wasn't Messima paying DI Morton to put the kybosh on me, who the fuck was? And why? Of course, there was always the possibility, however far-fetched, that the bugger had turned into a proper copper. Either way, it was all very unsettling. I looked down and saw my cup was still full to the brim and stone cold.

I hoofed it back to the Tube station and had my shave, all the while thinking of the close shave I'd already had that morning. It was hard to say which cut closer to the bone.

I took the Bakerloo Line down to Piccadilly Circus, came up by the Pavilion cinema, nipped over the road, and hopped the first bus turning up Shaftesbury Avenue. I jumped off at the bottom of Frith Street and quick-marched up towards Old Compton Street and on into Moronis, the newsagents, where I bought a copy *The Stage*, my usual camouflage when in Soho. I also bought a bunch of picture postcards of London; well-known landmarks such as Big Ben, Piccadilly Circus, and Trafalgar Square, and Londoners in uniform, policemen, guardsmen, Pearly Kings and Queens, Beefeaters, all the usual parade of colourful characters so beloved by tourists. Postcards have always been a favourite of mine. Keep it cryptic and it's marvellous what you can hide in plain English. Mission accomplished, I ventured next door into Patisserie Valerie for a cup of coffee and a bun.

Even at that time of the morning the backstage gossip was going full blast and, given the speed the knives were going in and out, it'd be a bloody wonder there'd be any actors left alive in London come nightfall. Despite the ritual massacre going on all around me, I managed to squeeze out enough table-space to address the postcards without too much coffee spilling on them. I quickly killed my pastry and raised the curtain for Act Two. I ordered another coffee, drank it down and waved for another, then another. Ten minutes later, when the nice waitress asked if I wanted yet another, I said 'no' and added just loud enough that what my horrible hangover really needed was 'the hair of the dog.' I made a pantomime of looking at my wristwatch and shaking my head, muttering on and on about the absurdity of official pub-opening hours, then arched my eyebrows as the solution visibly dawned upon me. I scooped up the postcards, paid my bill, left a nice tip for the nice waitress, then nipped round the corner, up into Dean Street.

I knew at least a dozen pairs of eyeballs would've swivelled after me as I left the cafe, but I'd planned on that. I needed a reason to be seen going where I was going. I did however steer clear of Greek and Bateman Streets, as in my humble opinion my star turn as a fledgling corner-man the previous day couldn't be bettered and I didn't want to give any critics any chance to rethink my performance. Also, being seen on the same street as Harry "Rabbit" twice in two days could be seen as being one time too many.

I skirted round the puddles, did a tango around a line of battered dustbins standing sentry duty outside one of the restaurants, and pushed open a badly scuffed blue door that led straight onto a dimly lit stairwell that smelled of cats' piss, boiled cabbage, and vomit. Though, after the night I'd had in the cemetery, it felt strangely comforting to be back in the land of what otherwise passed for normal in Soho. On the top floor was a club run by a Cypriot that catered for layabouts and minor villains, but on the floor below that was Sylvia's, a members-only drinking club that opened for business every day at ten in the morning.

If you were granted admission, that was.

The only people allowed in were the ones Sylvia hadn't taken an instant dislike to, had banned, or had had bodily thrown out. Problem was, you never knew your status until you tried to enter, when you were either welcomed with a warm smile or she swore at you in Russian and George, the six-foot-four barman—who was also her minder—told you in no uncertain terms to fuck off out of it.

That morning, however, Sylvia, as ever, elegantly perched on her corner stool near the entrance to the bar, greeted me by gently touching me on the arm and offering up her cheeks to be pecked in sequence. Then she scolded me for me having deserted her for so long.

I took a quick butcher's into the dimly lit, smoke-filled room to see who was in and who might be trouble even at that time of the morning. There were ten or twelve people, mostly men, mostly sloshed, although whether still hung-over from the previous night or freshly acquired with the dawn was debatable.

I recognised one or two faces and a well-known ginger that was holding court at the other end of the bar. I'd been introduced to him once. He reckoned himself a painter of life's tortured reality, but he didn't nod and I didn't wave.

I turned back to Sylvia, who really was a work of art.

She'd been a famous beauty once, but now she was what people referred to as being on the wrong side of forty. In truth, she was well past sixty, but she was still a 'looker' in my book, and a lovely lady. She was as small as a bird, with delicate little bones and skin as translucent as porcelain, and she always wore her hair pulled tight back off her face, in a severe bun. It was rumoured she'd once danced with the Follies in New York and Paris, and had even been painted by Augustus John, though quite when all that'd been no one thought it polite to ask.

I ordered a double Whisky and offered to buy her a large gin, but she graciously declined, as did George, who was busily wiping a glass when I extended my offer of a tipple to him. I lit two cigarettes and handed one to Sylvia and we both pretended to flirt a little, then she demurely lowered her eyes and told me I should perhaps be going or she wouldn't be responsible for the consequences. I smiled a genuinely warm smile and leaned in as if whispering some more sweet nothings and spoke softly and quickly so only she could hear. I said I was in dire need of a favour and asked if she could spare a few moments, *sub rosa*, so to speak.

She threw back her head, exposing her wondrous neck, laughed a tinkly laugh, gave me the briefest of nods, and then gently drew me to her. I explained I needed information concerning the activities of a certain person who probably hadn't ever been in her club, but who might've frequented Soho's more esoteric haunts. I suggested it was possible she'd heard things she hadn't attached any importance to, but that those whispers might well spell the difference between life and death for me. I said I knew her discretion was legendary and that in no way did I mean to cause her any trouble.

She simply leaned forward and closed my lips with her fingertips. "With me, my darling Jethro, your past is your credit. If you weren't in desperate need, I know you'd never have asked." She turned her head a fraction and said, "George, no one." Then, a study in understated elegance, she slid off her stool, stepped behind the bar, and pulled back a curtain, revealing a passageway. She didn't crook her finger at me, but then she didn't need to; the angle of her neck said it all.

I followed and let the curtain fall behind me.

I stepped along a narrow passageway, then through a door that led into a tiny drawing room. It was exquisitely furnished, something from another time and another place, the profusion of beautiful objects giving it the feel of an artist's atelier. The first thing that hit me was the profusion of framed paintings and drawings on the walls. One of them, a charcoal drawing, stood out like an old friend in a crowd. It was a sketch I'd done of Sylvia sitting on her stool in the bar early the year war broke out, and there it was in a lovely little gilt-frame nestled amongst real masterpieces.

I looked around the room. There was an armchair, a long couch that in a push could double as a bed, and a couple of side-tables—one covered with photographs in silver frames, the other a vase of flowers and a telephone. There was a lovely antique sideboard with rows of porcelain vases on top, that held everything from dried flowers to old painting brushes and drawing implements. There was even a little bathroom with toilet, off. It was an oasis of beauty amidst all the endless soot, squalor, and grime of Soho, and I'd never once had the slightest inkling about the place. "Help yourself to a drink, darling boy," she said, softly. "I just need a moment. Tell me how I can help."

I stood my side of the half-closed door. "It concerns those rumours about Nigel Fox, the MP that died under mysterious circumstances. I think someone's trying to fit me in the frame for it, Sylvia, only I have no earthly idea why. So I came to see you on the off-chance you or someone may have heard Fox's name mentioned in regard to questionable behaviour, whether it be booze, gambling, girls, boys, white powder, or running black-market nylons or Whisky. All I need to know is whether the bloke was on the straight and narrow or if he was bent— and, if so, in what direction."

She came back into the room wearing a pale pink silk dressing gown that set off her eyes and hair beautifully. She offered no comment, nor did she raise one of her beautifully applied eyebrows, she just nodded. "Consider it done," she said. "I'll ask around very discreetly. How is one supposed to get in touch with you? If you were seen coming back to the club anytime soon, people might say you've taken up as a drunkard or that, at the very least, you've become my latest paramour."

"I'd be flattered if people were to think that," I said.

She smiled. "Either way, my darling Jethro, I think this calls for a little more discretion than usual." She turned and pointed to the telephone, the silk dressing gown rustling and swirling about her ankles. "I really don't think you should call me here."

"I do believe I have a solution," I said, producing a couple of picture postcards from my inside pocket. I handed them to her, one of each type. I'd already addressed them to a PO Box at a newsagent's off the Edgware Road run by one of "Buggy" Billy's first ever hand-off boys on his market stall. The bloke was also a twice-weekly regular at the Victory Cafe and would slip Joanie any mail that'd come for "Buggy" or me whenever he popped in, which over the years had proved a very handy little arrangement for all concerned.

"If you should find that Nigel Fox was up to anything, Sylvia, just send a postcard of one of the London characters in costume—it'll tell me the man was other than he portrayed himself to be. If you can possibly add a word or two about what he liked or what he leaned towards, so much the better. However, if you hear he wasn't bent in any way, just send one of the postcards showing one of the popular landmarks. Fox always said he wanted to make London a safer place to visit."

She nodded, glanced at the postcards, and put them in a drawer in the sideboard. She moved across to the window and sat on the couch, and leaned back against the cushions, letting her dressing gown fall from her shoulders. The pale morning light caught the lines and curves of her face and neck beautifully. "Now come and sit here by me a while, my darling Jethro," she said, her voice as soft as silk, "I want you to do another drawing of me. I want to be sure you haven't lost your touch."

About an hour later, I left by the way I'd come.

George, the barman, still wiping dry the same wineglass, by the look of it, gave me a very odd look.

I didn't stop to ask him what he meant by it. He looked busy enough, as it was.

One of the many amazing things about women is their ability to get hold of secrets and, if need be, keep a firm hold on them even unto the grave. It's how they're made; they hold things together for the good of all: families, clans, businesses—whole cultures, sometimes. It's always been the women that preserve and keep safe, never the men. The men are usually all off somewhere, busy marauding and pillaging, searching for even more things that need holding. Men always seem to want to climb up some ladder or other and they give the game away as much by what's on their faces as what can be read by their actions. That's why men can always easily be pried open and preyed upon by dint of their ambitions and wants. A woman, on the other hand, whatever the implied benefit or threat, will look you in the face and be unfathomable; you'll never know what it is she really wants or what it is she's really after. And although it's a well-known fact men can never take their eyes off women, they rarely if ever see for want of looking, which is why women also make the best spies: they're literally hidden in not-so-plain sight.

And if Sylvia was one such accomplished mistress of mystery, the next old flame I had to call on had succeeded in taking it to a whole new level.

Her real name was Elizabeth Anderson. She favoured 'Lilibet' for short, but I always called her 'Shanghai Lily.' We'd been puffing away on a cigarette in the dark, in her bed, in her posh private flat, having just shared just about everything else a balmy London night has to offer. I'd been spinning her some yarn about an old china I'd known on the boats, before the War, and the age-old Cockney rhyming slang tickled her fancy and she asked me, right then and there, whether I'd now rate her as an old china, as well. I laughed and told her straight as how 'old china' simply wouldn't do her justice and said I'd call her 'Shanghai Lily' instead, on account of her being a dead ringer for Marlene Dietrich in the looks and legs department. "Same meaning," I said, "only tons more special." And by and by the nickname became a bond of sorts, like a secret handshake, and if I ever got the message by postcard, telegram, or telephone that 'Shanghai Lily' sent her regards, I dropped just about everything and went in search of her.

I'd first set eyes on her, one gloriously fine day, long before the War, when she was exiting the Burlington Arcade and I was sashaying down Bond Street, past all the high-class art galleries and jewellery shops, with a little too much time on my hands. I just stood there in the street, mouth agape, stunned by beauty. I was much younger, of course, and only very recently come under the tutelage of "Buggy" Billy, but I was already old enough to know she was a Grade 'A' knockout. I followed her for the next several hours, ending up in Hatton Garden of all places, where another golden opportunity then presented itself, out of the blue. Only this one involved the offices of a certain very select company of diamond traders and, not for the last time, I had to choose between what quickly became the two passions of my life. The fact I almost came a cropper because of an excess amount of dynamite entering late into the equation is, as they say, another story, but the upshot was that when I looked round for Lily—not that I knew that was her name— London had completely swallowed her up again.

I next caught sight of her some years later when I was a newly commissioned Fourth-Officer of the Cunard-White Star Line aboard the good ship R.M.S. *Queen Mary* on its way across the Atlantic to New York. And not to mince words, but I followed her again, all around the decks, then all around Manhattan. Then I followed her back across the Atlantic to Southampton and eventually all the way back up to London, by which time fascination had turned into obsession. But then, as well you know, beauty of a particular sort garners fools more easily than gold.

Always has.

Always will.

As time went by, I found out she ran a small but very, very exclusive employment and placement agency, one that dealt exclusively in the placing of ladies of the right sort into the right sort of positions: everything from ladies' companions to personal secretaries. Even nannies, if required. Many of the ladies spoke more than one language, all had been to finishing school, and the whisper was there were even a good few European blue bloods amongst them. Needless to say, all the ladies were uncommonly beautiful, which of course explained why it was not uncommon that a good number of them also ended up receiving offers of marriage from their employers.

From what I could glean, a lot of her business came from embassies and foreign trade legations, and big American companies, as well as extremely wealthy and influential businessmen. Institutions and individuals for whom money was never any issue. As I explained it to Ray, years later, the fees were such that if you had to inquire about them, you obviously weren't the sort of client the service looked to attract. But, then, Lily offered the *crème de la crème*, as the French so cleverly say. Her girls were nothing at all like the strings of brasses Darby Messima brought in from abroad. Lily's business was as different as the uppermost top drawer could ever be from the bottom of the barrel. Messima might've had half of West End Central in his pocket and a fair bit of Scotland Yard, too, but Lily being Lily would've had a little black book of private telephone numbers to call if ever the need arose, and every single one of them the ex-directory number of some VIP in Westminster, Whitehall or the City. Not that she ever told me any of this. Let's just say that, then as now, I had my ways of finding things out. I never did find out who the 'money man' was behind it all or what the relationship was between the two of them, not that that was really any of my business.

I never did visit Lily's establishment. I mean, what would I want with a nanny? Then the War broke out and the world turned and took me with it. Then thankfully the War ended and soon after VE Day, as so often seems to happen in London, what happened once happened again and there she was, walking across Piccadilly from Fortnum's, heading in the direction of the Arcade. Only this time I had the money and a body of experience to back up my desires.

Eventually the world turned again. Only this time she took me with her. A voyage of discovery no man could ever forget or would ever want to.

"So, my 'china boy', it is so very good to see you again. To what do I owe the pleasure? My secretary said you had an urgent message for Shanghai Lily."

I'd rung her office in Knightsbridge first thing and asked for an appointment and after the line went dead for a moment I'd been told to come round just before lunchtime. And there she was again, enough to unsettle the gyroscopes on an eighty-thousand-ton dead-weight ocean-going liner, let alone a Cockney lad like me, sea legs or no. She was one of those rare women that never seem to age at all and looked absolutely stunning whether she was clothed in a towel or the very latest Paris had to offer. I'd once told her she could wear a boiler suit and still make it appear the very height of fashion.

"Hello, Lily, love," I said. "Thanks for seeing me. Not to mince words, but I'm in a spot of trouble and need to ask for your help.

I also know time is money in your business and wouldn't want any of your ladies to go without or think they were being taken advantage of. I have sufficient funds and I'll pay whatever you deem is the proper rate for any time or effort expended."

She nodded, to acknowledge my visit was business, not personal. "Do go on," she said.

"Thing is, Lily, I know your ladies must hear things as they go about their business, and maybe they've already heard what it is I'm looking to find out, but as yet are unaware of its importance." So then I told her everything, bar the fact I'd actually done the Meridian Mansions job. Other than that I was completely candid with her. I mean, she knew all too well I'd been a high-class cat burglar and jewel thief and had even called on me herself, once or twice, to regain certain legal papers or photographs she believed should more rightfully be in her possession. And I'd rifled the odd safe and cracked a few strong boxes for her, and happily so. After all, she'd unlocked things in me.

Lily sat silent for a moment or two, her face inscrutable, unreadable. "I'll see what I can do for you, Jethro," she said. "It's a little out of our usual line, so I make no promises." Then her face broke into a smile and it was like sunshine dissolving shadows. "Will you stay for lunch?" she asked. "I can have my secretary bring in some cold-cuts, some cheese, and some wine."

"I could eat a horse," I said. "Thanks for agreeing to help, Lily."

"That's what friends are for my dear, darling 'china boy.' I can also assure you it won't be horse that you eat. The father of one of the girls supplies meat to the Café Royal, Simpson's in the Strand, and Harrods Food Hall, amongst others." She smiled an all-too-knowing smile. "As well you know, it always pays to have secret contacts in all the right places."

I couldn't help but break into a smile then. After all, that was the very reason I'd come.

A TEA-ROSE BY ANY OTHER NAME

The night Sid Field came up with the idea that 'Harvey' the invisible rabbit should also take a bow at the end of the performance, there were twice the usual number of curtain calls and the applause seemed to go on for hours. It was a great bit of theatre. Everyone backstage knew then that Sid would make the same call every night for the rest of the run. I remember it because that very same night I went in search of an old friend whose stock-in-trade was also invisibility, but who wouldn't have been caught dead in dyed rabbit fur, whatever the colour.

I declined a drink with the lads after the show, said I had a gyppy tummy and needed an early night. Then I dropped by the stage-door, to pick up a couple of parcels I'd left earlier. "Come for me packages, Fred," I said, as I slid a packet of fags across the counter by way of thanks. Fred motioned with his eyes for me to come round into his cubbyhole. "What's up," I asked. "You okay?"

"Couple of blokes in asking after you earlier, Jeffro. Plainclothes coppers by the look of them. Flashed what could've been warrant cards at me, but I didn't look too closely. They tend to get a bit funny if you do. Wanted to know if you worked here and if so for how long. I said as how you always pulled your weight, got on with people. Seemed to satisfy them."

"Thanks, Fred," I said. "It's probably me being cited in some rich divorce case, eh?" I forced a chuckle and gave him the bent-eye to show it was nothing that either of us need worry about.

He tapped the side of his nose. "Nod's as good as a wink to a blind man, Jeffro, it'll go no further."

"Night, then, Fred. Thanks, again."

And with that I walked up into Soho.

Piccadilly Circus, my first destination, was a mere hundred yards due west of the Prince of Wales, but that night I had reason to go by a more circuitous route. When I got as far as Broadwick Street, I zigzagged left through half a dozen streets, which got me to Glasshouse Street and back down to the Circus. By which time I'd dispensed with the cardboard boxes and brown-paper wrapping in various dustbins and was wearing the hat, overcoat, horn-rimmed glasses, and false moustache I'd had parcelled away. The moustache wouldn't have stood up too well to the harsh light of day, but in the kaleidoscope of shadows of a London night it did just fine. The entire transformation, completed, as the French are wont to say, *à pied*. I also changed my gait just enough for it not to be me and added a slight brogue to my voice and, hey presto, I was to all intents and purposes an out-of-towner from north of the border. And with me thus newly-garbed, I hurriedly descended into the Underground as per someone hoping to catch a last train, did a quick circuit round the ticket hall, and came up again outside Messrs. Swan & Edgar, corner of Piccadilly and Regent Street.

They say that if you hang around Piccadilly Circus long enough, you'll eventually see everyone you've ever known. Funny that, because when I stood for a moment in the shadow of the department store, I could've sworn I saw Bob Miller coming up from the station entrance by the Criterion Theatre. He peered round as if looking for someone then went back down again, but the sighting was pushed out of mind as someone bumped up against me and asked whether I wanted a good time. "Not tonight," I muttered, and the lady sashayed off and told me in extremely pointed language where I could put my hat. After that, three more brasses approached me in as many minutes, each time from a different direction. And each time I declined their offers of a good time, only to be told once more in no uncertain terms what I could go and do to myself. One brass shouted at me that she never liked doing it with mean Scots gits, anyway, which wasn't much of a review, but at least it played to the veracity of my accent. I told the woman straight that I had other fish to fry. It stopped her dead for a moment, then she caught on and she told me I was hanging around the wrong part of the fucking fish shop.

One thing I noticed was that most of the brasses seemed to be making much more of an effort with their make-up and dress, always a sure sign of increased competition and commerce. Truth was, though, it was probably due to the fact all the electric signs round the Circus had been turned on again the previous April. It's a well-known fact that lighting plays a large part in the success of any theatrical enterprise. And the official 'switch-on' after ten years of mandated darkness had drawn huge crowds and, as you can well imagine, business around Soho hadn't looked back since.

I drifted across to that part of the 'Dilly known as 'the Arches' and stood looking at the statue of Eros, frozen for eternity with his bow and arrow pointed up Shaftesbury Avenue. Silhouetted by the neon lights, I waited to be noticed. Three-quarters of the 'Dilly were worked by regular brasses, whereas the darkest area, where I now was, was the preserve of the lavender boys— some of them dressed as women. On first appearance, a few were quite passable, at least enough for them not to draw the attention of any vice squad coppers that deigned to work the same hours they did.

It wasn't long—about the time it took to straighten a seam or a wig— before I sensed and then heard high-heeled footsteps tripping towards me, although a blind man could've smelled the cheap perfume from a mile off. "Eye-eye," I said to myself. "Curtain up."

"Hello, dear, have you a light by any chance?" The voice was soft and breathy, only a good deal more tentative than a regular brass would've been. "Or are you perhaps looking for a very special time?"

I turned round slowly and said quietly, "I'm looking for Glover."

"Never heard of whoever it is," the would-be lady said, lifting her face up for me to admire. "Now how about that light, dear?"

I ignored the well-practised flutter of the false eyelashes. "Look, love," I said, my voice flat but with a slight edge. "I'm no copper, no *sharpy*, and I'm not vice squad. I'm just an old china of Glover's from the good old, bad old days, only she called herself Doris back then."

"And she called you Jock, I suppose. Doris, you say?"

"Yes, from her days on the boats. The *Queen Mary*. New York run."

There was immediate sea change. "Why didn't you say you knew Auntie D? Silly, wasting a girl's time. Any friend of Doris is a..." The voice of my newfound friend trailed off and I was treated to a lip-sticky red smile and another battering from the false eyelashes, which went on for only as long as it took to ensure I really was immune to such charms. "D's taken over the old Hat Box, in the alley off lower St Martin's Lane, next to the public lavvies. Know where I mean?"

I nodded.

"Only, it's called The Blueboy now."

I held out a quid.

She glanced at it, then looked around hurriedly to see if there was a copper hiding in the shadows nearby. She gave a firm shake of the head. "What you trying to do, get me arrested? Not in the light for heaven's sake." She leaned in towards me, touched my arm. "Walk up towards Windmill Street and stop on the corner and light a cigarette. I'll brush past you in a minute." She tottered off, but before she got too far I checked that I still had my wallet. Satisfied, I followed in her wake and duly handed off the pound note.

As I said before, the right little titbit is always an earner in Soho.

Like me, Glover had earned himself a medal in the war. His was for conspicuous gallantry, which far outranked mine, and was one of the very few such medals awarded to the men of the Merchant Navy. No one had seemed to mind being saved by a ginger or even cared that he coloured his hair like a tart when they were going down for the third time and he fished them out of the sea and up onto a life raft. His hands and arms had been very badly burned from the flaming oil on the water, but he continued fishing blokes out regardless. Afterwards, it was whispered he was just crazed and desperate to find his lover amongst all the seamen all bobbing up and down between the icy depths below and the deadly inferno above. Whatever the reason, pushing a 'Dan buoy' before him and splashing like a madman, he ferried fifteen or more blackened, bloodied men from out of the burning sea over towards a Carley float. Returning again and again into the oily smoke, until someone pulled him back from the wall of flame. He wore long gloves ever afterwards, both indoors and out, to cover the terrible scars.

People said that it was the grateful parents of a young deck-officer he'd saved who gave Doris the money to set up his club in Soho. Didn't know if it was true or not, but someone put up the money, and a pretty-penny it must've been, too. What I did know was that if there was anyone in queer London who knew what was what, it was Glover, hence my need to find The Blueboy.

Glover—or Doris I should say—hadn't seemed to have aged much. Or perhaps it was just the lighting again, along with the best wig and make-up money could buy. As I'd hoped, he—I mean *she*—welcomed me into her private withdrawing room with open arms.

"Hello, Jethro, you *bona omi*, you," she said in a voice made purposefully low and gravelly before resuming her trademark breathy Irish lilt. "Long time, no *vada*, darling. What fair wind, pray, has brought you washing up my shores I'm glad to say?"

"Nice to see you, too, Doris," I said. "You're looking very lovely."

She pretended surprise, but as with women the world over, she much appreciated the compliment. I meant it, too. She looked as unashamedly resplendent as ever she'd done, as if she'd just stepped off a music hall stage to rapturous applause. She wore a long-sleeved, floor-length, sea-blue velvet evening number that complemented her red hair beautifully and accentuated a womanly figure that was a tribute to British corsetry and padding.

She stopped, mid-bustle, and peered at me. "You look worried tonight, darling. Whatever is the matter with you? If I didn't know you better, I'd say you looked scared. Haunted, even. And that's not at all like you, is it, dear."

I nodded. "There's never keeping any secrets from you, Doris."

"It's my stock-in-trade, Jethro, dear. You know that. So as much as I know you love me for who I am, I also know you wouldn't be here if you weren't already up to your neck in *shinola*. So, come on. Out with it, pronto."

"That's the trouble," I said. "I'm boxing shadows at the moment. All I know is, someone's trying to put me in the frame for something that could well get me hung. You know I don't mind a fight, but when you can't see who or what it is you're fighting, it's as bad as being on the convoys. You never know if the next moment's going to be your last."

The image of feminine softness so artfully contrived suddenly hardened into steel inside a blue velvet glove. She made a sign with her hand to ward off the evil eye. "Well that's me all over: your friendly port in a storm. I promised you I'd always do anything for you. You just tell your Auntie Doris how she can help."

"Someone's trying to stitch me up for the death of Nigel Fox, the MP that died in questionable circumstances. And I had nothing to do with it, Doris; God's honest. But as no one's ever going to believe me if it all goes to shit, I've got to try get to the bottom of it myself. I need to find out if there's any truth in any of those nasty rumours about him. A public figure that high up, dropping money or his trousers on a regular basis, someone, somewhere, is bound to have heard something."

She threw me a look. "I'd have taken you at your word, Jethro. No need to bring the Almighty into it; life's complicated enough as it is. Anyway, just consider it done, dear. If the gentleman in question was *baddering the palone* anywhere in the Quarter or was after fresh young chicken or a bit of rough over Mayfair, Belgravia, or Chelsea way, I'll be sure and find out. What's the best way for a girl to get in touch with you these days?"

I produced some more picture postcards of London from out my jacket pocket and handed them to her. She studied each of them in turn, front and back. "Bit daring, these. What you trying to do, put saucy French pictures out of business? I can see you've already stamped and addressed them. How very thoughtful, save me the trouble. And don't tell me, but if Fox was queer I send the picture of the man in the skirt, the beefy Beefeater, and if he's in the clear, a proper *omi*, I send the wide open spaces of Trafalgar Square?"

"You always were a step ahead, Doris."

"The heels I wear, darling, I have to be, or I'd end up dealing with more than a run in my nylon stockings. Now, how about a little drinky-poo? I need one after all this, Jethro, dear, even if you don't."

"I owe you, Doris."

She batted her heavily black mascara-covered eyelashes, each one as long as the hairs on a long-handled sable watercolour brush. "No, no, Jethro, you'll never owe your Auntie Doris a thing. If it wasn't for you fighting off that awful mob of wild crazies looking to cut off more than my red hair that time near 42nd Street, in New York, I'd have lost more than my good name."

"It's the same with narrow-minded people the world over, Doris. They're always best avoided. I'll have a Whisky if you've got one."

She opened a Chinese lacquered cupboard that probably had a twin in the Victoria and Albert Museum and held up a bottle of single malt that most men in London would've given up their eyeteeth for. "Only the very best for our Jethro. Now come sit down and tell me more. A girl in my position needs to know who and what she might be up against one day."

So I told her as much as I dared, which was more than enough it seems, as she turned round and lifted a blue tea-cosy from off a side-table. Underneath, there was a red telephone without a dial, like the ones I'd seen used by Colonel Walsingham of MI5. It was a direct line to a special exchange for the exclusive use of very, very important VIPs. "Bloody hell, Doris. How on earth did you get your hands on one of those?"

"I never know which will get me the bigger laugh: saying it goes with the décor or that it matches my hair. Suffice to say it was put in for one of my very special regulars, so he can be contacted if there's ever urgent need. Much more discreet than sending someone round from Special Branch." She got up in a swish and a swirl of velvet and went over to a small antique desk, uncapped a blue onyx fountain pen, and wrote something on a blue note-card. She waved the ink dry as she walked back towards me. "Call if it's life or death, and if it isn't me that answers, just say you have news my sister is ill and needs to see me." At the top of the card was a letter 'D' printed in dark blue. Underneath, in ultramarine ink, Doris had written three lines of numbers and letters, all meaningless. I looked up at her, the obvious question plastered on my face. "It's all backwards, like back-slang," she said. "First line is the private telephone number here. Next is the number of the house, the street name and district, where I live. Bottom line is my home telephone number. Easy enough to read, but it'd look like gibberish to most people."

I looked at the card again, and nodded. "I see," I said. "I'm only surprised you didn't translate it into Morse code, as you were, without doubt, one of the very best radio operators ever to sail the Seven Seas."

"Dot-dot-dit-dot. Dot-dot-dit. Dit-dot-dit-dot. Dit-dot- …"

"F.U.C. beginning K. Yes, I get it, Doris," I said. "And I love you, too."

THE ONCE COMING MAN

Ray always said you could glean a lot from the better linens as long as you always made allowances for each newspaper's political bias and then separated likely fact from probable fiction. Do that, he said, and you stood a pretty good chance of getting hold of a real fact or two, maybe more. The million-dollar question then being, of course, whether or not the Right Honourable Nigel Fox, Member of Parliament for Gonerby North, truly was the feckless, immoral and adulterous bastard of journalistic record.

From the pictures you saw of him in the linens and all the society magazines, Nigel Fox MP wasn't what you'd call handsome. He was broad in face, stocky of body, and looked more like a farmer than a politician, especially with his ruddy complexion and shock of unruly fair hair. Yet once he started speaking his mind on the matters of the day, he was magnetic to men and women alike, and loved and loathed in equal measure.

The political pundits and cartoonists had a field day with him and likened him and his early rise to prominence to everyone from Lloyd George to the young Churchill, even the young Sir Oswald Mosley. Some called him a flagrant opportunist; others said he was nothing but a publicity-seeking cad. The one point everyone seemed to agree on though was that he was a young man in a hurry. What set him apart, too, was that other than the good people who resided and voted in Gonersby North, Nigel

Fox's self-elected constituency was the professional working man, be he managing director, bank manager, doctor, solicitor, or chartered accountant.

As an avowed Tory and a member of His Majesty's Government in Opposition, Fox had little truck with Labour's drive to nationalise everything. As far as he was concerned, the Nation's businesses were much better off kept in private hands and the only sector of public life where the Government had a duty to intercede was in the case of law and order. A cause he'd been strongly associated with ever since he himself had been attacked and robbed after attending a late-night session at the House of Commons. The fact that it occurred on Tothill Street, in the very shadow of Westminster Abbey, gave him his bully pulpit, and his persistent bating of Clement Attlee during Question Time on issues relating to crime in the capital soon became—as the newspapers all dubbed it— 'a festering thorn in the Prime Minister's side.' The thrust of Fox's questions, admonitions, and rebuttals always hit on the same sore point: Why had the Labour Government failed so lamentably to adopt all necessary measures to combat the marked rise of crime in the nation's capital? Was the Prime Minister—or for that matter his Home Secretary—aware of public concern with the alarming increase in cases of robbery with violence by armed men in London? How many such cases had been reported since the end of the War, and in how many instances had the culprits been convicted? Was it not really astonishing that so many crimes of this nature should escape solution? Could nothing be done to tighten up public security in this regard? He was relentless with it.

Fox was always so effective in making his points, it was rumoured that Winston Churchill had regularly sent him handwritten notes on how to further press home his arguments. Naturally, Fox very quickly became the darling of both the Metropolitan and City police forces, as well as the favourite politician of all involved in finance on a large scale—whether it was the acquisition of it, the banking of it, or simply the moving of it from point 'A' to point 'B.' Burglaries, bank robberies, and wage shipment heists were all too common occurrences in the Smoke and in and around the Home Counties, the majority of them unsolved, and all of them very discomforting to the gentlemen who ran the huge insurance companies that had to pay out on all the losses.

Personally, I could've cared less for his politics or his 'new policing' bills. It was the posh dinners and society balls he went to that interested me, especially the big important dos with all of London in attendance—the ones always reported on in the linens and upper-crust magazines—as that invariably meant he'd be partnered by his wife, a tall blonde lady, who not only brought the lustre of inherited wealth and influence to her husband's future political prospects, but who always made sure to catch all eyes with the radiance of her jewellery and her dazzling smile. She was extremely good looking, too, though I didn't fancy her myself. She seemed a little too cold and aloof for my taste. Too overly tailored and wholly unobtainable, like Greta Garbo in her prime.

I'd be lying too if I didn't also cop to the fact that the brass cheek of doing the drum of England's rising star of 'law and order' and of half-inching his beautiful wife's cache of top-grade tomfoolery, at one and the same time, very definitely had its attractions. I mean, what a way to prove to myself—and to Ray—that I was back in business and at the very top of my game.

Anyway, it'd all seemed like a very good idea at the time.

But as the old Yiddish saying goes, "If you want to make God laugh, make plans." Life being what it is, it's never too long before a tailor-made bolt of lightning comes right out of the blue and sends you for a Burton.

MEMORIES OF TIMES GONE BY

I had reason to go for a drink after that Saturday night's performance of *Harvey*. What with Sylvia, Lily, and Glover all agreeing to help, I was feeling better than I had in weeks. I was still a mere pawn in the game, but at least I now had three extra pieces on my side of the board, though whether any of them would turn out to be knights, bishops or castles I couldn't say. I tried to remember how many queens a player was allowed to have.

That's the trouble, though. Let your mind wander for a single second and life slaps you smack in the face with a wet fish. I'd just turned the corner opposite the Comedy Theatre when two shapes stepped from out of the shadows, and by the cut of their suits and style of their hats they were both from West End Central's not so plainclothes division. "A little word with you, sunshine." I looked round and noticed a police car parked up the street, but the coppers didn't usher me in that direction, they just pushed me up against a nearby wall. There was no show of warrant cards, just names and ranks ground out between tightly clenched teeth. Detective-sergeant this, detective-constable that, all to impress upon me the fact that this was their manor I was treading on.

The smaller of the two men spoke first.

"It's Jethro, isn't it?" It wasn't a question. "We've been meaning to have a word with you about the rumour you're back in the game and did a tasty little jewel job that could well have you swinging from the wrong end of a rope."

I looked from one to the other of them, my face a blank.

"Don't be a smart arse," said the big one. "You know the job we're talking about. That big block of luxury flats in South Kensington."

I just stared back at him so I'd be sure to remember his face. "So we're going to play the old dumb routine, are we?" He half turned away, then swivelled back, and punched me hard in the stomach.

I doubled up.

He brought his knee up fast in an obviously well-practised movement, but being equally well practised I leaned to one side just enough to take the blow on my shoulder rather than full in the face. "Got your fucking attention now, have we, toe-rag?" he sneered.

I just kept my head down and grunted.

Detective-sergeant short arse leaned over and said, "We can make it all go away for a price. We was thinking a couple of hundred quid should do for starters. More as we get to know one another better."

The big sod went to knee me again, but I saw it coming and just fell backwards onto the pavement, which almost caused him to lose balance. He covered it well though by swinging his body round. Then, balance regained, he stood, feet firmly planted, and rolled his shoulders and took off his hat and did smart-looking things to the brim. "That's the proper place for you, you piece of shit. Down in the gutter. So just you remember, we know where you work and we know where you live. You can expect to see a lot of us."

"Count on it," piped in short arse.

Then they both strolled away.

I stayed on the ground till they got back into the police car. Then I got up and dusted myself down. The street was as deserted, as if a bomb had just fallen. "Tossers," I said to the chill night air. "West End Central must really be going downhill if that's the best they can muster." Shaking my head at the folly of amateurs I continued on down Panton Street, crossed over the Haymarket, in search of a good drink.

Young Bob Miller must've noticed the look on my face, if not my dishevelled appearance, because he immediately came over and offered to buy me a pint, which I of course accepted. He seemed very keen to know my plans, whether I was going to stay on the team for the rest of the run. "What? Me leave a hit show where I get to see Sid Field perform every night? I should cocoa," I said. "What about you? Still fancy being an electrician, do you?"

He said he'd settled to being a stage-hand and that if he got his full ticket he'd stay on the team for the duration too.

I asked him what his girlfriend thought about it all.

He paused a moment and said she was very pleased he'd managed to get himself squared away so well in London. Out of the blue he suggested that one night maybe he and his girl could meet up with me and mine, and all of us go have a drink somewhere. "That'd be nice," I said, already thinking how to tango out of this without giving offence. "Ah, but there's the rub, isn't it?" I said with a chuckle. "How do I decide which lovely lady to bring, there being so many? I'll have to sleep on it and get back to you."

And with that I downed my pint, waved a cheery 'cheerio' and hoofed it out the door. I kept a wary eye out, but as I did most nights after a stint at the Elizabeth, I turned up Lower Regent Street making a beeline towards Piccadilly Circus and a Bakerloo Line train back home. I had another long night ahead of me in Kensal Green Cemetery, and I wanted a quick wash and some cups of coffee before I hit the road again.

I even remember thinking I should oil the bicycle-chain, help keep it from rusting.

Of course, even with the old saw, "bad things happen in threes," you never see the second one coming. There was no screech of tyres, no telltale brake lights, just a long black motorcar seen out the corner of my eye, the sound of footsteps on the pavement behind me, a black bag thrown over my head, and the speedy application of a leather cosh. "Here we go again," I said to myself, wondering who in hell was going to be the dark at the end of this tunnel.

"Bloody hell, Tommy, what did you have to hit me so bloody hard for?" I was slumped on a settee in some room, somewhere, with Tommy Nutkins' ugly mug staring down at me. He helped pull me upright.

"Mr Spot's orders, Jethro. It's the fastest way if you don't want to mess about with chloroform."

"Well it fucking hurt. You know I don't deserve this." I wondered if it was Tommy getting his own back for when I'd once had to brain him.

"Mr Spot thought you were being followed, Jethro, and he wanted you in the motor and away in the blink of an eye."

"Give him a drink, Tommy. Help wake him up."

I peered up into the cold, wolf-like eyes of Mr Jack Spot. "Blimey, Jack. You only had to ask," I said, rubbing my head.

"I did. Sent Tommy round with a note, asking all polite. I'm a patient man, Jethro, but even with you that patience stretches only so far."

Tommy stuck a glass in my hand. "Here, get this down your neck."

I was still a bit dizzy. Not quite as dizzy as I was letting on, mind you, but like a boxer that's just been knocked down, you never fully get to your feet until the count of nine. You use the time to recover. Finally, I sat up and took a sip of Whisky and gathered what thoughts I could. Jack Spot and me had boxed heads many times. The trick of course with anyone that outweighs you is to never let yourself get wrong-footed. Only trouble was, given Spottsy's supposed concerns about me being followed, I didn't even know what weight-class we were fighting in, let alone what round it was.

Leopards might never change their spots, but Jack Spot had changed since the failed Heath Row bullion caper the previous July. It didn't all happen at once — you never see a face age when you see it every day—but over time it becomes unmistakable. He was much quicker to take offence and much more suspicious of people in general and, outside of Tommy Nutkins and Moses Goldring—his accountant and right-hand man—I seemed to be one of the few people he still trusted. Probably because I'd not only taken part in the Heath Row job, but when it'd all gone wrong, it'd been me that saved Tommy from being nabbed by the coppers, then set him up with a watertight alibi. Plus, I wasn't in on the raid for the money, I was paying Jack back a big favour he'd recently done for me. There was no profit in me grassing him up. I was kosher and he knew it. And, as in all things, always follow the money.

The simple truth was that if Spottsy had succeeded with the bullion robbery, there would've never been any stopping him. He'd have had the funds to buy all the muscle and influence he'd have ever needed and would've ruled London's roost for years all but unopposed. That's why he'd planned the Heath Row job so very, very carefully and had handpicked each man. No one but himself was ever privy to the whole plan; each man knew only their own part in it until the very day of the job. Yet, even after all that, the police had been lying in wait ready to pounce. No one knew who'd given the game away and not knowing was still driving Spottsy nuts. Now here I was, face-to-face, with a man who'd been denied what he thought was his rightful title: 'Boss of the Underworld.'

I braced myself for the worst.

"Get him a refill, Tommy. Jethro needs to know he's among friends. He's looking far too worried about something at the moment. Can't think why."

Tommy reached in and took my glass away, while Spottsy held court.

"That Sid Field's bloody funny, isn't he? Tommy and me popped in to see him and that invisible rabbit of his, earlier tonight. Laughed our bloomin' heads off, we did. I ask you, 'Pooka,' what kind of daft word is that? Shows you how too much drinking will have you seeing things. That's why I never touch the stuff myself, muddles the thought processes."

Tommy handed me another large Whisky. "Drink up, Jethro, you look like you need it."

As I put my lips to the glass, I chanced a quick look round. It was a small room, too small for what was happening in it, but it was clean and tidy, nothing flash, just the usual bog-standard utility furniture. But also no knickknacks or family pictures. It was almost as if nobody lived there.

"It's Tommy's place, Jethro," Jack said, noticing my wandering eyes, "for whenever he needs to disappear for a bit, or as now when I want a private word and want to keep it private. How's your head? Alright, is it?"

"It'll mend," I said, swirling the Whisky around my glass. Then a thought struck me. "Mind if I ask you something, Jack?"

He nodded.

"Did you by any chance send anyone round the theatre asking about me?"

"Why would I need to do that, Jethro? I know where you live."

"True, Jack, true. You said you wanted a word?"

"Yes, I have a favour to ask of you."

I had a fair idea what was coming, but all the same I dreaded having to give an answer. "Er, what's that, Jack?"

"I remembered how very good you were at finding things that didn't want to be found, like you did that time for that Mr Zaretsky, and I have a mind to put those talents of yours to use again. For a proper fee, of course. I'm no chiseller."

I sat there holding onto the Whisky glass as if it were a buoy in a tidal surge and tried to hold my hand steady. "You mean them red books I found for Mr Zaretsky and, what was it called, *Cabal*?"

"Yes. Good memory. The Jewish Business League. Only there's this posh lady that's had her solicitor seek me out. Neither of them Jewish, but their money's kosher enough. They are too— I checked them out. Anyway, this lady wants her missing jewellery back, no questions asked. Of course, I told her solicitor the tom's probably all been broken up by now, but he said his client's intent on retrieving whatever she can, as it's apparently of great sentimental value. So I said I'd look into it, which is where you come in."

I said nothing, just kept my face as stiff as a kid's paper-maché mask.

Spottsy reached into his overcoat and pulled out a fat brown envelope, which he threw down onto the settee beside me. "There's a grand there, for starters," he said. He held out a hand, like a surgeon would to a nurse, and Tommy produced a photograph out of thin air and handed it to him. "This here is a colour photograph of the jewellery in question, courtesy of the lady's insurance company."

It was the photograph Ray had told me about. It wasn't too bad as 8x10 photos go, but it didn't do the pieces justice. There was no depth to the emeralds, no flash of fire to the diamonds. I did my best to act my part. "I'm no detective, Jack, but it's the Meridian Mansions haul, must be," I said. "That diamond and emerald suite the linens all said was insured for two hundred grand, the same loot the Yard and half of London have been looking for, for weeks. But, as you said, it's all so bloody hot it's probably already been broken up and shipped out the country. There's little chance of anyone finding that little lot, and I'm certainly in no position to."

"That may very well be, Jethro, but no one knows for sure. I certainly don't. That's why I want no stone left unturned in the search for the stuff."

I shot him a look to see if he was joking, but it was plain he wasn't. "I know it's not what she or you want to hear, Jack, but it's all long gone. It's always hard putting a price on sentiment."

"Well she has," he said. "She'll double the reward offered by the insurers."

I looked up and shook my head at the futility of the task, but Spottsy pointedly ignored me.

"So what I want from you, Jethro, is for you to find a certain person who's thought to have knowledge of the affair, that person being 'Monkey' Jim." Spottsy paused to let the name sink in. I tried my damndest not to sink with it. "You see the other thing I remembered, Jethro, was that I once heard whisper, way back before the War, that you and Jimmy Mooney had been seen drinking together a fair bit. A little fact locked away for a rainy day suddenly brought to mind again when I heard news as how Harry Mooney has also gone AWOL. So with him gone out the picture, I thought of that old saw "set a thief to catch a thief" and came up with you."

I just stared at him, a chill seeping ever deeper into my bones. "Harry 'Rabbit' gone missing?" I spluttered. "But I...I only just saw him recently."

"Apparently he's not been seen anywhere round Soho these last four, five days, which is highly unusual for him. Ask me, him and his brother have probably just fucked off somewhere. They were always an odd pair, them two. Though it must be catching. A lot of people seem to have suddenly gone on their holidays recently. Anyway, be a good lad and see what you can find out. There's ten grand in it for you if you find me either one of the Mooney brothers. A lot more if you should come up with the sparklers yourself."

I jumped in feet first. I had no other choice. "I can't do it. I can't take your money, Jack. It's true I did knock around with Jimmy Mooney for a bit, before the War, but I haven't seen hide nor hair of him in years. Didn't even know he'd got out of prison early until I heard whisper of it the other day."

The air chilled so fast I suddenly felt very hot round the collar.

"I don't think I quite heard you right, Jethro," Jack said, his voice low and menacing. "You can't help me or you won't help me?" It went dead quiet again and then he exploded. "You two-faced, malingering Cockney bastard. And there was me thinking you were someone I could still count on. Fuck me, what was I thinking of? Fuck you, you tosser. I don't usually go round asking people nicely, you know? I just fuckin' tell 'em what I want done and when I want it fuckin' done and if they don't fuckin' hop to it, I cut their fuckin' balls off and stick 'em in their fuckin' mouths."

Again I had no choice. "It's not just the Mooney brothers, Jack. I daren't get mixed up in any of that Mansions business. It'd get round London faster than a dog biting its arse if I was to start nosing around. I'd have the Shadow Mob and Messima's boys on me faster than flies round shit. As it is, I've already had coppers badgering me at home and in the street. Plain fact is someone's trying to drop me in the cart for something I haven't done. Messima, probably. Why, I don't know, unless he found out I was in on the Heath Row bullion job with you and he's getting back at me for it."

His eyes blazing, spittle forming at the corners of his mouth, Spottsy leaned his face in towards me. "Fuckin' Messima again, is it? Got your balls in a ringer again, has he? And it's my fuckin' fault, is it? Well fuck the little Maltese tosspot and fuck you, Jethro. I thought you had some fuckin' bottle left in you." He shook his fist and then shook his head. "How wrong could I fuckin' be? Tommy, take this piece of shit out and drop it somewhere. He couldn't find his own fuckin' arsehole to wipe it, this one. Just get him out of my fuckin' sight. I'll waste no more time on the tosser."

Tommy drove in silence for the first mile or so, then when we'd turned onto what sounded like a main road, he told me to take the black bag from off me head. "Sorry about the bag, Jethro, but Spottsy wants his and my bolt-holes known only to the two of us. He's very wary about everyone at the moment. It's odd times, with odd things happening all over the place. Can't put a finger on it as yet and neither can Spottsy. Like this race card of creepers your name's on. What's all that bollocks about?"

I shrugged my shoulders and kept my eyes glued to the twin cones of light pushing aside the darkness ahead. There was nothing to say. I'd just made an enemy of one of the most powerful villains in the Smoke, and if ever he wanted me topped, the man he'd have do it was the very man driving the motorcar—my old china, Tommy Nutkins.

"He'll get over it eventually, Jethro. You know what he's like when his pride's hurt. He's like a wounded animal. What with all the harassment from the boys in blue after the Heath Row job went south and his St Botolph's Club being forced to close soon after, he can't afford to lose any more face—it'd be the end of him. On top of which, having every fuckin' layabout in London trying to muscle in on every little bit of business just to test whether he's still got his balls or not, it's been very wearing." Tommy tapped the area over his heart. "I'm tooled up all the time now, never knowing who or what might be round the next corner. I tell you, the mere mention of Messima sets Spottsy off cursing something chronic. Especially since he heard word the little Maltese bastard has been having private meetings with every other gang boss north of the water. So he knows something really big must be up, but he has no fuckin' idea what it is, and that's gnawing away at his insides like nobody's fuckin' business. It's all but given him an ulcer. Then, today, out the fuckin' blue, Messima sends word via Harry McShane of the Upton Park mob that he wants to meet with him, personally; no minders, just the two of them, Spottsy and Messima; Spottsy to pick the time and place. As I said, it's all very odd."

"That's not just odd, Tommy," I said. "That's fucking unheard of."

COCKLES AND MUSSELS
ALIVE, ALIVE-O

Tommy dropped me on Lisson Grove, a few blocks short of Church Street, and I started walking home. I glanced at my wristwatch in the light of a lamp-post. If I got my skates on, I could still cycle out to Kensal Green Cemetery. But, in truth, given the news about Harry "Rabbit," I was in no mood. I turned into Church Street, saw the feint glow of the Apostles off in the distance and stepped up my pace. Even with it being the arse-end of Saturday night, I needed to get in touch with Ray, see if he'd heard anything.

I stepped inside 'Matthew,' sorted out some coppers, and started dialling. Ray and I had a code for unscheduled telephone calls of some urgency: a single ring, followed by a call of three rings, then another of two rings, then pick up. So I dialled Ray's home number, the first two times pressing button 'B' to get my pennies back, and on the third call, third ring, I heard a click and the tinny sound of echoing silence.

"It's Matthew, Father," I said into the void.

"Yes, Matthew, my son. Something must be troubling you."

"Had trouble sleeping. Heard my rabbit's gone missing."

"Sorry to have to tell you, Matthew, but your rabbit's dead."

"Dead? What? You mean dead, as in gone to heaven?"

"I'm afraid so, my son. There's always much more in heaven and Earth than can ever be dreamt of. Best get some sleep for now. There's another long day ahead for us all tomorrow and tomorrow. Pray for guidance. Father Fabrikant will take confession at noon at the church of the Holy Fisherman."

"Thank you, Father."

"Bless you, my son."

'Tubby' Isaac's jellied-eel stall just outside Aldgate Tube station, corner of Middlesex Street—or Petticoat Lane, as it's more commonly known—is a venerable East End landmark. And there may well be wheels on the cart, but the pitch has been sacrosanct since just after the end of the First World War, when old 'Tubby' Isaac Brenner started selling jellied eels and shellfish to London's hungry masses. Solly Gritzman, his old assistant, worked the stall now, 'Tubby' having long gone on to better things in America. And in all of Petticoat Lane, seething as it was with people of all stripes, colours, and persuasions, there was no better place to hide in plain sight than in a crowd of noshers noisily eating their way through plates of cockles and mussels, jellied eels, prawns, whelks, or rollmops. It may not have been the feeding of the five thousand come rain or shine, every day, including Sundays, but it was close.

"Plate of jellied eels, please, Solly."

"Hello, Jeffro," he said. "Haven't seen you around these parts for a bit. You after that old china of yours, 'Buggy' Billy, 'cos if you are, you've just missed him. Came by a good half-hour ago, he did. Took a jam-pot full of rollmop-herrings for his dinner on the train; had his suitcase with him and everything. Off up to Norwich on business, he said he was. Left his stall for them lads of his to run."

"Got no business with that old tosser, Solly, just journeyed out to the Lane for a plate of your wondrous jellied eels; best nosh in all of Aldgate."

"Es gezunterheyt…may you eat in continued good health."

"Yes. Ta, Solly," I said, tucking into my plate of jellied eels. I checked my wristwatch and glanced around, all casual like, but there was no sign of the man I'd come to see. Then just as the clock of St Botolph's church began to strike twelve, I heard someone behind me say, "Plate of prawns and a couple of roll-mop herrings, please, Solly."

"Hello, Mr Fabrikant, long time, no see."

And so with Ray now having successfully consigned all things 'Buggy' Billy to a suitcase in the Left Luggage office at Liverpool Street Station, all I had to do was drift to a less-crowded spot along the wall of the Aldgate Exchange pub and await my dinner companion, one Moisha Fabrikant.

"Just keep your back to me, my old cock. I'll do the talking."

I coughed, scratched an ear in acknowledgement, and slowed my eating down to a walk instead of a canter.

"Word is Harry 'Rabbit' got bundled off a Soho street by three men in a big black motorcar late Monday afternoon. No sign of him anywhere for days, then early last night a brass and her john came across his body tied to a chair in a disused warehouse over Wapping way, his tongue half cut out. According to one of the ambulance men, he died of shock rather than loss of blood, though how they can tell that sort of thing beats me. Harry's death has angered a lot of very heavy 'faces'; corner-men are supposed to be like Switzerland, hands off to one and all. There'll be bloody hell to pay when they find out who did it. Needless to say, the Sweeney have been at it hard and heavy this morning, pulling in snouts and 'faces' left, right, and centre. Word is they're fearful it's the first moves in a big turf war, which of course they want to put a stop to dead quick."

I pictured a dead Harry 'Rabbit' and came over, all dizzy, grateful beyond measure that at that moment I had the pub wall to hold me up. "But why the fuck would anyone want to cut his tongue out? Harry's ability to rabbit was his livelihood; everyone knew that. There was no one better."

"To get him to speak, obviously, spill the beans on 'Monkey' Jim's whereabouts. Says how very desperate some people still are to find him."

"I'll murder that swine, Messima," I said.

"And with good reason. But it could be any bunch of cowboys that did for Harry given the price Messima put on his brother's head. And when you think of all the work Messima put Harry "Rabbit's" way, it doesn't add up. It'd be like cutting his own nose off to spite his face."

"I'll kill whoever did kill Harry Mooney. Maybe jump off a roof myself, because I can't help thinking now that it was me that caused his death. Loads of people saw me talking to him that time in Soho."

"Don't be daft, Jethro. That was well-handled. You covered it with all that business about the stage scenery. You were watertight. So don't go blaming yourself; that way lies madness."

"Well I'm already fucking good and mad, so a bit more won't hurt."

"Steady, old son, steady. What's done is done. Leave it be for now. We'll see to it later, when we know more. If nothing else, it says 'Monkey' Jim must still be alive somewhere. Your only job now is to find him and help save his hide. What else was it you called me about? Spottsy, was it? Bit of bother?"

"Yes, he had me coshed senseless just to attract my attention. Said he'd been tasked by Mrs Fox's solicitor to find the missing Meridian Mansions jewellery. Big surprise being she's putting up as much again as the insurers." Moisha Fabrikant whistled appreciatively. "Spottsy wants me to find them. Said how he remembered what I did for Mr Zaretsky and *Cabal*. He did his nut when I told him I couldn't help. Afterwards, on the way home, Tommy told me Messima's been having private meetings with the guv'nors of all the gangs, north of the water. No minders, just him and the top man. Spottsy got asked yesterday via word from Harry McShane, boss of the Upton Park mob." Ray gave another little a whistle of surprise. "So what's it all about?" I said. But the only sound I heard was the urgent scratch of wooden fork across paper plate, which told me Ray was thinking and furiously so.

As good as they tasted, I suddenly found I had no stomach for jellied eels and I spat out what was left onto my plate, bone and all. Then I heard Moisha cough loud enough to draw phlegm from the back of his throat and heard him spit whatever it was he'd come up with onto the ground beside him. "Excuse me," he muttered, turned his back and leaned against the pub wall and carried on with his eating. I put my paper plate down on the pavement, wiped my mouth with the back of my hand, lit a fag, and leaned back against the wall myself.

"Alright, try this on for size," Ray whispered, over his shoulder. "What you just said about Messima puts a lot of things into perspective, bits and pieces I've heard but haven't been able to put together until now. And I tell you a turf war is the very last thing Messima wants. He knows all too well how very unstable things have been around town since Spottsy's mob slipped a peg or two after the Heath Row debacle, and the one thing he wants to avoid is everyone fighting over who controls what rackets when and where. There'd be far too much blood spilled over the cobbles if that happened, which would end up bringing the full force of Scotland Yard down hard on everyone's head. So I reckon the cunning swine is trying to get all the gangs to come to an agreement of some sort. That's the only way I see fits all the facts."

It was me that gave a little whistle then. "Cunning swine is right. He puts it all together and ends up the boss of it all, even if only pulling strings from behind the curtain."

"Exactly. He ends up 'Boss of the Underworld' without all the bother of having to stand on the cobbles and take on all comers. And, as ever, brilliant timing on his part. Hold on. What's this?" Ray turned in the direction of a flurry in the crowd, a whisper visibly forming on the wind. "Alright, the Apostles at midnight, if need be, but split up now, see what we can hear."

The news was very bad. It seemed another old mate of mine, "Tosh" Collis, had been discovered dead on the foreshore down by Tower Bridge. "Tosh," a legend even amongst London's

fraternity of cat burglars. "Tosh," born into a one of the oldest
family's of 'toshers' still working the river and scouring the mud
and the sewers in the hope of finding lost valuables. "Tosh," who
as a teenager had got out of all the mud and the shit and scaled
the heights and rooftops of the Smoke with a fearlessness and
a daring that'd left the rest of us open-mouthed in admiration.
"Tosh," who'd been right up there with "Monkey" Jim, who'd
been amongst the best of the very best, found drowned in the
mud at the river's edge, dead as a smoked kipper on a plate.

"Tosh" had also been one of the names featured on the list of
creepers linked to the Meridian Mansions job.

Six names now cut down to five.

I caught sight of Ray in the crowd, his face a grim mask,
so I knew he must've also heard the news, but when he caught
my eye, he gave a slight shake of his head. Then he waggled
an ear and ran a finger and thumb quickly up and down his
nose, twice— a hand signal used by race course tic-tac men
that meant "wolf at the door" and that I should scarper in the
opposite direction in considerably less than two shakes of lamb's
tail. I rolled my shoulders, all nonchalant like, then turned and
started eeling my way back through the crowd as fast as my two
legs could carry me.

"Oi, you, Jethro, get your arse back here and be fucking
quick about it. I want a fucking word with you, scumbag."

NOTICE IS HEREBY SERVED

Of all the coppers in all the world, why did it have to be Detective Chief Inspector Robert Browno of Scotland Yard's Flying Squad? Not a man to be taken lightly by anyone on either side of the law, and certainly not by me. He was built like a brick shit-house, had a head like a battering ram, and was a bull in any china shop he was sent into. Needless to say, the people that mattered considered him a copper's copper, but then a steady stream of high-profile arrests and convictions has always been a sure way to curry favour with Old Bailey judges and the Commissioner of Police.

The crowd parted as Browno strode forward, much like the Red Sea must've done for Moses, and I still might've chanced hoofing it if it wasn't for the fact his sneaky detective-sergeant had already sneaked up behind me and stuck an arm-lock on me. I could've taken him, one hand tied behind my back, but not only did he have the element of surprise, he also had something stuck hard in my ribs that felt like a revolver. Browno didn't even glance at me as he thundered past. "In the back of the motorcar, you tosser, and no fucking trouble or I'll have him snap your fucking arm in two."

Browno's voice barely ever rose above a gravelly whisper, but if you were the one he had in his sights you would've heard him above the noise of a Cup Final crowd. Every 'face' in the Smoke kept a wary eye out for him. He was always double dodgy and could be decidedly deadly.

One thing I knew about him, that very few others did, was that Colonel Walsingham of MI5 also had something on Browno, by which device he directed rather than diverted the detective's focus to whatever ends he desired. My last runin with Browno had been under very different circumstances, but he didn't recognise me that time. I'd been strapped to a chair, bollock-naked, my face streaked with dried blood, mud, and spittle, and he was very instrumental in saving me from a fate worse than death. It's funny how the world turns, sometimes.

I got pushed into the back of the motorcar, next to Browno; Sergeant 'Strong-arm' got in the front next to the driver.

"Alright, driver," Browno growled, "go down to Prescot Street, then pull in just before the Goods Depot and get out and have a cigarette. And you go with him, Sergeant, and keep him honest. I'll wave a hand out the window when I want you both back."

The driver didn't say a word, just executed a U-turn without any regard for whatever other traffic was abroad on Aldgate High Street and sped off in the direction of the Mint. "Yes, sir," was all Detective-Sergeant Strong-arm could muster. Meanwhile, I sat in absolute silence, keeping a very still tongue in my head. I'm no steamer.

We arrived outside the Goods Depot in short order to find the street all but deserted. The police car pulled in to the kerb and everyone went to their respective corners. Browno didn't say a word, he just sat and waited for his men to exit the police car and move far enough away for them not to be able to overhear. I just braced myself for the backhand across the face I knew would soon be coming my way.

"You still have a fucking red card on you, you jammy bastard. I don't know why, don't fucking care, but when I heard your name mentioned again I went and searched out your file. Why the fuck anyone at Special Branch would have their eyes on you, I have no idea. It's restricted even from me. So you must've done something for someone important—grass someone up, probably. Whatever it was, the upshot is I can't touch you, for now, but one thing's for fucking sure: you're going to help me out now, sunshine, or I'll knock your fucking block off, just for starters. That understood?"

I nodded my head, pleased to find it still attached to my shoulders. "Got it," I said. "But help you in what way, exactly, Mr Browno?"

"This so-called list of Meridian Mansions creepers you're on, what the fuck's that all about when it's at home? 'Tosh' Collis's name was on the list and now 'Tosh' Collis is dead and drowned down by Tower Beach. I should fucking cocoa. He was a fucking fish that one, born on a barge, an old winkle-boat for his fucking cradle. He could've fallen in the river by a sewer outlet and still come up smelling of fucking roses. Him, drown? Not even head-fucking-first into a butt of Malmsey wine. Him and his jewellery capers gave me fucking heartburn for years, and I never did catch the little fucker at it. All which earned him my grudging respect, if nothing else. So give. What's it all about? What the fuck's going on?"

"I don't know, Mr Browno. Really, I don't. It's years since I saw 'Tosh'— same with the others. But ever since word got round about that bloody list, everyone and their mother's son thinks I'm back in the game."

"Well, are you, scumbag? Never any smoke without fucking fire."

"I'm not at it, Mr Browno. My bottle's gone for that lark. I'm a full-time stage-hand down the Prince of Wales at present and that's more than enough to keep me happy."

"Who the fuck do you think you're talking to? Some agony aunt in the fucking linens? Don't give me any of your sob stories. There's something very nasty brewing in the Smoke and unless you want me to detain you, you better cough up something here and now and be fucking quick about it."

I'm no 'grass,' but I couldn't afford to be banged up. Not for a week. Not even for a day. Especially not with all that was going on. "Er, I can't tell you what I don't know, Mr Browno, but something I have heard is that Darby Messima's having private meetings with the bosses of every gang north of the water; no minders, just him and the top man. What it means, I don't know, but it sounds odd."

"Fucking unheard of, you mean, but I already heard about that from my snouts. Ever heard of someone or something called 'Norto'?"

I shook my head.

"What about Harry Mooney? You hear he was found dead last night?"

"Yes, I did. Very sad. It was the talk of the market."

"Think there's any connection between the two deaths?"

"There very may well be, Mr Browno. I don't know."

"Well let me put a little something in your shell-like. I just heard from a little birdie, there's whisper about a 'notice' being put out on you, just like as probably happened with 'Tosh' Collis. So if I were you, sunshine, I'd start watching my step very, very carefully."

I just stared at him, for the life of me not knowing what to say, and Browno just stared back at me, his face expressionless, his piggy eyes like bits of broken glass. He shook his head at me and slowly rolled down the window.

He stuck a brown-leather-gloved hand out through the opening. Browno's sergeant and driver must've been on the lookout for him, because I immediately heard them hot-footing it back to the police car. Of course, I didn't see it coming, but you never do, do you? Browno gave me a back-hander right across the bridge of my nose and before I knew what'd hit me there was blood everywhere.

"Try to bribe me, you piece of shit," he growled. "You fucking useless, know-nothing scumbag. Get the fuck out of my police car. Who the fuck do you think you are, trying it on? I shit lowlifes like you for breakfast. Sergeant, scrape this turd out from under my shoes and let's get on after some real villains, not this fucking no-face, fucking nobody."

Two sets of nicotine-stained hands yanked me from out the back of the police car and dropped me straight in the gutter. And when they all got in the motorcar again, the driver executed another tyre-screeching U-turn, and the Flying Squad's finest exited Down Stage Right.

I lay in the muck and the puddles thinking about what'd just happened. I can't say which I was more surprised about: Browno warning me or the way he'd covered-up the whole incident from his men. Either way, that red card that'd originated with my service to Walsingham was still working its magic, but even that couldn't save me from the 'notice' someone had put out on me. It was nothing at all like that given to an actor who'd died on stage. A 'notice' was a piece of paper with your name scribbled on that'd been thrust—along with the appropriate thirty pieces of silver—into the hands of a hired killer.

Not the sort of news anyone ever wants to hear.

I tried to staunch the blood still pouring from my nose, brushed myself down as best as I could, rolled my shoulders to ease the ache, and trudged back up towards Aldgate Tube station. Not wanting to scare the daylights out of fellow passengers on the Metropolitan Line, I headed for the pub on the corner to try and clean myself up. My half-eaten plate of jellied eels was still on the pavement where I'd left it a thousand years before—surprising, really, as I thought the local cats or rats would've had it away long before now.

There was no sign anywhere of Moisha Fabrikant.

I went inside the pub and borrowed a dishrag and went into the Gents toilets and washed the blood from my face and hands and did what I could to dab the dried blood from off the front of my coat. No one in the pub said anything. No one commiserated with me or offered to buy me a drink, so I bought myself a pint to pay for my use of the facilities. People looked away whenever I happened to glance up, but they'd already seen what they needed to see before they eeled away to whisper the latest bit of tittle-tattle into whichever ear it was they whispered such things into. Having your collar felt and your nose bloodied by the police was an everyday occurrence in the East End, all part of the cost of living, but seeing evidence of the law going out of their way to nobble a 5-to-1 runner in a much-fancied race, now that was definitely news.

TAKE UP ARMS

I took the Tube back to Edgware Road, never quite able to shake the feeling I was being followed, and as the train slid into the station, I readied myself for an old dodge. Exiting the carriage along with half a dozen other people, I immediately knelt down and undid and redid a shoelace, my eye on the sliding doors, then just as they were about to close I stepped back inside the carriage. I glanced round and caught sight of one or two faces a mite more interested in my travel plans than might be considered normal, so I waggled my ear and logged them to memory.

I got off at the next stop, Paddington, mainline railway station, took to the stairs marked 'No Entrance,' jumped the centre barrier, and sprinted up the escalator. I dropped my ticket and an extra threepenny-bit into the open palm of the ticket collector and headed for the stairs up into the main station concourse. I hot-footed over to Platform 1, went into the ticket office through one door and straight out the other into the covered carriageway where taxis dropped off their passengers. I slowed enough to mingle and walked along the pavement until I could slip back inside the station. I took the footbridge that led over to the local line platforms on the far side, which in turn brought me to a maintenance door, just past where the footbridge opens out into a wide corridor. Then I was in and through and down the stairs that led onto the ramp for incoming taxis. After which it was a case of holding to the shadows and zigzagging over onto where London Road runs parallel to the station and up and over a fence, down onto the embankment, along the canal, over the walkway, up onto North Wharf Road, and so round to my lock-up.

I needed a wash and a change of clothes and some time to think. I also needed a handgun. I decided on the Colt .38 revolver rather than the 9mm Browning automatic, needing absolute reliability more than the extra rounds. If everyone and their mother's son were going round all tooled-up, I didn't want to be the only one not properly dressed for the occasion, especially as it now seemed someone had decided to have me measured for a pine box.

I got out a tin of Spam and a tin of baked beans from my store-cupboard, cut the meat into slices, and fried the lot over a Primus stove. The only thing missing: a couple of pieces of fried-bread, which I made up for by having several mugs of tea sweetened with condensed milk and eating my way through half a packet of digestive biscuits. Weekly ration be blowed. I always get a bit peckish when there's a growing chill of danger in the air, a holdover no doubt from my days on the convoys.

The other thing I'd learned at sea was that once you'd had your fill of food and drink you tried to get your fill of sleep, as you never knew what the morrow would bring. So I set up the camp bed, set the alarm clock, turned out the light and went straight off to sleep. The dreams I had, had me running all over London, from all manner of shadowy creatures, an awful lot of them with the faces of Messima, Spottsy or Browno. There were other faces in the shadows, too, but I couldn't make any of them out. Somewhere, deep down inside, though, I knew they were all the faces of the men I'd have to kill.

I slept the sleep of the dead and was raring to go when the alarm went off just after eleven. I made myself another pot of coffee and got myself dressed and properly kitted-out: newly-filled Thermos flask, newly-honed Fairbairn-Sykes Commando knife in a leather sheath, newly-oiled Colt .38 revolver in a shoulder-holster, Kriegsmarine night-glasses and bird-book in the saddle-bag. Then I stuck on the old cycle-clips, got on the old bicycle and became just another faceless worker wending his weary way home after another long night's slog in one of London's many restaurants and clubs.

My work, though, was only just beginning.

My own rising sea of troubles and the murders of "Tosh" Collis and Harry Mooney made it even more imperative I find "Monkey" Jim, if he was still alive, that was. And so once I'd caught up with Ray by telephone at midnight, I had another long night at Kensal Green Cemetery ahead of me.

To get myself stretched and limbered for what was to come, I cycled hard and fast up the Harrow Road and then cut through the back streets so I'd come out the other end of Church Street. I turned into the street and saw the Apostles off in the distance, standing like hallowed guardians of the gate.

Church Street looked pathetic in that way street markets do when denuded of jostling crowds of people. The street still smelled of Saturday's market, as a lot of the leftover rubbish wouldn't be cleared until Monday. As ever, the odd cat was chasing the odd rat, odd fast-moving shadows cast for the very briefest of seconds against the odd brick wall. There was a large furniture lorry parked outside Jordan's department store—ready for its regular run out to the furniture factories in High Wycombe—as well as the usual motley collection of motorcars and delivery vans parked up and down either side of the street. And other than the fact the light bulb inside 'Mark' was out, everything seemed normal.

It's times like that, though, that give me the willies.

I cycled on past the Apostles, almost as far as Penfold Street, just to give that end of Church Street the once-over, then turned a circle and slowly cycled back towards the West London Stadium, where I dismounted. I leaned the bike against the wall next to the telephone-boxes, switched off my headlamp and tail lamp and, nosing the night air, glanced up and down the street again. Then I stepped into the darkness inside 'Mark,' did the business of dialling three times, and waited for Ray to pick-up the receiver at his end.

"It's Mark," I said into the silence. "Thanks, for the warning."

"Sorry I couldn't warn you any sooner. Very glad you didn't get yourself banged up. How did the rest of your Sabbath go?"

Ray was very intrigued Browno had warned me and had all but broken my nose to cover it from his men. He was also very concerned about the 'notice' put out on me and that I'd been followed, but it was the word 'Norto' that really got him to thinking. It was the first he'd ever heard of it.

"This 'Norto' business," he asked, "did Browno say what it was about? Whether it stood for anything or was anyone's name?"

"No, it was just that one time, that one question."

"Okay, got it logged. Now what I've managed to piece together is this. Last three, four weeks it seems all manner of faces have upped and disappeared from the Smoke. There's some talk of it being three blokes in a motorcar behind it all, though no one's saying who it might be. 'Monkey' Jim was one of the first to disappear and the only thing making me think he's still alive is the fact that Messima is still offering big money to find him. We know what happened to 'Tosh' Collis and Harry 'Rabbit,' but where it gets truly odd is that a couple of goons who worked for Messima, a couple of his minders and one of his drivers, have also recently turned up dead. It's more than enough to have started a gang war at any other time, but so far, nothing. On the surface, everything appears to be normal."

"Calm before the storm?" I asked.

"Don't know, but something about the deaths of 'Tosh' Collis and Harry 'Rabbit' gives me heartburn. It's not so much the punishment fitting the crime, as the punishment exactly matching the person. Add to that the whispers about various well-known faces being smacked way, way above any normally accepted levels of retribution, and it says to me and my suspicious mind they're all explicit warnings of some kind. But to what end or purpose, I have no idea." He was silent for a bit. "Anyway, given the 'notice' on you and knowing you as I do, I know you've already got yourself well tooled-up," he said, flatly. "Only just you remember this, and you remember it good. We don't want you ending up at the wrong end of the hangman's noose. It's the very thing we've been trying to avoid."

"Believe you me," I said, "I wish to hell shooters weren't necessary. You know how much I hate the bloody things, but it's their bloody game, so I'm playing by their bloody rules."

"All I'm saying, old cock, is you go careful."

"Funny, that's what Browno said," I said. "Er, got to go, looks like I've got some unexpected company."

TWO WHEELS GOOD,
FOUR WHEELS BAD

I was out of 'Mark' and scooting the bike, one foot on the peddle, the other madly kicking the pavement even before the door of the telephone-box had started to close. I'd caught sight of something out the corner of my eye, a big black motorcar moving up the street from the direction of Edgware Road, its headlights and sidelights off, moving oh so very, very slowly, like a cat stalking its prey. I wouldn't have seen it, but for the changing patterns of light from the lamp-posts along the street being reflected on the motorcar's windscreen. And in considerably less time than it takes a heart to beat, I was up and onto the saddle, peddling like mad.

I didn't look behind me. If I was wrong I'd get in a little more exercise. If I was right I needed to get as much distance between me and my pursuers as was humanly possible. I didn't even have time to switch on the bicycle's headlamp, which meant I had to keep my wits well about me. What with rubbish from the market still strewn all around the place and potholes everywhere, I could go arse over tit at any moment.

Headlight beams as big as an anti-aircraft searchlight battery suddenly thrust back the darkness and threw my jagged shadow along the road in front of me. I cut right and peddled like billy-o to get to the second turning on the left, before the motor could reach the corner and turn down after me.

My only plan was to look for a friendly bombsite or a hole big enough for me to crawl into. In the interests of time, however, I settled for a little cobblers shop. The street was dark, but there was still the danger of me being silhouetted against the streetlights at the far end. I skidded to a stop, dropped the bike in the gutter, and stepped smartly into the little recess of the shop doorway, flattening myself against the door. The fast-moving beams of light stopped for a moment at the end of the street and then moved on. I gave it a few seconds for the curtains of darkness to fall back into place, then peddled along the street, steering clear of any and all lamp-posts. I'd almost reached the end when I saw the thrusting headlight beams again. Even with the speed it was going I couldn't see how the motorcar could've gone around the block so quickly. So I was off the bike again in a flash and hugged the nearest wall just as it sped by.

It hit me then: there must've been two motors, parked either end of Church Street, waiting for me to arrive home. I hadn't clocked the second one, as I'd cycled in from Lisson Grove, which told me it must've been hidden down by the side of the Duke of York pub. I cursed myself for being so blind and pushed down hard on the pedals, my plan now to make for the railway cutting a block or two north of Church Street. It was only a small section of the marshalling yards that served Marylebone Station—just four lines across at that point and used mostly for commuter-line rolling-stock rather than the larger main-line carriages destined for Rugby, Sheffield and Manchester—but it was a big enough hole for me to hide in till morning. And if push came to shove it'd be a good way out of the Smoke. My first task, though, was to get there in one piece, my only strategy to keep heading in the opposite direction of my pursuers.

I passed Jordan's department store again and cut left back onto Church Street making a beeline for the corner of Salisbury

Street, and I was but halfway there when I saw beams of light fingering the walls of the street, the other side of the West London Stadium. I knew I couldn't make the corner in time, so I braked hard, yanked the back-wheel around, and headed back the way I'd just come, praying I could get off Church Street before I was caught in the headlights. Bugger it, why were there never any friendly beat-coppers around when you needed one?

I was almost back at the corner, readying myself for the turn, when another big black motor turned into the street from Lisson Grove. Half-blinded, I braked hard as it roared past, its headlights reflecting off the windscreen and chrome radiator of the other motorcar, barrelling towards it from the other end of the street. There was a screech of brakes and the squeal of tyres shredding rubber and a loud bang that probably meant that one of the motors had collided with the furniture van.

I shot through the covered alleyway that led into Plympton Street and chanced a quick look over my shoulder, only to see one of the motorcars turning down after me, its engine roaring, its headlights blazing, fully intent on running me over. Just as quickly it slowed to a crawl, the driver at last realising that with barely a foot or so either side there was little or no room for manoeuvre and certainly no room for mistakes.

I saw the bloke's ashen face. He saw mine. He snarled and gunned the engine. I hit the brakes. Let the bike drop. Had my jacket unbuttoned, the Colt drawn and cocked. My feet firmly planted. And was crouching down into a two-handed shooting stance before you could say 'boo' to a Christmas goose. All of it done in one fluid motion, just as I'd been taught to do in a previous lifetime by a very wily firearms instructor called Mr Carter.

I aimed at the seething mass of light and chrome and fired off two quick shots, a double-tap, hoping to hit the radiator or engine block, or at the very least take out one of the headlights. Then I aimed a little higher and got off two shots at the windscreen, aiming to deter the driver.

The effect was quite dramatic, even if I say so myself. The big black motor bucked like a horse and careened against one side of the narrow alleyway before scraping itself against the opposite wall. The driver wrestled like mad with his steering wheel and had all but gained control as the motorcar shot out from the covered alleyway and ran straight into the twin metal bollards set into the road to stop anything wider than a market barrow from using the cut-through. The motorcar stopped dead. The driver's head and shoulders came bursting through the windscreen. By then I'd already re-holstered the Colt, scooped up my bicycle, and was speeding towards Broadly Street, each turn of the peddles taking me farther and farther away from the marshalling yard.

"That's torn it," I said to myself. In less than a minute, it'd gone from peaceful tranquillity, or as much as is ever possible when you live within earshot of a main railway line terminus, to what must've sounded to the sleeping denizens of Church Street like the re-staging of the night raid on Dieppe. It was enough to have awakened the dead, as was increasingly evident by the trail of bedroom lights and twitching curtains I seemed to be leaving in my wake. It was odds on somebody would've been disgruntled enough to dial '999' and put in a call to the police.

Which of course begged the eternal question: Whither goest thou?

Deciding against Lisson Grove, as it was too well lit, I turned right into Broadly Street, which would afford me dark streets aplenty. It would also bring me in short order to "Buggy" Billy's drum—a place that'd offered me refuge on countless occasions—only I couldn't chance being caught off the bike, standing there on the pavement, knocking on his front door like a madman. If my pursuers saw me, they'd be all over me like flies on dog shit and, if I involved "Buggy," they'd take him down too without a second thought. And the very last thing I wanted to do was take trouble to his door. The same went for Joanie and Barry. Even though my own home was just a few streets away, it might as well have been the other side of the moon. That's when I abandoned the idea of making for the marshalling yards and decided instead to head for the sanctuary of Paddington Green Police Station. DI 'Deadeye' Morton had asked that I drop by at my earliest convenience and now seemed as good a time as any. I'd worry about what to do with my shooter when I got there; it'd be easy enough to drop into the canal.

Distant headlights and the sounds of a fast-approaching motorcar put paid to idle thought and I cut immediate left and mounted the pavement, slewed the bike to a stop between a parked van and the wall of a house, and melted into the bricks. The motorcar sped on down Broadly Street without any sign of slowing or stopping. "That was bloody good timing," I said to myself, wiping my brow with the back of my coat sleeve.

Cycling can be hard work sometimes.

I breathed deeply to try and get my heartbeat back down to something like normal before pushing off again. With that last motorcar now headed back towards Lisson Grove—there couldn't be three of the sods—I had a good few minutes clear to get myself to the far end of Bell Street and across the Edgware Road to the police station on the Harrow Road. And I remember thinking that with a little luck, I'd soon be home free.

I whizzed past the school and fixed my sights on Edgware Road Tube station off in the distance, put my head down, and went for it. I'd not gone but twenty yards when out the corner of my eye I saw this huge shape come hurtling at me from out of the darkness. Of course, it was far too late for me to do anything about it, the devious sods had turned off the headlights and sidelights again, and I think the motorcar's front wing had already clipped my back-wheel before I was even aware of it. All I remember is hearing the screech of tyres and the crash and crunch of twisted metal as I was thrown up into the air. There wasn't even time to cry out. Yet, the funny thing was, it also all seemed to happen in slow motion as well, just like people say always happens in accidents, and as I sailed past I clearly recall seeing the face of the driver and the bloke sitting behind him in the back seat.

I didn't wave.

COLD COMFORT

My eyelids fluttered as I shivered myself awake into a darkness as black as the black hole of Calcutta. I gulped in lungfulls of air made heavy by the smell of carbolic and the traces of the chloroform they'd used to keep me under. And that started me off coughing and retching like nobody's business. Echoes of the ungodly noise I was making crashed around me in waves, all but deafening me, and I squeezed my eyes shut and prayed the commotion would soon end. After a bit I opened my eyes to discover it was still as black as pitch, and when I tried to feel for the blindfold, I nearly poked my eye out. From which I deduced there was nothing pressed against my eyeballs but the darkness itself and I was lying in a crumpled heap in some deep, dark, dank cellar somewhere.

I was one mass of bumps, bruises, and swellings, but the pain said I was still very much alive, and that was welcome news. I rolled, very gingerly, over onto my back and tried to sit up, but from the sharp stabbing pains it was clear I'd cracked some ribs. After a few more tries, I managed to sit up, which said there were no ropes, shackles or chains restraining me, and that was more good news.

I patted the floor around me and found it cold to the touch. It was very deeply scratched in some places and as smooth as a baby's arse in others and, although a bit greasy, it was relatively free of rubbish. I tried to stand up but didn't have the strength. So I lay down again and waited. After about a million years I managed to get to my feet and I stood in complete darkness and tried to see through my ears, but the only sound I heard was my tortured breathing.

One skill you tend to develop in my line of work is the ability to judge the size and shape of a room with your eyes closed. So, right away, I sort of knew there was no proper doorway or windows to hand, just bare walls, a bare ceiling, and a bare floor. It wasn't too hard then for me to work out I was in a large metal container of some sort.

I squeezed my eyes shut and stood in my own self-imposed darkness and tried to keep my overly active imagination in check. Then, feeling a mite calmer, I opened my eyes and spied a patch of wall about the size of a biscuit tin that seemed lighter than the area all around it. I turned on the spot and spied a second patch of wall much the same. I slowly inched forward, in the darkness—arms held out in front of me—until I reached the wall, then I turned round again and paced out the length and breadth of my prison cell.

I leaned against a wall and scratched my head as much for human contact as to help me think. The old creeping saying, "The only way out is the way you came in," holds true more times than not, so I slowly felt my way, hand-over-hand, around the walls.

My foot collided with something that boomed like Big Ben and turned out to be a small oil-drum. I did some exploring with my fingers and found the metal drum had a lid on it. I cautiously lifted the lid and a very pungent odour of disinfectant mixed with piss and shit hit me smack in the face. I dropped the lid and for a moment the noise was as bad as the smell had been. It was very obvious then what the drum was supposed to be used for. It was also very plain I wasn't the first person to have come to that sad little realisation whilst all alone in the dark.

I continued on around the walls of my prison cell until I came to what had to be the doorway, though there was no handle, no hinges, no handy screw-heads, and no helpful keyhole. My imagination shrivelled to nothing in the face of the cold hard facts as then presented. Someone had stuffed me inside an industrial-sized meat-locker with no way out other than by a person outside pulling the handle of the roll and clasp lever lock mechanism bolted to the other side of the door. The picks and skels hidden in my shoes, my belt, and the lapels of my jacket were certainly no match for that. My revolver and knife, of course, were long gone. I had a nasty thought and felt for my belt. That was missing too. I reached down and found both sets of shoelaces gone. "Blimey," I said to myself, "a suicide watch and all, is it?" And for one brief moment I wondered about the poor sod that must've made such precautions necessary and pondered again why either of us had ended up in such a God-awful place.

My next little surprise came when I turned and knocked what sounded like a tin tray across the floor. I got down on my hands and knees and felt around and put my hand in a cold, wet puddle of something. I waved my hand gently from side to side a few inches above where I imagined the floor to be until my fingers touched an enamelled tin mug. I held it to my nose. It was tea, stewed enough to tan leather. I took a tentative sip of what few dregs were still left. It was stone cold, tasted rusty, but it was mighty welcome all the same, as was the sugar that'd congealed into a lump at the bottom of the mug. I stuck my finger in and scooped the sugar up and wolfed it down. I left the mug by the door. It'd been full of hot tea once upon a time and I hoped against hope it would be again.

And I shivered at the very thought of it.

I sat back down and tried to do some proper thinking. I could be anywhere. Smithfield meat market. Leadenhall produce market. A sausage or meat-pie factory somewhere on the outskirts of the city. Even a disused warehouse. I couldn't smell the river, so I didn't reckon I was anywhere near the Docks. One good thing, the walls weren't covered in rivulets of frozen water, which meant as cold as it was the meat-locker and me weren't being refrigerated. Another good thing, I hadn't been left hanging from a meat hook.

I had a brainwave and felt around the floor near where I'd found the tin mug hoping to find a crust of bread or something, but had no luck. I tried again, anyway, quartering the entire floor area of the meat-locker like a Flower-class corvette on patrol, but again came up with nothing.

I had a thought and turned and stared up at the two patches of pale shadow, and it may have just been my imagination or simply that my eyes had fully adjusted, but both shapes seemed lighter than before. I stared past them—an old trick— and began to make out dark lines running from top to bottom and side-to-side. And I began to make out the jagged holes and the metal grilles that'd been welded over them in all their horrible glory. I knew then if someone had gone to that much trouble they'd have also sited the meat-locker cum Jerry-made holding cell far enough away from regular commerce or foot traffic for any undue noise not to attract attention. I knew then that I could yell my head off, scream blue bloody murder, but it wouldn't matter a damn.

On a more positive note, the ventilation grilles said I wasn't meant to suffocate to death, and even though my stomach thought my throat had been cut, I also didn't think I was going to be left to starve to death either. It was also very clear by then that if whoever it was outside had wanted me dead, my throat would've already been slit from ear to ear and I'd have been left to fatten up earthworms over Hackney Marshes way.

Still, whichever way I looked at it, I was up shit creek without a paddle and I have to admit I felt the first uneasy stirrings of panic as my overly active imagination started pushing to get into the act again. So I did what I always do at such times: I got hold of myself and gave myself a right talking to. Well, someone had to, or I was finished before I even started. In the end, it all comes down to whether you think you're going to survive whatever's threatening you or not. And as my old dad used to say, God bless him, "Never say die."

"You can fuck this for a game of old soldiers," I shouted, loud enough for anyone outside my prison walls to hear. And as the harsh tinny echoes of "old soldiers" faded away into nothing, I sat cross-legged on the floor, my back against the wall, determined to fight the good fight, come what may. Not that I had much choice in the matter, but with my decision made, it wasn't long before I imagined I was back out among the rooftops and alleyways of the Smoke, padding back and forth over every blessed little thing that'd happened since I'd first espied 'Monkey' Jim climbing up from out the darkness below.

COTTONING ON

Some evil, callous bastard of a cowson banged out an urgent tattoo on the side of the meat-locker and my Smoke-filled thoughts were blown into a million pieces and me very nearly with them.

"Wakey! Wakey!" yelled a voice, doing a bad impression of Billy Cotton, the bandleader who'd just got his own show on the radio, Sunday afternoons. "Tea's up. So be so good as to back away from the door."

I suddenly realised how parched I was and how very, very cold it was. I had no idea how long I'd been locked inside. My wristwatch had long gone. The length of the bristles on my face felt like a good day's worth, maybe two, which meant at the very least I'd been there overnight and part of the following day. By my reckoning it was sometime Monday morning and only then did I realise I could actually see my hand in front of my face. I waved both my hands about to make sure it was me I was looking at.

"Back away from the door now, sunshine, we don't want any nonsense or I'll have to break your fuckin' fingers, just for starters."

"Just you try it," I muttered, before backing away. There was a click and snap as the big lever lock was pulled back, and suddenly there was a slim pillar of light that burned to the very back of my eye sockets. Then, just as quickly, the door banged shut again and I was thrust back into the darkness.

"Oi," I shouted. "What's going on? Why am I locked up in here?"

The stupid berk just banged all the harder on the outside of the meat-locker, all but breaking my eardrums. "You just drink your tea now, like a good boy," yelled the voice. "That's what it's fuckin' there for."

"Oi," I shouted, again. "Oi, you." But the only sound was my by now raspy voice echoing off the cold hard metal walls.

A long, thin, narrow rectangular shape seemed to want to linger on the inside of my eyelids forever and I did my best to blink it away. It was only then that I smelled the tea. I inched my way round to where the harsh sliver of daylight had been and got down on my hands and knees and let my fingers do the seeing. I all but yelped when my fingertips touched the scalding hot tin mug, but that was as much out of fear of me spilling the precious liquid as anything else. I slowly counted to ten, then firmly grasped the mug in both hands and just sat there in the gloomy darkness, my back against the wall again, warming my hands, as if by a fire.

After a bit, the rest of me would wait no longer for its share of warmth and I began to sip at the tea, even though it was still hot enough to burn my tongue. The stewed, sweet taste of the tea—as sweet to me then as any single malt had ever been—sent heat coursing into me, and I sat and supped and reflected some more on my situation and prospects.

For some weird reason though I couldn't seem to keep my thoughts from flopping into one another or disappearing off round a corner somewhere. Far, far away I heard a voice yelling "Wakey! Wakey!" again, then much closer to home I heard the sound of something hitting the floor with a clunk and a clatter.

Then the world was wet and full of darkness.

And the whole world and me ceased to exist.

Again.

There was sound before there was light, wave after wave of it ripping at the edges of my brain cells, all of it muffled and warped as if I was underwater. Not that I was back in the game yet, I was just coming and going with the tide, picking up snatches of whatever happened to float past. "Dozy sod is spark out." "Better him dopey than yelling his fuckin' head off." Silence. "So he's the one all the trouble's been over. Doesn't look like he's up to much, does he?" Short silence. "Tell that to the bloke whose head went through the fuckin' windscreen and the rest of them still in traction." Short silence. "Not having too much luck these days, are they, his drivers?" Long silence. "You put how many fuckin' barbiturates in his tea?" Silence. "Well, you told me as how he used to be a bit of a fly bugger, so I put in double the dose, didn't I?" "You stupid sod, that's enough to put a fuckin' horse to sleep." Long, long, silence. Different voice. "Listen you berks, use smelling salts, cups of coffee, anything. Throw a fuckin' bucket of water over him if you have to, but get him ready. He's the fuckin' star of the show." Long silence, with noises off. "Come on, sunshine. Show time. Wakey! Wakey!" "It's no use, he's still as dopey as old rope." "Fuck it, we'll just have to carry the bastard and fuckin' prop him up."

Next thing I knew I was being half-carried, half-dragged down a long, dimly lit corridor by a couple of heavy-set blokes in dark suits. They stopped when we got to a set of double doors and I stopped with them.

"Prisoner all present and correct," one of the blokes shouted.

"Right, bring him up," said a voice off.

The doors opened and they dragged me up some steps into the unknown. The light burned my eyes, but I was that hungry for the sight of anything that wasn't the inside of the meat-locker, I snatched butcher's hooks as opportunities arose, all the while fighting off the urge to sleep. All the same, it was a huge effort and it took a while for my eyes to start working properly. I found it easier, less dizzying, to blink and stare, blink and hold, give it time to develop, then blink and stare again, in the manner of a camera shutter.

First picture. I was in a small hall as might be used as a community centre or a meeting place for the Women's Institute or the Boy Scouts. Though, as the entire place reeked of cigarette smoke, Whisky, and sweat, and a couple of big, burly blokes were busy replenishing water jugs, and setting out fresh paper and pencils, I took it a meeting of a different sort hadn't long broken up.

Second picture. At the far end of the hall was a line of green baize-covered trestle-tables positioned end to end, with chairs along one side. Ten feet or so in front of that, to the left and right, were a couple of desks—card-tables really—each with its own chair.

Funny place to find a bridge school, I said to myself.

Third picture. I espied a chair next to one of the card-tables that looked to be a good deal more solid than the rest of the furniture. And, as I was carried ever closer to it, I focussed on it, and saw it was festooned with leather straps and bolted to the floor. Hang wire flex from it and it could've done duty as an electric chair, the very thought of which was enough to bring on the shakes. I squeezed my eyes tight shut and tried to stop from yelling out. And that's when the pictures in my mind began to crisp and burn and curl into ashes. I'd finally got the picture. I saw now I was in a courtroom of some sort. The whole set-up eerily similar to one I'd seen captured in a David Low cartoon in the *Daily Mirror* of a show trial in Russia, at the very moment the accused is being dragged out to be shot. I forget the caption, but it was along the lines of, '*You promised me a great show, Comrades, but I didn't laugh once.*'

They sat me down and strapped me into the wooden chair and put the blindfold on. I resisted, of course, or the parts of me I had any control over did, but even my normally sharp tongue couldn't seem to quite get itself round any of the words I had in mind and anyone listening must've thought I'd gone completely gaga.

A voice whispered in my ear that if I didn't shut my noise they'd stick a gag in my mouth.

So I just sat there, eyes closed behind the blindfold.

Some time later—I don't know how long—I heard the sounds of people coming back into the room. The chatter seemed so innocuous it could've been a theatre crowd returning to the auditorium after the intermission. It went on like that for a few minutes. Then an expectant hush descended on the room. And that's when the blindfold came off, and the curtain went up, and for some reason I found I just couldn't stop myself from yawning.

I looked at the 'faces' in front of me, each and every one of whom I knew by sight and or reputation, but who in the Smoke didn't? Every single one of them had been pictured in every Sunday linen going, and most of the dailies, too, at one time or another. They were the cream of London villainy, the leaders of every major gang working north of the water. And all of them sat in a line like they were at the Last Supper or something. The heads of London's Italian, Maltese, British, Irish, and Jewish mobs, as well as the head of the Diddikies, the King of the Gypsies—the real power behind the Upton Park mob. Seven faces that no one on God's green earth would've ever expected to see in the same room, let alone sitting together at the same table.

Jack Spot was sat at one end of the table, looking decidedly out of sorts. At the other end, looking very pleased with himself, was young Ronnie White, head of the King's Cross mob, now that his dad and two uncles had been banged-up for seventeen years apiece. And sitting smack dead centre was Darby Alphonse Solano Messima, Emperor of Soho, his eyes expressionless, his face a complete blank, a sure sign that something very bad was about to happen to someone. That someone, of course, being me.

I blinked and blinked and blinked again to try and bring my mind into some sort of focus. So picture this if you will: No jury box, no public gallery, in fact, no public, no audience, just blokes dressed in dark suits and ties, standing around the room like guards. I tried to clock their faces but didn't recognise a one. And as addled as my mind was, that sent up a bunch of distress rockets and flares, because none of the seven gang-bosses ever went anywhere without one or two of his top minders in tow. Which begged the obvious question. What the fuck was Messima up to now?

"Alright, let's fuckin' get on with it," said a voice that I think belonged to Jack Spot.

SEVEN PLUS TWO EQUALS NOUGHT

There was this bloke, stood by the card-table nearest me, waiting for me to compose myself, which in my case, I suppose, meant I shouldn't dribble too much. I hadn't noticed him before, but he had barrister written all over his dark blue chalk-stripe suit, as did his counterpart standing in starched collar, black jacket, and striped trousers over by the other card-table. I wondered how long ago it'd been since these two 'Johnnies' had been disbarred, and for what.

"If it please the court," said Chalk-stripe. "Due to the egregious nature of the crimes of which the prisoner stands accused, the chairman of the jury of judges, Mr Darby Messima, has asked if he may first say a few words."

While I pondered on the word "egregious," everyone else played their part and nodded or grunted their assent. Me, I'd already been cast as a mute witness at my own trial and, slow-witted though I may've been because of all the barbiturates still sloshing around inside me, it was obvious even to me the whole set up was a sham, if not an outright farce. A court of law? I should cocoa. It was a damned bloody kangaroo court, the result already well fixed.

Looking dapper as ever, in one of his more sober Savile Row suits, Messima got slowly to his feet. "My fellow judges, I find myself in a very difficult situation. It's well known I've had high regard for the accused's past reputation as a creeper, and I admit that over the years, tales of his rascality have occasioned in me the odd chuckle. I liked him and, like everyone else, I took him at his word when he said he was no longer in the burglary business. Still, given he was once a respected 'face,' I've treated him with proper respect whenever our paths have crossed. But that's me, isn't it? Always courteous to a fault. It's a veritable weakness of mine."

"Blimey O'Reilly," I said to myself. What's this? The Variety Club's Ancient Order of Water Rats charity dinner? What was Messima's game?

Messima turned both palms upwards as a sign of trustworthiness. "However, given the serious nature of the crimes he's been accused of, I can no longer allow past feelings to colour the issue and, in the interests of the justice to be served in this case, I must hereby excuse myself as a judge."

"What the fuck's that mean when it's at home?" said a voice.

"It means that due to possible conflict of interest and in the true spirit of justice, Mr Messima, as the presiding court official, has decided to abstain from participating in the final vote," said Chalk-stripe helpfully.

"That's it, exactly," Messima said, pointedly, pointing at me. "I don't want it ever said that I let my personal disappointments with this piece of shit in any way influence the court's fair and final judgement."

"Fair enough," said another voice. "Let's get on with it."

With Messima's impersonation of Pontius Pilate done and his hands duly washed of me, the two layabouts playing at being barristers set about trussing me up in ever more absurd sounding legal gobbledegook. I won't bore you with the back and forth between Chalk-stripe and his chinless counterpart as to whether in fact I'd done this or that, it doesn't really bear repeating. Needless to say, I was accused of the manslaughter of Harry Mooney. It being the contention of the court that I'd wanted to get my filthy hands on the reward money, and that Harry had died rather than cough-up the whereabouts of his dear, lost brother. Then, suitably emboldened by my sordid act, I'd murdered "Tosh" Collis in a jealous rage to stop him from succeeding where I'd proved myself such a conspicuous failure.

In addition, I was charged with having caused grievous bodily harm to a number of officials who'd been duly going about their court-appointed business. The cherry on the fish cake, as Ray used to say, was that I was also then accused of having been a long-standing 'grass' for Scotland Yard, the murmur in the court when that little titbit was read out sounding very nasty.

One thing I did find a bit odd, given that they'd thrown everything but the kitchen sink at me, was that at no time was I accused of having done the Meridian Mansions job or of being in any way responsible for the death of Nigel Fox MP. Funny that, especially as that whole business was supposedly the root of all the evil that'd transpired since.

Striped Trousers read out a pile of witness statements in support of the prosecution's case. On the first count, a boatload of people had seen me talking to Harry "Rabbit" on a street corner in Soho. Trousers even produced my missing copy of the *Evening Standard* and asked that it be entered as evidence against me. His point being that nowhere did it report any news item or show any classified listing in reference to any theatrical scenery company, bankrupt or otherwise. On the second count, people had sworn blind they'd seen me at various pubs along the river—all places known to have been frequented by "Tosh" Collis. (All damn lies, of course.) On the third count, no less than six people, all upstanding members of London's criminal community, had positively identified me as the malicious bastard who'd so violently resisted apprehension. The most damning evidence, however, was reserved for the heinous crime of me being a suspected 'grass.' Offered as proof was the fact I'd been seen to frequent a known haunt of CID officers working out of Paddington Green. Another report had me drinking tea with a senior detective from the same police station at the selfsame Bridge Cafe, and that a brown envelope, a payment obviously, had figured in our conversation. Further, there'd been additional sightings of me with detectives near the Haymarket and again near Aldgate Underground station. The real shocker came at the end, when Trousers spoke of my known close association with a Ghost Squad copper. I wondered just who in hell he could be referring to. Then he dropped the iron on me again, when he informed the court that because the copper in question had recently suffered an unfortunate accident and died, he couldn't be produced as a witness.

Regardless, it was all pretty damning evidence, if the looks on the faces of the seven judges there assembled were anything to go by, and I dare say if they could've hung me right there and then, they would've done, if only to save themselves any more bother.

"It's all merely circumstantial," was about all Chalk-stripe could offer up in my defence. But then, something odd: Jack Spot spoke up in my defence. Well, someone had to, as try as I might I was certainly in no condition to do so. It was hard enough for me even to stay awake.

"Hold on, hold on," Spottsy said. "I'll grant you, Jethro has at times been a feckless bastard and a right dodgy character to boot, but personally I have to say I don't give a tinker's cuss whether he has or has not given up the game as a creeper. What I do know from personal experience is that in the past he's not been entirely unhelpful to certain friends of mine. I also have it on good authority he's extremely loyal to anyone he calls family or friend. So for that alone, I can't see him topping "Tosh" Collis—they were as thick as thieves, back before the war. Same goes for Harry "Rabbit." Jethro palled around with his brother Jimmy back then, too. So as far as I'm concerned none of this manslaughter, murder stuff holds any water. It just doesn't add up."

I don't know which part of what Spottsy said lit the fuse under Messima, or whether it was because a few faces had mumbled their agreement, but Soho's "Little Caesar" came off his chair like a bloody V2 rocket. "There you go again, you see. That's exactly what I was talking about: you mustn't allow personal issues to fog the argument. So let me, as chairman of this here court, put some things into proper perspective." Messima pointed at me again. "For a start, why did this arsehole run if he had nothing to fuckin' hide? And in the second place, if he had nothing to hide, why did he need to go around all tooled up? That doesn't sound like a fuckin' West End stage hand, does it? And it weren't no fuckin' prop gun from no play he was carrying round in his pocket, either. It was a well-fuckin'-oiled Colt .38 revolver, and he all but topped several of the lads by shooting at them and their motorcar point blank. And shooters, may I remind you, are the very things we're all trying to avoid, for the simple reason the public fuckin' hates them. Then so do the politicians, who turn round and jerk the Yard's chain. Who in turn let loose the Heavy Mob, who then come and jerk our chains, looking to seize enough pop-guns and collar enough miscreants to satisfy public outrage. And all of it, I might add, a totally unnecessary disruption to business. So I repeat, this arsehole here presents a clear and current danger to the peace and prosperity of us all."

Like any good orator, Messima gave time for the chorus of nods and approval to subside, then went in for the kill.

"So apart from the fact Jethro was seen rabbiting to Harry 'Rabbit' not long before the late Mr Mooney went missing, and whether he was or was not dead jealous of 'Tosh' Collis, the fact remains this so-called loyal friend to his friends is a fuckin' 'grass' for the Yard. Or why else would the Yard have a file on him that we can't get our fuckin' hands on? I can get hold of stuff on bloody MPs. I can even get the starting prices on fuckin' Cabinet Ministers, but no fuckin' way can we get hold of Jethro's records, even after paying very good money to various otherwise highly respected officers of the law. There's nothing there—not even on all the jewel jobs he did before the war. It's as if he doesn't fuckin' exist. So what the hell does that suggest to you then?"

Chalk-stripe piped up again. "Excuse me for interrupting, Mr Messima, but a fellow judge has a question for you."

It was helpful Frankie Fullerton of Watney Street, Whitechapel, the cradle and crypt of London's more psychopathic villains. "Yes, true, Mr M, true. But what about Eddie Chapman, then? Does the same go for him? Only we've not been able to get hold of any police files on him, neither."

Again, Messima's voice was like silken thread pulling minds through the eye of his needle. "Yes, good question, Frankie. Does you credit for asking it. But I can tell you Eddie's a special case; he's very patriotic, he is, and very definitely no nark. Did special work for special people during the War." Messima tapped the side of his nose to emphasise what should be read between the lines. "All I can say is, I have my sources, and I know certain things other people don't, and I can tell you here and now Eddie's kosher. I hope that satisfies you." Grunts of acknowledgement sounded from up and down the table. "Right, where were we? Oh, yes, the court's only remaining business is to decide whether this piece of shit's guilty or not—a verdict I believe by now should be very clear to all of us. Then we simply need to reach agreement on what's to be done with the bastard."

Chalk-stripe and Striped Trousers both cleared their throats in preparation for closing arguments, but Messima waved them down.

"No. Hold on. This is as good a time as any to remind ourselves why we're all here. For years it's been the same old bloody game. We can squabble like kids over territory, fight it out on the cobbles like costers, for who sells what to who, even try to top one another to see who's got the biggest set of balls. But it begs the question: why? There's vastly more profit to be had with us banding together than there is with us banging heads and battling against each other. That's why I set up NORTO, the single aim of which is for us to control all crime in London. Put in simple terms: We all do the graft, we all share the profits. If there are differences between us, we discuss and resolve them. We establish our own rules and our own court, before which transgressors from both sides of the Law, coppers as well as con-merchants, can be put on trial and, if necessary, punished. All judgements determined by a single body, namely us; all justice dispensed by duly appointed minders drawn as the occasion demands from each of our various teams. No one ever need go round mob-handed. An attack on one is taken as an attack on the many. And, in retaliation, any such act draws the full wrath of the many down upon the guilty party. If I knew of any other way to do it, believe me I'd be doing it. All I know is, it'll work. It's what the Eye-ties have done in America and it's our turn now to make it work here. All we have to do is work to make it work, because the only ones who can fuck it all up are all sitting here at this table, as we're the only ones who have a vote."

"Very well put, Mr M. Very well put. Very Winston Churchill," muttered ever-helpful Frankie Fullerton, which occasioned another round of nods and approvals. And as if to quickly seal my fate, Messima turned and asked Chalk-stripe whether I had anything to say in my defence. I tried to say something, of course, but the words came out all wrong. I tell you, it's not helpful when you can't even say, "That's a fucking lie" or "I'm well innocent."

I know I must've managed to get a few words out though, because someone sniggered at me and said: "The dozy bugger can't even speak up for himself. That tells how you fuckin' guilty he is."

"Can't you see he's been fuckin' drugged, you berk?" sneered Spottsy, which occasioned a fair amount of muttering and murmuring from amongst the other judges.

Chalk-stripe quickly stepped in to forestall any more discussion and offered up a firm, "No, sir, the accused has nothing more to say." And with that said, Messima pushed hard for a verdict as regards my guilt and got five hands raised 'for,' none against, with Spottsy abstaining.

Messima then moved for a ten-minute recess so people could go for a pee before they came back and discussed final sentencing. It was a foregone conclusion I was going to be given the worst beating they could dish out. And when the decision was handed down that I should receive the maximum punishment permitted I have to admit it gave me pause, but I consoled myself with the fact no one had reached for the Black Cap, as was tradition with hanging judges.

Chalk-stripe got the last word in. Undeterred by his complete failure to render any sort of proper defence, he drew himself up to his full height and called out, "This session of the Shadow Court, duly authorised and represented by the administrative council of the North of the River Treaty Organisation, is now at an end."

It was the only sane thing I'd heard him say all afternoon, but by that point in the proceedings, I was that dog-tired I didn't much care. I was also being dragged bodily from the court. And I may well have been the star of the show, but I hadn't found too much to laugh about, either.

As they carted me off I remember thinking: What the hell had got Messima so worked up that he'd want me dead and buried? True, I had done a fair bit of creeping on his manor without his say-so, even after I'd told him and everyone else I'd given up the creeping game for good. True, I had helped Jack Spot with his Heath Row caper. But add it all up, and it shouldn't have amounted to much more than a good striping with a razor. A hundred stitches, say. All over the body, if lucky. All on the face, if not. I could see Messima having all my fingers broken, maybe both my arms, too, even a total kneecap job, but him wanting me stone dead was something new and different.

They dropped me into some black hole and, despite the bitter cold, I went out like a light. And with what happened next, maybe I should've stayed dead to the world and saved an awful lot of people an awful lot of trouble. Might've saved a good few lives, too.

'PITCHER', 'SHIPMAN' AND 'BUMAREE'

Something sharp went up my nose and ran around my head, and I came to curled up on my side on a wet patch of concrete. I blinked and found I was in what looked to be an abandoned warehouse. I could smell the river this time. The smoke from oil-fired engines and coal-fed boilers, the whiffs from gas-works and soap factory, the acrid reek of chemicals and the tang of boiled tar, all of it overlaid with the lingering aroma of spices, and the stench of rotting vegetation and river mud. I could hear the river, too. A whole panoply of sounds. Horns hooting, whistles blowing, winches whining, heavy chains rattling, cranes and gantries clanking, steam-hammers thumping. And way, way off, above the endless screeching of the ever-present flocks of gulls, I fancied I could even hear men calling and shouting, on boat and barge and riverbank.

I sniffed it all in as if it were food, then took in a great lung-full of air and rolled over onto my back. There were three of them looking down at me with all the interest you might accord a rat in a trap. The dark suits and ties had all gone; instead they wore khaki-coloured boiler suits and rubber boots.

"He's awake, Mr. Bumaree," said the one who looked like a weasel.

"Indeed he is, Mr. Shipman," said the one with hair as black as coal.

"Shall we begin?" said the third one—a big bugger, built like a boxer, who had a shaved head and broken nose.

"Please do, Mr. Pitcher. I believe you have first call on each carcass when it arrives," said the weasel called Shipman. Then, without a word, he and Bumaree stepped in and stood on my hands, just as Pitcher stomped down hard, all but rupturing my stomach. My head came off the floor, as did my legs and feet and, as I gasped for air, they looped ropes around my wrists and started dragging me backwards across the concrete. I heard the rattle and clink of chains through a block and with the ropes holding me now secured to a metal ring, they began hoisting me upright, all but pulling my arms out of their sockets. They hoisted me up just high enough for the toe of each shoe to touch the ground and left me to hang, which meant the only way I could ease the strain from off my arms even for a second was to stretch all the more. And in what seemed like moments, the pain was beyond belief, and I was sweating cobs and it was all I could do to gasp, let alone curse the fuckers.

Shipman, the brains of the outfit, stood front and centre to be sure he had my undivided attention. "You're destined for pig-food, old cock, but in what condition you're in when we finally cut you up and stuff you through a mincing machine depends entirely on what you tell us. I can promise you one thing, though: none of it's going be too pleasant."

Given what I'd heard said in that pathetic imitation of a court thrown together by Messima, I fully expected they'd do me with 'the mark of the nark'—a long jagged razor cut ending at one of the corners of my mouth—and thus marked to be forever shunned by all criminals everywhere. But without any warning, Pitcher started laying into me with a length of thick rubber cable, each blow landing like a punch from a fifteen-stone heavyweight, and I snapped my head away to try and shield it. Then Bumaree stepped in and started whacking at me. And the two of them went at it something fierce, first one, then the other, until the dull thuds and slaps of rubber cable hitting my flesh sounded like a champion boxer working-out on a heavy bag.

Shipman shouted above all the noise, most of it by that time coming from me. "We're just softening you up to start with. Help warm up the blood, get the bruises going." I think he wanted to say more, but one of the bastards thrashing me within an inch of my life mistimed his stroke and a glancing blow hit me smack on the temple and I went spark out. As they'd done before, they used smelling salts to bring me round and a bucket of water, too, by the feel of it, because I was dripping wet this time and much more so than would've resulted from the rivers of sweat running down my body. I may have pissed in my pants, too, I don't know. I know I felt like I'd been run over by a team of dray-horses. I was just one heaving mass of red welts and purple and blue-coloured bruises. I only hoped both my kidneys were still in one piece because they hurt like buggery.

Someone reached in, pushed up an eyelid, and when they were sure I was back in the land of the almost living, Shipman addressed me again.

"Alright, sunshine. What we want to know is this: where's your old mate Jimmy Mooney, or 'Monkey' Jim as he's also called? And don't worry. We're not going to threaten to cut your tongue out. We don't know if your heart would stand it once we started hacking at it with a hacksaw. No, we've got some special things lined up for you, old cock." He held up a pair of nasty-looking crocodile clips attached to two lengths of electrical flex. "How about a bit of cooking? Bit of current through these and we could fry your balls as hard as pickled walnuts. Or if that's not to your taste, we could bubble the skin from off your hands in boiling water. Your choice." He set aside the thick-wire flex and picked up a bag of tools and pulled out a rusty old hammer or maybe it wasn't rust on the hammerhead, but dried, crusted blood. "If you prefer, we could try a bit of carpentry. Hammer and nails or hammer and chisel, hand-drill, hacksaw, pair of pliers—whatever we got in the bag. Do interesting things to your hands. Fuck up your knees and your ankles, so you'd always walk funny—if you could walk at all, that is. How does that sound?"

It sounded fucking awful, but I didn't let on. "Fuck you," I mumbled, trying hard not to dribble down my chest. I don't know if he heard me or not, as Shipman darted in, fast, flashed his razor, and striped me a quick one across the chest, all but slicing off a nipple. Blood sprayed out from me like fizz from a shook-up bottle of Tizer, which at least said my heart was still going strong even if I wasn't. All I wanted to do then was get one good kick at his face. Break the bastard's nose. Probably the last thing I'd ever do, but at least it'd give him something to remember me by.

Then out the red-rimmed blackened blue there was a crash and a bang of a big heavy door being slammed shut and the sound of some heavy-footed sod coming closer and closer. Then this deep voice I hadn't heard before, said, "Oi, I've got the 'notice' on this piece of shit: he's all bought and paid for. So just stand back, because this one's all fucking mine."

Shipman turned to address the newcomer. "Fuck off, you. Who the fuck do you think you are? We're not taking orders from the likes of you."

"Well, as of this moment, 'Mr. Maytum', you are," said the bloke. "As are your two little pals. And you'll all do as I say or I'll blow your fucking heads off here and now." I couldn't see the shotgun, but by the looks on the faces of Messrs. Pitcher, Shipman and Bumaree, they could. "You tossers have stirred things up something awful at the very moment Mr. Messima is trying to demonstrate to everyone that London can be properly handled. These recent fucking mad escapades of yours have caused a lot of heartburn. A lot of very important 'faces' are extremely unhappy about Harry Mooney being found dead in the manner he was; same with that 'Tosh' Collis bloke. You stupid berks went and topped him before he'd even been tried and sentenced. Made it appear like Mr Messima doesn't know his arse from his fucking elbow, which made him very unhappy—unhappiness, which he then expressed in no uncertain terms to your own guv'nor, young Mr Ronald White, who's now also none too happy, as it lost him a good deal of face. So I'm here to take you three dozy pricks in hand until things calm down. And you all do as I say or, I repeat, I'll blow your fucking heads off. I trust we understood one another?" The three blind mice all nodded, mutely, but they looked none too happy about it. "Right, then," said the new bloke in charge, "let's fucking get it done. You two miscreants cut this piece of shit down and stick him in the van outside. He's for the river, he is. As for you, Mr. Maytum, you're to go disappear up West and keep out of trouble until you're called for— Mr. White's orders, with Mr. Messima's compliments."

It's funny what your eyes fix on sometimes to try and help distance you from whatever pain's wracking your whole body, but as they were cutting me down and bundling me into the wheelbarrow, I noticed they each had this little tattoo on the back of whichever hand they favoured—on that fleshy bit of skin just between thumb and forefinger. Nothing too flash, just two intertwined letter O's. Me, I'd never fancied tattoos, even when I was a sailor, as however small or discrete, a tattoo's always an identifying mark, and there was never any room for that in my line of work.

Me and my wandering mind, it'll be the death of me, yet. I didn't see it coming, but then you never do. The new bloke strode forward, a dark blur without a face, and he snatched the thick rubber cable from out of Pitcher's hand and he smacked me a wicked cross-blow, smack on the temple, and I went out like a fucking light. Again.

THE UNMOURNING WATER

I fell into a blackness that consumed me whole, no trouble at all. The darkness was endless and the nightmare unending and it confined and restricted me so that I couldn't move a bloody muscle, let alone a finger. And even when I tried to open my eyes it was as if there were pennies already laid atop them, two copper pennies ready to pay the ferryman to ferry me over the River Styx.

And as I journeyed across the dark face of the water, long jagged slashes of light rent the unending murky blackness, and wave after wave of sound pricked and poked and lapped at the edges of an awakening I knew would be without pity. Then the liquid black nothingness faded to a murk-filled muddy brown, and in a flash I was delivered, wet and foul, covered in slime and shit and crying for air.

I opened my eyes and was lost again. Bound, head, hand and foot, to a wooden piling on the river foreshore and the entire world was the river and the dark water was swirling at my feet and fast rising, impatient to encircle my legs and tug at my unmoving body. My poor, purple-bruised, battered body that'd soon be nothing but a shapeless bulging sack of broken bits hidden among an unending forest of wooden jetty supports, and me unable to cry out or beg for mercy for the cloth gag tied tight over my mouth.

I stared at the dim lights on the far bank until one by one they too faded, consumed by the unrelenting waves of blackness, and I closed my eyes again for the last time, became just another something in the river. And as my body began to bloat and float away on the tide, long-fingered, dark-veined hands stretched and stretched to catch and hold me, embrace and comfort me as I drowned in sorrow at the waste and the pity of it all. And I looked into the all-enveloping darkness again and saw the face of my mother grown old beyond age and felt my father's strong riverman's arms holding my last breath clear of the unmourning water that was the river.

Then there was nothing until, without any preamble at all, the darkness was ripped asunder and I was born again mewling and puking to the pitiless screeching of flocks of angry gulls. And, in the shadows, I heard something retching as if its very guts were spilling from its body. Such awful sounds, such horrible sounds, that I could do nothing but cry out in alarm.

And then silence and everything blacker than pitch and sodden wet through and I coughed and spluttered to rid myself of the foul bitter river mud still inside my mouth. I heard my teeth chattering like pennies rapped on a counter top and felt my entire body shivering. And I knew it was me I'd heard and that it was me that was alive. But in truth I had no idea of who or what I was. Or how I still came to have breath in my body.

After the first death there's nothing but the startled cry of rebirth. Suddenly, there you are again, pulled from out the dark and as large as life, lungs screaming for air and, amazingly, it's no dream, no dream, you really are alive and kicking, and maybe not as much you'd like to be, but more than enough to be going on with. And you hear the voice of your dear old dad saying, "Never say die, old son," and you can do nothing but cry out in joy at the very prospect of reliving a life.

All of a sudden there was a sound of voices. And squelching sounds, sticky wet sounds, sucking sounds. Then someone turned me over and wiped the foul-smelling river mud from off my face, mouth, and eyes, and I could see again.

"Fuckin' hell, Jethro, I thought you was a right gonner that time."

"Hello, Jack. Fancy seeing you here," a tiny, faraway voice said.

"Give us a hand, Tommy. We best get him out of sight and fast. There's going to be hell to pay if anyone sees he's still alive."

"Tommy, Tommy, Tommy. Hello, me old china," said the strange little voice that reminded me of someone I once knew a long, long time ago. Then it all went black again. Just like it'd been before I first came into the world.

ENTREATIES

Tommy's drum was all ship-shape and Bristol fashion, but that was only to be expected. We'd both learned on the boats that keeping everything stowed away neat and tidy is far less work in the end than letting things pile up on top of you. And I say it was his drum, but as I was to learn, it was just one of several boltholes he'd set up around the Smoke as a precaution against rainy days. I'd done no less. A lock-up, shed, railway arch, backroom, back of a shop, office, flat or house, any sort of space that didn't call too much attention to itself. Any place you could have a kip, a wash, a nosh, and a change of clothes. Add a fold of cash and a weapon or two and you were more than ready to face the world when it next came knocking.

Not that I was in any condition to comment on Tommy's place when they carried me in; I was still very much spark out of it. I was also soaked through and caked with mud from head to foot and they just stood me on the kitchen lino while Tommy held me upright and Spottsy pulled my coat and trousers off. My shirt was plastered to my body, so they peeled that off me like a banana skin and dropped it on the floor. My vest and underpants came off the same way. My belt and tie had long gone and my shoes and one of my socks were stuck back in the mud somewhere, and I stood there bollock-naked, on the lino, shivering like a jelly on a cold enamel plate.

They bundled me up in a couple blankets, plonked me down in an armchair, and stuck a pair of Tommy's huge woollen socks on my feet. Tommy took the bundle of clothes away to try and sponge the worst of the mud off. Spottsy, surprisingly, as nimble-fingered as a Boy Scout, soon got a fire going in the grate, while I just sat there and began to thaw out. And I must have drifted off for a bit, because when I opened my eyes again, the fire was roaring away like a witch-burning and Tommy had rustled up some mugs of hot sweet tea, mine laced with Whisky. I gulped down the tea, hungry for the warmth, then drifted off for a bit, only to wake with a start at the sound of voices in muffled discussion and the fire settled and glowing a deep red. I peered out from my shell of blankets and maybe I moved or made a sound or something, but they turned and looked at me, as one. There was an odd look on their faces. I have no idea what my face must've looked like.

"Thought you was a gonner that time, Jethro, and no mistake," Spottsy said shaking his head. "And that was before we clocked the cuts and bruises all over your body. It's a bloody marvel there was anything left of you to save. I've seen cow carcasses down Smithfield Market in better shape. Tommy did the best he could with that nasty gash across your chest."

Tommy nodded a hello and held up his Whisky and waggled it in mute question. The glass looked very tiny in his ham-sized fist. I nodded back and he poured me one.

I had to cup both hands around the glass to make sure I found my lips.

"I would've been a goner, too," I croaked, "if it wasn't for the two of you rescuing me. Don't know how I can ever repay you."

Spottsy shook his head again. "Wasn't us that saved you, old cock. Tommy and me were merely the ambulance boys. Tommy took a call at the club, some bloke with a message that a close friend of mine was in desperate need down Wapping Docks way. Described exactly where you were to be found, but didn't give his name, just rang off."

"Yes, so me and Jack tooled over in the Jag and there you were, by King Harold's Wharf. We thought you were dead," Tommy added helpfully.

I looked Spottsy straight in the eyes. "No messing, Jack, thanks a million. Thing is, I thought you were really pissed off with me on account of that business with them missing diamonds."

Spottsy held my gaze, eye for eye. "I was, and I dare say I still am, but me being pissed with you and me pissing on your grave are two entirely different things. And what I do or not do with you is my business and none of Messima's. As for whoever it was telephoned the club, someone up there must really like you. Don't know who it was and don't need to. There's never any need to look a gift horse in the mouth once it's passed the post. But know this: I never held with you being topped. On my mother's life I didn't, and I said so very loudly, but for whatever reason nobody wanted to listen, and I was out-voted. I still owe you for what you did for my Jewish friends in *Cabal*, and they put it on me to keep an eye out for you. I also very much appreciate what you did for Tommy after the Heath Row business. You've always been as dodgy as a cartload of monkeys and always will be, but you're no 'grass,' no back-stabber, and no murderer, neither."

"All the same, thanks, Jack," I said.

"You're welcome," he said. "And if it gave me the chance to stick two fingers up at Messima's bloody Shadow Court, we both come out ahead."

"Is that what it's called? Shadow Court?"

"Yes, that's its name. I tell you, Jethro, this whole business has put the shits up people something chronic. The Ghost Squad's bad enough, what with coppers pretending to be villains. But this, setting thieves to catch or kill thieves—and coppers, too, from what I've heard—upsets every rule there is. And as cunning as that little Malteser is, one thing I know for sure: he's not big enough or clever enough to have put it all together himself. The couple of tame MPs he's got in his pocket don't have the clout. My one certainly doesn't. So it says someone somewhere draws enough weight for Messima to think he can get away with it all."

I started shivering, though whether from cold or a portent of what was yet to come, I couldn't say. Tommy stuck another blanket around me. Jack heaped more coal onto the fire. "Even in that first meeting Messima had with me about NORTO, he was like a cat with fuckin' canary feathers sticking out both sides of his mouth. Like one of them Brains Trust people on the radio who can never stop talking about bloody history, as if we haven't all had enough of that to last us a lifetime. Said he got the idea for NORTO from this NATO lark everyone's been going on about, that the North Atlantic Treaty Organisation was how countries that fought and won the war as Allies have come together to win the peace. History in the making, he said it was. A lesson for us all, if only we were smart enough to learn from it. Smart enough? I nearly nutted the little Malt bastard." Spittle started forming at the edges of Spottsy's mouth; I didn't think it was proper to mention it. "Messima have an original idea? I should cocoa. His lips fuckin' move when he reads the fuckin' label on an HP sauce bottle."

Spottsy sniffed and pulled out a silver drinking flask from his camel hair overcoat, now looking very much the worse for the dried mud caked to it. He took a long swig of lemonade, his tipple of choice, as alcohol dimmed the brain and he always wanted his head clear for business. "What really got me, though, was the smug look on his boat that says he knows he's on a winner and can't lose because the fix is well in place."

Tommy threw in his two-penny worth then. "Well, whoever it was helped Messima set up the bloody thing, now he's got all the other top gangs in it with him. He's top-dog, for sure, and we all ignore that at our peril."

Spottsy sighed. "Unfortunately, Tommy's dead right, Jethro, and that means you've got no choice now but to disappear out of the Smoke and quick. The way Messima's got the Shadow Court set up, neither Tommy nor me can be seen helping you or, by general agreement, all the other gangs can move in on my manor and take me and mine out the game for good. Ain't that right Tommy?"

Tommy grunted his confirmation, but at the same time slipped me the 'bent eye' that said he had his own thoughts on the matter.

"'Thing is, Jethro, I've still got to finger whoever grassed up the Heath Row job, and I know in my water it's going to be someone close. So I daren't risk anyone in my mob knowing you're alive or that Tommy and me, knowing that fact, haven't immediately grassed you up to NORTO. So, for all our sakes, it's best you stay dead for a bit or you'll end up dead for real—a fate Tommy and me would likely suffer soon after. Tommy will get you fixed up with some more clothes. Tell him what else you need. A shooter. Anything. There'll be another grand to tide you over, but that's all I can do for now. I've got problems of my own to sort out. So rest up here for the rest of the night and then, after tomorrow, just lose yourself as best you can. And despite all those rumours about you and 'Buggy' Billy having a falling-out, let's just say if I come up with anything, I'll follow my nose and get a message to you via him. Okay?"

I nodded. Trust Jack to see through my little ruse, but anyone that really knew us knew "Buggy" Billy and me were joined at the hip, and always would be. Tommy nodded his agreement, before disappearing off into the tiny kitchen to open some tins he had stocked in the larder, and in short order produced a dinner for the three of us that would've done any five-shilling restaurant proud. By then he'd also changed into a clean suit identical to the one that'd been covered in mud. He had on clean shoes, too. And before they went back to the club, he'd make a quick detour to Edgware Road, so Spottsy could also change into a suit and coat exactly like the ones he'd been wearing.

As they say, old habits die hard. Spottsy had once been

accused of cutting a bloke to ribbons in a nasty gang war over control of on-course betting. And one Saturday, at Epsom racecourse, after he'd sorted some people out with his razor and the police had finally moved in to sort out the mess, he'd quietly disappeared into the crowd. Twenty minutes later, he was stopped by the police and questioned about the incident and he simply pointed to his pristine suit and shirt cuffs and said it must be a case of mistaken identity as there was no blood on him anywhere. He was let off with a caution. But then, as I said, boltholes are very handy things, even if only a nearby caravan.

Planning ahead, it's called.

Spottsy looked at his wristwatch. "Right, let's get off. If Tommy and me aren't back at the club soon, questions will be asked. I'll walk round the corner to the Jag. Tommy, give it five minutes, then follow."

"Right, Guv'nor," said Tommy, starting to clear up.

"Jethro, you go safe. And don't fuckin' well be seen by anybody."

"I'll be like a ghost," I said. "Won't be hard. I'm meant to be dead."

Spottsy chuckled, but there was no humour in it. When he'd gone, Tommy asked me was there anything else I needed before he left.

"Yes, a tin of boot-blacking to help change the colour of my Barnet, and I'll need to get myself on a narrow boat going down the Regents Canal, towards the Grand Union Basin. I've got to get to my own lock-up and I daren't chance the roads anywhere around Edgware Road or Paddington."

"Very wise," he said. "I can rustle us up a canal boat, no problem. And being the better seaman, I also better be the steerer as well."

I shook my head. "No, Tommy, grand of you to offer, but I can't let you put yourself at risk, not after what Spottsy just said about NORTO."

Tommy gave me a look worthy of Ray Karmin. "I'll be buggered if I'm going to let Messima or anyone else put the shits up me. Hitler's bloody 'wolf packs' couldn't do it and I'm too old to let anyone start now. And if you think I'm going to let you handle a narrow boat by yourself, in your condition, you can bloody well think again. It can be done, but you know it's best with two of us working it. This way it'll make for a much smoother passage and attract a lot less attention. And from the Kingsland Basin or City Road Basin, it'd be what? Eight, nine miles to Paddington? It won't take us too long. So I don't want to hear any more about it. It's the two of us, and that's final. There's tins of food in the larder, blacking under the sink, the boiler's full, so there's plenty of hot water. So get some sleep and remember to get some ointment on them bruises. See you later."

"Thanks, Tommy," I said. "For everything."

"Don't mention it," he said. "Be lucky."

And then he quietly slipped away to join Spottsy in the Jag.

I threw some Epsom Salts into the bath, soaked my bruised and battered body, tried to avoid looking at all the damage that'd been inflicted upon me, then almost frightened myself to death by awaking with a start an hour or so later in muddy water gone freezing cold. I rinsed off, towelled myself warm, patted the stiches across my chest dry, slathered ointment everywhere on me coloured dark blue, yellow, or purple, then set about staining my hair black with boot polish. That done, I scrunched my hair up, parted it on the opposite side to how I normally comb it, and hacked at it with a pair of scissors. When I checked the results in the mirror I still looked like death warmed up, but with my swollen face and bloodshot and bruised eyes, I didn't look like me exactly, which was encouraging. I did remind myself of someone, though I couldn't say who it was. I scratched my chin. The three- or four-day-old beard could certainly wait another day or three or more before it went to meet its maker. What else? I reached under the sink again and looked for a roll of cotton wool—always on hand in certain circles to help stem the blood from razor cuts, large or small. I tore off a couple of bits, rolled them between my fingers, flattened them, and stuck them down each side of my gums. I looked at myself again. The effect was utterly startling. It was the face of the bloke in the Scotland Yard 'HAVE YOU SEEN THIS MAN?' poster.

NARROWING THE ODDS

Tommy returned just after dusk the next day carrying a big brown paper parcel and wearing a boiler suit with 'Co-op' embroidered on the pocket. "That face rings a bell," he said, looking at the new me.

"Hopefully, not the ones they've got on the front of police cars," I said. He handed me the parcel.

"There's another set of 'Co-op' overalls in there," he said pointing to the parcel, "as well as a shirt, trousers, vest, long-johns, socks, and a pair of boots for when we leave. You'll also find the grand Spottsy promised you. The rest of your kit is in a van I've got parked round the corner—a nice little London Co-operative Society delivery van I have use of from time to time."

"The old Harry Houdini trick: the tailor-made invisibility of uniforms. Works every time. And, knowing you, I bet that little delivery van could give even a souped-up police Railton a run for its money, if it had to."

Tommy tapped the side of his nose. "Goes faster than one of Houdini's vanishing elephants, that's for sure," he said. "How are you feeling? Get yourself rested, did you?"

"Yes, I did. Thanks, Tommy," I said. "Slept most of the time, but still stiff as buggery and very, very sore. A few badly bruised or cracked ribs, but luckily no other bones broken. The nasty cut on my chest, of course. Thanks for sewing me up, by the way, some of your best work. So, walking wounded all present and correct, sir, and ready to shove off when you are."

"No, it's Convoy rules, Jethro: sleep all you can when you can, eat all you can when you can. You look a darn sight better than you did, but you still look like something the cat dragged in. So get some food down your neck, get another good night's sleep, and we'll set off before first light. I've got us a narrow boat moored at City Road Basin, just this side of the Islington Tunnel. We can be on the boat and moving before everyone else is up and about. So you put the kettle on and I'll fix the grub. I got a loaf of bread and some black pudding; the pig's blood will do you good. I also scrounged you up a fresh egg. Had to kill to get it, but if it helps build you up, it'll be worth it."

Tommy did the business and I attacked my food as a ravenous dog would a bone, not having realised until that moment just how incredibly hungry I was. As I forked the last piece of black pudding into my mouth I chewed something over. "Were you there, Tommy, in Shadow Court? Only, it's all still a bit of a blur."

He looked up, finished wiping his plate clean with his fried-bread. "No, me and all the other top minders were all busy keeping an eye on one another in the banquet room of a big hotel in Bloomsbury, down near the Museum. No man's land. Every gang leader had to send his top man as a guarantee, so to show willing, Messima sent two, Ralphie and Reggie."

"What, Tweedle-dum and Tweedle-dee?"

"Yes, eight of us in all, all locked in, as it were, until we each got word our respective Guv'nor was safe home. Everyone was quite pleasant considering how very wary we usually all are of one another. But no one got out of order; we all ended up playing poker for matchsticks."

"I won't ask who won what," I said, and I told Tommy about Messrs. Pitcher, Shipman and Bumaree and what'd happened in the warehouse. And about the fourth man that'd arrived out of the blue and taken charge—the bastard who'd left me tied to a wooden jetty support in the river, with the tide making.

The bastard who'd left me for dead.

"Odd bloody nicknames. They mean anything?"

"Someone's obviously got a very twisted sense of humour. 'Pitcher' is the name given a Smithfield market porter who unloads meat carcasses from off a lorry; 'Shipman' is the bloke who cuts and weighs the meat; a 'Bumaree' drops whatever meat has been sold onto a wheelbarrow and carts it away.

"From your description, the weasel with the chiv, the one you said called himself 'Shipman,' sounds like Eddie Maytum, top hit man for the King's Cross mob and a very nasty piece of work all round. And if that's the case, that makes his two little playmates Jimmy Pottle, another well known 'chiv artist' from Islington, and Bobby Boyle, ex-boxer from Clerkenwell—a right thug known to favour brass knuckledusters and rusty hammers. But neither the Islington nor the Clerkenwell gangs ever move a muscle without the say-so from King's Cross. They're all one and the same mob, as near as buggery. Can't say I can place the fourth man, the big bloke you said put you in the water, but from how you describe him, it could well have been me."

"The same coat and hat size, that's for sure. But a favour, Tommy: if you should ever hear anything about that big geezer—anything at all—keep tabs on him for me, will you? For later?"

"Thinking of serving it up cold?"

"Revenge as cold as the Baltic Sea in winter."

Tommy nodded. "Nobody lasts long in them waters."

The way Tommy drove the Co-op van down the Commercial Road you'd have thought it was an Alvis or a Bentley Continental—he was that smooth going up and down the gears. I stared out at the cold, indifferent streets of East London and found myself flinching at the oddest things: the empty windows of a bombed-out warehouse staring back at me, a dark alley leading into a deeper darkness, a black motorcar lurking in a

side-street. And it was in those fleeting moments that I began
to admit to myself just how very badly I'd been beaten up and
how very near to death I'd come. It felt as if I'd been stripped
bare of whatever it is in a person helps keep the world at bay. In
my time, I'd been at death's door any number of occasions and
by luck or God's grace had survived, but that first step back into
real life never gets any easier.

We turned up into Commercial Street, headed for the City
Road, and so came to Wharf Road and the City Road Basin.
The van went into a nearby lock-up, as did our Co-op overalls,
and we both got kitted-out in flat cap and blue serge coat as
befitted hardworking boatmen. I added a dab or two of soot to
obscure my face even more. Tommy, carrying another change
of clothes in a battered cardboard suitcase, unlocked the iron-
gate onto the towpath, and we made our way down to the canal.
I shivered as we got closer to the water's edge and hesitated,
even though the water was barely three or four feet deep.
Tommy touched my arm and said quietly, "It's like getting back
on a horse that's thrown you. I could barely look at the sea after
that time you saved me from drowning; it looked too much
like my empty grave." Then he slapped me on the shoulder and
introduced me to the good narrow boat *Phoenix No. 7*.

I smiled and took both the name and number as good omens.

The *Phoenix* was steel-hulled and slightly smaller than a
standard-length boat, a mere 56 footer, but she had a 15 hp
diesel motor and was perfect for quietly moving cases of Whisky
and gin or other in-demand black market items from one
end of the Smoke to the other. Even though the Government
had nationalised all the big rail, road, and canal carriers the
previous year, there was still more than enough room on the
canals for small firms to operate, not that Tommy or Spottsy
ever regarded themselves or their enterprises in that light.

We set about navigating the first lock, waited for both the
boat and us to go up in the world, then we were away towards
the eastern approach to the Islington Tunnel, almost a thousand

yards of self-imposed darkness, which to my relief I managed to handle no sweat. We emerged into the flat, grey light of early morning—the sky already overcast—and slid under the bridges at Caledonian Road and York Way and made for the lock at St Pancras. Then it was up to Camden and through the locks at Kentish Town, Hawley, and Hampstead Road. And with Tommy standing and steering on the little platform at the stern and me up and out and onto the bank, as was called for, we pootled along at four miles per hour, two men in a boat, the back-side of London silently sliding by. We settled into the rhythm and speed of the canal and hardly spoke until we'd cleared all the locks and it was a straight run on to Little Venice. We passed the zoological gardens on the left. The racket the animals were making even at that time of the morning, you'd have though the Crazy Gang were in residence.

After Little Venice, just before it enters the Maida Tunnel, the Regents Canal passes under Lisson Grove, and I found myself getting more and more tense the closer we got to the scene of my recent abduction. And by the time we slid into the tunnel, I was shivering almost uncontrollably. "I'm not bloody having this," I said to myself and I shook my head to clear it of all the dark images trying to crowd in on me, and I took myself into the little cabin aft, turned up the oil-lamp, set the Primus-stove and made a pot of tea. And in short order we had mugs of hot tea cupped in our hands to help stave off the chill as we busied ourselves eyeing both sides of the bank for any early worms up and about in the shadows.

Tommy eased off the speed as we came out into Browning's Pool and said, "I'll swing around the island and bring her in to the opposite bank. You do the ropes, then get back inside and wait." Tommy berthed the *Phoenix* alongside the towpath that ran parallel with Warwick Crescent and I secured ropes, fore and aft, then disappeared into the little cabin.

Tommy walked up the towpath to Delaware Terrace, went into the Toll Offices, paid the necessary fees, and arranged for a month's mooring at Paddington Basin. I don't know how much money changed hands, but what would've normally taken an hour or so to sort out was completed in ten minutes. Then Tommy came back with two bacon sandwiches from the Bridge Cafe, fired up the diesel, and steered the *Phoenix* down into Paddington Basin, taking us under Bishop's Road Bridge and making straight for a berth not a narrow boat's length from Wharf Road: the location of my secret lock-up.

We sat inside the cabin, scoffing our second breakfast of the day, and downing endless mugs of tea.

"What name will you use when you call?" Tommy knew I had definite plans for the boat, but he didn't press for details.

I thought for a bit. "Marley. Yes, that seems appropriate, but Charley, not Jacob. Charley Marley; a mate of yours, down from Manchester."

"The Twelve Disciples?" he asked.

I nodded.

"Fair enough," he said. "I'll be there every midnight on from when I get your first message. Remember the numbers?"

I nodded again.

He looked at his wristwatch. "Two and a half hours from start to finish. Not too bad, considering. We'll make a proper sailor of you yet." He turned and tapped the barometer. "And good timing, too, as it seems we're in for some heavy rain."

He was right. Not twenty minutes later it started raining hard and, as people all over London were hurriedly unfurling umbrellas or scurrying for cover, I took the opportunity to nip out onto the bank. I made my way along the canal-path, and went up the steps and through the iron gate to street level. Then I slipped back down into North Wharf Road and eeled my way round to the lock-up. For appearances' sake, Tommy stayed aboard the *Phoenix* for another half-hour, during which time he changed into his street clothes. Then he locked everything up, made his way over to Paddington Station, and took a Tube back into town.

Meanwhile, I had to find some way of meeting up with Ray Karmin without bumping into any of the local faces. And I couldn't wait until dark to do it, as having found myself newly resurrected, time itself seemed to be of the very essence.

SHOCKING NEWS

So there I was, sitting in the old Austin 'growler,' pulled over to the side of the road, the 'For Hire' sign off, me peering impatiently through the windscreen, as if waiting for a fare to return from an errand. I had the heater going full blast, as I'd been feeling the cold a lot more since I'd all but caught my death in the Thames. And, other than hoping to catch sight of Ray, I was hoping the spirit gum on my moustache wouldn't come unglued. I chanced another look at my wristwatch. Raymond Karmin, scholar, was nothing if not punctual in all he did, whereas as "Buggy" Billy you never knew from one moment to the next where the hell he'd pop up once he'd vacated his market stall. All of it Ray's way of ensuring that he always presented two entirely different faces to the world.

I sniffed and wiped my nose, and there he was standing by the kerb outside the British Museum, about to cross Great Russell Street. He looked right, looked left, and I tapped out "dash-dash-dot," "dash-dash-dot" on the car horn. "D" for "danger" in Morse code. He looked left again and at that exact moment I trundled forward.

He raised his umbrella to hail the taxi, and bingo.

Ray leaned into the front of cab and just stared at me like he was seeing a ghost—which I suppose he was. Then, like any other punter, he got in the back.

"Right, sir. Sloane Square it is," I yelled over my shoulder, pushing the flag down to set the meter going, and off we went. Though of course we weren't going anywhere near Chelsea, not with me dressed as Albert, the old cabby, and Ray resplendent in all his velvet-collared finery. But the taxicab was the only place I could think of where the two of us could be sure to have a talk in private. Riding in plain sight, I suppose you could call it.

Ray rapped loudly on the glass partition with a half-crown coin, as much to give vent to emotion as catch my ear. "God's holy trousers, Jethro. I heard very reliable rumours you were dead. So, as good as it undoubtedly is to see you alive and kicking, what the hell happened?"

We more or less motored round in circles until I'd brought him up to speed. I told him about the chase through the streets, the meat-locker, Shadow Court, what followed in the warehouse, me being tied underneath a wooden pier in the river like a pirate of old, the mysterious telephone call, Spottsy and Tommy saving me, and Messima's plans for NORTO. And when I dropped him at Euston Station, so he could get another cab home and change into clobber a little more appropriate to our current needs, Ray looked like he could do with a drink.

I knew I could.

"I want to call a few people," he said, "see what I can ferret out. We'll meet up later."

We decided on The Hope and Anchor, the other side of Shepherds Bush, far end of the Goldhawk Road. Given the troubled waters we were in, we needed an island well off the usual trade routes and, in all the times we'd been to The Hope, we'd never once seen any known 'faces' there. The other good thing about the pub was that it was close to Stamford Brook Tube station, which meant that if you took a District Line train from Edgware Road it only required one change at Earl's Court. Point being, Mr Moisha Fabrikant would be travelling by Underground.

I parked the cab in a side-street, went into the pub, and tucked myself away in a corner of the public bar. I wet-nursed a half-pint, rolled and smoked a prile of cigarettes, read the *Standard* from back to front and back again, and began to get a bad case of the itches. It wasn't like Ray—either as himself or as Moisha Fabrikant—to be diabolically late. I was jumpy as a bucketful of eels, as it was, and behind my disguise I must've aged a year for every overdue minute that ticked by. We had this agreement to abandon ship if either one of us was ever more than an hour late for a meeting. After which, the missing party would leave a message at the Victory Cafe. Only, with me now supposed to be dead, that wasn't even remotely possible.

Ray had told me in the cab how Joanie had taken the news of my death. Apparently she'd gone deathly white, bitten her lip until it bled, and then shut the cafe and thrown everyone out. Afterwards, Bubs told "Buggy" that later that night Joanie had asked to be taken over to Hackney, where she'd walked up and down the bombed-out, ghost-filled streets for hours on end—a thing she'd vowed she'd never do after the Blitz had taken our mum and dad. I knew all too well the demons that would've been waiting for her there and, at that moment, feeling her pain, I think I hated myself even more than I hated the bastards that'd brought me so low. Mercifully, I was saved any more self-loathing by a movement out the corner of my eye and as I blinked my way back to the noise and lights of the pub the shabby figure of Moisha Fabrikant edged his way slowly but purposefully through the crowd.

My relief at seeing him was enormous, but we played our parts and went through the usual pantomime of surprise at seeing one another, with me nodding acceptance of his mimed offer of a pint. And as Moisha got in the drinks, I folded up the evening paper and wiped the table clean with my coat-sleeve, sitting there with an expectant look on my face.

The look on his, however, told me something very nasty was in the wind.

"Hello, Albert, me old cock," Moisha said, placing a Whisky and chaser down in front of me. He sat down, sipped his drinks, and we chatted the usual inanities about horses, greyhounds, and football teams and waited for any and all interest around us to dampen down. Then he gave me the 'bent eye' and, glasses in hand, we both leaned forward just enough for each to hear the other's whispers.

"It's bad," he said as an opener. "I went out to make some calls from the Apostles before I came and noticed loads of new faces hanging around the West London Stadium. Same all along Church Street and down the Edgware Road as far as Praed Street." He sipped at his Whisky to give time for his words to sink in. "Word on the street is most people believe you dead and flushed down the river on last Monday's late tide. Only, a stubborn few are now asking questions about whether you had nine lives or not, as no one seems to have seen your dead body."

"Well, they can't have it," I said, scratching. "I'm still using it."

"Yes, but you know how Messima hates loose ends. People might start to think he hasn't got things tied up as tightly as he'd have them believe, and that'd never do. The very idea you might still be alive must have him really spooked. That's why he's got eyes out everywhere and why there's even a 'notice' on your ghost, at double the going-rate, if it or you should turn up anywhere. All of which means you're going to be double-dead if anyone even remotely thinks they recognise you and fancies their chances at serving your head up on a plate."

Ray's voice warped and melted into the pub walls. I sat there, staring into nothing. And I don't know whether I spoke aloud or simply heard a voice in my head, either way, I said, "I'm going to have each and every one of them bastards that sat on that jury and, save for Spottsy, they're all dead men." I blinked and blinked and stared at Ray without really seeing him.

Ray must've recognised the look in my eyes for what it was, because he leaned forward and gently patted the air between us with the flat of his hand. "Easy does it, old son. Easy does it. Death comes quick enough for us all, there's no need to go looking for it." He paused and tapped a finger up and down on the folded-up copy of the *Standard*. "Saw it, then, did you?"

I shook my head. "Saw what?" I said. "Same old bloody nonsense every day. Don't know why I bother to read it sometimes."

"It was the Prince of Wales you were working at, wasn't it?"

I went stone cold before I even finished nodding my head. "Why, what happened?" I said, my voice suddenly hoarse. "Didn't see anything." He reached for my *Standard* and thumbed through it until he found the two-and-a-half-inch, two-column news item he was looking for. He stabbed at the sub-head and I leaned forward, sliding the specs down my nose so I could read more clearly. 'FREAK ACCIDENT DARKENS THEATRE'. I don't know how I'd missed it. I read on and then looked up, my eyes fixed on a point somewhere over Ray's shoulder. "Yes, I knew him. Bob Miller, nice bloke, never any side to him, always pulled his weight, stood his round. Saw him around Soho a few times. Odd, that, him supposedly being electrocuted by a dimmer-board that wasn't earthed properly. It's true what the theatre management says, he was only a trainee stage-hand and wasn't authorised or qualified to go near the lights, but from what I witnessed of him I'd say he knew as much about the wiring as the chief electrician. He was mad-keen on all things electric; had been since he was a nipper. Even wanted to be an electrical engineer at one point. It just doesn't add up, doesn't add up at all." I looked back at Ray. "I can see by the look on your face you don't think it was an accident either."

Ray shook his head. "I also suspect it was no accident he turned up working at the same theatre as you, which says he was probably Shadow Mob, sent by Scotland Yard to keep tabs on you. So maybe, just maybe, when you went missing, your young Mr Miller set out to find you and got too close for someone's comfort and they fried him for it."

I sat there lost in thought. Bob Miller, a Ghost Squad copper. All the questions he'd asked, all the times I'd seen him round Soho: it all suddenly fit. He was the Ghost Squad copper Striped Trousers had referred to back in Shadow Court, and now he'd been murdered all on account of me. And all of a sudden there it was, as big as day, the straw that broke this camel's back. "You're right," I said. "And if he got topped, I'll bet a pound to a fucking penny it was done by the same bastards that tried to top me: Pitcher, Shipman, and Bumaree, and that other big fucker—whoever he is. Well, fuck that for a game of soldiers. They're all dead men now, too. Each and every fucking one of them. On my old dad's life, they are."

I began to scratch at the red-hot itch that seemed to be spreading all over my body; the itches of the stiches on my chest had nothing on it. I may have even started pulling at my false whiskers, I don't know. All I know is was seeing red, lots and lots of red, buckets of it, rivers of it. "I'm going to gut the fuckers. I'm going to get hold of each and every one of them and slit them from their bellies right up to their fucking throats, even if I end up dead as a fucking mackerel in the process."

Ray peered at me over the edge of his beer glass and shook his head. "Hold on, hold on," he said, "no need to take the bloody lead off the roof, not when everyone's already out looking to kill you or your shadow on sight. You'd be dead before you even started. Just calm down a moment and listen. I've never steered you wrong before and I won't start now. You've got to stay calm, old son. Box clever and get yourself fit. As even under that disguise you still don't look at all like your normal self. So you've got to get out of sight and stay out of sight for a good two weeks or more until you're well and truly out of mind. If you want to get revenge you've got to keep a cool head and stay sharp. Revenge is always best..."

"...served cold. Yes, I know, Ray," I said, my voice dull, my eyes flat, and if not exactly sullen and mutinous, then pretty close to it.

OUT OF SIGHT

Moisha stretched his shoulders and got to his feet. "I need a pee after that little outpouring, after which I'll get in another round so we can celebrate your most recent resurrection all over again. Meanwhile, you just think about where you can safely park yourself for the next couple of weeks."

I sat and thought and tried to get myself grounded. Ray returned with another tray of drinks, and we both sat there lost in thought, sipping the fiery Whisky and downing the watery beer.

It was Ray who broke the silence. "You can't go round any of your girlfriends, as it'd put them in too much danger. Tommy's drum is out, even if you knew where it was; so is the canal boat, at least for now. He and Spottsy have already done more than enough to get themselves topped. And you going back to your place or anywhere near Joanie or the cafe is strictly verboten. It's very clear this NORTO mob don't follow any rules. They'll go after anyone, family or friend, if they think they can use them to get to you. If they were even to smell you'd been within a mile of Church Street, they'd have Joanie spirited away and pinned to a factory floor somewhere just waiting for you to reappear. So for the time being, believe you me, her believing you dead is her only protection."

I nodded. I'd been down the exact same roads, and every one of them had led to the very same dead-ends. "What about you?" I asked. "You be okay, will you? Everyone knows 'Buggy' Billy and me were—I mean are—fast friends, despite us trying to pretend otherwise."

"Don't you worry about me none," Ray said. "They may well be watching 'Buggy' Billy's every move, but they don't know Moisha Fabrikant from a hole in the wall. But if it makes you feel any easier, I'll be sure to have 'Buggy' always go round mob-handed with some of the lads from the market. Another thing, not that it matters much at the moment, but when I asked my learned colleagues down the British Museum Library whether anyone had heard anything untoward about Nigel Fox, in the City or elsewhere, there was nothing. Not a peep. It seems his wife is the one that attended to business; Fox never set foot inside Lloyds. She's the underwriter or 'name' as they call them. He didn't give tuppence for any of it. Politics at Westminster and a Ministry in Whitehall were all he ever cared about."

"Must be nice not having to work for a living," I said, the incidents at Meridian Mansions a million years in the past. "Me, I'm just working on how to stay alive. I know I've got to give Paddington a wide berth given the number of eyes you say are on the streets, but I can't stay as old Albert for two whole weeks without using the lock-up. So I was thinking Glover's drum would be the ticket. It's off the beaten track, and he told me to think of his place as a port in a storm. No one would ever put the two of us together, and Glover could easily get hold of anything I need in the disguise department."

Ray thought for a moment. "Yes, good thinking. Tommy Nutkins is the only other person that knows Glover is part of your past and, from what you've told me, the two of them would both rather drown themselves than grass you up. All right, Glover's place it is. Leave the taxi in a near-by street and I'll have some of the lads come round with a pick-up lorry and tow it somewhere safe."

I thought of the streets round Primrose Hill near where Glover lived and rattled off a couple of names. "Tell them to box the compass. The cab won't be too far. I'll put a cardboard sign on the dashboard saying it's broken down, though it'll be the usual loose distributor cap."

Ray nodded and my plan of inaction was set. He downed what remained of his Whisky. "How about a ride back to Marylebone Station? That is if you think old Albert won't mind taking a single pin as a fare?"

"Given the circumstances," I said, "it's the very least he could do."

I dropped Moisha outside Marylebone Station, near enough for him to walk home, and just far enough away from our usual haunts for there to be no reason for anyone to give either of us a second look. I wasn't too concerned about myself. As Albert, the old cabby, I was all but invisible amongst all the other black cabs that served the station. But you can never be too sure when Sod's Law will up and hit you on the head. So I went through the motions with the flag and Ray tendered a handful of coins for the fare. He leaned in towards me as if proffering a tip. "There's an envelope with five hundred quid on the back seat that should help tide you over, and always more when you need it," he said. "Be lucky, old cock. Go safe, until next." Then he turned and walked off into the station and I watched the remarkable transformation he could effect with nothing more than a slight change in his walk and his bearing. The dirty old stained mackintosh was now neatly folded over his arm, the tartan scarf inside the pocket—even his battered Trilby hat had been coaxed into something a little more presentable. And the man that'd been Moisha Fabrikant for the last several hours walked in through one door of the station and then walked out another as Raymond Karmin and was gone into the night.

I kept the flag down and the 'For Hire' sign off and motored on along the Marylebone Road for a bit, then turned down into a deserted Bloomsbury until I found a line of out-of-the-way telephone-boxes, back of the British Museum. I chose one, dropped two pennies in the slot, gave the night operator the emergency telephone number Glover had given me and got ready to press button 'A,' hoping against hope that Glover was in and not out gallivanting about and that I wouldn't have to think up a Plan 'B.'

The line clicked and clacked a good deal more than was usual and then it rang, or rather buzzed, at the other end, and then there was an empty silence. "Yes?" said a voice that was neither fish nor fowl.

I blessed Dame Fortune for smiling one more time and pushed button 'A.' "It's the Distressed Seaman's Benevolent Society," I said in as neutra-sounding a voice as I could manage. "I was hoping for a donation."

There was a long pause, longer even than the previous empty silence. "Make it four," the voice said, then the line went dead.

I exited the telephone-box and limped back across the pavement to the cab, very relieved that the next couple of weeks were almost as good as sorted. I was eager to get the itchy whiskers from off my face and a spring back in my step, but I had four hours to kill until I could turn up at Glover's. The petrol gauge showed there wasn't nearly enough for me to keep on driving about the whole time, so I motored sedately up to Primrose Hill and, after going round the houses for a bit, found a suitable spot midway between lamp-posts.

I put up the cardboard sign saying 'broken down'—the one I always had with me in the taxi—on the dashboard. Then I climbed in the back of the cab, settled myself down on the floor, threw a blanket over myself, and slept the sleep of the just until my inner-clock woke me just before four. Then, once I'd determined the coast was clear, I left the old taxi for "Buggy" Billy's boys to pick-up on the morrow and slipped through the shadows to Glover's house, which, like the rest of London, was shrouded in darkness.

ISLANDS IN THE BACK STREETS

Glover—or Doris, I should say—looked to have done very well for herself. It was a nice Georgian three-storey house, four including the basement. I climbed the steps to the front door, the gloss paint and big brass doorknocker gleaming in the dim light of the lamp-posts. I gave the door the very gentlest of taps and it opened soundlessly onto a darkened hallway. The perfect welcome for an out-of-hours caller as it meant I wasn't silhouetted against the light. But as Doris had learned the hard way, discretion was always the better part of common sense, especially if you valued your privacy.

She knew I'd arrive on the dot and had been ready waiting. I took three steps into the hallway and stood and paused for Doris to close the door behind me. "The door to your right, darling," she said quietly, and I turned and went into the drawing room.

The light was low, the curtains closed, a coal fire lit. There was even a bottle of The Glenlivet and some sandwiches beckoning on a silver tray. "Thanks, Doris," I said, turning round. She was in full *slap*, full *drag* and coifed *shyker*, which is to say she was fully made-up and dressed to the nines in another fetching, long dark blue number with matching full-length silk gloves. But not too unusual, given the hours she kept; four in the morning to her was just the end of the working day.

"Stone the crows, Jethro, dear; if that's supposed to be a disguise, it's not at all becoming. Them *oglefakes* on yer *onk* make you look dreadful."

The cotton wool I'd had inside my cheeks had long gone, as had the white wig, but I still had on old Albert's old coat, flat-cap, spectacles and whiskers. "I'm supposed to be dead," I said.

"You're not kidding, darling." She poured a drink and handed it to me. "Which is why the long pause when you telephoned. Not often I get a call from the other side, but you're a hard one to kill, as well I know. Even so, I've been a bag of bloody nerves all night. And, by the look of you, you could do with some *mangarie*, a good wash, and a proper night's kip. So upstairs with you now, *khazi*'s on the right, your room's on the left. We can chat tomorrow. And don't you worry, darling. I gave the maid the night off: she's downstairs in her dinky *latty*, so you won't be disturbed, even by me."

"Thanks, Doris," I said. "I didn't know who else to turn to."

"Whist, now. Enough. How long do you need to stay?" she asked.

"At least a couple of weeks," I said, quietly.

She blinked and blinked, as if suddenly in deep thought.

I got the gist immediately. Given the circumstances, it was much too much of me to ask of her. The danger was too great. And not wanting to prolong the agony any further, I stepped into the silence. "Only, thinking about it now, Doris, I really shouldn't even be here. If anyone were to find out you'd helped me, it's you who'd be in real danger then, not just me. So just tonight and tomorrow will do if that's alright."

I put down my drink.

She blinked again and then threw me a withering look. "Whist, you silly man, drink up. You can stay here as long as you need to, because if you're trying to tell me it's Messima that's got it in for you, well I knew that, you daft trollop, when you dropped in to the Blueboy club out of the blue." I just nodded and tried not to look too surprised. "And whether there's a 'notice' out on you or not, I don't give a tinker's cuss about his *naff* thugs or anyone else's. You'd be surprised who treads the lavender path to my little blue door. There's any number of VIPs partial to a little bit of *bona*, so I'm *lills* off, I am. Or those same VIPs can very quickly ensure that said nasty people find themselves in a very sorry world of troubles. And that goes for Mr high-and-bloody-mighty Darby bloody Messima, too, so no need to worry your little head on my account, darling."

"Thanks, Doris," I said softly.

"Yes," she said, "you already said that. What do you think I've got, cloth ears?" She was quite worked up, for Doris. Though whether it was to allay her fears or mine, I couldn't say. She held out the tray with the sandwiches and I took two. "So what are we going to do with you for two whole weeks?" she said as she moved on around the room, restlessly pausing here and there— touching things, moving things. "Don't mind me, darling," she said, "it's just the Bette Davis in me." She turned as if struck by a sudden thought. "I know. I'll call in sick, give my lazy cow of a maid the entire weekend off, and look after you myself. The *naff polones* down the Blueboy will all just think I'm having a dirty weekend." She paused. "Should do my reputation a world of good." She pushed a stray red curl back behind her ear. "I could probably push it as far as Tuesday, but after that they'd all start asking too many questions. So even if I do go back to the club, I'll need another reason to keep the nosy sods at bay."

Doris went back to touching things and moving things from mantelpiece to sideboard to side-table and back again, and I just stood there, sipping my drink, eating my sandwiches, rather enjoying her performance. Suddenly she stopped sashaying around the room and stood staring at an old photograph in a silver frame. "Wait a minute," she said, turning to look me up and down again. She studied the photograph in the silver frame even more closely. "What would you say to you having your *ends* done in a centre-parting?"

"Er, I dare say I wouldn't mind, why?"

"Can I call you father?" she asked.

HOW'S YER FATHER?

So that was it: I was cast as Doris's old dad recuperating from a hernia operation. I had to give Albert's white wig a short back and sides and darken it up a bit, as well as part the hair down the middle. Then I had to shape and trim the old false moustache so it looked less like a walrus and more like Neville Chamberlain. Doris gave me an old pinstripe suit to wear and the pick of the men's clothes she said she only ever wore for funerals of past acquaintances that weren't theatrically inclined—mostly old salts like me she'd known on the boats. Doris also came up with another pair of *oglefakes* she said were a little more becoming to the man I was becoming, my new disguise in case her maid ever caught sight of me shuffling stoop-shouldered to or from the bathroom.

I had the house to myself most evenings, as it turned out Doris's maid, another redhead of indeterminate age and gender, also acted as her dresser and always accompanied her to and from the Blueboy club. A taxi came to pick them both up at five o'clock every evening and brought them home again, often times as late as three or four the following morning. It was only later I learned the cab was part of a private taxi service for VIP club members— again, all owned and run by Doris.

She asked if I needed anything special, so I asked if she could get me a skipping rope and a set of dumbbells. And in short order, she produced a skipping rope, a pair of old wooden

Indian clubs, and a chest-expander, although I don't think any of it was hers. That little lot, a few press-ups, and a bit of shadowboxing was more than enough to help get me back into shape.

The days and nights passed in their own sweet time. I slept a lot. Read a lot. Listened to the radio. Exercised when I had a mind to. Then pulled my socks up and went at it hard, as if in training for a prize fight. And, all the while, I went back over past events until I couldn't remember a time when I hadn't been caught up in the whole sorry mess that'd started the night of the Meridian Mansions caper. And whatever Messima was up to with NORTO and his secret courts, it seemed that all roads led, if not to Rome, then back to that block of flats in South Kensington.

Doris scotched one rumour for me. "Fox wasn't camp, dear," she'd told me one afternoon, in between nattering on about all the boats we'd served on together. "It's as I said in the postcard I sent you. There's not a word, not a whisper, not a whiff, anywhere in lavender-scented London. *Nishta*. Not to say anyone's a hundred per cent snowy white, darling. No one ever is. There's always some fresh fruit or some old *quean* ready to dish the dirt and ruin some poor *omi*'s reputation, even if only to hint at something too *naff* for words. It's how we're all made, darling: spiteful when spat on, shitty when shat on. It's how the world turns."

And the world did turn. And, just as the doctor ordered, my bruises slowly healed, and me with them. And the better I felt, the more I realised the huge debt I owed Ray, which is why I felt bad about having to break my promise to him. But I had no choice in the matter. Before I could even think about tracking down 'Monkey' Jim, it was vital I get to my lock-up in Paddington Basin and attend to some business in Church Street. After all, I'd also made a promise to myself that I'd find some way of messing up Messima and his bloody schemes even if it bloody well killed me.

"Here, put this *capello* on, Jethro, make you look *trés bona*, much better than wearing that *naff* old flat-cap of yours. And for goodness' sake throw that tatty old silk muffler away. It's filthy dirty. Here's a nice blue scarf; help keep you nice and warm. You better also take a walking stick to remind you to slow down as you go." Doris gave me another quick look up and down to ensure I'd got my hat and wig on straight and that my disguise as her old dad would pass muster under the fluorescent lights. She'd had the overcoat cleaned, my shoes polished, and my trousers pressed, and even if I say so myself, I didn't look at all bad for an old bloke on the mend. Then Doris helped me down the front steps to the waiting cab—she'd given her maid the night off again so it was just the two of us—and we taxied on over to Paddington Station through the back-doubles of North London.

The weirdest part of the whole journey was when the taxi turned off Sutherland Avenue onto the Harrow Road and went on down to Bishops Bridge Road. And there it all was, my old stomping ground. Tube station and Turkish baths, off in the distance. Paddington Green Police Station, its blue lamp trying to push back the night. The Bridge Cafe, close enough for me to touch. And all of it part of another world I'd left behind a million years ago.

The cab turned into the one-way street that led down to the station ticketing office and pulled into the kerb, but Doris didn't get out of the taxi and, as I turned round to close the door and lean in through the window to say goodbye, she leaned forward and kissed me on the cheek. "Bye, da," she said, in her trademark Irish lilt. "Get better. Go safe. Write me when you can."

Then as we waited for the taxi driver to come round and retrieve the suitcase from the luggage compartment, she squeezed my hand and whispered under her breath, "Be a *bona omi*, Jethro. Don't go and get yourself killed. I don't want to have to put on a bloody gent's whistle for you, darling." Then she pressed some half-crowns into my hand and said loudly,

"Give them to the porter, Da, and remember your ticket's in your overcoat pocket." Then she smiled, blew me a kiss, leaned back, and was lost to the shadows inside the cab.

The taxi moved off just as a porter came up with his trolley. Doris gave a last blue be-gloved royal wave before being whisked away into the darkening night. And I nodded to the porter and pointed up at the sign directing people to the main waiting room on Platform 1 and off he trundled, me bringing up the rear, walking stick, posh hat, scarf, and all. I tipped the bloke and then sat in the waiting room, my head down as if dozing, and waited an hour or more until everyone who'd been in there when I'd first arrived had all gone off to catch their trains.

I waited another good half-hour until it was good and dark outside, then I stood up and went out into the pale flat yellow light of the station concourse and, with my battered cardboard suitcase and walking stick in hand, made my way along the platform and over the walkway through to the other side of the station and exited onto London Street. Nobody paid me any heed, but then again, amidst all the hustle and bustle of a major railway terminus, why ever should they?

I trudged up the ramp, past the Royal Mail sorting office and the dozens and dozens of mail trolleys being loaded up ready for that night's mail trains, and headed for Bishops Bridge Road. I lowered my head against the bitterly cold wind that whistled up from the railway tracks on the far side of the bridge and headed for the lock-up; just another slow-moving shadow in a soon to be increasingly busy London night.

THE WILL WHICH SAYS

I moved silently down dark shadow-filled streets, past row after row of blank-faced houses and buildings I'd known all my life, and all of it as indifferent to my passing as if I'd been a torn piece of paper blown by the wind. I anchored myself to a soil-pipe and ascended.

I went from rooftop to rooftop until I found a point where the shadows cast by chimney after cockeyed chimney gave me perfect cover, and I lay stretched-out on the tiles. As per usual I was kitted-out from head to foot in black drab, my face and neck underneath my balaclava blackened with soot so no sliver of skin would show pale against the dark.

Way off to my left, the streetlights along the Edgware Road did their best to throw a sickly yellow glow up into the night sky. But all the streets of my old manor were now as deadly as a newly laid minefield to me —my drum on Church Street, like a ticking bomb. And as the world turned, revealing anew above me the eternal procession of the stars, I lay in wait for all the houses around me to settle to sleep, my eyes slowly blinking, slowly blinking.

There were certain very important items I needed inside the flat, little things that'd greatly ease my passage if I had to do a runner. A money-belt with diamonds sewn into the lining. A driver's license, a ration book, an identity card, a passport, a merchant seaman's pay-book and a union card—all in the name of a bloke I knew who'd been lost at sea and all of which would secure me a berth on almost any ship in the Port of London. I also needed to get a butcher's at the mail I knew that Joanie— despite all the stories of my death—would've placed, religiously, on the kitchen table each day to await my return. A small, insignificant act, but a totem of hope that as with proverbs and old wives' sayings is sometimes the only thing that keeps you going through the worst of times.

I was still sailing blind, without a compass, and by my reckoning there were only two marker-buoys worth their salt: "Monkey" Jim and the dead MP, Nigel Fox. Come hell or high water, I was going to run Jimmy Mooney to ground, but I still had to find out how Fox figured into everything. And now that Doris had shut the door on him being queer, it all came down to what Sylvia or Lily had managed to find out. The other big problem was my sister, Joanie. Her senses were better than any alarm system, so there was no way I could use the stairs and chance us meeting on the landing outside her flat. It'd blow the whole caper sky high—and her and me with it—which was why, as weird as it sounds, I had no choice but to break in to my own drum.

My flat looked dead, like a film set waiting for a bank of 'brights' to bring it to life, but the lights were still on in Joanie and Barry's flat.

I had no choice, therefore, but to wait.

An hour passed and the lights finally went out and I counted to a hundred to focus my mind. Then I was up and zigzagging across the rooftops, clinging to the deepest, darkest shadows as I would the rungs on a ladder, never moving in a straight line, knowing from long experience that, up on the tiles, the long way round is often much the safest course between two points. But then, as "Monkey" Jim had told me years before, even crows find it prudent to fly round in circles at night.

I held a bird's eye view of the whole manor in my mind's eye and sent my senses flying in and out of the streets and alleyways and out across the rooftops. I knew there'd be beady eyes lurking deep in the shadows even at that time of the night. The money Messima had put on my head was just too tempting for people to ignore, and there were hard-cases aplenty running round the Smoke for whom killing me would be just part of another night's work. Unlike all the muscle for hire, though, I knew every nook and cranny of the manor, as well as every brick and tile of the building I called home.

The locals all thought the house was rented out to Joanie and me by a very understanding landlord, but only Joanie and me knew I owned the entire building that comprised the Victory Cafe and the two flats situated above it, lock, stock and barrel. And only I knew there were dozens of tiny metal studs and six-inch nails set into the back wall of the house in a seemingly random pattern that'd provide solid purchase if ever I had need to exit in a hurry.

There was another little refinement I'd added, for the simple reason that I'd been burgled myself the previous year. If you examined the sash-windows front and back, they all looked as if they'd been nailed shut, and even if you tried using the window-catches they wouldn't budge. That is, unless you knew how to disengage the hidden metal rods that held the windows securely in place. There were two air-vents situated beneath each window. Indoors, you slid the 'open-close' knobs sideways. Outside, you slid two metal studs chased in between the bricks either to the left or right.

And that was how, in the dead of night, I came to find myself spread-eagled against the back wall of my house just below my own bedroom window. I slid the studs sideways and attended to the sash-window and before you could say Jack Robinson I was inside.

I flicked on the narrow beam of my pencil torch and cut the darkness in half and retrieved the money-belt, diamonds and documents from their hiding places. Then I made my way to the kitchen and saw the neat, little pile of letters and postcards waiting for me on the kitchen table. I gentled across the kitchen floor, stuck the glim between my teeth, stared down at all the envelopes and postcards, blinked twice, and seared the position of every piece of mail into my memory. I noticed the handwriting on one of the envelopes was Joanie's. She always had a distinct way with capital letters. I wondered why she'd written. She'd only ever done that during the war when I was away at sea. I didn't have time to puzzle over it, though, so I rifled through the rest of the pile.

First, I picked up the postcard Glover had sent me, a saucy seaside number by Donald McGill, showing two drunken sailors just about managing to hold each other upright. The caption read: '*Why ishtit we always looshe our she-legs on dry land?*' and I could see Joanie looking at it and trying not to cry at the reminder of happier times. The message on the back was innocent enough, but its meaning would've been clear even if I hadn't already heard it from Doris's own lips: '*Nothing on the horizon, not a cloud in the sky, food awful, no need ever to visit. Go to Blackpool instead. x x x D.*'

The second postcard was one I'd given Sylvia, a photo of Trafalgar Square, taken, by the look of the buses and motorcars, sometime in the early Thirties. '*On the square,*' was all it said, accompanied by the initial '*S.*'

It was the third postcard that set the cat back amongst the pigeons, as it were. It was from Lily. But again, it wasn't one of the postcards I'd originally bought. It was a picture of a pussycat and a canary cohabiting together in a wicker basket. On the back it said, '*Thought you'd like to know, the cat didn't walk alone he had a little friend. Love, it seems, still conquers all. Love, SL.*'

Blimey.

Landfall. Solid ground, at last. So the rumour about Fox having had a mistress, looked to have some truth to it. Not much, but something. Only problem was it opened up a whole new can of possible worms. Was his affair the real reason he'd ended up being topped? The wronged-wife turns up out of the blue and lets herself into the flat with her own key, ready to confront her cheating husband and his dishy young girlfriend. He's by himself, head in hands, having discovered the burglary. She finds out all her jewellery's gone. It tips her over the edge, so to speak. They argue, they fight, he slaps her face, she hits him over the head with a poker, he staggers and falls, hits his head on the andirons, she drags him over to the balcony and up and over he goes. She clears up all the mess and disappears back into the night. Hell hath no fury and all that. I'd seen many a play and many a film with all but that exact plot.

It was a definite possibility.

I shook my head. "Who am I kidding?" I said to myself. Then I stopped dead. I'd heard a sound, a handle turning, a click of a lock, and imagined rather than felt a rush of warm air, followed by urgent steps on the stairs. In an instant, I had the mail all back in a pile and was gone and back out the window and pressed against the outside wall before Joanie unlocked the door to the flat and threw on the lights. "Jethro, Jethro, Jethro are you there? Jethro, I know you're there. Speak to me, for pity's sake, speak." I heard her come to the window. She pushed and pulled and tried to force it open, but the retaining rods held it firmly in place and she beat at the window with her fists and let out a cry of such despair as should've melted stone.

I knew, though, there was no way she'd have heard me. I'd moved in time with the pattern of noises that always ran through the house on a cold night and I'd stayed well clear of any floorboards that were prone to creak. It was clear, though, she'd sensed something. That something that exists between brothers and sisters that only those brothers and sisters know.

I sensed Joanie above me and imagined her just staring out the window into the night, but with the light on in the room still, I couldn't risk any movement. I was stuck solid, spread-eagled against the brickwork, and I blinked and blinked and abandoned all further thought and committed myself into my hands and feet and I clung to the studs and the nail-heads and tried to separate myself from the growing pain in my fingers, hands, arms, legs, feet, and toes, and tried to forget everything that wasn't the wall. I knew all too well anyone out there in the darkness who'd seen the lights in the flat blaze on would have their eyes sharp focussed on the house and any movement on my part would have them on me like flies on a rotting corpse.

In less than a minute I was totally numb. The only sounds: the blood coursing through my ears like a mill race and Joanie crying her eyes out at the window a couple of feet above my head. Her sobs cut me like a blunted knife and sawed at my will, and when she cried out my name again I almost fell off the wall. I began to shake with the strain of holding on. So I started to count to ten. "One, two, three, four…" Just like you do when you promise yourself "I'll just carry this heavy suitcase another ten more steps, then put it down and rest awhile, before I carry on again." Only you never do stop, you continue to count yourself further and further along the seemingly endless road, your heart fit to burst and every nerve and sinew in you screaming until…until everything goes dark.

The light was off! Joanie had gone back down to her flat.

Thank God.

Only trouble was I found I couldn't move a muscle. Not a one. And I cursed and cursed and wailed and wailed and when that didn't work I blinked and blinked and squeezed my eyes tight shut and breathed and breathed and tried to calm myself, and then willed myself out of my body. And, detached and disinterested, I looked down on myself and saw I was anchored to my body as if by a silver cord and ever so slowly the frozen cogs inside my head began to turn and I began to focus and to get a grip. I didn't have too many options. Even if I could get my fingers to let go, the drop down onto the Victory Cafe's motley collection of dustbins and pig-bins thirty feet below would be enough to break my neck, even as it broke my fall. It'd also wake up the entire manor and announce my whereabouts to all and sundry assassins, which was none too appealing. I needed a 'Plan B.'

Feet first. That was it. Get my feet moving first. Then let my hands follow. And not downwards, no, but across to the nearest soil-pipe. Then up onto the roof and away. Sounded easy enough. Any fool could do it. Or anyone idiotic enough to have got himself stuck on the bloody wall in the first place. All I had to do was do it. I pictured the pattern of studs and nail-heads I'd hammered into the wall, held it in my mind, measured angles, inches, feet, and then willed my left foot to move across the rough surface of the bricks.

Everything inside me concentrated on my numb unfeeling left foot, willing the black canvas plimsoll to scrape just nine inches to the left. Nine inches. Not a lot. Not even as much as a foot. Then another nine inches, then another, and then another stud, then another, and all of a sudden my hands and feet knew exactly what to do and where to place themselves and before I knew it I had them clasped hard around the soil-pipe. And I went up it like a rat escaping the plague and was gone, scurrying back across the rooftops, ever deeper into the cold, indifferent shadows of the dark London night.

WORMWOOD, WORMWOOD

I kipped long and hard to catch up on my sleep and it was late afternoon when I at last eased the *Phoenix* away from Paddington Basin. The sky was grey, the clouds were lowering their utmost, and the drizzle was turning to rain, which meant the Sou'wester I was wearing to hide my face didn't look at all out of place. I wanted to reach my destination just before dusk, the time all towpaths closed, so a narrow boat tying up for the night wouldn't seem out of the ordinary. It wasn't that far as the crow flies, and at my top speed of four miles an hour I'd be there in forty minutes or less. That'd be much too soon. So even with the open canal calling, I throttled back on the engine.

I steered hard to starboard, which took me under Bishops Road Bridge and back into Browning's Pool, then veered to port, to pass under Paddington Bridge, and headed for Ha'penny Bridge. From there the canal curved left and then right, passing Paddington Hospital, before it wended its way up to Carlton Bridge. I had to be a bit careful at that point—the channel narrowed for a good half-mile as it ran past the back of a line of terrace houses on the Harrow Road. And after that white-knuckle experience, I motored happily on under Kensal Green Bridge, past the Narrow Boat pub, and on towards the gas works and the two huge gasometers that overshadowed the canal.

Slowly sliding into view on the opposite bank were all seventy-plus acres of the vast cemetery, its wild profusion neatly fenced in with ornamental iron railings. At the halfway mark, there was a landing stage that'd once served as a disembarkation point for the soon-to-be-buried dead, but for obvious reasons I passed it by. In the approaching dusk, the cemetery looked otherworldly and dead eerie, its mad profusion of trees, bushes, headstones, and mausoleums, a complete contrast to the bleakness of Wormwood Scrubs on the opposite bank. I eased off the speed for the last few furlongs and pulled in the other side of Mitre Bridge, just beyond the far end of the cemetery. The towpath was open to the public along that whole stretch of the canal, and I saw a couple of people making for the steps up to Scrubbs Lane, but they didn't seem too interested in me and in true boatman style I gave them nary a look.

I set about securing the narrow boat, fore and aft, set a warning light, then went back inside the tiny cabin and made myself some tea and had a fry-up. I nipped outside, went through the motions demanded of a life afloat, then went back inside, turned down the oil lamps, and pushed away the infernal sounds of the Old Oak Common marshalling yards up ahead. Then I catnapped until just gone eleven. I got up, splashed my face with cold water, and then got dressed—from head to toe, in black—so I could go creep 'softlee, softlee' and catch myself a monkey.

And so there I was, in the dead of night, come again to All Souls Cemetery, Kensal Green, the last resting-place of a couple hundred thousand of the great, the good, and the downright rotten. Church of England, mostly, but with ground off to one side for Dissenters and those that followed rites of their own devising, as well as a separate cemetery for Catholics. At the western edge of the cemetery proper was the West London Crematorium, built just before the War for those souls whose elected path to eternity was to become as ashes. It was there, on a brief visit I'd made during the hours of daylight, that I'd chanced upon the key to finding "Monkey" Jim on a memorial wall near the crematorium's Gardens of Remembrance. I'd been standing in the guise of an American tourist, looking out towards the Scrubs, thinking of Jimmy Mooney shouting himself sober, and I'd turned and there it was, a marble wall plaque showing the names of his wife, his daughters, and his sister, alongside the dates of their respective births and the date of their deaths.

That's when I recalled the rumours about there not having been enough left of the four Mooney women to fill a single coffin and how Harry had taken it upon himself to have the remains cremated, because Jimmy hadn't been in a fit state to decide anything. There'd been bitter words afterwards—Jimmy having wanted a proper church burial—and the two of them had fallen out, or so the story went. But Jimmy being Jimmy, I knew he'd visit the spot as often as he could, just to be able stand in front of the plaque and touch something good amidst all the horror he'd had to endure. I knew, too, that if he couldn't do it in the light of day, he'd venture forth in the dark of night. And that was why, as had always been my plan, I was going be there every night until he appeared, like me, a ghost doomed to walk the dark London night.

I lay in wait, still as a newly-chiselled name on a gravestone, and thought back to all the many nights I'd spent up on the roof of the Anglican Chapel, a quarter of a mile away, peering endlessly through binoculars, just watching and waiting for movement where there shouldn't be any. I'd probably still be up there but for my visit to the cemetery in broad daylight.

I'd been waiting just over an hour, my ears doing their best to see into the darkness, when I heard a twig break underfoot. I let the silence die then dashed noisily out into an open space near some rose bushes I'd noted earlier and turned to face the shadow I knew would come at me from out of the dark. The figure lunged forward and I stepped aside and parried his knife arm with my forearm and pushed him to the ground and stepped back and away. He curled up ready to take a kicking, but once he'd realised it wasn't coming, he rolled over and got to his feet. I took a step back and lit a match and held it cupped in my hand and up to my face. He looked at me, blinked, and then looked again, his brain working out who it was I reminded him of. I winked and said my name, the penny dropped, and I blew out the flickering flame, consigning us both again to the dark.

"Christ, Jeffro, I heard you were dead. You almost scared me half to death, you silly sod." His voice sounded like whispers from a newly dug grave. "How did you know I was here? No, don't tell me, there's only one person could've told you and now he's dead, too. Because of you, was it?"

He came at me, fuelled by rage this time, the knife sweeping back and forth in front of him, and I feinted right, went low, and swept my left leg out and knocked him off his feet again. He landed heavily, rolled into a rose bush, cursed, scrambled back up, then came at me a third time, knife held low.

I couldn't blame him. I'm the same. I see nothing but red when I think someone's hurt someone I call family or friend. But I could see he was losing steam. So I didn't faff about. I just did what I'd been taught to do and stepped in with my forearms crossed and blocked his knife arm just above the wrist. Pressing down, I slid my right hand round, grabbed his wrist with both hands, and twisted hard, pushing him off balance. I kept hold of his arm as he fell to the ground and twisted it, forcing the blade from his hand. Then I held him face down in the wet grass. "Easy now, Jimmy. You know it's never been my game to top anyone that didn't have it coming and your Harry certainly didn't, he was a master at what he did. Same as you." I paused to let us both catch a breath. "Remember 'Romulus' and 'Remus,' the names you called each other as kids?" His shoulders heaved and he went rigid, then his whole body went limp and he began sob. "Well, Harry did when I threw the names at him, which is why he threw me a clue as to your whereabouts in a way no one else would've had the wit to catch, but he was always clever that way."

With everything that'd been balled up inside him now all but spent, Jimmy's voice was barely a whisper of a whisper.

"So you're not after me and the bleedin' sparklers, like all them other sods? Sparklers I haven't got or have ever bloody seen. Sparklers what they went and killed Harry for."

"No, Jimmy, that's not why I came to find you. Someone put a bunch of creepers in the frame for the Mansions job around the time a price was put on your head, all done presumably to take the spotlight from off of you. So Don, 'Tosh', 'Shifty', Eddie, Eric and me, we all ended up with the Ghost Squad up our arses. Then your Harry turned up dead. So did 'Tosh.' Ever since when they've done their utmost to put me out the game for good. So, just like you, I've been living like a ghost. And me, I'm hell-bent on finding out just who the fuck's behind it all. And the thing is, Jimmy, it all seems to be tied up with a job you're reputed to have done at Meridian Mansions. That's the reason I came to find you. There's no one else can help sort all this shit out. So have you got that? I'm going to ease up now, going to let go of your arms. Okay?"

He made pulling-himself-together noises and I kept up the bunny to comfort him as much as keep us both on track. "When I heard you were out of prison, I knew it had to be you, Jimmy. Who else could've pulled off a seven-storey climb in the dark?" He rolled over and sat up and wiped his eyes on the back of his turtles. I held out a hand and he took it and I pulled him upright. "Sorry I had to do that. Let's get out of here, find a place we can talk."

Ten minutes walk later we were sitting, snug as two bugs in a rug, inside a little wooden hut, a kettle going on a kerosene-stove for some hot cocoa, an oil-stove for warmth. Two big oil-lamps threw our shadows against the walls, but with a blackout curtain still pinned in place over the little window and cut strips of lino tacked all round the edges of the door, from outside, you'd have never known anyone was at home.

I told Jimmy about Shadow Court and the three blokes that'd done for Harry and all I knew about the death of 'Tosh' Collis. He didn't say anything, just continued to potter about. I looked at him and almost didn't recognise him. He'd lost a fair bit of weight, his hair had gone grey, and he'd grown a scraggy beard that was all salt and pepper. Gone was the sleek 'Monkey' Jim I'd known as a lad. He seemed more badger than fox, now. Just another faceless face.

He saw me staring at him. "Changed, 'aint I?" he said, rubbing a hand across his face and chin. "Add a pair of binns, flat cap, scruffy clothes, a lift in one of me shoes, a trusty walking stick, and it's hardly surprising no one's twigged me yet. Not that I visit any of me old haunts anymore, but I still manage to get out and about when I've a need."

He told me he'd been in a pub out Ealing way when he'd overheard the news about Harry and 'Tosh' both being found dead. "Couldn't get out the soddin' place fast enough. Someone saw me throwing up outside and called me a dirty old drunk, but I'd only popped in for a couple of bottles of R. Whites lemonade, don't touch beer or the hard stuff any longer."

Turned out Jimmy had been living in the very hut we were sitting in. Hidden in plain sight on an allotment smack in the middle of two dozen other such garden allotments situated along the edge of Little Wormwood Scrubs, not far from the canal. Just one of the million and more allotments that'd sprung up all over the country when the Ministry of Agriculture had urged everyone to 'Dig for Victory' during the War. Almost everyone did, too, growing potatoes, tomatoes, carrots, cabbages, broad-beans, anything that could help nourish the national pot. And with food rationing still rampant throughout the land, a good few people had simply carried on gardening.

It'd been Harry 'Rabbit's' allotment, originally. He'd started growing carrots after Government scientists let on they were good for the eyes. Jimmy told me how Harry loved going down the allotment after long days on the streets of Soho. No noise, no crowds, no evil eyes in the shadows. He loved the peace and quiet, the sounds of the birds, and had even taken up bird spotting. "Brought me down here to let me bawl me eyes out when the ladies died," Jimmy said, pouring us both some hot cocoa. "It worked its magic on me, as well. A little place where I could let things be, and even if just a little hut and a couple of rows of carrots and runner beans, better than any church. A little piece of heaven on earth."

"I never did believe all that nonsense about you and your brother falling out," I said.

"We did that to put people off. If they thought we was at each other's throats, they wouldn't go on at him to get to me, and vice-versa. It worked, too, until Messima's boys got hold of him that first time. They told him if he didn't let on where I could be found, they'd find me themselves, then make him watch as they cut me thumbs off and stuck 'em up my arse. I can only imagine what they threatened him with when I went to ground after the Mansions job."

I bit down hard on my tongue to keep from asking about Messima. Jimmy misread the look on my face, pushed aside a pile of sacking, and pulled out a half bottle of Scotch from a flowerpot. "Every time I feel as if I'd go mad if I don't have a swig of this I think of Harry. Then I put it away. No man ever had a better brother." He twisted the cap off the Whisky and poured some into my cocoa. "Here, that'll help sweeten it," he said. He thrust the bottle at me. "You better have it all. Safer that way."

I saluted him with the bottle, slipped it inside my coat, and pulled out a packet of cigarettes. "So it was you that did Meridian Mansions?" I said, lighting a fag and handing it to him.

He took the 'Harry Rag,' nodded, and took a couple of puffs and drew the tobacco smoke deep down inside. "Tried to give these bleeders up inside, an' all," he said staring at the cigarette cupped in his hand. "No bleedin' chance of that, though." He coughed long and loud and stubbed out the fag. "Now all this. Poor Harry dead, his body God knows where. 'Tosh' done for. You supposed to be dead and drowned. It's as bad as the bleedin'

Blitz." He stared at me hard, almost as if to reassure himself I wasn't really a ghost.

I just stayed stumm and sipped me cocoa, praying he wouldn't clam up.

"Whole bloody world went down the shitter again after that Mansions job. When I saw in the *Standard*, that the flat where that MP died was the same drum I'd done, I went stoppo, long before anyone began calling it murder or there was one bloody word about any tom that'd gone missing. I knew they'd come looking for me then. Never thought for one moment they'd do for Harry, though, the bastards." He waggled two fingers urgently in front of his mouth and I handed him another fag and lit it for him. "I did the job, just like I was told, and it all went as smooth as a baby's arse. In, out, Bob's yer uncle, no one any the wiser. I mean, it wasn't as if I was sent in to nick any friggin' diamond jewellery, was it?"

I all but fell off my chair when he said that. I know I almost dropped my cocoa. "Excuse me, Jimmy, but what the fuck do you mean you weren't sent in to pinch Mrs Fox's jewellery? Why else would Darby Messima have torn up half of London trying to find you?"

MONKEY'S TALE

I felt like I'd been hit by a heavyweight. I tried to think. To see straight. Okay, so Jimmy hadn't gone in to nick Mrs Fox's diamond jewellery. And knowing him as I did there was no way in hell he'd have murdered Fox. All of which meant he probably knew even less about things than I did, which was a huge letdown. Ever since Ray had figured out Jimmy was the mystery 'midnight plumber' at Meridian Mansions, I'd counted on him filling in the missing bits of the puzzle. He was the key to everything, and I'd focussed on nothing else. In some ways it was what'd helped get me through my time inside the meat-locker and the nightmare afterwards. And, looking back on it, beatings and drownings aside, I don't think I felt more at a loss than I did at that moment.

I rubbed my tired old eyes and poured some more Whisky into what was left of my cocoa. I stared at the label, the lure of finding sweet oblivion at the bottom of the bottle suddenly a very enticing prospect, but I looked over at Jimmy and thought better of it and slipped the Whisky back inside my pocket. I raised my mug. "To 'Tosh' and Harry," I said, my voice hoarse. "May they both rest in peace on whatever rooftops and street corners they now inhabit."

"To 'Tosh' and Harry," echoed a gravelly voice, a good deal more hoarse than my own, "may they both rest in peace."

"There's never any peace for the wicked," I said to myself. I not only had me to worry about now, I had Jimmy to consider as well, and the hard truth was we both had to get out of the Smoke and fast. Given all that'd happened, I had to see Jimmy right, but how? I was as much a bloody ghost as he was. And I know I was tired, but I must've started muttering to myself, because I heard this raspy whisper as if in reply to something. I looked up.

"Straight up, Jeffro, there was never one bleedin' word said about there being any tom in the flat, on my life there wasn't. It was supposed to be a quick in-and-out job, nothing more than any locksmith would've done, and two hundred and fifty nicker in my hand for my trouble."

"So you scoped out the place, did a walk-by?"

"No, it was a rush job—never did see the Mansions in daylight, still haven't. It was late one Sunday night, I was just sitting in one of my locals over Ealing way, minding my own business, they'd just called last orders, and this gangster pops up out of nowhere and steers me straight outside. Tells me there's this special job needs doing, urgent, and there's a motorcar waiting with all the necessary gear: harness, turtles, plimsolls, black balaclava, the lot. So then he stuffs a roll of fivers in me pocket. 'On account a certain gentleman said I should first ask you nice,' he says. Then he opens his coat and shows me a big bleedin' shooter. 'Or I could insist,' he says. So, of course, I'm no steamer, I nodded me head dead quick and off we went."

I blinked and saw myself climbing up the back service-stairs of the Mansions at the exact same moment Jimmy was being bundled into the gangster's motorcar. It sent a shiver up my spine thinking how very close we'd come to stepping on each other's shadow and of the serendipity of it all.

"And they drove you straight to the Mansions?"

He nodded. "Then this gangster bloke all but pushes me down this ramp-way and tells me to do the padlock on the gate at the bottom and leave it open. Then I'm supposed to climb the pipes and get into the seventh floor flat, south side. 'Just open up the front door, leave it on the latch,' he says. 'Then into the corridor and open the push-door to the back service-stairs, wedge it open, and come down.' Only then he says, 'And nothing half-inched or fingered or your brother's life's forfeit.' Now that wasn't called for, was it, Jeffro? No cause for him to go and threaten Harry like that. I'm no bleedin' amateur; I can keep me mouth shut. I mean it wasn't as if I hadn't already done a dodgy job for them not that long previous. No complaints, that time."

My ears almost came out my head at the mention of an earlier job. "This…er…other job you did, Jimmy, set up by the same 'face,' was it?"

"Yes. That job gave me the willies and no mistake. And again, no choice in the matter, but there never is when it's Darby Messima doing the asking."

I had to swallow before I could get the words out. "Messima, you say? Are you sure about that, Jimmy? Messima was behind both jobs?"

"'Course I am. Been in the game too friggin' long not to know who's behind what. Messima always uses the same few gangsters to pull a gang together when he wants to keep his distance from everything."

"So what was this other job you did for Messima?" I said, my throat suddenly as dry as bone.

"I did the 'Bladder,' didn't I?"

"You blagged Scotland bleedin' Yard? You've got to be kidding?"

"God's honest truth, Jeffro, I did the old 'Bladder and Lard,' didn't I. Came away clean as a whistle, too."

"What in hell's name for, Jimmy? There's nothing there worth nicking, unless it's the keys to the fucking cells."

"Well, Messima or someone wanted something inside real bad, and given how it played out, I'd say he's not only got a bunch of coppers in his pocket, he's got some of the 'Bladder's' top brass tucked in there as well."

"Blimey," I said, getting a sudden second wind. "When was all this?"

"Few months back. Couple of weeks after I was let out the Scrubs. Also a Sunday night, as it happens. Same gangster had me teamed with a real hard man. Never seen the bloke before. Real cool customer. Ex-military, I'd say. They had the two of us kitted-out in pukka Electricity Board uniforms, peaked-caps, badges, clipboards, the lot. We even had an official-looking van with all the proper kit in the back. And there we were, well gone midnight, parked near Derby Gate, a truncheon's throw from Canon Row Police Station—me as jumpy as a cat with its tail caught in a mangle, Chummy just calmly checking his wristwatch every few minutes. Then, off in the distance, them lights atop of the gate into the 'Bladder' flicker and go out. 'Five minutes,' he says. And before I know it, he's driven us straight into the inner courtyard, where he parks right next to all these bleedin' police cars. Next thing, we're inside the old 'Bladder' itself, the whole place lit by oil-lamps and coppers marching around with hand-torches. Dead eerie, it was, like Bela Lugosi's bleedin' castle. Hated going in there, I did, as I've always hated the soddin' place." He shivered at the memory of it and went quiet.

I sat there, my cocoa gone cold in my hand, and tried to steer into the skid and keep him on track. "That's why the architect built it to look like Macbeth's bloody castle. What with the turret towers and everything. It's meant to impress old Joe Public and put the wind up people like you and me. Even the marble they used was quarried by convicts doing hard labour in Dartmoor Prison. So what happened then, Jimmy?"

He blinked back to life. "Never thought of it like that. I hope the architect fellah rots in hell. Anyway, these two coppers, a sergeant and a constable, met us and signed us in. 'The power's on elsewhere in the area,' says Chummy, loud enough for everyone to hear, 'Scotland House seems to be okay, so the problem must be here inside Central. Better take a look at the Electric Intake Room.' So they escort us into the bowels of the place. Like a bleedin' rabbit warren in there it is, corridors going off in all directions. It was even worse down in the basement: electric conduit running every which way, meters, fuse boxes, switches, and levers all over the wall, as well as some big heavy-duty jobs for setting off the air raid alarms all round London. I tell you it was all I could do not to smash the bloody things with a spanner. Fat lot of good they'd been. Next thing, one of the coppers opens up a set of doors with 'danger – high voltage' stencilled across the front, and lo and behold, it's the main junction boxes all bunched together in a wired-off enclosure. So on go the turtles and, while I held the torch, Chummy pokes around, mumbles about AC/DC rectifiers, watts this, watts that, capacitors and blown fuses. 'Main power line into the building seems to be in order,' he says, 'so it's probably one of the circuit breakers upstairs that's shorted-out and overloaded the rest. In which case, we best check out the circuit boxes on each floor.' So I just cough and nod my head like a good electrician's mate."

"The copper in charge says to the other one, 'Okay, I'll take it from here, you get back to your duty.' Next minute, we're back on the ground floor and up the marble stairway to one floor, then another, everything still in darkness, the copper leading the way. We turn a couple of corners, and then halfway along he shines his torch at an office door. 'The utility room containing the circuit boxes is at the far end of this corridor. It'll be open. I'll be there in twenty minutes. If anyone should ask, just say I was taken short and had to visit the gents.' And off he walks."

"The copper left the two of you alone in the Yard? Unbelievable."

"There's more. Quick as a flash, Chummy produces a set of keys from out his pocket and opens up the door to the office. It's not very big, but obviously belongs to somebody important, as there's pictures on the walls, carpet on the floor. Chummy hands me his glim, goes behind the desk, unlocks a drawer, and pulls out a sealed envelope, which he stuffs in his pocket. We exit sharpish, he re-locks the door and we nip along the corridor to where there's this other door with 'danger – high voltage stencilled on it. Turns out to be a room not much bigger than a broom closet, but we both crowd in. Chummy rips open the envelope and pulls out what looks to be a typewritten note, a cigarette lighter, and, of all things, another key. He reads the note and I see it's got a little diagram on it, but Chummy just nods and stuffs everything back in his pocket. 'Right,' he says, 'Follow me.'

"Next second he's striding up the corridor, torch in hand, with me trotting behind. We reach the far end, go round a corner, and he stops by this lobby area, where there's a secretary's desk, covered typewriter, and stuff. He checks his bit of paper, shines a light on a big mahogany door, and out comes the key from his pocket and in we go."

"Unbelievable," I said.

"I can't bleedin' believe it either, and I was there," he said, reaching for his mug of cocoa. He took a sip, which must've been stone cold, but he didn't seem to notice, and just wiped his mouth and continued on with his tale. "Only, this office we're in now is about four times the size of the previous one and much more posh. Big glass-fronted bureau, padded-leather chairs, big knee-hole desk at the head of a long glass-covered table; oriental carpet, portraits on the wall, Royal coat-of-arms over the windows. Come to think of it, the ceiling in one corner of the room was rounded, so it had to be one of them offices in one of them corner towers overlooking the Thames. There was also this large wall chart showing where crimes had been committed in London and the number of arrests made the previous day. Very disturbing to see, it was, but Chummy didn't even give it a glance, he just says, 'Safe's in the corner, to your right. So do the business and be quick about it.' And there it was: a monster Moser 400 from before the First World War, big as brass, as black as coal, and as solid as the Rock of Gibraltar. Right bastards to open they are, usually, but as is well known in certain circles, as the old man specialised in them, I cut me teeth on the sods, didn't I?"

"An old Moser 400 Series? What did you do, the old spindle tap routine, just like you taught me? The safe maker's nasty little secret?"

"Exactly. I knew then why it was me that was there, doing the blag. Afterwards, I even had the funny thought Messima might've helped arrange my early release on purpose, so I'd be on hand for the job. Wouldn't put it past the bastard. Anyway, I knelt down and did the Moser, clicked it, clocked it, tapped it with the magic rubber hammer, and Bob's yer uncle, *Opensesame.*

"Even Chummy was impressed at the speed of it. 'Look for a duck-egg blue folder with a wide red band around it,' he says. And there it was on the top shelf. So I hand Chummy the folder and he opens it and pulls out a couple a sheets of typewritten paper. He gives them a quick butcher's, lays them side by side, and tells me to come and hold a glim steady in each hand, and shine them down on top of the desk. Then he pulls out what I'd thought was a lighter, only it turns out it's a teeny-tiny little camera, and he snaps each page three times. Then he puts the typewritten sheets back in the folder, stretches the red band back around it, and hands it to me. 'Put it back exactly as you found it; same with the dials on the safe.' So I did. And he locks up the office and back we go to the utility room and wait. No friggin' sweat at all."

I sat there, shaking my head, not wanting to believe it could've been that simple. Someone on the inside, a Trojan horse in the shape of a little green Electricity Board van, a couple of uniforms, a bag of tools, couple of glims and a clipboard. And a camera of the sort you just didn't pick up on the Charing Cross Road on a Saturday morning. "So…er…what happened then, Jimmy?" But of course the only question on my mind was, what the hell was inside the safe that was so important to risk blagging the Yard?

"Copper comes back, doesn't say or ask a thing, just marches us back down to the basement, and we just stand around for a couple of minutes not saying nuffink. Time drags like it's wearing chains and Chummy and the copper can't seem to keep from looking at their wristwatches. All of a sudden as if by magic all the lights come back on. I can see the copper's relieved, but from then on I keep my head well down. We all troop back up to the ground floor, then, of all things, the bloke in charge, all spit and polished buttons, is so pleased, he stops us and wants to talk the hind legs off a friggin' donkey. He asks us which depot we're from, offers us a cup of tea in the canteen, suddenly can't do enough for us. But Chummy, cool as a cucumber, says something about Lotts Road power station and that it's urgent we get on and check out an electricity sub-station further along the Embankment. Then away we go, like two thieves in the night, and all with the blessings and thanks of the 'Bladder and Lard's' night duty officer."

"Un-fucking-believable," I said. "Don't suppose you know whose safe it was you blagged, Jimmy, or what was on those typewritten sheets."

I said it more as a statement than a question, but he blew his nose loudly into an old spotted handkerchief and said, "It was the Police Commissioner's safe, wasn't it? His name and rank were on a brass plaque on the desk, not that that was enough to deter whoever planned the blag."

Fucking hell. If that was true, even partially true, it completely redrew the underworld map of London, as it said the person Messima had in his pocket had to come from the very highest ranks of the Met. Who else could've known about the old Moser safe or what was in it, let alone get hold of a duplicate key to the Police Commissioner's office? Whoever it was, it wasn't anyone to be trifled with, that was for sure.

"Monkey" Jim's tale had given shape and substance to a very dark shadow that'd been looming over everything since the very start of the caper. But as big a part of the puzzle as it undoubtedly was, in many ways it'd only added to our problems, because if Messima had managed to 'straighten' someone at the very top of the Yard's hierarchy of thief-takers, who in hell in London could be trusted on either side of the law?

TWO MEN IN A BOAT

It's an ill wind that blows nobody any good and that goes double if it blows you a second wind. Thanks to "Monkey" Jim's tale, the game was afoot again. But as the game of chess teaches you, the only sure way out of any mess is to go on the attack, let loose the dogs of war, as it were. Or as my old mum used to say, "Faint heart never won fine coconut at the funfair."

First order of battle was to ensure our position was safe, and as it stood, two men in a potting shed on a public allotment was one man too many. Two men working a narrow boat, however, was par for the course and much the safer option. So as dawn stole upon us, I asked Jimmy whether he was up for a little voyage and suggested it might be a good idea if we both decamped to the *Phoenix* before any of the other allotment holders turned up. I knew people could be very possessive about their own-grown vegetables, and anything out of the ordinary could waken even the blindest of men from sleep and have them asking questions—or, worse, commenting on it later in some pub or cafe— and that we didn't need.

Jimmy saw the wisdom in us joining forces and was quite tickled when I explained that in the old days narrow boats had been called 'Monkey' boats. "Just think of it as your home away from home," I said.

"Aye, aye, captain," he said.

And so as the morning mists crept over the cold dead ground of the cemetery on the other side of the canal, we got busy loading wooden boxes with extra food and whatever else might come in handy. Root vegetables, mostly, but Jimmy still had a few more surprises up his sleeve.

He pushed aside some sacking from a stack of flowerpots and pulled out a well-oiled Browning Hi-Power 9mm automatic, all nicely wrapped in chamois leather. "Here, Jeffro," he said. "If we're going to fight the good fight, you might as well have this. I only kept it in case someone came calling, though knowing me I'd have probably blown me bleedin' foot off with it. Must've belonged to 'Tosh,' as Harry never held with them and I certainly don't."

I knew how he felt. I couldn't stand the bloody things myself, but in this case I regarded the pistol as a necessary evil and clicked the safety, racked the slide to see if there was one up the spout, and then checked the contents of the ammunition clip. "You saying 'Tosh' and Harry 'Rabbit' actually knew one another?" I said, as casually as I could.

"Yes, him and 'Tosh' got on like two houses on fire, though no one was ever supposed to know. But 'Tosh' wasn't daft. He knew Harry had the best eyes in the business. So, every now and then, Harry acted as a 'crow' for him. Chelsea, Belgravia, the Boltons—anywhere where the occupants would be away in the country for the weekend. Harry got a hundred nicker in his hand whether 'Tosh' pulled a result or not, more if a job turned out extra tasty. Kept it dead quiet, he did, as he wasn't supposed to pull capers with anyone on account of him being the ace corner-man. Now you mention it, though, maybe that's what did for them both in the end."

I slipped the Browning inside my jacket. "Harry and 'Tosh': partners in crime. Who'd have thought it?" I said. I know I never had.

Jimmy lent me an old mackintosh and flat cap so I wouldn't stick out like a sore thumb dressed all in black in the light of morning. And in the end we did two trips back and forth along the towpath. Our last task being to put down a plank and run Jimmy's little 125cc BSA Bantam motorcycle up onto the foredeck of the *Phoenix*. I stowed it next to my rusty Raleigh bicycle, secured both machines with rope, and covered them over with a tarp. Then we cast off and motored some four miles along the canal, Jimmy's mouth fully agape for a good fifteen minutes at the sight of the aqueduct that took us high over the North Circular Road.

"I've lived in London all my life," he said, "and never knew that bleeder was there."

"As I said," I said, "travel helps broaden the mind."

And he laughed and I laughed and a lot of shadows were cast onto the surface of the waters and left to dissolve and drown in our wake. Then round the very next bend we found the perfect mooring spot right next to Sudbury golf course. "A hidey-hole in one," I said. "Maybe our luck's changing."

It was a good spot, easy to see who was out and about on the links, as well as anyone on the towpath for a half a mile or so in either direction. It was a short distance from a Tube station and a line of telephone-boxes, as well as a main road that led down to Western Avenue and a fast route in and out of London. So all in all it was nigh on perfect for our needs. And while Jimmy repaired to the little cabin in the stern and stowed away the rest of his gear, I put on the flat cap and blue serge jacket and walked back to Piggery Bridge to pay a week's mooring fees, pick up a loaf of bread and some milk.

I also took the opportunity to do a quick reconnoitre of the area.

When I got back we had some tea and toast, before we both turned in. I locked up, put the Browning under my pillow, and slept the sleep of the dead, and didn't wake until late afternoon. I shook Jimmy awake and went and did my ablutions. I had a walk up and down the towpath to check things out again, and when I got back I lit the oil-lamps, set the kettle back on the stove, pulled some tins out the larder, and as the night closed in around us, I did us a fry up. We could've been two castaways on a desert island.

"I slept like a bloody log, I did," Jimmy said. "Best kip I've had in ages. All the watching, listening, never knowing what's coming round the corner, me nerves have been stretched thinner than banjo strings. So doing anything normal is a proper tonic. What I mean to say, Jeffro, is ta, ever so."

I raised my mug of tea. "Confusion to all our enemies."

He raised his tea in salute, but didn't smile. "And we've got enough of them bastards to last several bleedin' lifetimes, what with half of London out looking to nobble us. It's a racing cert someone's going down for the count."

"Well, it's not going to be us with our faces down on the canvas, Jimmy. Not if I have anything to do with it. Believe you me, I'm going to find some way to fuck up them and their games, even if it kills me."

"Well let's do what we have to do to make sure it never comes to that," he said. "I've stood at too many gravesides for one lifetime."

"Amen to that," I said, "but as we stand now, my old china, I'm blowed if I know where to begin. I'd always hoped you'd be able to shed some light on what happened at the Mansions when that Nigel Fox MP went arse over tit off the balcony, but I bet you never even saw him that night you B-and E'd the place, did you?"

"No, never did see the bloke. It was only when they showed pictures of him in the linens that I knew for sure it was his drum I'd done. And that's only because I'd seen all these photographs of him and his missus on top of the huge 'joanna' that was in the living room. I even remember thinking, 'the size of that thing, how in hell did they get that bleeder up the stairs?'"

I'd noticed the photographs in the silver frames too, all lined up, as they were, in serried ranks on top of the grand piano. Fox with Winston Churchill, Fox and his wife next to a famous

actor and his equally famous actress wife, Fox victor in his first
by-election, Fox standing next to a copper outside the Houses
of Parliament.

"Point is, Jimmy, when he went over the side and ended up
dead as a doornail, he took a lot of us with him. You, me, Harry,
'Tosh,' and it's not as if I can just clean up the mess by marching
in to Messima's Shadow Court and shooting the bastard,
though I admit the thought has crossed my mind more than a
few times. No, I've got to put the finger on this shadowy 'brass-
hat' at Scotland Yard, the hidden power behind the Emperor
Messima's throne, because if I can find that out, there are ways
of getting even that kind of information to the right people—
people much better suited to sorting out this sort of mess than
my old mum's little boy."

"'Buggy' Billy knows some important people, does he?"

I looked at him. He may've looked much the worse for wear
but he was still as sharp as a tack. "Yes, you could say that. As you
can well imagine, in his time, 'Buggy's' crossed paths with people
from all walks of life. You know he's no copper's nark, but he
knows all too well how the game's played, and I happen to know
he knows a man who knows a man who can get word to certain
VIPs who walk the corridors of power if ever there's need."

Jimmy nodded and gave me the bent-eye. "Always reckoned
there was a lot more to that old scallywag than ever meets the
eye. Clever bloke like that was always bound to have more
sides to him than a tub of bleedin' bug powder, that's for sure.
I always suspected he had a secret path into Hatton Garden, if
not to pastures beyond." He tapped the side of his nose. "Give
'Buggy' Billy my best if ever we all live to see better times. Tell
him his secret's safe with me, Jeffro, just as you was when he
sent you to me to learn the trade. I always rated him, you know.
He was always more than fair to me. A rough diamond he may
be, but always of the finest water."

"'Buggy' always reckoned you too, Jimmy," I said, softly. "He
often said as how you were the very best there was on the tiles

and there was no one else in all the Smoke he'd ever trust me with, in fair weather or foul."

He gave a little nod and smiled a little smile, and I swear there was a little flicker of the dapper Jimmy of old in his eyes. He sniffed up the cold in his nose and rubbed his hands together and I thought at first it was because he was feeling the damp, but given what he then proceeded to tell me, he might as well have been rubbing an old oil lamp from out of the *Arabian Nights*.

"So it being God's honest, Jeffro, what you just said about 'Buggy' Billy knowing some important people, I'll let you in on a little secret of my own. Thing is, these past few weeks and months there's been nobody on God's green I could talk to, let alone trust."

Silence descended upon us like a dead hand, a thing it often does, I've noticed, whenever matters of life or death are about to be imparted.

"You can trust 'Buggy' as you would me. You know that," I said.

"Didn't think there was any reason to burden you with it, Jeffro. I thought it'd only weigh as heavily on you as it has on me. I mean, who'd believe me if I told them? Me, an ex-drunkard, ex-convict, press-ganged into thieving again by the Emperor bloody Messima. Nobody. That's who. And who'd believe you, as good as you once were? You, an ex-'face,' ex-seaman turned jobbing stage-hand? Again, nobody, 'cos we're both of us at the bottom of the shit heap, craftsmen creepers though we may once have been."

I nodded and shook my head and made the kind of encouraging noises you do when something terribly important is trying to struggle and squeeze its way from the depths of the dark out into the light.

"The fing is, Jeffro, I know who the bleeder is, don't I? The one you're after putting the finger on. This mystery man Messima's got down the Yard."

I blinked and time just stopped dead and me with it.

"I also know where the brass-hatted bastard lives, because I've been and done his drum, haven't I."

The silence stretched fully into eternity then snapped and the only sound left in the whole wide world was the tick-tick-ticking of my wristwatch.

"I know all about the place," he said, nodding his head in emphasis. "Everything from his friggin' alarm system, to his telephone number, as well as which nights of the week he's off out to one of his bleedin' lodge meetings. What's more, Jeffro, there's this contraption inside the house that shows he and Messima have been at it together for bleedin' months, if not longer."

I just stared at Jimmy, open-mouthed, the tick tick ticking of my wristwatch now as loud as a night train thundering over the points.

"Well I had to do something, Jeffro. This hanging about, waiting for the chopper to drop on the back of me head got on my nerves something chronic." He puffed on his fag and then blinked, suddenly struck by a thought. He peered at his wristwatch, then snatched at my arm and looked at mine. "Is today a Tuesday, by any chance?"

MIDNIGHT PLUMBERS

'*Who dares not stir by day must walk by night.*' The creepers' motto as uttered by the Bastard in Shakespeare's *King John*, and my favourite of all the pithy sayings we all of us nick from the Immortal Bard from time to time. And very apt for the daring-do we were going to dare to do that very night.

After a bit of to-ing and fro-ing we managed to off-load Jimmy's little Bantam and my trusty old Raleigh bicycle and off we went along the towpath to do battle. First thing on the night's agenda was to get myself to a telephone-box and give Ray a call. I did the whole 'call three times, let it ring once, twice, and three times' business and he picked up right on cue. He had to pick himself up from off the floor when I told him what Jimmy had just told me about the very bent copper very high-up at the Yard. He whistled in amazement when I gave him name and rank.

"Well, that certainly explains it," he said. "Messima having a VIP that high up, that deep in his pocket, explains why he'd ever think he could get away with Shadow Court. Right. I'll see what I can find out from my end. Go safe."

"Yes, cheers," I said as I put down the phone and faded back into the night. Our hastily made plan called for Jimmy and me to get our arses out to Kensington High Street. The Bantam was only good for one-up and what we had in mind required transport for two, so out of necessity we had to do everything in stages and Jimmy had gone on ahead to a little lock-up he had squirreled away down Ealing Broadway. And even as he'd sat astride the little 125cc BSA motorbike, just like the ones used by the General Post Office's telegram delivery service, I marvelled again at his ability to disappear into the background in front of my very eyes.

The bike had been re-built after an accident, and Jimmy had picked it up for a song, second-hand, not long after he'd got out of prison. It had the telltale fairings at the front, saddlebags at the rear, and the official GPO red had been painted over battleship grey. In the dark, you could easily be forgiven for thinking it was out on official business, especially as Jimmy also wore official-looking goggles and helmet and regulation blue serge tunic. There was no way he could be mistaken for an eighteen, nineteen-year-old—the age of most delivery riders— but nine times out of ten, even with him sporting his pathetic imitation of a beard, most policeman would never have noticed. And just as well, really, as Jimmy had managed to hide a full set of burglary tools in and around the Bantam's frame, fairings, and saddlebags.

He'd always had a fancy for motorbikes. In fact, it was from him I'd once acquired a big Arial Square Four, a lovely bike that'd gone to meet its maker, saving me from going to meet mine. I have to admit, though, that when at last I arrived at the lock-up he had hidden away in a stretch of railway arches, I was completely bowled over by what he had in store. It was a pre-war Reliant three-wheeler, 10cwt van, painted dark green, complete with signage for 'Roman Bros. Plumbers.' (I had a much-needed chuckle at that.) Just imagine the front-half of a motorbike sticking out the front of a tiny van, the body part of which is supported on two standard-size spoke-wheels at the rear, and you'll get the idea. When fully loaded, its 4-cylinder, 750cc engine wasn't exactly designed for a quick getaway, but it served its purpose well enough, and that's as much as you can ask of most things.

So there we were, two grey ghosts, shadows of our former selves, maybe, but both of us ready to play the bastard if need be, on our way to break into the home of Messima's mysterious Mr Big. I'd asked Jimmy how on God's green he'd managed to get hold of that little titbit.

"Easy enough," he said. "Stole a business card from off his office desk that time I stole into the 'Bladder,' after which I took myself off to the public library down Ealing Broadway and looked him up. Started with *Who's Who* and there he was, a right toff. School, college, clubs, hobbies, the lot. Family with a history of money and a pile in the country, only not the eldest son, so he didn't inherit. But more than a few bob lying about. Certainly enough for him not to have to work if he didn't want to. Odd, though, him choosing to be a copper. I ask you, where's the appeal in that? So then I did all the usual magazines and linens, found pictures of him in uniform, a few of him done up like a dog's dinner at various police charity events, boxing usually, a couple more photos of him at posh dos and banquets. After that it was simply a question of hanging around outside his various clubs in St James's, all weathers, until I managed to get a butcher's at him in the flesh. Then it was a case of me shadowing him on the Bantam until he finally led me back to his drum, then keeping watch until I'd got his routines down pat."

I shook my head in wonder. That little lot would've taken weeks and weeks of hard, diligent work, and he'd done it all while there was a gangland 'notice' out on him. I eyed my old teacher with a renewed respect.

Melbury Road is as good an address as any can be found in central London, situated as it is just below Holland Park and just off the Kensington High Street. I knew it well, as would anyone that loved drawing and painting as much as I did. In late-Victorian times the street was a veritable artists' colony, famous for the likes of Luke Fides, Marcus Stone, G F Watts.

Most of London would've passed by without knowing or caring, unless sunlight sparkling from off one of the many huge studio windows happened to catch someone's eye. But one house had very definitely caught our eyes, as could be attested by the binoculars that Jimmy and I continually passed back and forth between us.

"Very nice pair of binoculars, these," I said, "but then the Jerries always did make the best ones. Cameras, too. Loot Alley, was it?"

"Yes. Cost me an arm and three legs, but well worth it."

"I once had a pair myself, until they went for a Burton."

"It's as I feared," Jimmy said, his voice like a rustle of leaves. "The friggin' window's closed tight shut this time. Hopefully, though, the little adjustments I made to the alarm on my last visit will have escaped detection."

"From your lips to God's ears," I whispered.

We were parked in the little three-wheeler van not far from where Abbotsbury Road doglegs into Melbury Road, and it was immediately apparent we had a problem. There was a bloody lamp-post right outside the house I was about to break into that lit everything up like a film set. 'Sod's law,' it's called in the trade. No creeper likes to work all lit up, but we both knew how vital the creep was. Hard evidence brought to light and placed in the right hands could mean all the difference to us, even be the difference between life and death. Plus, if what Jimmy had told me he'd stumbled upon inside the house was even half-true, there was no choice; it had to be done.

As if reading my mind, Jimmy said, "Never planned on doing the creep that first time. I'm no steamer, I knew the risks—but right out the blue, there he was, Messima, come calling at the house. At first, I was like a cat on hot bricks not knowing what to do. Then after he left, I thought to myself just maybe there's something inside the house worth having, something that could help drop Messima and his little brass-hatted friend in the shitter."

"Still, a bit bloody dicey going in on the spur like that," I said.

"Drawn like a moth to a friggin' flame. Had no choice once I spied the little side window was open. Couldn't miss that. So, as I had me tools on the Bantam, I waited until the house went dark, then in I went." He paused. "Apprentice's Rules, is it?"

"Yes," I said, "just like the old days. You stand watch outside the drum while I go inside and bang about." It was the smart thing to do, of course, because if things did go wrong for any reason, only one of us would have to face the music. "Same warning signal: three rings and off; another three rings and I'm off out the place like there's no tomorrow. Telephone-box is just round the corner. Got enough pennies in case you need to make the call?"

He nodded the once, wiped a hand across his tired face, and sniffed up the cold in his nose. "Never saw it before, strikes me a lot of these redbrick houses round here look like bits of the bleedin' 'Bladder.' Fair gives me the friggin' shivers."

"That's because the bloke who designed Scotland Yard also did the house we're looking at, as well as a good few others round here. Bloke by the name of Norman Shaw, and if ever anyone believed an Englishman's home was his castle, it was him; always built his buildings to impress themselves upon the local peasantry, did Shaw."

"He's still a bastard," Jimmy said levelly. "And it still amazes me the things you find in them books you read. So, okay then, tell yer old teacher how you read the house you're about to burgle."

"Façade's some eighty, ninety feet wide; sides of the house, forty, maybe fifty feet deep; the entire top floor comprising the main studio with attendant galleries, drawing-room and or library, off. At ground floor left, huge reception room with a fifteen-foot-high ceiling if it's an inch, which would also suggest there're one or two similar-sized rooms at the rear. Can't say what's round the back, but given what you say is the size of the garden, probably a lot of big picture windows, a couple of double French doors, maybe, all barred tight shut no doubt. The rest of the living accommodations—bedrooms, bathrooms, etcetera— will be to the right. The kitchen and servants' quarters probably on the ground floor and or in the basement, if there is one."

Jimmy nodded. "Cellar extends left, full length of the house; kitchen and semi-basement flat open onto the kitchen garden on the right. That's where the husband and wife couple that tends to the house live. Point to remember: careful of the steps that lead down below ground level, there's an ornamental iron railing to stop people from tripping and falling, so watch yer step. Okay. Next thing: how do you plan on getting in?"

I sniffed up the cold in my nose. "Well, for starters, disregarding the eight-foot-high perimeter wall, even without the bloody lamp-post, the three big oriel windows at the front are all latticed, so there's no going in through them. Same with the drain-pipes, either side the front door—far too spindly, far too exposed. Drainpipe that runs up the side of the chimney on the right isn't much better, but it's doable. Best bet's where the tiny bathroom wing abuts the main building. Round window, second floor, is too tiny, probably doesn't open anyway and again far too exposed, so given the extra cover provided by the fruit trees in the garden, I'd go in via the small window on the first floor."

"Nine out of ten, Jeffro, nine out of ten. Cat's-eyes coupled with a creeper's brain; a real criminal combination—which was exactly how "Buggy" Billy first described you to me."

I grinned. Jimmy never gave 'ten out of ten' for anything, even to himself. "Always leave room for improvement," he'd say. But I'll tell you this for nothing, I wouldn't have gone anywhere near the house if it'd been me in his shoes. Creeping a top politician's place was one thing; creeping the home of one of the country's top policemen was quite another and worth 'ten out of ten' for sheer bloody bottle any day of the week. It went against every rule in the book. It wasn't quite up there with killing a copper, but it was close. A copper's home and family were supposed to be off limits, otherwise it'd be no-holds-barred, all-out war. It hit me then, I was in Jimmy's shoes, with little or no room for manoeuvre. Stuck between a proverbial rock and a hard place.

"I can see now how your walking stick came in very handy," I said.

"That's why I lent it to you." He turned and narrowed his eyes at me. "To business then. As it's Tuesday night, our Mr. Watts is no doubt out building sandcastles in the air with his brother Freemasons, while the couple that do for him are out on their weekly visit to the pictures, followed by a quick one down the pub. Only problem is we weren't here to see them leave, so we can't be sure this isn't the one night everyone's decided to stay home. So final decision to do the creep is up to you, depending on what you see and hear once you're over the wall." Jimmy tapped his wristwatch. "If you go now, you've still got a window of fifty minutes, an hour ten minutes tops. Got yer socks?"

I nodded.

"Be lucky," he said.

WALK IN, CREEP OUT

The 'walk-in' stick was a marvellous bit of kit Jimmy had dreamed up while inside the Scrubs. It consisted of five metal tubes that slid each one inside the other, like a telescope, that when pulled out to their full combined length formed a metal pole just over eleven feet long. Every fifteen inches or so, he'd drilled holes in the tubes through which you pushed a long metal bolt. The bolts then acted as the rungs of a ladder. The stick hooked onto a window ledge by means of its crooked handle, which was covered in rubberized tape to give added purchase. To complete its appearance as an invalid's walking stick, he stuck a thick rubber ferrule on the end. The weight of it was the only giveaway to the stick's true purpose, but to my mind that only made it all the more handy if ever you had sudden need of a weapon.

I exited the van, slipped across the road, and headed for a clump of shadows. I lobbed the stick over the perimeter wall into a patch of grass Jimmy had assured me was there, and I was up and over before my own shadow had time to fall on the pavement. Extracting myself from a bush, mercifully devoid of thorns, I retrieved the stick, and stood stock-still. The hallway lights were on. There were one or two ground-floor lights on, but there were no lights on upstairs that I could see and, importantly, no moving shadows anywhere. There was no gramophone playing or radio set blaring, and there were no dogs barking, which was all to the good. The only things to be heard were the normal sounds of a London night.

I checked the rear of the house and, satisfied it was all clear, I made my way back to the tiny bathroom wing. And I had the 'walk-in' stick extended, the crosswise bolts inserted, and the crooked handle up and hooked onto the window ledge above before you could say 'P.C.49.'

I climbed in a slow, steady motion so as not to dislodge the 'walk-in' stick's crooked handle from its perch. It worked a treat, too, and I wondered and not for the last time why no one else had come up with such a brilliantly simple aid to burglary. Jimmy went up in my estimation even further when I saw how he'd altered the alarm circuit by the judicious introduction of tiny lengths of wire secured beneath the circuit connector plates in the outer casing frame and the window proper. He'd also nobbled the window-catch with nothing more than a length of fishing line and a small nail positioned to act as a pulley-point. All I had to do was connect a new loop of wire to the two tiny wire terminals he'd left protruding out of the exterior woodwork, give a little pull on the fishing line, and it was 'opensesame.'

I did the business, eased back the window, and, happily, no alarm went peeling out into the night. I reached down and slipped off the pair socks I had on over my plimsolls, rolled them up, and stuck them and any dirt they'd picked up into a pocket. It always paid to be neat and not leave a trail of mud in your wake. Then I climbed in through the tiny bathroom window, leaving the walk-in stick to dangle down the side of the building.

I closed the window and just stood there, in the darkness, slowly breathing in and out. Then on an out-breath I sent my sixth sense flying throughout the house and waited. I blinked, almost dreamily. Felt the air. Nodded. The place was good and empty. One funny thing, though, given who'd once lived and painted there, I'd expected to feel something from the house's fabled past, but it felt as flat as a pancake. There was no fizzy feeling in the air as when the very darkness itself seems to sparkle, as often occurs in houses where something of a person's greatness seems to have seeped into the very walls, floors, and ceilings. And I know it may sound fanciful, but when you've stolen into as many dwellings as I have, believe you me, no two houses or even rooms ever feel quite the same.

I exited the bathroom and headed down a narrow corridor to a door that Jimmy had told me opened onto the stairs. The house seemed even bigger inside than I'd imagined, so I adjusted my senses accordingly and got to work. I slipped down the stairs to the front door, to find it double-locked and dead-latched, and all very commendable, as you can never be too careful, can you? I decided against bolting the door from the inside, which I do to give myself extra time to get away if the lawful occupants should ever arrive home unexpectedly. The whole idea of this creep was to be fast in and fast out, with no signs left anywhere that might suggest a recent burglary.

I hotfooted it back up the stairs to the top-floor landing, but surprised myself by turning left towards the main painting studio. Blimey, the things your brain will do to you sometimes. Truth was, I felt much like Jimmy had done; it was as if I was being drawn to it. I mean, I couldn't not have a peep at the place where the great man had slaved so long and so hard to produce works of such unabashed beauty, now could I? Not when it was highly unlikely I'd be passing that way ever again. Anyway, at most, it'd be no more than a minute or two's detour.

I flashed the glim and imagine my disappointment when I saw the place was devoid of paintings of any kind and that it'd been fitted out as a gymnasium. There was a full-size badminton court, exercise rings hanging from the ceiling, wall-bars, wooden-horse, sets of Indian clubs, the works. It was larger than the tiny bedroom I'd had at Doris's, that was for sure. I didn't know this Ernest Harold Percival Watts, Deputy

Assistant Commissioner of Police—for that's whose house it was I was burgling—from a bloody hole in the wall, but I knew right then and there I was dealing with a right Philistine.

I all but ran from what'd once been one of the finest painting studios in all of London and sped back along the corridor to where Jimmy had told me I'd find Watts' inner sanctum. I took a deep breath, calmed myself, opened the door very gingerly, but knew immediately it was a different kettle of fish, entirely.

For a start, I didn't need the glim. There were about half dozen standard lamps and table lamps bathing everything in the room in a rich, warm, welcoming glow, and if Jimmy hadn't already forewarned me the lights might be on, I'm sure I'd have turned and done a runner. Light is always best avoided on a creep. And maybe Watts had reason to want to shun the light too, as the huge oriel window at the front and the two large side windows that would've drawn in natural light from sun-up to sundown, were all covered by heavy drapes thick enough to keep daylight permanently at bay. It was as effective a blackout as any I'd seen during the War, or, indeed, inside any theatre.

The room was far longer than it was wide with very high ceilings, all of it beautifully appointed—the ceiling mouldings, light fittings and exposed woodwork, a celebration of the Arts and Crafts Movement at its finest. Fitted bookcases all but covered all four walls. Three of them boasting the usual serried ranks of muted leather bindings, the mark of well-appointed libraries and law chambers the world over; however, the bookshelves covering most of the far wall presented a profusion of coloured-spines that more resembled a display of newly published books down the House of Foyles, on Charing Cross Road. The only visual relief to which came from the elegantly carved mahogany chimneybreast and mantelpiece on which stood a stunning early-nineteenth-century French gold and onyx ormolu clock.

Four wooden library ladders were positioned each side of the room, each one guided to its task by a set of wheels set in a brass rail that marked the edge of the wooden parquet flooring. What caught the eye though was a huge Oriental carpet a common beat copper would never have been allowed to stand on, let alone buy even with ten years' wages, and the massive mahogany library desk that stood, dead centre, like some tropical island seen against an expanse of red sky at dusk. On the far side of the desk was a lovely caramel-coloured leather chesterfield sofa strewn with cushions that matched the colours of the carpet perfectly. On the far side of that was a nice Victorian walnut davenport with drawers. All it needed was a roaring fire, an attentive butler to attend to my worldly needs and I could've lost myself there for a year and a day, no trouble.

Only trouble, I didn't have an hour, let alone a day.

I looked at the array of brightly coloured book-spines and it instantly brought out the jackdaw in me. They were all modern first editions and all of them mystery and detective stories, thrillers, or adventure yarns.

I scanned the shelves and, at first, couldn't see any sort of order. Then I blinked and the pattern emerged. They ran in sequence, A to Z, by author's last name, but they'd also been grouped by country of origin; British authors, in the main, but also American and French.

Watts seemed to have a copy of every mystery ever published in Britain. From Agatha Christie to Edgar Wallace. From her *Murder on the Orient Express* to his *The Four Just Men*. My eyes darted left and right like a hungry blackbird eyeing a swarm of flies: Allingham, Ambler, Bentley, Buchan, Charteris, Chesterton, Collins, Greene, Hornung, Maugham, Sayers; all the greats.

I found myself inexplicably drawn to the works of Eric Ambler. The titles all but screaming at me: *The Dark Frontier, Uncommon Danger, Epitaph for a Spy, Cause for Alarm, The Mask of Dimitrios, The Army of the Shadows, Journey Into Fear.* I scratched my chin. If that wasn't the story of my life since that fateful night at Meridian Mansions, I didn't know what was.

I stepped back for one last all-encompassing look-see. There was a whole section devoted to Conan Doyle, the immortal Sherlock forever bound in lovely gold-tooled Moroccan leather. All of Charles Dickens had received the same treatment.

There was also shelf after shelf dedicated to real rather than imaginary crimes: biographies and memoirs of villains from both sides of the law; records of infamous court cases and criminal trials; histories of robbery, histories of murder; all the usual suspects, from The Ripper to Dr. Crippen. All of it supplemented by veritable reams of jottings by this Commissioner of Police or that Chief Constable of somewhere or other. Scotland Yard's finest, mostly; recently retired detectives proceeding down memory lane in uniform with whistle and truncheon, followed by their inevitable promotion into the plainclothes and souped-up motorcars of the CID. Boring stuff, most of it, about events and people long gone. Still, taken all in all, it was a remarkably comprehensive collection of books. And I remember thinking that perhaps this DAC Watts of Scotland Yard wasn't such a Philistine after all.

"Just because a person likes reading mystery novels," I said to myself, "doesn't mean they can't also be a bit of a mystery themselves."

FOR WHOM THE BELL TOLLS

A sudden nagging thought took Centre Stage. There were no telephones, not even an old-fashioned candlestick model as was still used in many places. I'd assumed that Watts, as befits a man of his rank, would've had any number of telephones close to hand, fingers on the pulse of the nation's capital and all that. I went back out into the dim light of the landing and flashed the glim. An unexpected depth of shadow revealed an alcove a little further up the corridor. It seemed Mr Watts liked to separate business from pleasure.

The alcove was large enough to hold a suite of office furniture: black leather, chrome-steel chair; black-slab table; small filing cabinet. It was all very modern and business-like and a world away from what was in the library. On the tabletop, each piece lined up perfectly, was a black leather-edged blotter, a black onyx pen set, a square glass ashtray, square-faced clock, a black-leather bound desk diary, and a stack of headed notepaper bearing the legend: '*From the Desk of E. H. P. Watts, Deputy Assistant Commissioner 'L', Metropolitan Police.*

There was also a large silver-frame containing a photograph of a severe-looking, silver-haired lady alongside a typewritten note. I leaned in for a closer look. The note was from '*Winterbrook House, Wallingford, Berkshire*' and was signed by '*Agatha Christie,*' no less, saying how very pleased she was that so eminent a policeman had enjoyed her books so much and she thanked him for his professional appraisal regarding Chief Inspector Taverner in *A Crooked House*, her forty-ninth book. "I don't know if that's a piece of the puzzle," I said to myself, "but I'm sure it fits in somewhere."

Pride of place on the tabletop, however, went to four telephones: one black, one red, one green, one cream. I just hoped one of them matched the telephone number Jimmy had scrawled on a piece of paper in his pocket.

It struck me then; the alcove must've been where Jimmy had stood, cloaked only in darkness, listening to Watts replay the same bits of conversation over and over again in the library. "If the trick-cyclist who had me under observation back in the Scrubs hadn't used a dictating machine, I wouldn't have known what it was, let alone been able to believe my ears," he'd said to me that night back in the potting shed. Given the circumstances, and knowing all too well how sound plays tricks with you in the dark, it must've been very unsettling. I peered underneath the desk, but there were no wires. No hidden microphone or speaker. And no sign at all of a dictating machine, just four tubular chromium-steel table-legs gleaming in the torch beam. I returned to the library for a closer look at the big mahogany desk.

It was like a partner's desk, only twice the size. The sort of thing you might see in a fine country house or better public library. As large as it was, though, like everything else, it fit the room perfectly. It had beautifully proportioned pedestals, the leaf-shaped brass fittings and gilt-tooled green leather insert as finely crafted as anything you'd see on display down the Victoria and Albert museum. The desktop was covered in books on art, all stacked in small, neat piles. Off to one side were a number of dictionaries and reference books held between a pair of very solid-looking bookends. There was a pipe rack festooned with pipes of all sorts and sizes, a tobacco jar, a large glass ashtray, and a red-lacquer fountain pen. I noted the position of everything, memorized it, and waggled my ear—an old trick.

At each end of the desk there was a long centre-drawer flanked by four drawers on the left and two drawers and a double-sized drawer on the right. It was the two big bottom drawers I was interested in, as I knew the inner workings of a Dictaphone were often hidden away inside a desk, along with the wax cylinders used to make the recordings. I put my money on it being the one farthest from the door.

I went over, knelt down, and picked the lock. The machine inside was about the size of a small suitcase—say 18" deep, 12" wide, and 8" high. It looked like one, too, in that it was contained in its own brown leatherette-covered wooden carrying case complete with metal catches and plastic handle. It didn't resemble any Dictaphone I'd ever seen, more like a cross between a 'Teasmade' and a small radio set. "Might even be a bloody radio, for all I know," I said to myself. Trouble was, I'd never even heard of the manufacturer 'Webster-Chicago' so I couldn't be sure of anything.

I picked the locks on the other two drawers above and inside the top one were a dozen or so three-inch-square boxes bearing the legend Webster-Chicago *Recording Wire*. So much for wax cylinders. Jimmy was right, though, about Watts having a recording machine.

I opened a box. The metal spool inside resembled a fishing reel and was about the size of a tin of shoe polish, only hollow. It said on the spool the 3,600 feet of stainless steel wire was good for thirty minutes recording. I slipped it back in its box, opened another that had the letters 'DM' written on it in neat capital letters, but it was empty. I closed the drawer, pulled open the one below and found the machine's removable hard cover-top inside. More importantly, there was a set of 'Special Instructions' stapled to it on how to operate the Webster-Chicago *Electronic Memory*. I gave them a quick read through, then took a closer look at the machine itself. The rear casing was of cast metal and consisted of a circular recess for a wire spool and a circular drum, about the size of a bread plate, into which you fed the recording wire, and a control lever that could be turned to "Run," "Stop," or "Rewind." The front section was slanted for ease of access and had four big switches, two either side of the built-in speaker. The switches were marked "Record and Listen," "Volume," "Output," "Tone and Off." There was also a tiny indicator light and two small sockets, labelled "Input" and "Output," with leads leading off.

I turned the switch, marked "Tone and Off" but nothing happened. So I turned it back to its original position, then felt around under the desk and touched upon a button, which I pushed.

Again nothing.

I stared at the recorder, turned the "Tone and Off" switch again, and this time a red light came on and the spools began to turn and I heard Messima's voice. I quickly pushed the button again and the spools stopped moving. I felt a bead of sweat on my forehead; the very last thing I wanted to do was erase what was on the recording machine by mistake. I read the instructions again and fiddled about until I worked out how to rewind the wire spool and remove it. I rifled through the top drawer, pulled out another used spool at random, and substituted it for the one that'd been on the machine. I put that all-important spool into the empty box and slipped it inside my pocket.

I peered at the desk and tried to imagine the likely path of any electrical leads or wires and it was only then I noticed the end of the bookend facing me was really a speaker, the fabric-cover a perfect match for the bookend's wooden veneer. That's when the blinders came off and I realised that one of the pipes standing in the wooden rack wasn't a pipe at all, but a microphone. Simple, but very effective; Messima wouldn't have had a bloody clue his conversation was being recorded. And that was the exact moment one of the telephones out on the landing began to ring.

Ring-ring. Ring-ring.

I didn't wait for the third ring; I was already on my toes, making fast for the stairs. Only, the telephone kept on ringing—five, six, seven rings, more—which meant it wasn't Jimmy trying to warn me. Someone else was calling the house. Finally it stopped and I breathed a sigh of relief. Then out the blue, a loud voice said, "Are you sure you wouldn't like me to accompany you into the house, sir?" Then a second voice, less strident than the first, said, "That won't be necessary, Sergeant. Thank you, that will be all for tonight."

My first instinct was to make a dash for the windows, if only to seek refuge behind the heavy velvet curtains, but I willed myself to slow down so as to check all the drawers were closed and locked. And in truth it seemed a whole hour passed before I heard the police sergeant say, "I'll bid you a good night then, sir."

Then I heard, or rather imagined, the sounds of the front door being closed and bolted, the overcoat, hat, gloves, and attendant paraphernalia of 'the craft' being dispensed with. I waggled my ear again and stared at the desk to ensure it matched the picture in my head; I moved a book a hair, the fountain pen a smidge, until everything was ship-shape. Then I heard the scuff of well-heeled shoes on polished marble floor and the quiet tattoo of approaching footsteps upon the carpeted stairs and I dived for the floor.

I dug into a pocket, pulled out a boiled-sweet, unwrapped it, and stuck in my mouth. I got myself into as comfortable a position as I could manage in the time, settled to it, closed my eyes, switched off, then as of long practice I began to see through my ears. Watts opened the door and crossed the carpet. He stopped, picked up a glass decanter, and poured himself a drink. I smelled the brandy and then heard a series of sounds as he went through the whole blasted ceremony of packing and lighting a pipe. I heard the scrape of a match, caught the brief tang of sulphur, and then endured a whole parade of puffing and sucking sounds. He seemed to take the devil's own time before he drew his first contented puffs. I just hoped to God I didn't start coughing.

I sensed him coming closer and heard a key catch the metal surround of a keyhole and prayed to heaven he wasn't going to do what he then did, which was turn the key and unlock and open the drawer containing the wire-recorder. My nerves were stretched thinner than piano wires as it was, but when he switched the machine on, they all but snapped. Watts walking down memory lane listening to whatever had passed between him and Messima was probably a nightly ritual, along with his nightcap, but it was curtains for me if he rumbled I'd switched wire spools. And that was the exact moment the phone rang three times then stopped. It was Jimmy trying to warn me— too little too late, but better late than never if it helped distract Watts.

"Who the Dickens?" Watts muttered, irritably. The telephone began ringing again, as if to answer him.

Ring-ring, ring-ring, ring-ring.

It stopped again and the house fell into an ominous silence. Watts didn't move and neither did I. I could sense him just standing there by the desk. I could even smell the Trumpers aftershave cologne he was wearing.

I began to count numbers off in my head to try and stay calm.

The telephone on the landing began ringing again—once, twice, three times—then it stopped dead again and so did my heart. "Damn," he said, as he switched off the recording machine and closed the desk drawer. Then he went out into the corridor, picked up one of the telephones, and repeatedly banged the receiver-hook up and down and waited for the operator to answer. "Hello, operator, this is an EHP unlisted number, Kensington 6669. Did you just try to put a call through to me? No? You're sure? Yes, good night."

I heard him dial another number.

"Hello, Whitehall 1212 exchange, DAC-'L' here, did you just try and contact me about anything? No? Then will you also please check to see if any HO alerts have been issued since eighteen hundred hours? Nothing at all? You're sure? No. Thank you. Good night." He banged down the receiver. "Some damn idiot calling the wrong number."

He came back into the room. He poured himself another large brandy, then suddenly he was by the desk again and I heard the key catch the brass surround of the keyhole again and my heart stopped dead again. Then I heard him turn the key and lock the drawer and it took everything in me not to let out a huge sigh of relief. Then there was a loud click and even with my eyes tight shut and me curled in a ball, I could tell the room had brightened considerably, and I sensed rather than saw him reclining comfortably on his bloody chesterfield, getting ready to read one of his bloody books. Did the sod never sleep? Didn't he have a proper job to go to in the morning?

That was when I felt the first awful stirrings of cramp in my left leg. Then, as night surely follows day, the cramps began creeping into all my limbs, pins and needles began pricking me, and bit-by-bit I felt bits of me going dead. To try calm myself, as of old, I thought of a number of at least six figures and started counting backwards. "One million, two hundred and—"

I felt my eyelids flutter open and knew I was awake even though it was as black as a coalhole. For a moment I had to think who I was, let alone where I was. Then I was hit by a wave of nausea as something deep down inside remembered waking up to the bitter blackness of the meat-locker. "Oh God, no," I croaked, "not again."

From out of nowhere I heard the tick-tocking of the ormalu clock on the mantelpiece, and once I'd oriented myself to the sound I stole back into the present. I tried to stir myself, but found I couldn't move a muscle. I was stuck solid, as if buried up to my neck in concrete.

I slowed my breathing and slowly pushed away my growing sense of panic. Then I flexed and stretched fingers, hands, neck, shoulders, arms, and legs. Tiny, infinitesimal movements at first, then inch by painful inch, increasingly larger ones, until I'd managed at last to massage some semblance of life back into my all but dead and useless limbs. And after what seemed like an eternity, I crawled out from under the desk and lay spread-eagled on the lush expanse of Oriental carpet until I was sure enough blood had circulated for me not to fall over when I eventually tried to stand up.

I shivered violently, as much to shake off any lingering nightmares as dispense with the feelings of inadequacy that always attend such a close a call. Had I snored, coughed or sneezed while sparked out, I could've very easily woken up in a police cell. Not a pleasant thought. First golden rule is never fall asleep in the middle of a creep, not ever. As with sleeping on sentry duty, it could get you shot. It's only superseded by golden rule number two: always make good your exit. And I still had that to do without walking into walls, blundering into Watts, or disturbing his housekeeper or handyman.

I stretched, tentatively at first, and then fully, and ever so slowly got to my knees. I reached into my pocket and eased out the glim. I had to chance a quick flash of light to orient myself, as in total darkness it's hard to know which way is up, let alone what's to the right or left of you. But the bloody thing didn't work. I shook it, shook it again. Not even a glimmer. So I shook it again, daft I know, but third time's the charm.

Not a sausage. Total darkness.

The glim must've been on all the time it was in my pocket, the battery now as dead as a fucking dodo. And that'd never happened before, not ever. I was really losing my touch. I stuffed the dead torch back in my pocket and held the back of my hand up to where I guessed my eyes were, pulled back the cuff of my turtle, and stared unseeingly at the luminous dial on my wristwatch. It looked to be just gone four or five. I felt for the little square box in my pocket. At least that hadn't been a dream. I got slowly to my feet, pictured the room in my mind, oriented myself by feeling along the edge of the desk, then having reached what had to be the far corner I set my compass and with hands held out in front of me at waist-height, I slow-stepped through the pitch-black darkness in the direction of the door.

I have no recollection of how I actually got out and away from Watts' house. It certainly took me long enough—a good hour or more—and even though it was all done as if in a dream, something in me must've been awake enough for me not to fall over, brain myself, and wake up the entire household. I do remember Jimmy was as glad to see me come looming up out of the dark as I was to see him. And from the way he stroked and patted his 'walk-in-stick,' he was as glad that was back in his possession, too.

"Jesus, Mary and Joseph, Jethro, I'd all but given you up for dead," he said, his raspy voice made all the more hoarse from five or more hours of swallowing down fears for my safety.

"Rumours of my death continue to be much exaggerated," I said, "but that was too bloody close for comfort." I held up the little box containing the wire-spool. "Even for this."

"Is that it?" he asked.

I nodded, and we both looked at it as if expecting it to give up its secrets right then and there. I stuck the box back in my pocket.

"Here," he said, handing me the plastic cup from the top of the Thermos flask. "Have some of this. You look like you need it."

And as I sipped the tea, he told me how he'd seen the police-car conveying Watts turn into the street and as quick as a startled rabbit he'd scurried round to the phone box on the corner of Ilchester Place, only to find Watts' telephone line engaged. "All but had a bloody heart-attack, Jeffro," he said, barely able to contain himself. "All I could do was keep on trying the soddin' number until I finally got through and heard it ringing. Even did it a third time to make sure. Anyway, well done." He glanced at his wristwatch. "Nearly half-five, we can be on the road in a few minutes. Better not kick-start this old crate round here though or we'll risk waking the dead. Best push it closer in the direction of Kensington High Street, just to be on the safe side."

We drove back to Jimmy's lock-up and got our heads down for a couple of hours on a couple of tarps spread out on the floor. Later that same morning, after a swig of tea brewed on a tiny primus stove, I slipped out to the General Post Office in Ealing Broadway and sent off a brief telegram to 'Mr S. Bosanquet, Esq.,' after which, needing some decent grub and some proper kip, we motored back up the Ealing Road—Jimmy on the Bantam, me driving the Reliant three-wheeler van with my old rusty bicycle safely stowed in back.

We split up when we got to Piggery Bridge, Jimmy riding on ahead to Ballot Box Bridge, a mile or so away, so he could wheel the Bantam in from the towpath gate there, while I took a right and parked the van alongside Wembley Cemetery. I cycled the short distance to the shops, where I picked up a bottle of milk, a loaf of bread, midday-editions of *The Star* and *Standard*, and then wheeled the bike in from that end. And apart from the paw-prints of some overly inquisitive dog, there were no other telltale scuffs or footmarks in the dustings of bug-powder we'd left at various points along the canal bank and on the *Phoenix*. It all seemed secure enough. So we had a fry-up, washed down by lashings of tea, and finished the lot off with some bread and jam. Then we read the linens to help clear our minds and tried to ignore the little square box sitting on the table in front of us. The way the two of us kept staring at it you'd have thought it was a hand grenade about to go off.

"Best get that soddin' thing to whoever can use it to do us some good."

"My thoughts exactly," I said. "Let's hope it's not just Messima and Watts reciting a laundry list. Anyway, that telegram I sent should've done the trick. I'll be off when it gets dark, so best get my head down again for a couple of hours. I've got a feeling it could be another very long night."

I slept the sleep of the just, awoke around five o'clock, had a quick wash and brush up, put on a change of clothes, and bid "Monkey" Jim adieu, leaving him the Browning revolver for company. And as dusk brought the swirling mists back to the dark-mirrored surface of the canal, I disappeared off down the towpath in the direction of the cemetery and a gap in the wall that gave me access to the street where the van was parked.

Jimmy, of course, presumed that the whole process of me getting the little wire-recording spool into the right hands started and ended with "Buggy" Billy. I didn't want to lie to him, so I just tapped the side of my nose as if to say, "Ask no questions and I'll tell you no lies," and he'd nodded the once and tapped his nose.

"On the QT it is then."

And never was a truer word left unspoken, for "on the QT" fit Simon Bosanquet to a 'T,' and if ever anyone was hidden in the folds of a cloak with attendant dagger, it was he. Officially, he was the Assistant Deputy Assistant Liaison Officer between the Home Office and Scotland Yard. Unofficially, he was an officer of some very special branch of Special Branch and in truth was ever hugger-mugger with Colonel Walsingham of MI5 and in every way was the velvet glove to his boss's iron fist. But Simon was the only trump card I had in my hand, and I had no choice but to try bring him into play.

SIMON BOSANQUET, BART.

So there I was, an hour or so later, driving up and down the King's Road, Chelsea, waiting for the lights to go on in Simon's house. I parked the little three-wheeler van several streets away and walked back carrying a small battered cardboard suitcase. I turned the corner into the tree-lined square, stopped and crouched down as if to tie an errant shoelace, and went from humble plumber to North Thames Gas Board official by exchanging cloth-cap and scarf for a peaked-hat and a pair of heavy-rimmed National Health spectacles. I stood up, opened my raincoat to reveal a dark blue serge suit— complete with official NTGB tie and enamel lapel badge—and then proceeded on with the purposeful air of a man on an important mission. Any reports or evidence of a gas leak permitted a Gas Board official to enter into any premises in the land at any hour of the day or night, and to use any and all means necessary in the implementation of his duty—all of it without the signed authorisation of a local magistrate. And if not quite the draconian powers granted the officers of His Majesty's Customs and Excise, they were no less effective for that.

I lifted the brass knocker and banged on the front door.

Simon saw through the disguise immediately, the telegram in his hand having clued him in.

'COUSIN HANNEY ARRIVES LONDON LATE THIS PM STOP REQUIRES ASSISTANCE STOP'

But quick as a flash and loud enough for any noisy neighbour to hear, he said, "Thank you for coming out so quickly. I do hope this turns out to be a false alarm, but if there's any chance of a gas leak, it of course needs to be attended to immediately. Do come in."

I tipped my hat, wiped my feet, and crossed the threshold back into the shadowy world that exists on the other side of the looking-glass.

Even after a long, hard day of ensuring the nation could sleep securely in their beds for yet another night, Simon Bosanquet was as impeccably dressed as ever. From the tip of his hand-made shoes to the telling stripes of his tie, he was the very model of a modern major spy-catcher. He was Eton, Balliol, the Guards, and Whites. And though to all intents and purposes he was merely a policeman, he was also a Baronet—a title he'd inherited from his father. Not that I ever saw him lord it over anyone, but as Walsingham himself had once explained to me, Simon Bosanquet, Bart., only ever used his title when obliged to attend some state occasion or society function. As one amongst many, he was then all but rendered invisible. Perfect cover for a spy.

As per usual, he didn't beat about the bush. "Good God, man," he said, pumping my hand up and down. "I was told you'd been killed in some gangland feud." He ushered me through into the drawing room and sat me down. "So you can well imagine my reaction when I read your telegram. 'Cousin Hanney', indeed. It's very good to see you're still alive, Jethro."

"That makes two of us," I said, sipping appreciatively at the single malt he'd thrust into my hand. "Not to beat about the bush, Simon, but I'm up to my neck in something extremely nasty. And even though I wouldn't normally have bothered you, certain aspects of it recently come to light touch directly upon your world. So I'm here in the hope that if I can help scratch your back, you might in turn scratch mine."

"Absent the usual constraints regarding DORA, I'll do whatever I can, Jethro—you know that. Needless to say, you turning up out of the blue like this sparks my interest no end. I promise, not a single word until you've finished whatever it is you've come to tell me."

Did I say "merely a copper?"

Simon was that clever, he could've been a barrister. He could listen with the best of them and squeeze out more truth than ever you'd intended to reveal, but I'd counted on him being smart, just as I counted on him being an honest copper through and through. So I took a sip of Whisky and told him everything I thought he needed to know and, as you do when you're really trying to convince someone, I began with a question.

"Do you remember that so-called suicide of Nigel Fox MP, the rumours of a huge cache of jewellery that went missing, and the cries of murder most foul that followed soon after?"

He nodded.

"Well, within days, a list of creepers thought capable of pulling off the job appeared out of nowhere, with my name prominent amongst them, even though it's widely known I gave up the game for good after the war."

Simon didn't bat an eye, even though he knew my claim of having retired as a cat burglar was somewhat at variance with the facts, but as he was one of only three men in all of London in possession of that knowledge there was no need for the truth to get in the way of a good story. So I carried on with my tale and told him about the eruption of violence in the London underworld, the likes of which hadn't been seen since the Thirties, when the Sabinis fought to take over control of the West End. I told him about the scores of people who'd been lifted off the street and badly beaten up, and of the people who'd been killed in such particularly unpleasant ways, as to suggest it was done as a warning to the entire East End, and the death 'notices' put out on 'Monkey' Jim and me.

I told him about NORTO and Shadow Court, about being captured, incarcerated and sentenced to death, then being tied, hand and foot, to a jetty support in the river with the tide fast making. I didn't bring 'Spottsy' and Tommy Nutkins into it—didn't think it necessary—but I did briefly sketch in the bit about me commandeering a canal boat and hunting for "Monkey" Jim amongst the dead at Kensal Green Cemetery. After which I jumped to the episode about Jimmy and some mystery villain dressed up as Electricity Board employees doing someone's safe at the Yard so they could photograph some secret document that was inside. I stopped there and Simon got to his feet and rang down the safety curtain and called for an intermission.

He didn't come right out and ask whether I'd been involved in the original burglary of Fox's flat or not—he chose to let that sleeping dog lie undisturbed. Neither of us wanted to be lied to by the other. And as to the implication of police corruption at the topmost level at Scotland Yard, I fully expected him to be shaken by the revelation, but he covered it well.

"Is this friend of yours, 'Monkey' Jim, sure which building he was taken into? North and Central look very similar."

"It was the Norman Shaw building. He's certain of that."

"The awkward thing is, Jethro, only Deputy Assistant Commissioners and above have locks on their office doors in Scotland House or Central. Added to which, the Police Commissioner is the only person with a corner office, such as you describe. I think we therefore have to assume the safe in question was his. As to the duck-egg blue folder secured by a wide red band, it indicates that the information contained therein was classified as 'Most Restricted and Top Secret.'" He paused for the very briefest of pauses. "Did your friend by any chance happen to see the contents of the document as it was being photographed?"

"I asked him that very question. He said it looked like a list of names. Thirty or forty or so, men's mostly, but there were women's names as well— each name paired with a different town or city, but no postal addresses or telephone numbers or anything."

"Do you happen to know when this burglary at the Yard took place?"

I thought for a bit. "Jimmy never mentioned any specific date, but I do remember him saying this gangster first approached him on a Sunday night, some three weeks after he was let out on parole. He told me he was released the beginning of June. And I happen to know the 6th was a Monday, because that night I had my weekly game of chess with Ray Karmin and we toasted to the memory of all those who fell on D-Day, 1944. So that'd make Jimmy's first Sunday out of prison, the 5th." I counted the dates off on my fingers. "So by my reckoning they blagged Scotland Yard the night of June 26th or, failing that, the following Sunday, 3rd of July, but no later. Is it important?"

Simon stared off into space, his face suddenly as expressionless as a slab of new Portland stone. I knew the look, so I just kept stumm and sipped my Whisky. He'd been trained from birth to keep his head while people all around him were losing theirs, but I'd watched him stiffen as my tale had unwound and saw his eyes take on that odd, flat look that men of action seem to exhibit when denied immediate opportunity to let loose their dogs of war. The break in at the Yard was the first shoe to drop, but when and if the second shoe dropped depended entirely on what Simon said or did next.

"*Quis custodiet ipsos custodes?*" he whispered. He looked down and shook his head and squeezed the bridge of his nose, a mannerism I'd seen Colonel Walsingham use when troubled by events. "This is unimaginably bad news you've brought me, Jethro."

"What's that mean," I asked, "that thing you just said in Latin?"

"Er, 'Who watches the watchers?'" he said, almost absent-mindedly.

"Very pertinent," I said, knowing we'd reached the moment of truth.

Simon nodded, his decision made. "I suspect the document that they photographed was a list of the police officers currently seconded to the Special Duty Group, or 'Ghost Squad,' as it's often called. There's only one copy that's known to exist, which is why it's kept in the Police Commissioner's safe and has such a high security clearance; even the original typewriter ribbon would've been destroyed. The Deputy Assistant Commissioner (Crime), the man who originated the idea of the secret undercover group, isn't even privy to the full information; all he knows are the code names. The same goes for the four senior detectives in charge of the day-to-day running of SDG."

It was my turn to stare into space then. Acquiring the real names of every member of Ghost Squad was the unholy grail, the key to untold power. Whoever could pull that off would have more face than all the other gang bosses put together. He'd be all conquering. Deep down inside I must've known the truth of it. From the first moment Jimmy had told me about the blag, it had to be something so hugely important it'd forever change the game in the Smoke, or why else would Messima have taken such an enormous risk?

"That list is a veritable death sentence for any copper identified as Ghost Squad," I said. "So, whoever's got it mustn't have been able to put too many two and twos together, otherwise it'd be wholesale slaughter out there."

Simon looked at me, his face a blank, his voice a dry monotone, all emotion already spent. "The killings started the second week in July. Since then, five Special Duty Group undercover policemen have been killed in the most horrific and horrible of ways. No doubt as a direct warning to the other members of the Ghost Squad—an exact parallel of recent events in the East End. Scotland Yard hasn't released the real names of the dead officers and in all probability, as things stand, they won't. Each murder has been officially recorded under the name each officer assumed when on duty."

"What about the families," I asked. "Haven't they got a right to know?"

"The view from the top, by which I mean the Home Office,

is that if news of the deaths got out beyond a very small circle of people, there are those within the Metropolitan Police Force who would likely take matters into their own hands and exact immediate revenge against any number of criminals, whether they were complicit or not. In which case things could very quickly get out of hand, even lead to a complete breakdown in law and order, which in turn would mean troops on the streets. And that's something the Government simply will not countenance. I'm certain, though, no one's even remotely considered the possibility that it's someone at Scotland Yard who's secretly behind all the violence."

"So 'Monkey' Jim and the other bloke couldn't have pulled off the job at the Yard without inside help of some sort?"

"No. Impossible. They wouldn't have known what to look for, let alone where to find it. They must've had help from inside, and probably from more than one source. But as to whether the left hand knew what the right hand was doing and who on duty that night knew what crime was being committed would be difficult to prove. Policemen also close ranks in the face of any enquiry and, with over sixteen hundred officers at the Yard itself, it could be very hard to pin down. From what I understand, though, no more than a dozen very senior officers even knew of the list's existence."

I just looked at him and waited, my face now a perfect blank.

"However, accusing any officer, especially one of command rank, is fraught with difficulties. The powers-that-be are very reluctant even to begin the process, as once an official accusation has been made it can forever blight a person's reputation. So the higher up the chain someone is, the more circumspect any investigation needs to be. Mud sticks for a very long time, and, believe me, the criminal fraternity aren't above using it to besmirch a good copper's reputation and effectively ruin his future career."

I tried to feel sorry for all the police officers whose careers had been ruined, but found I didn't feel very much at all. Not when compared to all the people innocent of the charges made against them who'd ended up serving long prison sentences.

"Even I have to be careful who I talk to and what questions I ask, Jethro. Especially at the Yard. My official position is seen as being somewhat lowly, so the channels open to me are very much pre-proscribed. All of which means that any enquiries beyond my normal duties would only cause more questions to be asked. And I don't want to alert anyone unduly."

I was struck by the similarities between Scotland Yard and London's criminal underworld: two huge pyramids with everyone supposed to remain in their appointed places until such time circumstance moved them up or out or down. No, much too static a picture. It's more like two beehives all abuzz and roiling. All eyes on the centre of power. All eyes always on the 'bees and honey'. The money. The funding that made the different worlds go round.

"The one problem I see, Jethro, is that most of what you've said is hearsay and would at best be considered circumstantial in any court of law. And if as you say we are in fact dealing with the commission of a very serious crime by a very senior officer of Scotland Yard, then before any sort of official enquiry could begin we'd need to be able to supply some pretty damning testimony or irrefutable evidence in support of any such accusations."

It was time to drop the second shoe. "Don't think that I've suddenly gone Dolally, Simon," I said, "but as to the subject of irrefutable evidence, could you by any stretch of the imagination get your hands on a Webster-Chicago wire-recording machine? By which I mean as soon as possible?"

He looked at me sharply, then, his own pointed questions barely held in check. "As it happens, Jethro, we do have one or two Webcor 180s at the office in Queen Anne's Gate. A lot of Government departments have them on a trial basis, courtesy of our American cousins. Why do you ask?"

"I did wonder," I said, producing the little box containing

the wire-spool from Watts' recording machine, "because if this little thingumijig has got recorded on it what I believe it has, it's going to be all the proof you need to get the ball rolling, if not knock all the pins over in one go." It was also the exact moment I chose to lay down my one remaining trump card, the name of Ernest H. P. Watts, Deputy Assistant Commissioner ('L' Division). It wasn't perhaps as spectacular as producing a white rabbit from out of a top hat, but it did the trick: it won me the hand I'd set out to play. I held up the wire spool. "This is what Watts had on his recording machine. I substituted another one for it. I haven't listened to it, but there's a better than even chance it's the right one. If not, I'll have a ton of dried egg on my face, and I'll disappear for good and you'll never see me again. But if it does have on it what Jimmy Mooney says he heard, then you've got to give me your word you'll act on it and not just sweep it under the carpet because it's to do with some Scotland Yard VIP. Otherwise, there's no way in hell Jimmy or me are ever going to be able to live a normal life, not with an MP's murder still hanging over us both and having to deal with the very dangerous people still hunting the missing jewellery."

Simon nodded, not taking his eyes off mine for a second. "You have my word on it, Jethro," he said. "If this friend of yours is right, it's a remarkable bit of sleuthing on his part. Is this Jimmy Mooney trustworthy?"

"I'd trust him with my life, Simon," I said. "The same I do you."

There was no more beating about the bush after that. "I'll be back in thirty minutes. Make yourself comfortable. You know where everything is." And with that he roared off into the night in his handmade Bristol motorcar. It didn't quite sound like a Spitfire taking off, but it was close.

He made it back with several minutes to spare, not a hair out of place, with not one recording machine, but two. He held out both carrying cases. "Marshall Plan dollars at work," he said. "American-made goods, on account— a whole shipload of them, voltage suitably altered, all to do with getting a foothold in future European business markets."

I didn't say a word, just watched him load the wire spool and twiddle the appropriate knobs and switch on. Then he pushed the lever to "Run" and, "hey presto," it was as if Darby Messima and Watts were in the room with us.

We'd only been listening for about five minutes when he suddenly stood up and switched the thing off. I looked at him daft, suspicious that even after all he'd said it was all too damning for my ears to hear, and I'd suddenly become *persona non grata*.

I couldn't have been more wrong.

"It's all so very damning," Simon said, already setting up the second machine. "We need to make another recording, right away."

"Good idea," I said, the penny nowhere near to dropping. He set up the second machine and we sat there for a full twenty minutes, hardly daring to believe what we were hearing as the curtain was slowly pulled back not only on the outlandish scheme concocted by Messrs. Messima and Watts, but also the tragic events that'd led to the untimely death of Nigel Fox MP.

After the wire spool had run its course, we both sat in silence, lost in thought.

"How in hell's name did Darby Messima and a Deputy Assistant Commissioner at Scotland Yard come to be mixed up with one another?" I said, out loud. "I mean, it's well known there are some really bad apples at the Yard, but I can't even begin to put Messima and Watts together. Talk about an odd couple. It's obvious Watts isn't short of money, so why do it? Do you think he had any idea who he was getting into bed with?"

"Only too clearly, Jethro," he said. "The question is why?" He leaned forward and quietly dropped a couple of heavy printer's shoes right on top of my head. "Do you think you could sneak back into Watts' house tonight and return this wire spool to his desk drawer?" he asked.

"Return it? Tonight? Stroll on, Simon," I said, almost coming out of my chair. "You've got to be joking."

"I've never been more serious, Jethro," he said, leaning back and smoothing his tie. "If Watts has already discovered the spool is missing, sooner or later he's going to accuse Messima of stealing it, at which point there's no telling what would happen. Watts would come to a sudden and very sticky end, probably." He paused to let me ponder that little titbit and then really chilled me to the bone. "And while such a conclusion is not entirely without its appeal, we'd never know for sure the full extent of Watts' role in all this or how fully the Yard's been penetrated or how it all ties in to Messima, the Shadow Court, and NORTO. So, of necessity, Jethro, we must play by Walsingham's Rules."

I leaned forward, lamb to the slaughter; I couldn't help myself. "We contain it, take immediate steps to control it, but if that proves impractical, we cut away anything that might one day prove useful and destroy whatever else of it is left."

I sat back and loosened my tie—probably from relief, now I come to think of it. I knew from personal experience that's how business got done on the other side of the looking-glass. There was never any room for half measures. Yet wasn't that exactly what I'd counted on happening ever since I'd first had the idea of drawing Simon into the tangled web of terror woven by the two would-be 'Napoleons of Crime,' Messima and Watts?

"And there was me thinking I'd left all that cloak and dagger nonsense far, far behind me," I said, almost wistfully.

"That's where you're wrong," Simon, said, pointing to my North Thames Gas Board uniform. "You're wearing the cloak of subterfuge even as we speak and the dagger of mortal danger is already pointed at your throat." His face was still a blank mask. Then all of a sudden it cracked open into the very warmest of smiles. "And, no, I haven't taken leave of my senses, Jethro, or lost my regard for you. Far from it. There are few other men with whom I'd rather march into battle. As Colonel

Walsingham would say, your singular skills exactly match the present need. It'd be foolish of me not to put them to good use. And don't worry, Jethro, I'm coming with you this time."

It was as good a notice as ever I'd had. I could already see extracts from it on all the playbills. So, I thought, "Right monkey. In for a penny, in for a pound."

"All right, Simon," I said. "Let's go and burgle Mr Watts' house. Only, speaking of daggers, I have another favour to ask of you."

WHAT SIMON SAID

"I need to make a quick telephone call," Simon said. "I won't be a tick. You know where the Knockando is." He disappeared out of the room and I sat there, lost to the world for a moment, savouring the single malt's lovely nose, pleased that my measure of the man hadn't been out by a single inch but wondering what in hell Simon was conjuring up now. I didn't have to wait long to find out, and I knew by the look on his face he was already three steps ahead into whatever plan was about to be executed.

"I just called Central Clearing Office to check on the whereabouts of DAC Watts. He's listed as having caught a train to Manchester from Euston Station early this morning. He's gone to give a speech on 'A New Approach to the Civil Business of Policing' at an invitation-only Chamber of Commerce dinner at the Town Hall." Simon looked at his wristwatch, "A speech he's giving even as we speak." He paused again. "All of which means he's not at home and won't be back until tomorrow midday at the very earliest."

"How very civil of him," I said, sarcastically, "considering how much he's already done to bugger up things in London."

"One good thing, Jethro. It's unlikely Watts had either the time or the inclination to listen to the conversation again, not with a seven o'clock train to catch. So we can be pretty confident he still doesn't know it's missing."

"That still leaves his cook-cum-housekeeper, butler-cum-handyman at home ready to bar both window and door," I said.

"Hungry?" he asked, changing the subject.

"I could eat a horse," I said, trying to remember who I'd said that to in some previous lifetime.

"I think I can do a little better than that," he said. "There was a delivery from Harrods earlier today."

"Whatever would we all do without Harrods?" I said, suddenly thinking of Shanghai Lily. It's funny, the connections your mind makes sometimes. Anyway, in short order, we were sitting in Simon's dining room enjoying a cold supper of rabbit, lettuce and tomatoes, bread and cheese, washed down with a nice glass of claret, and I wondered what Joanie would do to me if I were to set up regular deliveries from Harrods instead of availing myself of the delights of the Victory Cafe. Between mouthfuls, Simon explained how he intended to get me into Watts' inner sanctum, and, unfortunately, even I had to admit there was definite method to his madness.

"It worked well for 'Monkey' Jim at Scotland Yard, you employed it yourself tonight, and we worked a similar ruse that time at BLESS House. Do you remember?"

"How could I not?" I said. "It's been 'Plan B' ever since the Greeks built wooden horses."

"As you once said to me yourself, Jethro, 'No one who's really good is ever above stealing a really good idea.'" He ushered me out into the hallway. "Here," he said, handing me a Trilby hat, "better put this on until you're in the motorcar; you can put your peaked-cap back on when we get to where we're going. You better bring the rest of your Gas Board paraphernalia with you, too." He paused for the briefest of moments and reached for something on the top of a table in the hallway. "You better have this, as well—not that I think you'll need it tonight." He handed me a beautiful, brand new, black-coated carbon steel Fairbairn-Sykes Commando knife, in a black leather sheath. "One of the many good ideas I've stolen from you. New army-issue, from a good friend in the Artists Rifles, but no less deadly for that. A gift to replace the one you said was mislaid."

I looked at him. "I didn't mean for you to give me—"

"Thus far, I've only ever used it to help change a fuse in plug, Jethro," he said, smiling. "I'm sure, in time, you'll be able to put it to better use."

Simon pointed the nose of the Bristol out towards Hammersmith and drove us to what at first glance appeared to be a small factory. High walls hid anything but the top floor of the building, but he drove straight round the back, in through some open gates, and on into a closed yard. A shadow appeared out of nowhere and the gates were shut behind us, so it seemed we'd been expected. It was then that I got a better sense of the place. It looked like a main garage or motor depot, as I could see the outlines of lorries, cars and vans of all makes, shapes and sizes, even a few single-decker buses.

Simon parked away from the building and told me to stay put. Then he got out and walked over to what looked to be the main office. As he'd explained on the drive over, it was yet another one of MI5's little set-ups, this particular hush-hush outfit specialising in the surreptitious and clandestine entry of all sorts and sizes of premises, either public or private. So I had a good idea what was coming, but it was still a bit of surprise when not five minutes later there emerged from out the depths of the garage a convoy of two medium-sized Bedford vans, one pulling a small trailer, and a small Austin 8 van, each vehicle fully liveried in the colours and insignia of the North Thames Gas Board. The little Austin 8 broke out of line and headed straight towards me. Simon flashed the headlights and drove right up to the door of the Bristol, screening me from the other two vans, and signalled me to get in. I slid from the motorcar to the van, stuck the NTGB peaked-cap on my head, and with another flash of headlights, the convoy sped off into the night.

"Supposing Watts makes enquires about the gas leak afterwards, won't he smell a rat?" I asked, as we neared Melbury Street.

Simon shook his head. "To all intents and purposes the visit will have been from the North Thames Gas Board. By tomorrow, midday, all the official paperwork will be in perfect order— from depot level all the way through to the north London head office. Time, date, incident code, number of personnel on duty, number of vehicles deployed, number of dwellings visited, inspector's 'end of incident' log. Colonel Walsingham's a stickler for such details, but then he would be. He was the one that initiated 'Special Access Group' after the war, employing much of what he'd gleaned from SOE. You met 'Keys' Cruickshank last year; he runs the whole show from down in his basement at Central Registry, motor depot and all."

"I might've known it," I said. "There's not a building the length and breadth of Great Britain that old 'Keys' couldn't get in and out of if he so desired. He was in the Special Operations Executive, too, wasn't he? Part of old Winston Churchill's plan to take the fight to the enemy? I forgot that with you lot, day is night and night is day and the desired end justifies any means." I shook my head in admiration and envy. "And all you had to do to call out the armoured cavalry was pick up the telephone and ask?"

He nodded.

"It's all right for some," I said, staring out into the night. "I could've robbed all of London blind, ten times over, if I'd had even half that mob behind me."

We got back to Simon's house a little after twelve, but neither of us was ready to call it a night, and so we sat in the drawing room—it was never the kitchen with Simon—and chatted over a hot cup of cocoa.

"Well, I thought that went rather well," he said.

"Darn sight easier than when I did it by myself. I thought

the little touch of rousing half the street with the generator and lights was masterly."

"There's always safety in numbers, Jethro. If we'd just alighted upon Watts' house, he might, as you said, have smelled a rat, as opposed to the entire neighbourhood now convinced they smelled gas. It'll be the subject of local gossip for weeks. It's marvellous what a little tampering with the gas main can achieve. A little fluctuation in pressure is all that's required, unless of course it's ever necessary to bring down a whole building."

"Charming," I said. "And they call me a hooligan. I have to say, though, the way you had your man first knock on the door and get the housekeeper and her husband all worried about a possible gas leak and then beckon us over with our torches and smoke pots and other gas snooping paraphernalia was worthy of Harry Houdini. The only thing in the world the housekeeper wanted to see at that point was more North Thames Gas Board uniforms coming to the rescue. Then the way you ushered everyone down into the basement, then the kitchen— brilliant. It gave me all the time I needed to nip upstairs and do the business. I had to pick the lock on his library door this time, but that didn't hold me up too long; it was making sure I got each wire spool back into its original box that took real concentration. Even then, when I finally did get back outside, I had to think hard whether I'd remembered to lock the door to his study on my way out. I'm sure I did though." I chuckled.

"What's so funny?" he asked.

"Rich, isn't it? I'm supposed to be dead, victim of a homicide, and if everything I've told you about this whole rotten business were taken as being my dying declarations, it could all be admitted as evidence in court. All to do, as Ray Karmin once explained to me, with the religious awe one's supposed to experience when approaching death being held equal to the sanction of an oath. All of which says to me, I'm still worth more dead than alive as far as this bloody caper is concerned."

"That's much too high a price to pay, Jethro, but it does raise the question: Will your friend, 'Monkey' Jim, be worried that you're not back before midnight?"

"No, we counted on it taking a bit of time to get things going. So he'll potter about the canal boat for the first three days, after which he'll take what he needs and return to his allotment across from Kensal Green Cemetery. If there's no word after another couple of days, he'll move on to his lock-up near Ealing Broadway. After the week's up, and if he still hasn't heard from me, he'll know he's on his own again and he'll scarper for good. I left a few things with him that could help him get out of the country."

"His life is still in danger then?"

"Very much so, as is mine, even though I'm supposed to be dead. There's still a 'notice' out on him and if not shot on sight he'd be lifted right off the street and dealt with in ways too unpleasant to contemplate."

Simon thought for a while. "Look, why don't you stay in the guest room for tonight? I need to make some more enquires in the morning, so I'll be up and out by seven. But I'll be back around lunchtime. It just so happens that we have a safe-house over near Ealing Common. It's well appointed, comfortable, in its own grounds; I can have a cook laid on. Both you and Jimmy Mooney could stay there for the immediate future, or at least until such time as we figure out how best to play this thing through. More importantly, you'd both be safe. There'd be an armed guard twenty-four hours a day. Not policemen, ex-army. What do you say?"

Having not been born yesterday, I of course said yes. I'd seen inside one of Walsingham's little homes away from home once before when he'd had Ray Karmin in what he called "protective custody." I knew I'd still have to square it away with Jimmy, though, because if he felt it was a substitute prison, he'd never agree to it. But whichever way I looked at it, it was a far better result than any I could've hoped for, a real sanctuary in the Smoke.

"I'm going to turn in, Jethro," he said. Then he paused. "Look, however disquieting I might find this dreadful business, thank you for bringing it to my attention so soon after you yourself first learned of it. You can be sure I'll apprise Colonel Walsingham of the facts at the very first opportunity. Thank you, too, for your help earlier tonight." He held out his hand.

I shook it. "Thank you for taking me seriously, Simon. There's millions out there that wouldn't have."

"More fool, they." He smiled. "I'll show you to your room."

"Er—I'll come up, see where the room is, but if you don't mind, Simon, I'd like to stay down here for a bit longer and listen to the wire recording again. There's something I'm missing that keeps niggling me and won't let go. I don't know what, but if I listen again and sleep on it, it might just help dislodge it."

"Of course. Let me set the machine up for you, but please excuse me if I don't join you. I'll no doubt be hearing the damn thing over and over again in countless meetings over the next few weeks. Just remember to rewind the spool at the end and to switch off the machine so it doesn't overheat and blow a valve. Oh, and one more thing: Should you perchance need to make any telephone calls—to your friend Raymond Karmin, or to anyone else, for that matter—use the red telephone in the study. It goes through a secure government exchange. Other than that, it's standard procedure. Local London calls you can dial yourself and if you need to make a trunk call, dial 'O' for the operator and give the number. However, there'll be no record of any calls made and you can be guaranteed no one will be listening in."

"Thanks, Simon," I said. "You must've been reading my mind."

"Oh, and help yourself to the Knockando," he added.

I was certain he'd been mind-reading, then.

REVELATIONS

I poured myself another dram of Scotland's blessed twilight wine and tried to gather my thoughts. What was it I was still missing? I stared down at the little machine on the table, its little red eye staring back into my two red-rimmed eyes. It'd been a long day bracketed by two even longer nights. I turned the switch to 'Run', but stayed standing, I suppose in a vague hope that I'd think better on my feet; but before I knew it, I found myself pacing back and forth from one end of the carpet to the other, like an animal in a cage.

The recording starts with background noise, then after about fifteen seconds or so a man clears his throat. It's Watts. He calmly states the time and date, and soon afterwards there's the sound of someone politely knocking on a door.

"Yes, come in."

"The gentleman in question, sir."

"Thank you, Fry. Show the gentleman in and then that will be all for tonight. I'll see my guest out myself, when we've finished."

"Yes, sir. Thank you, sir. I'll bid you a good night then, sir."

The door closes. There's more background noise, and then a third voice—unmistakeably that of Darby Messima—says, "A very nice place you've got here, Ernest. Been in the family long, has it?"

At first Watts can hardly contain himself. "How dare you come barging into my house like this, uninvited and unbidden. It goes well beyond the realms of all decent behaviour, if not good manners. Damn it, Messima, we agreed at the very beginning that I would be the one to contact you if ever it became necessary and that you would never under any circumstances attempt to contact me. That was our agreement. It makes this unheralded visit of yours quite unforgivable. Good God, man, I'm not some ruffian from off the streets or one if your simpering cohorts that go in fear or in thrall of you; I'm a VIP civil servant and should be afforded that courtesy even by you."

The silky voice of Darby Messima then takes Centre Stage.

Hearing it again made me shiver.

The body, it seems, keeps its own memories.

"Hold your horses, Ernest. There's no call for you to go flying off the handle like that, no call for you to treat a business colleague in such a manner. I can assure you that if needs didn't seriously must, I would never have called round like this and certainly not at this time of night. It's just that recent events make it imperative we have a little chat."

"But we have nothing whatsoever to discuss, Messima."

"Oh, but we do, Earnest. We do. There's still the little matter of the late Nigel Fox MP, the shadow of whose unfortunate and untimely death continues to fall across us all, especially now it's been officially classified as murder, and the 'Bladder,' excuse me, Scotland Yard is pulling all of London apart in a concerted effort to find the murderer and bring him to justice."

"But I wasn't responsible for Fox's death, as well you know."

"I'm not saying you were, Ernest, not saying you were."

"It was an accident. A horrible accident. Fox slipped or tripped or collapsed or had a heart attack, I don't know. What I do know is he suddenly became extremely agitated and started shouting and waving his fist at me. He got up and dashed around the dining table to confront me. And, as I said, he slipped or something, and fell and hit his head on the fireplace surround."

"Yes, that's very well put, Ernest, very well put. I'm sure it could've happened just like that. As I'm also sure that given the appropriate inducements, any jury of twelve just men would conclude that that is indeed what occurred that dreadful night."

"But why would you even suggest that anyone would need convincing otherwise, Messima? It's the truth, I tell you. You were there, you saw it."

"Ah, but I didn't actually see what happened, did I, Ernest? I'd excused myself to go visit the lavatory and was out the room when whatever occurred, occurred. I did hear the commotion and rushed back into the room as soon as was decently possible. When, as you said, there he was on the floor by the fireplace, as dead as a proverbial doornail. I mean, what could I say? I just took your word for it, didn't I? I'm sure you didn't mean to kill him. I'm sure it was an awful accident, just like you said."

"But it was an accident. The man just wouldn't listen to reason. The more I tried to explain my radical new approach towards curbing crime in London, the more agitated he became. When you left the room he went off like a Roman candle and started yelling at me. Accusing me of tricking him into attending the meeting and aghast that of all people it was you that'd turned out to be the surprise dinner guest. He got more and more angry about it all. Said he absolutely refused to even consider such an outlandish scheme. I tried to tell him that it would achieve all the things he himself had been fighting for—and in the shortest possible time—but bloody fool of a man that he was, he just wouldn't listen. And then there he was, suddenly, dead on the floor."

"Ah, but there's the rub, Ernest: truth doesn't always carry the day—not down the Old Bailey, nor anywhere else— especially when death in strange circumstances is concerned. The law proves to be very fickle then, as many unfortunates have found out to their cost. That's why it's always best to avoid the full panoply of the law when seeking justice. It's far better to use more direct and more reliable means, much in the manner that you yourself proposed when you and me first met. Do you remember what you said? I wrote it down, afterwards, so

I wouldn't forget. Got it on a piece of paper in my wallet. Hold on, I'll quote you."

Messima clears his throat and reads aloud. "'Society can never fully eradicate crime, so it behoves the powers that be to adopt whatever methods may be necessary to reduce incidents of crime to more acceptable levels.' After which you added, 'After all, isn't that all we ask of any police force, to reduce the incidents of crime?' A clever point, that, Ernest, but to press it home all the more you even quoted the mission of Scotland Yard itself, which I had someone look up afterwards."

Messima clears his throat and reads aloud again. "'The primary object of an efficient police is the prevention of crime;the detection and punishment of offenders who have committed crime is secondary.' That's the ticket, but you didn't stop there, did you? Oh no, because then came the real kicker. 'And, if the end is lawful, does that not also justify the means? In which case, who better to police the criminals, than the criminals themselves?' It's all marvellous stuff, Ernest, marvellous. Only then you delivered your absolute knockout punch, didn't you? 'It's a far better idea,' you said, 'to set a thief to police a thief, than to have a policeman pretend to be crook.' The words of a true visionary. Very Churchillian, in my humble opinion."

This time it's Watts who clears his throat before he speaks, his voice all but cracking from suppressed emotion. "If it's so visionary, why in heaven's name hasn't anyone else seen the wisdom of it? Tell me that."

There's another long pause, then from out the void comes Messima's oily voice, a mere whisper, but full of understanding, and all consoling. "What is it they say, Ernest? That a prophet is never recognised in his own land."

It's plain Watts pretty much despises Messima, and yet here he is, in his inner sanctum, alone with the self-styled Emperor of Soho, the one man in all London that's not only acknowledged his radical new vision for dealing with crime, but who's also helped put it into practice. And as Messima's gift of the gab works its silken magic, Watts' whole demeanour changes, his animosity evaporates. You hear it happening in the silence.

After what seems an age, Messima speaks again, the very voice of reason and reasonability. "Please understand, Ernest, the only reason I'm here is to ensure you haven't changed your mind about your vision, what with Fox's death having been officially classified as murder. I simply need your assurance that you're not losing your bottle, because if you were, like, that could prove very unfortunate, even life changing. I need to know you're going to keep your nerve and keep on sending me them little titbits of news about what the Yard's up to so that I can duck and dive and dodge and weave with the best of them, and keep any and all aggravation down to an absolute minimum. That's all, Ernest. No one outside this room need ever know about what really happened that night."

There's another long pause. This time, the voice is reminiscent of a man gentling a horse. "I promised you I'd take care of it all, clean up the mess, smooth things over, and I have done. I've been as good as my word, making sure that you and me are kept well out of it, and that any loose ends get well tied off. There's no record of us ever having been at the private room in the restaurant. As it just so happens I own the place. I also have the personal diary that he always carried on his person. I even have the invitation card you sent; it was still on a table in his hallway. And anyone that leant a hand that night, let's just say, they've been encouraged to take a very long holiday. There's no one now that can place you and me and Fox together that night, or any other night for that matter. You're in the clear, Ernest. And there's nothing you need worry yourself about now, other than how best to help NORTO succeed."

I wondered what Messima would've said or done at that point had he known that everything he was saying was being recorded. Watts wasn't about to tell him; that was for sure. He was a bit fly himself, was Watts, but then you needed to be if you were dealing with Darby Messima and had any hope of coming away with all your fingers and limbs still intact.

"Yes, thank you, Darby. For all you've done. And you have his diary, too. How very thoughtful. How very thorough of you. This incident with Fox has been so...so very distressing."

There's more, of course, mostly Messima extracting what he needs from Watts now that his bitter pill of blackmail has been successfully sugar coated and swallowed. He tells Watts that they must stick to their guns, regardless of what occurs at Scotland Yard or what gets reported in the newspapers. Messima's also very clear about the need for continued secret trials and public punishments. Messima, ever the keen student of Napoleon Bonaparte, likens it to the time of "the Terror" during the French Revolution. "It's nothing more than a temporary, but very necessary, clearing out of all the wrong elements, for the good of all." But what chills the most is when Messima touches upon the Ghost Squad officers that NORTO has been able to identify. "I'd only intended of course that each of the sods be given a good smacking. Off the force for a year or so, no one permanently crippled, just something they'd remember for life. Unfortunately, accidents do happen. But however tragic their deaths and all the others may have been, it's not been for nought. It went a long way in helping establish the authority of NORTO. People round the Smoke have really sat up and taken notice, for once." He pauses, briefly, before he delivers his coup de grace. "But that's life, isn't it, Ernest? You can't have a plate of scrambled without first cracking a few eggs."

I reached down and stopped the wire in the machine. It'd been staring me in the face the whole time. I'd always thought the reason Messima had put a price on "Monkey" Jim's head, then kept redoubling it, was because he wanted to get his hands on the missing Meridian Mansions jewellery—and there had to be some truth in that—but what I now realised was that Jimmy Mooney was the one missing link in the chain that could place Messima's mob at the Mansions the night of Nigel Fox's death.

And if anything in life was certain, it was that Messima always made dead sure he was at least twice removed from any and all mayhem or carnage conjured up in his name. Plausible deniability was the be-all and end-all of the law as far as he and his brief were concerned. All those snippets I'd heard about Messima's regular driver and one or two of his usual minders having gone missing were now all pieces that fit into the puzzle.

Messima had to ensure that "Monkey" Jim was silenced forever or the whole bloody house of cards could come tumbling down and him with it. He and Ernest H. P. Watts, Deputy Assistant Commissioner (Legal), were a right pair. The two of them, busy cloaking their words in feigned friendship, pointing a dagger at each other's throat with one hand, while holding a loaded gun at London's heart with the other.

A SACK OF POTATOES, FALLING

It was well-gone half-past lunchtime when Simon returned home and, as I was to learn, he'd spent most of the morning wearing his civil servant's hat rather than his copper's helmet. Once he'd divested himself of his bowler, umbrella, and various sets of keys, he produced a well-thumbed buff-coloured file from out the folds of his black leather briefcase and waved it at me as if it was a winning ticket at the Derby. "Sorry I'm late," he said. "I'll fix us a bite to eat first, then we can we talk." And sure enough, within minutes we were both munching away happily on cheese and pickle sandwiches, washed down with ginger beer.

"I needed this," I said.

"We both did," he said. "This is all very taxing." He pointed to the buff folder lying on the table. "I had to go a good deal round the houses to get hold of that," he said between mouthfuls. "It's not the full report, not even the full autopsy—it's the Home Office briefing paper. It makes for interesting reading, nevertheless. I also managed to acquire a full set of police photographs."

He handed me the file on Nigel Fox MP, deceased.

Home Office ministers and under-secretaries of State being a busy lot, the report was brief, to the point, and dryer than toast—the dead man's life and death reduced to a series of short, pithy typescript paragraphs under suitably cryptic headings. It gave his family background, his education, war service, a list of his clubs, which was all to be expected, but it also touched upon his medical history, his personal finances, even his marriage. There was a section marked 'Confidential Record'—complied by MI5, no doubt —on his political affiliations at university, as well as the results of his later positive vetting as an MP and his subsequent security clearances. Next came highlights of his Parliamentary career, the issues he'd sought to champion, and a quick rundown of his major speeches, with footnotes as to the relevant dates and issue numbers of *Hansard* should any reader be disposed to delve deeper. Following that was a copy of the police report detailing the incident when Fox had been attacked and robbed in the street after attending a late-night session at the House. Appended to this was a series of graphs and tables, courtesy of the Met's very own Statistics Branch, showing the extent and nature of violent crimes, up to and including murder, committed in the capital since the end of the war. The single incident that'd precipitated Fox's crusade against the rising wave of crime helpfully marked in red ink.

The report got down to brass tacks with a timeline of known events of the dead man's last day and the latest thinking on the question initially at the back of everyone's mind: "Was the murder in any way politically motivated?"

The most telling fact, of course, was that Fox had been dead for at least two to three hours before his body had impacted with terra firma some eighty feet below the balcony of his flat. That alone had given sufficient grounds for the case to be reclassified as one of murder. The report then concluded with brief summaries on the key findings of the two pathologists and analysis of all bloodstains and fingerprints found at the murder scene.

It was the police photographs, though, that really caught my attention, despite the ever-present police detective or constable dutifully standing in the frame to give scale. The first set showed the interior of Fox's apartment: the hallway, living room, dining room, kitchen, bedrooms, study, balcony etc., with additional close-ups of whatever was deemed to be of particular interest. Bloodstains mostly. A second set showed the door to the flat, the corridor outside, the door of the lift that served both apartments and the push-door that opened onto the service stairwell cum fire escape. The rest comprised exterior shots of the front, sides and rear of the building at full elevation and ground level, shots of the ramps leading down to the underground garage and the service yard, plus various close-ups of the landscaped area at the front of the building where Fox's body had been found.

"I suppose Messima had hoped a fall onto concrete from that height would've more than put paid to the issue," I said, finishing off my cheese sandwich. "I don't suppose he or any of his goons had ever given Meridian Mansions as much as a second glance before that night."

"I very much doubt it," Simon said. "Otherwise they would've done their damndest to ensure the body fell onto the concrete apron and not the privet hedging that rims the building. As it was, it was sheer luck it helped cushion the body from the full impact of the fall. All the same, what strikes me is that both pathologists were alerted to the likelihood of foul play by the simple fact there was little or no bleeding from any of the many scratches inflicted on Fox's hands and face when his body got entangled in the bushes." He shook his head at the serendipity of it all, swirled the ginger beer round and around in his glass, and downed it in one.

Having eyes as sharp as scalpels wasn't the half of it: it was a bloody wonder what the two pathologists had been able to determine from their examinations of Fox's body. Even though the skull exhibited a large round fracture, they'd each concluded separately that Fox had died as a result of an earlier blow to the head occasioned some hours before the body's fall from the balcony; maybe as few as two hours, but certainly no more than five or six. They'd both also looked very closely at where the skin had or hadn't discoloured or gone all purplish and where and to what extent the blood had pooled and congealed inside the body. From their observations they'd not only been able to establish the approximate time of death. They'd also been able to determine conclusively that the body had been moved post-mortem. What the two of them hadn't been able to agree on was the extent to which the dead body had been manhandled. The first pathologist was of the opinion Fox had died in the flat, probably in the kitchen, and that his body had then been moved from there to the balcony and thence pushed over the side. The second pathologist, however, was of the opinion Fox had died elsewhere and that his body had been transported to the flat, where it'd been moved from room to room, tampered with even further—by which he meant it'd been subjected to even more trauma—before being dropped from seven floors up.

Simon produced another bottle of ginger beer, as if from out of thin air, and topped up both our glasses. "For someone that revels in so much bloodletting," he said, reflectively, "I find it ironic it was a simple question of lividity that put paid to all of Messima's attempts to muddy the water."

I almost said, "He'd be dead livid with himself if he knew," but I let it pass. "Queering the pitch is as mother's milk to Messima," I said. "He'll throw out a bucket of red herrings, put up a smoke-screen, anything that'll help confuse the issue, cover his tracks, or help put a shine on his alibi."

Simon nodded. "Messima no doubt counting on the fact that Scotland Yard would be under such immense pressure to resolve the case, they'd follow whichever line of evidence offered the least resistance. What a remarkably cold and calculating bastard he is."

"He's been called a lot worse," I said. I tapped the pile of photographs. "Thing is, none of his usual disposal methods would've worked this time; he couldn't just drop Fox's body in the river or chop it into pieces and bury it over Hackney Marshes way. Even the Emperor Messima would've known there'd be far too many questions asked following the sudden disappearance of an MP. No, the safest course of action was to try and make it look like Fox had never left Meridian Mansions."

I spread the photographs out on the mahogany dining room table. "They must've used a van to transport the body, rather than one of Messima's motorcars," I said. Then a thought struck me. "Come to think of it, Jimmy did say he saw an ambulance pass as he was being driven from the Mansions." (I didn't think it proper to mention it was me that'd seen it; it'd only complicate things unnecessarily.) "There's dozens of war surplus ambulances around town, converted into fish and chip vans, ice cream vans, you name it. Even hearses. It might've even been a proper ambulance; Messima's certainly got enough pull to get hold of one, but given what was said in the pathology reports about "cold shortening" and all the rest of it, my money's on an ice cream van or a meat lorry, anything that'd help keep the body cold."

Simon nodded. "The muscle shrinkage and hardening of the flesh mentioned in both reports would certainly seem to support that."

"I think we can also take it they had dinner in Soho. Messima's got a whole string of clubs and restaurants in the Quarter, and he could've arranged a discreet little private backroom somewhere with a snap of his fingers and just as easily arranged for the body to be carted off afterwards. It would've been easy for them to wrap the body up in a tablecloth, a carpet, or a tarp or something, then pack it round with ice or keep it in a cold store until such time as they could move it." I pointed to a photograph showing the façade of Meridian Mansions, then at another showing the hidden ramp leading down to the rear service yard. "They couldn't risk taking the body in through the main entrance as, day or night, there's always someone on duty at the front desk, and that's not even counting the building manager who lives in a small flat off the lobby. The only sure way in would've been down one of the side ramps, round the back, and up the rear service stairs. It explains why it was so urgent they get hold of 'Monkey' Jim." I pointed to the likely sequence of events. "He climbed up here, got in through a window there, unlocked the front door to the flat, and left it open. Then he wedges open the push-door to the service-stairs, nips down all the way to the bottom, and 'Bob's yer uncle.' He pushes the door open and is met by God knows who, whereupon he's immediately blindfold so he can't recognise anyone and bundled back up the ramp into a waiting motorcar and whisked away into the night."

Simon nodded again. "Meanwhile, Messima has all the time he needs to work on the finer points. The two glasses, the open bottles of wine, the two different brands of cigarette-ends in the ashtray, the table set for two, the food on the plates to match the contents later found in Fox's stomach. Everything, a horribly distorted mirror of the events that'd occurred earlier that evening. And all of it designed to suggest that Fox had had a late-night visitor that he himself had smuggled in up the back stairs."

"Not to mention the whole sordid question of whether it was a man or a woman he'd had up there and whether his death was a result of a lover's tiff or a violent argument that later drove him to bash out a suicide note on his typewriter and then top himself out of remorse."

I found myself thinking of the days following Fox's death, when the police had requested that anyone who'd been in the vicinity at the time should come forward. Soon after which, they'd produced the curly-haired bloke on the 'HAVE YOU SEEN THIS MAN?' poster that may or may not have been me. Only it wasn't me, was it, because they'd been after the 'queer basher' who they thought had bashed Fox's head in, staged the suicide note, and thrown his body from the balcony. Another penny dropped then. The police of course would've seen the missing jewellery as the perfect motive for murder. Not that Messima or any of his goons knew about any missing jewellery when they messed up the place; they'd just wanted to stage the scene for the police. I shook my head to clear it of shadows.

"I think you're right, Jethro. It explains the blood in the kitchen, in the bedroom, and on the balcony rail—not to mention the red wine spilled on the dining table and all over the floor, as well as the smashed picture frames strewn everywhere."

"And all of it stage-managed no doubt by Messima's two hard-men, Messrs. Tweedledum and Tweedledee, not that either of them would've been the ones to carry Fox's body up seven flights of stairs. They would've had a heart attack, though, when they found it was all central heating and there was no mantelpiece or fireplace handy for them to re-enact the accident that'd killed Fox. That's probably why the place ended up looking such a bloody mess: they were irritated at having to think for themselves. Though, as dim as they undoubtedly are, I wouldn't put it past either of them to slice open their own arms with a razor so they could scatter drops of fresh blood around the place. Even if what they're rumoured to have done for Messima in the past is only half true, having to put up with a few stitches and a bandaged arm for a week would be a walk in the park for those two."

"And but for science, they very well might've succeeded. Have you had enough, Jethro?"

Had I had enough? Too bloody right. I'd been to hell and back. Jimmy, too. And then it happened, just as it does sometimes when I'm creeping—time seemed to slow down and all but come to a stop and all I could see in my mind's eye was Nigel Fox MP falling to earth like a sack of potatoes just like that time, back in the Bridge Cafe, when I'd first read about events at Meridian Mansions in the midday copies of *The Star*, *News*, and *Standard*. God knows how many people had died since then and for what?

"Jethro?"

"Er, yes, thanks, Simon, lovely grub, went down a treat. As for all this— reading all the details, seeing the photographs—

there's almost too much of it to swallow. A lot of food for thought, that's for sure."

"Yes," he said. "I've been thinking long and hard myself since last night. I'm pretty sure I know how Watts and Messima crossed one another's paths. Watts is Deputy Assistant Commissioner Legal, and Department 'L' deals mainly with civil business and legal matters. It's responsible for a multiplicity of statutes, statutory regulations and byelaws, and is concerned more with matters of 'nuisance' and 'disorder' than crime, *per se*. To put it into context, there are four other departments besides 'L' that make up Scotland Yard: Departments 'A', 'B', and 'C', and The Receiver's Office. 'A' is in charge of administration and discipline, 'B' in charge of anything and everything to do with traffic and public carriage. 'C' deals exclusively with crime and comprises the C.I.D. at the Yard, the Fingerprint Bureau, the Criminal Record Office, Special Branch, as well as all the C.I.D. officers that serve the twenty-three London Area Divisions that make up the Metropolitan Police District, not counting the three Dockyard Divisions and the River Police. It's 'C' who are the real thief-takers and who deal with Messima and his ilk on a daily basis. They're the ones the public immediately think of whenever Scotland Yard gets mentioned. It's 'C' in the form of the Flying Squad, the Murder Squad, the Ghost Squad that bags all the headlines."

"I can't say I've ever given the rest of the Met a moment's thought," I said. "Like any bureaucracy or government office the world over, they're all but invisible to outsiders."

"Invisible and unsung. No guts, no glory. The good people of Department 'L' don't even warrant a standard-issue truncheon; let alone a police whistle. For them, it's all rubber stamps, fountain pens, and forms in triplicate. 'L' is responsible for the distribution of betting and gaming licenses, the granting of liquor licenses, club licenses, and firearm licenses—all issues very close to Messima's heart. What's even more significant is that 'L' also deals with all matters to do with alien registration and deportation, which means that Watts' office would've been directly involved in the whole kerfuffle over the deportation of Messima's brother. Watts is more civil servant than police officer, and even though he's DAC- 'L', he also holds the civil service rank of Assistant Secretary. There are a dozen different ways Messima's name could've crossed his desk. And as we heard on the wire recording, it was Watts who first approached Messima. It was Watts who first dreamt up the whole lunatic scheme to control crime in the capital."

"And so the stage was set. Enter Ernest Watts—Stage Right—offering up all of London on a silver salver. Enter Darby Messima—Stage Left—a knife in one hand, a razor in the other, eager to carve out a larger empire for himself."

"Each one with something the other desperately craved: Watts, the keys to Scotland Yard, and Messima, the keys to the London underworld."

"That explains how and why they met," I said, "but what in hell compelled Watts to come up with such a mad idea in the first place? It's not as if he's hard up for money. What did he have to gain by it all?"

"I have no idea, Jethro. I can only assume Watts convinced himself that the end justified the means and that whatever the cost it would ultimately be to the benefit of all. I assure you we'll get to the bottom of it when we do finally interrogate him. As I said, though, we first have to assess the extent of the damage, then put together a watertight case that will stand up in court."

I took my leave soon afterwards. We'd done with all the thinking; it was action that was called for now. Simon had to start putting wheels into motion, and do it all on the QT, the grinding gears of justice in matters *sub rosa* moving even more mysteriously than anything adjudged by the Law Lords. Me, I had to get back to "Monkey" Jim, hopefully still waiting for me aboard the good ship *Phoenix*. I needed to bring him up to date on all that'd happened and then get him and me squared away at the safe house. After which I had to try and get things sorted out in the big bad Smoke, once and for all, as all this 'shadow only ever able to move by night' malarkey was getting very old.

I made my way towards the front door, but Simon stopped me in the hallway. "Here," he said. "You better put this hat on again. No reason to take any unnecessary chances of someone recognising you."

"Thanks," I said, turning to go, but I stopped again, on the threshold, struck by a sudden thought. "Excuse me for asking, Simon, but what does Colonel Walsingham think about all this?"

"He's in Washington, DC, at the moment, Jethro, in talks with his counterpart at the FBI on matters of long standing. I sent him a coded telex about everything this morning and hope to be talking to him on the trans-Atlantic telephone link this evening."

"Just asking," I said. "Only considering what we're up against—not knowing who to trust and such, even at the Yard— it'd be very good if he could pull some strings. Doesn't he know the Commissioner personally?"

"That, he does. He knows a lot of people, both highborn and low."

"Present company included, I suppose," I said.

Simon smiled, but then his face clouded. "It was from Colonel Walsingham that I first learned you were dead. He heard about it from one of his many secret sources."

"DCI Browno, probably. He's got his nose in everywhere, that one."

"No, Detective Chief Inspector Browno heard of your death the same moment I did. I will say this, though: Colonel Walsingham will be delighted when he finds out you're still alive and kicking."

"You can say that again," I said, knowing full well DCI Browno wouldn't have given a toss either way.

WHEELS TURNING WITHIN

I drove the little three-wheeler back up towards Sudbury, but I can't remember too much about the journey, which says it must've been pretty uneventful—a nice change, for once. I parked by Wembley Cemetery again and walked down to the small parade of shops, this side of Pooley Bridge, where I bought some milk, a loaf of bread, and a late afternoon edition of the *Evening Standard*. One of the headlines near the bottom of the front page immediately caught my eye. 'GANGSTER'S HEADLESS CORPSE DRAGGED FROM THAMES.' I skimmed my eyes over the piece. No names as yet, and not much else to report other than the deceased was thought to have been a man in his mid-twenties and of slight build. The fact that whoever had done the deed had left both hands on the body said they didn't care if in due time the authorities found out the bloke's real identity—the severed head was the real message, the soundless spread of terror and fear. Villain or Ghost Squad member, I pitied the poor sod, whoever he'd been.

The light had begun to flatten and fade and the shadows begin to linger longer as I walked the last furlong or so along the towpath. I could tell Jimmy was aboard from the tiny wisps of smoke coming from the chimney and the fact that his little motorbike was obviously still under the tarpaulin cover. It all looked nice and normal. I began to whistle a little tune he and I used to use as a signal way back before the War. A few bars was all it took for the tarp to move and Jimmy to pop his head out, a grin on his face, a gun in his hand. He also had the pair of binoculars hanging from his neck. In truth, I hadn't twigged that he'd been under there, but I didn't let on.

"Hello, Jeffro, good to see back. Excuse the welcome, only I didn't recognise the titfer."

It was only then I realised I had on the hat Simon had lent me. The NTGB peaked cap was probably still on the floor of his Bristol; shows just how much I'd had on my mind.

Jimmy let the Browning dangle down by his side. "The thing's not even loaded," he said. "I took the bullets out first, just like you showed me, so I wouldn't blow me bleedin' toes off. Still, if it hadn't been you on the path, the other bloke wouldn't have known that, would he?"

"Let's go murder a cup of tea instead," I said. "Only, I've got a lot to tell you."

So while downing enough tea to sink a battleship and keeping myself buoyed up with lashings of bread and jam, I spent the next half-hour telling Jimmy all that'd happened. Suitably edited, of course, it was enough for him to know buttons had been pushed, wheels had started to turn, and that in time strings would be pulled. He, of course, still put it all down to "Buggy" Billy, and there was no good reason to disavow him of the fact.

Give him his due. He just sat there in silence, taking it all in, nodding or shaking his head as need be, not saying a single word until I'd finished. "So as you can see, Jimmy," I said, "it's no bloody wonder Messima was after you. You're probably the only one left alive outside of the 'Tweedles' who could link him with Fox at Meridian Mansions and Watts at the Yard. And as the 'Tweedles' are still both alive and kicking, I can only think they must have something big on Messima tucked away in a strong box somewhere that'd bring him and his whole evil empire down if he ever had the two of them topped. At that level of villainy, it's only prudent to have some high-priced solicitor standing by ready to send whatever damning evidence it is off to the Sunday linens if he doesn't receive your pre-arranged weekly telephone call." He nodded. And I changed the subject. "Now about this safe-house business."

Jimmy took to his new digs like a duck to water. "This is a bit of all right," he said after his first look around. "The high walls, especially. Nice and private, help keep all the riff-raff out." Even I laughed at that. You could almost see all the worries and fears he'd been carrying lift from off his shoulders. The keepers, as Simon called them, were military men all, even the cook, but they didn't act at all like guards or jailers—more like minders. For a start, they gave us both a set of keys so that we could come and go as we pleased and left us to our own devices mostly or joined in a game of table tennis or gin rummy or whatever else it was took our fancy. They even filled up the tank of the little Bantam so either one of us could pop out if we wished and added a book of petrol coupons and a pass that said the rider was travelling on official business.

To my knowledge, Jimmy never once sallied forth during those all-too-brief weeks he and I spent at the big house just off Ealing Common. Even with the cage door open and with me gone many a night and day, he preferred to stay snug in his room or cooped up with a book. "I'm sleeping like a bloody log, I am, too. Even better than when I was with you on the old narrow boat," he told me. "I never even friggin' dreamed how scared stiff I was, deep down. Sometimes I had barely enough bottle left to take the next breath, let alone the next friggin' step. I was a dead duck just waiting for the chop; it was only a matter of time before I was a bleedin' gonner. Then up you popped out of nowhere, back in the cemetery, and now here I am, an ex-jailbird, as happy as a lark in a gilded cage."

The new arrangement suited me down to the ground, too. I even had use of a private telephone, though I never once used it. I preferred the call box on the other side of the Common, the corner of Elm Avenue, near the church— a mere five-minute stroll, but a whole world away.

As knackered as I'd been that night I stayed at Simon's house, I'd made a dozen or more telephone calls trying to get word to Tommy Nutkins before I'd finally packed it in and gone off up to bed. The early hours of the morning are the best time to catch some people. Even so, I knew it was a long shot I'd actually get him. I tried spielers, gambling clubs, nightclubs—all the places Jack Spot still had a hand in, now that his St Botolph's Club had been forced to close—but the answer was always the same.

"No, Tommy's not been in. Any message?"

And I'd mutter, "Just tell him his old mate from Manchester, Charley Marley, called."

I'd left the same message at various gymnasiums, slot machine arcades, billiard-halls, and private drinking clubs the next morning. All Tommy had to do was walk in somewhere and be given one of the messages; all I had to do was take another late-night walk before bedtime.

I stood inside the telephone-box on the edge of the Common and watched the second-hand on my wristwatch sweep round to join the hour and minute hands in a moment of prayer. It was almost midnight. It was cold, and I had to think for a second before I could recall the sequence of numbers. Daft, I know, as I'd used them many times over the years, as had Tommy. And I pictured him waiting in a nice, warm telephone kiosk; one of the dozen wooden kiosks to the left of the big double doors inside the all-night Post Office, just off Trafalgar Square. He'd have a gloved finger pressed down on the hook and the telephone already pressed to his ear. Just waiting.

I tried to think how long it was since he'd disembarked the *Phoenix* and slipped over to Paddington Station. It felt like years, and yet it'd only been a matter of days.

I tell you, time can be a right bugger, sometimes, the games it plays with your head.

I picked up the receiver, got the familiar 'burring' sound, dropped two pennies into the slot, and dialled WHI-7601, the number of the first of the twelve telephone kiosks that made up the Disciples. The intermittent buzz I heard in my ear meant the number was engaged; as, too, were Whitehall 7602, 7603 and 7604. It was obviously a busy night out there in the Smoke. I tried the number of the kiosk next in line, heard it ringing, then I heard a voice say, "T for Tommy in trap number '5'." I pressed button 'A'. "Hello, Tommy," I said. "Thanks for coming out on such a bloody cold night."

"Gezundheit!" he said. "Good to know you're still alive and kicking; only I had been wondering. How's tricks, out there, in the big bad world?"

"Progressing nicely," I said. "Even better than I could've wished for."

"Well, if it's wishes you're after, cop a load of this. I've found the bleeder that all but did for you in the river, haven't I? Seems there's this pub he's known to frequent certain nights of the week."

"You'll be starring with Sabu in *The Thief of Bagdad* next."

"I'm not shaving my head for nobody, but I have got the old Co-op van standing by all ready to go. All we've got to do is pick a night and wait for the bastard to show. I could pick you up tomorrow, if you like. Just give me a time and place. I could do with a good night out."

I had a quick think. "Cleopatra's Needle," I said, and gave him a half-hour spread. "Thanks, Tommy. You're a brick."

"Got one of those an' all," he said. "All the better to bash the fucker's head in with, pardon my French."

I had to laugh. First, a plumber's van. Then a North Thames Gas Board lorry. And now a Co-operative Society van. I wondered where in hell I'd be without the wheels of commerce to carry me forward.

TWO EYES FOR AN EYE

I could pick out the silhouette of the bloke from up against a soot-blackened wall if I had to, so often had I seen it in my nightmares. Height, build, his way of moving was all but etched on the inside of my eyelids. I waited, hardly daring to breathe, as still as any cat had been since the dawn of time readying to pounce on a rat. And a fleeting shadow on a shadow, in the cold, grey, flat light of late afternoon—a dark streak of something barely seen out the corner of his eye—I erupted from my hiding place and hit him hard and fast with a weighted leather cosh, twice behind the ear, and down he went like a ton of pig iron.

Lights out. Fuses blown.

Very next thing—though in truth Tommy and me had to expend a good deal of effort arranging it—it was him that was gagged and bound to the selfsame wooden pier support I'd once been lashed to. Only this time there was no old Father Thames lapping hungrily at the foot of the wharf ready to embrace and devour him, there was only the green slime-slicked forest of wooden piles and rusted metal stanchions that'd soon stand sentry to his watery tomb. Difference being, I wanted him to have sufficient time to contemplate his past misdeeds before he drowned a cold and very miserable death. Fair's fair. Two eyes for an eye—and two arms, two legs and a head as well while you're at it.

It was well known the river could smell especially bad at that part of the tideway, but the pong was so bloody awful that even with a handkerchief tied over my nose, bandit-style, I badly wanted to throw up. Tommy, too, by the disgusting grunting noises he was making.

"I'll be glad when I've had enough of this," I'd said to myself, over and over, as we'd trudged across the stinking mud, wary we might be spotted at any moment. But now with the bloke at last fully secured to the pier support, I unstopped the bottle of smelling salts I'd had safe in my pocket and wafted them, to-and-fro, under the nose of my very soon to be ex-would-be executioner.

The coughing and retching of the condemned man returning to consciousness began right on cue. And as I waited for the effects of the smelling salts to subside, I nodded to Tommy and he retreated back across the mud and up the old stairs back to street level. Not so much out of respect for the soon-to-be departed, but to have a quiet smoke and to keep a lookout on anyone that might be loitering outside The Town of Ramsgate public house, or the Red Cow, as it was still known to anyone with half-a-memory. I turned and looked at my catch of the day, all nicely trussed up and ready for the gutting. And my catch stared back at me from out of the grim dark ominous gloom beneath the pier, his disbelieving eyes as glassy and as black as obsidian. I tell you, it's quite amazing how expressive the old mince pies can be sometimes. You can tell so much from so little: alarm, confusion, fear, entreaty, begging, even anger and defiance.

"Good afternoon," I said, evenly. "Just wanted to inform you it's not the Shadow Court that's done for you; it's me that's your judge, jury, and executioner." I removed some bits of disguise and leaned in so he could get a better look. "Remember me, do you, you bastard? The bloke you were supposed to do away with? Well I'm back from the dead and what you should've known about me, sunshine, is that no man ever gets a second chance to top me." I righted the wool cap on my head and for tidiness' sake adjusted the gag around his mouth and pulled it even tighter. "It should help keep the water out, at first. After that it's hard to say whether you'll drown or simply suffocate. Should be an interesting experience though, either way. But afraid I can't linger, must be off."

I turned to go and as I did, there was a small explosion of muffled expletives from behind me.

I just walked away, across the expanse of river mud. But the racket only seemed to increase. I stopped and turned round. Even then, I had to stare hard to see him, as from ten feet away he was barely visible even to me. I cupped an ear.

"You talking to me?" I said.

A sound drifted across from somewhere deep in the forest of tarred and blackened wooden pilings.

"'Cos as far as I'm concerned you're already a dead man," I said without rancour and turned to go again. This time the clamour increased with each step I took. I shook my head resignedly and turned and slopped back over the mud towards the jetty and became one again with the shadowy netherworld.

"So what is it you want to say that's so important?" His eyes blinked out a non-stop S.O.S. "This better be good," I said, prying the gag from his mouth with a gloved finger. "I'd hate to think you'd wasted any more of my time." And I stood there ready to stuff the gag back in if he started screaming and hollering, but he didn't; he just draw in lung-full after lung-full of foul-smelling river air, and very sensible of him, too, considering. I have to admit though even I was finding it very hard not to cough at all the stench of things already rotting in the river. I glared at him. "Speak now or forever hold your fucking peace."

He coughed and retched and shook his head. "What was in your jacket pocket when they found you?" he said, his voice raspy but oddly unwavering.

I looked him straight and could see from the dull-whites of his eyes he was staring back at me. "Tell you," he said, "a penny-piece in a twist of oilcloth; penny with a big scratch across the King's head." He waited for the navigation lights to blink on.

But they didn't. In truth, I didn't know what the hell he was babbling on about.

"Well, you blew that chance, sunshine," I said, disgustedly. "A bleedin' penny for my thoughts, after all the bloody nonsense that's gone on? I should cocoa." I began to stuff the gag back in his mouth, but he shook head from side to side.

"It was a sign…only thing I could think of…was being watched…I'm …"

But I'd lost all interest in his ravings. A dank bitter cold wind was blowing up from beyond Gravesend, trying to outrun the incoming tide, and I didn't want it to warm my heart any. "Good riddance to bad rubbish," I said. "The river can fucking have you."

The gag went in hard and fast then, and I left him there lashed to the same jetty support I'd been roped to, never once looking back.

But that's me all over. I hate drawn-out goodbyes.

The London Docks were on a scale all their own. And what with the never-ending tide of dockers, going on or coming off shift, as well as wave upon wave of seamen newly arrived from ports the world over, it was impossible for anyone to know everyone; the endless sea of faces was just too vast, too ever-changing. Not that Tommy or me were too worried about being spotted. Bundled up as we both were, even our own mothers wouldn't have recognised us. We'd wiped the mud off our clothes as best we could, but stains are badges of office for anyone that works the river and uniforms are ever a boon to invisibility. In my case, add a putty nose, beard, woollen watch cap pulled over fair hair still dyed black, and I was well lost in the crowd.

"Killing a man's always thirsty work," I said. "Or so I've been told."

Tommy raised his eyebrows as he handed me a Scotch and chaser, then changed the subject. "Good to be in here. The wind coming up off the river was enough to strip the barnacles from off the belly of a tugboat."

"Needed this," I said. "Cheers to a good day's work done. Tying up a loose end like that really makes me feel I'm starting to get somewhere at last. " I took a long sip of Scotch and a longer swig of beer. "Stupid sod had a chance to appeal to my better nature and instead went on about him stuffing pennies into pockets. He'd obviously already gone round the bleedin' twist."

"Kept himself in shape, that's for sure," said Tommy. "You can tell a lot lugging someone through the mud. Hard, no flab. Army, at some point, I shouldn't wonder. Never come across him before all this, though. What was that you said about pennies?"

"Reckons he stuffed a penny inside my jacket pocket as a message. Dead daft, really. I mean whoever remembers one penny from another? Said he put it in a twist of oilcloth or something."

Tommy scratched his chin. "I did find a bit of oilcloth in one of your jacket pockets that time I was sponging off the worst of the river mud. You were covered from head to foot in it, smelled something awful. Come to think of it now, I did pick a penny up off the bathroom floor when I was cleaning up the mess afterwards. And I only remember that because I noticed someone had gouged a big scratch across the face of it."

"Heads, I bet," I said, starting to scratch my own chin. And just as fate decrees sometimes, I overheard someone ask the barman for some coppers for some change for the telephone. The pennies dropped then.

"Fucking hell, Tommy. He's a bleedin' copper. It must've been him came back and saved me after I'd been left to drown."

"That'd make him the same bloke what called Spottsy on the blower and gave him the nod about where we'd find you."

"Jesus, Mary, and Joseph Stalin, I think I've only just gone and murdered one of Scotland Yard's very own Shadow Mob, haven't I?"

It's not often I stun myself silly with a sudden insight. And as if in slow motion, I looked at my wristwatch and shook my head, but Tommy—who could always move surprisingly fast for such a big bugger—was already at the bar asking for a quick butcher's at the tide-tables. His big fingers rifled through the tiny pages until he found the date, then he ran a finger down the index of tide points along the river. He glanced up at the clock behind the bar, then back at me.

"I'll do the driving," he said. "You get ready to go swimming."

A PENNY FOR THEM

Under Tommy's skilled hands the Co-op van went through the darkening streets faster than a burning bat out of hell, and any old lag abroad that night would've been forgiven for thinking it one of the Flying Squad's very own souped-up 'X'-cars out on the hunt. We'd both of us agreed there was no way we could reach the wharf from Wapping Old Stairs given that the river would already be running high and hard, so we'd decided on "Plan B."

"Plan B," however, had one very large flaw. It was just our bloody luck the wharf we were heading for was at the end of Wapping High Street that hadn't been totally flattened in the Blitz. There were whole stretches of empty warehouses—some burned-out shells, others only partly-destroyed, all of them waiting to be razed to the ground—any one of which would've made access to the river that much easier. That's always the problem though with any "Plan B," it's never your first choice.

Next thing I knew, we were skidding to a halt, the scream of tortured rubber bouncing off the all-too-solid warehouse walls that stretched both sides of that particular stretch of Wapping High Street, and I was out and running, crowbar in one hand, ten-pound sledgehammer in the other. Only, I came face to face with three big 'monkeys'—three huge padlocks holding down two heavy metal clasps, two locked on one clasp, one on the other, and me with no time or the proper tools to pick my way into any of them. So I just let loose at the single padlock with the sledgehammer. And I was about to take a swing at the other two when a hand the size of a prize ham plucked the hammer from out my grip, and without a word, Tommy swung twice, hitting both shackles smack on the mark, and it was '*open-fucking-sesame*.' That done, the two of us got stuck in with crowbars and everything designed to deny unlawful entry into King Harold's Wharf "Storage and Warehousing" Company's despatch office came off the door in a tortured screech of splintering wood. Then I was off and running through the empty office, chasing shadows deep into the rat-warren of narrow-packed corridors that ran between the ten-foot-high stacked bales of this and stacked crates of that, the torch in my hand waving about like a Roman candle on Bonfire Night. And trusting Tommy to bring up the rear and still counting off the seconds in my head, I eeled my way through the serried walls of looming darkness and prayed I didn't end up in a dead end.

It was odds on time had already run out for the copper, but that's me all over—never say die—and I went at the nearest set of rear doors at full-tilt and had the locking-bar up and out of its restraining slots and open and was out and onto the wharf and running pell-mell even before I could orientate myself properly. Dusk was falling like a lead weight, and I had to be careful I didn't trip and brain myself silly, but I could hear the river already sloshing and sucking against the wooden pilings below, and I quickly rid myself of my coat, chose a spot, and jumped in. I snatched a deep breath as I went over the side— the inbred instinct of the sailor—and prayed that Tommy had read the tide-tables properly. If not, I'd break both legs on the rock and rubble-strewn foreshore below, but I hit a good seven or eight feet of water and was turned about and swimming towards the pier on my next lungful of air.

The pier's massive wooden pilings seemed to have taken on a life of their own, everything first all angling one way, next moment, everything all going the other. I swam to starboard, against the incoming tide, making for a spot three or so pilings in from the end. As I got in closer I tried to touch bottom and took in a mouthful of river for my sins. Fighting the desperate urge to swallow, I went under again, pushed upwards, broke the surface, coughed out water, and snatched another breath. But as I fought to swim in ever closer, it was only the brief but slippery purchase the riverbed gave me that allowed me to get in amongst the forest of pilings without being dashed to pieces. And I moved with each wave as it tried to push me off my feet, then held on for dear life as, its job done, it did its best to pull me back under.

I couldn't see much of anything in all the gloom, let alone the already dead or drowning copper; there was no body, no shapeless lump, no nothing. Then I heard him choking, gasping, and gurgling, and saw the round bobbing buoy that was his head as the waves dashed repeatedly up against his neck and mouth and chin. The wash from any passing lighter or launch would've been enough to swamp him and any passing tug would've finished him off for good. I pulled myself in closer, and that's when it got real tricky. What to do now? Go back under and cut the ropes that bound his chest and feet and hands? Or stay on the surface and try and keep his head out the water?

Holding on, one-handed, I pulled the Fairbairn-Sykes from its sheath at my waist and fought to get a purchase so I could cut the gag off without cutting his face or throat.

"Cough first before you breathe in or you'll choke," I shouted.

I went under, feeling for the rope that held his feet, and started sawing like there was no tomorrow. Then I was back up on the surface gasping for air and then back down again into the ice-cold darkness and filth of the river, sawing blindly, sawing madly, doing everything by feel, cutting as if by Braille. And at last I felt the copper's feet and legs move with the push of the tide and I was up and out and gasping for air again.

I slapped the bloke's face to keep him awake, keep him alive. If he was still alive, that was. And then I was under again, round the other side of the wooden piling, cutting, sawing, cutting, and sawing at the ropes that still bound him and his hands, and then he was free and floating, a shapeless lumpy mass of wet bedraggled rags, a something in the river that'd once been "a somebody."

I heard Tommy yelling from the jetty above, though how long he'd been shouting his head off I had no idea.

Time had no meaning down in the stinking, watery netherworld, nor eternities; the world was the river and the river was ancient and mighty, all-powerful and unforgiving, and didn't give a tinker's cuss about what I was doing or why. Man or beast, dead or dying, half-drowned or half-alive, it was indifferent and as of old merely wanted to claim whatever was its rightful treasure. And me, I was fighting the only thing in all London older than London itself: Old Father Thames, fighting to the death to deny it yet another sacrifice.

I slapped the copper's face again and squeezed and rubbed and squeezed and rubbed whatever part of him I could touch, and even in the liquid darkness I could see the bloke's flesh was ice-white with cold and as puckered as a corpse.

"Get hold the fuckin' rope." It was Tommy again, louder now than any river foghorn. "Jeffro, get hold the fuckin' rope or I'll come down there myself."

A torch beam cut through the curtains of darkness, reflecting back off the ink black surface of the river, throwing the front line of pilings into bleak, stark relief, and I swam out from under the pier, a hand under the copper's chin, pulling the whole shapeless floating mass behind me, doing my all to keep his mouth up and out the water.

Some hope. Some horror.

I saw the rope swinging back and forth, back and forth, a straw in the wind, and I raised an arm to catch the eye rather than clutch at the line. When Tommy saw me bobbing up and down in the inky blackness, a cork at the mercy of the waves, he swung the rope to port and let it wash back towards me. For the very briefest of moments I was back with him on the boats, on the convoys, in the cold, dead-cold water, hellfires all-consuming, sailors forever drowning and dying all around us. Then the rope was around the copper's body and the body was ascending to heaven and I was free of my burden.

I twisted and turned and fought against the pull of the ever-moving, still unmourning water, the river still coldly impatient for its due. And the line came down over the edge of the pier again— Tommy as expert with a rope as any Tom Mix or Will Hays. It came skipping over the waves towards me and I embraced it lovingly, and I too was pulled heavenward, as if resurrected all over again.

Then there I was on my hands and knees, on the dock, retching and coughing the river out of me, rubbing and pummelling myself to get my circulation going again. In the pale flat light of the hand-torch left lying on the concrete, I saw Tommy had picked the copper up from behind and had him held tight in a bear hug and was jumping up and down with him. The copper was a big bloke, but Tommy was bigger still, and as strong as a carthorse. Even though it looked like a dance of death, as enacted by shadows, I knew Tommy was doing his level best to squeeze river water out and pump life back in. There was a sudden barrage of choking coughs and Tommy instantly had the copper on the deck and was pressing the bloke's chest and lifting his arms like nobody's business.

And lo, there was breath. And lo, there was life.

And that was when Tommy growled, "Come on you lazy sod, you can't stay there all night. Get up off your friggin' hands and knees and help me roll him up in the carpet."

Tommy was always one to think ahead. He knew, dead or alive, we'd have to carry the copper back out and that what'd worked before would work again, and he'd brought the carpet from the van. We rolled the Ghost Squad copper up like a streak of jam in a pancake, and off we trudged back through the warehouse. We could do nothing but trust to luck and hope against hope that a nosy beat copper hadn't already noticed the

smashed-in door of the wharf company's office and called for
assistance from the police box at the far end of the high street.

It'd been tricky enough manhandling the copper across
the mud bank in broad daylight, but charting a course back
through the dark cavernous warehouse with only one fading
torch between us proved just as dodgy, and anyone spying on
us would've have thought we were more Laurel and Hardy
than Burke and Hare. But once we got into proper step, we
moved as if charmed and nothing and no one barred our way
and we moved from the safety of one dependable shadow to
the next. Life's like that, sometimes. Suddenly, right out of the
blue, every traffic light in your path somehow decides to turn to
green. And never being ones to look a gift-horse in the mouth,
neither Tommy or me once commented on our good fortune as
we barrelled up Wapping Lane and back onto Ratcliff Highway
and headed towards Hackney— and beyond —to Tommy's
hideaway.

'NIT-NAT-NATO'

The bloke whose job it'd been to kill me looked dead to the world. I wondered if I'd looked even half as bad when Tommy and Spottsy had fished me out the river. Tommy had pulled out all the stops to save him. He stripped and dried him, bundled him up in blankets, and stuck him in front of the fire in an armchair to help thaw him out. I'd given a hand where I could, but it was Tommy's drum, Tommy's tune. It'd been touch and go for a minute or two, but the copper seemed to be hanging on. And I have to say I was very glad of that; murder is never easy to shoulder.

"I'll be glad when I've had enough of this, Jeffro. First you, now him I'll need to find myself a larger gaff, anymore of this. Give up minding; do bed and breakfast instead, special rates for any old lag on the run. Get in the kitchen. Time to get some hot tea down his neck."

I went and put the kettle on. I needed some hot sweet tea, I don't know about anyone else. I mean it wasn't as if I hadn't been down in the river catching me death all over again.

"And make it strong and sweet enough to stand a spoon up in," Tommy called over his shoulder.

"Is there any other way?" I yelled back.

I tried to stop from shivering myself silly as I concentrated on making the tea. I was bundled up to the ears in some of Tommy's old clothes but still felt chilled to the bone. The two oiled-wool jumpers I had on one over the other smelled strongly of mothballs and the sea, as did the woollen-socks and blue serge trousers. I must've looked like a kid wearing his dad's cast-off clothes.

"What about putting a drop of Whisky in the tea?" I called out.

"Put some in yours and mine, but only extra sugar for him, for now."

"Aye, aye, that," I shouted. But then any port in a storm, even if it is only a bleedin' teacup.

"Right, let me get something off my chest, right away," I said, handing him his cup of tea. "I had no idea you were a copper when I lashed you to the pier, like you did me. As far as I was concerned you were just another black-hearted villain who fully deserved being offed. Why the fuck didn't you say who you were when I took the gag out? You're Ghost Squad, aren't you?"

The bugger wouldn't be rushed, though. He just concentrated on drinking his tea, didn't even deign to look up. I didn't know whether he'd gone 'Dolally' again or what, so I waited. Given what I'd just put him through, I suppose he deserved that at the very least.

"First. Thank you for jumping in to get me. I thought I was a gonner." He looked up. "As for telling you, I wasn't sure how you'd take it, to tell the truth. It's enough to get me topped in some circles and a good few cop-shops, as well, so I hear. But if you knew that I'd saved your life, I reckoned it'd do the trick."

"Well it very nearly fucking didn't, you stupid sod. I never even saw the copper coin or the twist of oil-skin." I nodded in Tommy's direction. "It's lucky for you he remembered seeing a penny on the floor afterwards, otherwise you'd have been dead and drowned by now."

He looked at me without resentment or rancour, a real cool customer. "It was all I could think of before I climbed down to save you. I didn't have much time. I knew someone would be watching me. You were my final test. All I had to do was top you and no more questions, I was on the team."

"Yes, in Messima's pocket until death you do part," growled Tommy.

"But why go out of your way to save me from being topped," I said, putting the all-important question to him again. "I'm nothing to you."

"Same reason you came back for me—there's them that deserve to die and them that don't. I may have had to break a few arms and legs, carve a few faces along the way to get in with Messima, but cold-blooded murder is way beyond my remit. So I did what I had to do to see you safe, then lost myself in the shadows, and as soon as I was able I made the telephone call."

"So it was you who called Spottsy at the club?"

He nodded. "Spot was the only one that spoke up for you. Said there was no way you'd have murdered Harry Mooney or 'Tosh' Collis. Said he couldn't comment on your so-called association with some Ghost Squad copper or about you being a 'grass,' but as for the other two, you had too high a regard for them to have done either of them in. So I reckoned a call to Spot would see you safe. Sorry I had to bash you so hard with the rubber cable back in the warehouse; it was the only way to keep those three tossers from doing even worse to you."

The light in the room seemed to change. And so did I. I stared at the bloke who'd first appeared from out the shadows as a dark shape limned in flame, a thing of nightmare that'd tormented me and left me to drown in darkness. Only the selfsame supposed horror had then returned to see me safe and leave me beached but alive. An act, I now realised, that could've cost him his own life. My executioner now revealed as my saviour.

The copper made a show of moving against his restraints. "Is this strictly necessary?"

"Same reason," I said. "Wasn't sure how you'd take it when you finally came round. You might've been as pissed with me as I was with you."

"You had cause," he said, levelly. "Someone obviously saw fit to fit you up, but I was never out to collar you. The one I'm after is the bastard behind Messima and the Shadow Court, as whoever it is, I reckon he's using the whole rotten set up as a cover to kill off Ghost Squad."

"It does have that smell about it, doesn't it?" I said. "Very nasty."

He shook his head and looked down at his hands and flexed them. "They've killed five Special Duty Group coppers that I've heard of. The poor sods are officially listed as being 'as yet unknown' victims of gang violence. The senior brass at the Yard don't know which way to bloody turn, but while they're all busy dithering, Rome burns and the poor sods out there in the cold are still getting thrown to the lions. That's why I mean to find the bastard behind it all and kill him with my bare hands."

"That makes us fellow travellers along Ratcliff Highway," I said, "because if I don't get to the bastard first, he deserves all the grief he gets when you do finally get your hands on him."

"Amen to that," said Tommy.

I blinked and in an instant all my seething rage was gone and it was as if we were all in a scene in a different play. It wasn't for me to tell the copper I knew who the real villain was. I didn't want to bugger up Simon Bosanquet's plans in any way. But I have to admit given all the shit I'd been put through I was sorely tempted to drop Watts in it. The better angel on my shoulder, however, helped bite my tongue.

I nodded to Tommy to unbuckle the belts binding the copper. It was very apparent Tommy and the copper were two of a kind. Big-hearted men, as tough as nails and relentless with it; the kind of man you'd want by your side when in a fight for your life; the only way to stop either of them from exacting their own particular brand of justice, to kill them stone dead. It wasn't often Tommy met his match. I'm sure the same went for the copper. And even I could see there was a growing mutual respect between them.

"You ex-military?" Tommy asked, unbuckling the belts.

"Military Police, Berlin. Finally got demobbed last year and went into the Force, where I immediately got hand-picked for Ghost Squad."

"Reckoned as much," said Tommy.

"You?"

"The Merch. Cunard, before the War. Convoys for the duration."

"Is that where you two...?"

"Yes," I said, interrupting their little tea party. "We go way back."

He turned to Tommy. "Thanks for reviving me."

"You're welcome."

"How long was I out of it?"

I glanced at the clock on the sideboard. "It's very early the day after."

He nodded. "I was on my way to a big meeting called by Messima when you two nobbled me. Seems he's very steamed about something. I'll have to think of some excuse why I never made it; say my old lady was taken bad or some such. I also better report in to the Yard. They're understandably very jumpy about the way some of us have been disappearing of late. Only thing that burns me is that I'll have to give up the game now, seeing as how the two of you have made me as Ghost Squad."

"Well there's nobody we're going to tell," I said. "There's no skin off our noses, you going after Messima. Only reason I'm still in the Smoke is to get to the bottom of the same barrel of shit you are. And the enemy of my enemy is my friend. So 'carry on MacDuff', and with our blessings."

"Yes," murmured Tommy. "Anything you do to bugger up Messima would be A-OK with my boss. In fact, I'm sure he'd be glad I helped you, not that I'm going to tell him. This is all on the QT. Another cup?"

The bloke nodded and handed his cup to Tommy. It was only then that I noticed the small tattoo at the base of his thumb that resembled two tiny circles overlapping one another.

The exact same markings I'd seen on the hands of the bastards who'd been about to work me over with rusty hammers and hand-drills. "Those three fuckers back at the warehouse had that same tattoo on the back of their hands," I said, my voice suddenly hoarse. "What's that mean when it's at home?"

"This," he said, rubbing at it with a forefinger as if to rub it out, "stands for NORTO, which is why the 'nought' and letter 'O' are linked together. It means you've handed out retribution, as ordered, for the good of keeping the peace in the Smoke— each act another link in the chain that binds all together. Each gang boss throws one of his top men into the pot to help dish out the prescribed punishment and so serve the greater good. Those three back at the warehouse were out of King's Cross, Islington, and Clerkenwell—all very nasty pieces of work. Do the business, as I was supposed to have done with you, and you get the tattoo, like special units in the Army. I tell you, it won't be long before every tearaway in London is sporting one."

"Spottsy's never asked me to get involved with any of this NORTO nonsense," growled Tommy. "He knows I'd fuckin' walk first rather than work for Messima."

"Is that why the tiny circular burn marks on people's bodies?" I asked.

"Yes. Alive or dead, it's a sign it was done on orders of NORTO. A small round tin gets heated white-hot—an empty Brasso tin seems to be the tool of choice—gets applied to the victim wherever appropriate. It's meant to ensure that no one gets any daft ideas about seeking revenge afterwards. Anyone tries it, the rest of the underworld drops on them like a ton of bricks."

"Bloody hell," said Tommy. "I know Spottsy carves an 'X' on a tosser's cheek when he deserves it, but going out your way to brand a bloke with a Brasso tin, that's way out of order."

"Sends a very effective message," said the copper. "Means few if any witnesses ever come forward to speak out against it. It's building up a huge wall of silence around the Secret Court and its dealings."

"Ever heard of the Walls of Jericho?" I said. "It's amazing what a bit of brass in the right hands can do. I think it's high time, though, we all had another cup of tea. After which, Tommy will get you sorted out with some clobber. Then, as they say, you're free to go about your business."

Tommy disappeared for a few minutes and when he came back I went into the kitchen and had a wash in the sink. When I returned to the living room the copper was dressed in one of Tommy's old suits. He also had a nice-looking hat and a raincoat that wouldn't have been out of place in West End Central. It all fit him much better than anything of Tommy's had ever done me, even down to the shoes.

Tommy held up the blindfold; we didn't need the copper knowing the exact whereabouts of Tommy's drum. But the bloke shook his head. "Not necessary. I won't be looking for either of you, so there'll be no dawn raids or smashed-in front doors, you have my word on that." He turned to look at me. "Only thing I'd ask of you, Jethro, is that you try and stay dead for the time being, otherwise I'm a gonner for sure, myself." He rubbed the bump on his head where I'd coshed him. "And no hard feelings, I'm sure it's been even more of a nasty business for you, whichever way you look at it."

I looked at Tommy, who gave it the nod. "Okay, then, we'll take you at your word. No hard feelings on either side. It can't have been that easy for you. Messima and the other gang leaders are no fools. Tommy will drop you somewhere out the way, near a Tube station. There's some money in your pocket to help tide you over. As for your motorcar, all we did was loosen the distributor cap, so it's probably still where you left it."

"Road goes both ways," said the copper. "Back in the real world, people know me as Coulton, 'Gus' Coulton, short for Augustus. When this is all over and done with, if either of you ever need a favour anytime, I'll see to it people look the other way."

"Amen to that," said Tommy.

ALTERING COURSE

Tommy drove down Minories to Tower Hill so we could pass by the Merchant Navy War Memorial on Trinity Square. He gave two beeps on the van's horn in salute—the sound signal anywhere on the Thames River for '*I'm altering my course to port*'—then went down to Upper Thames Street and back along the Victoria Embankment. Tommy inclined his head a fraction in my direction. "Just a word to the wise," he said. "Spottsy's been asking after the *Phoenix*. Only, he's expecting a few lorry loads of Whisky and wants to move it about on the QT. I'd told him you'd borrowed it for a bit and I wasn't exactly sure of your or its whereabouts. Don't get me wrong, he's okay about it, he knows you have need, and he told me again to try and help you where I could, but you know what he's like: a dog with a bone. So, I'd say sooner rather than later on the return of the narrow-boat."

"She's berthed back at Paddington Basin," I said. "Nice little boat. Took quite a shine to her. Do you think Jack would ever think of selling?"

"No chance. The amount of money he spent fitting out the *Phoenix*, you'd think he was going to retire to the South of France in it."

"Really?" I said. "Who'd have thought it, Spottsy the boatman?"

"He also asked me to ask you, when I next saw you, whether you'd had any luck regarding that missing jewellery he was on about. He knows you're still supposed to be dead and that, and he's not expecting miracles, it's just whether you had any ideas that might help him bring it to light. Only the solicitor acting on behalf of that dead MP's wife has been on to him again."

"And of course Spottsy's got to keep pulling rabbits out of his hat to keep his reputation intact, hasn't he?" I said, feeling the tiny wheels in the back of my mind start to turn. "Tell him I've not forgotten, only I've had my hands a bit full."

Tommy grunted. "Are you sure you don't want me drive you any farther? You'll be okay here, will you?"

"Yes. Thanks, Tommy. Back of the Savoy will do nicely; I've got a little runabout parked near there."

Tommy slowed to turn right and waited for a gap in the oncoming traffic—a seemingly unending stream of delivery vans, taxis and buses, even a bloody horse and cart, and wouldn't you know it but a copper wearing white armbands stepped off the pavement to direct traffic and wave us across. Tommy waved an acknowledgment, turned into Savoy Place, and pulled in to the kerb just beyond the Institute of Electrical Engineers, the same building the BBC had broadcast from back in the Twenties. I got out and made my way towards the little alleyway where many of the Savoy Hotel staff kept their bicycles and motorbikes. It was only a few steps up the street, but it was like crossing the border into another country. Tommy might well be one of my oldest mates, but in truth we lived in different worlds, served different masters, and some things are best left uncomplicated. I hadn't told Tommy about finding Jimmy Mooney or the safe house or anything, and certainly nothing at all about Simon Bosanquet or Colonel Walsingham, or Watts, or any of the rest of it. Tommy must've guessed I'd found whoever or whatever it was I'd been so intent on finding, because when he'd picked me up in the van the previous afternoon, he told me I seemed more like my old self, less haunted, less like something that'd been dragged in from out the shadows.

I retrieved the keys I'd left under the saddle, donned the helmet and jacket I'd locked away in the panniers, kick-started the engine, sat astride the little BSA Bantam, and snapped off a salute in Tommy's direction. He flashed his headlights in acknowledgement and drove up Savoy Hill with me following behind. At the junction with Savoy Street, Tommy bibbed his horn and turned back down towards the Embankment, so as to go back east, while I turned left, and left again onto the Strand, and headed west and slowly made my way back to Ealing Common.

Secure behind its high brick walls, the safe house shone like a beacon in the pale wintery sunlight of late afternoon. It was odd, but against the flat expanse of the Common, it really did seem like an island of sanctuary, and I have to say I was very glad to be back. Jimmy was right; it wasn't until you could cast off all your cares and woes—even if only for a moment—that you realised just how very tensed up you were about everything.

Even so, I certainly didn't expect the bollocking I got from Simon Bosanquet. He didn't exactly raise his voice, but it was his look of utter disappointment that cut me to the quick. "We agreed you'd call in by oh-two-hundred hours, Jethro, any night you weren't coming back, so that we'd know you were safe. It's not just the staff standing down for the night. People out there still suppose you dead, and with Messima and NORTO as murderous as ever in their dealings, you could all too easily end up being dead for real."

"I had me hands full, Simon," I said. "Honestly, I did. But I apologise. It won't happen again. I know how much you've gone out your way to help me. It's just that I stumbled upon a member of Ghost Squad who knows all about the deaths of his colleagues and is hell-bent on finding whoever is behind Messima and NORTO and killing them with his bare hands."

Simon raised an eyebrow, in him akin to someone removing the pin from a hand-grenade.

I patted the air with both hands. "No, no, I didn't let on I knew anything, not even a hint, but I'll admit I was sorely tempted. With this Ghost Squad bloke after him, Watts wouldn't have seen out the night."

"I'm very glad you resisted the urge to give the game away, Jethro, as we now have a plan in place to deal with Watts and, hopefully, NORTO, too."

"Colonel Walsingham back from America, is he?"

"Yes, and he'd very much like to talk to you."

"That's considerate of him," I said. "When?"

Simon consulted his wristwatch. "Well let's just say you have enough time to change into something a little more suitable."

I looked down at myself. I still had the Co-op overalls on over a set of Tommy's outsized clothes. "It's a very long story," I said.

"You better pop your head around the door and show your face to Mr Mooney; he's been worried sick about you, too."

"I'll do that," I said. "And, Simon, thanks again for everything."

Colonel Walsingham was dressed for dinner, immaculate as ever. He wore his bespoke clothes as lightly and as effortlessly as he wore his rank, but he made no less a forceful impression for all that. He was one of those men who inspire confidence in others merely by his presence, and he gave the impression that he could just as easily have directed an entire battle as lead a Commando unit on a night raid. He smiled warmly, gestured for me to sit down, and, without appearing to, scrutinized me with the measured appraisal of a man that'd sent men out to die and would do so again, unhesitatingly, should the need ever arise.

"Jethro, how very good it is to see you again," he said. "I was so very pleased when Simon called and told me you were alive, but if I may say, you look very much like you've been in the wars, and even more recently than I'd been led to believe." He threw a glance at Simon. "But I'm forgetting myself. A glass of the Glenlivet for you?" He poured generous measures all round, handed us our drinks, and gave a toast. "Chin, chin," he said, affably.

"Chin, chin," I said, raising my glass. "It's very good to see you, too, Colonel, despite the very odd circumstances."

"Yes, a very strange kettle of fish, Jethro. That's why I wanted to talk to you as soon as possible and why we're meeting here at the house rather than at my office in St Anne's Gate. The nature of the problem means that for the time being, at least, your involvement and that of your friend, Mr Mooney, must remain unofficial."

At that moment one of the telephones rang in the hallway.

"Would you like me to get that, sir?" Simon offered.

"No, I was expecting the call. Excuse me; I won't be a moment. Simon, would you be so good as to bring in the cheese and water biscuits I had May put out for us in the kitchen; she's off for the night, I have to fend for myself."

Colonel Walsingham and Simon Bosanquet both exited the room and I sat there taking it all in. I'd only been inside the place once before—the time I'd broken into the house only to find Walsingham sitting there, in the dark, waiting for me, pistol in hand. The handle of the Fairbairn-Sykes Commando knife I'd managed to throw, in a futile but very satisfying gesture of defiance, was still lodged in a cushion on the leather Chesterfield. It'd missed him by miles, as I'd intended, but he'd chosen to leave the knife stuck exactly where it was as a constant reminder for him to remain ever diligent, and decent fellow that he was, in return, he'd given me the Commando knife he'd carried in the war. I didn't think it was the right time to tell him I'd gone and lost it in battle.

I ran my eyes along the shelves of his built-in bookcases filled with books that spoke volumes to Walsingham's love of the history of politics and war. Then my gaze wandered over towards the oil painting on the wall opposite me. It was a portrait of Walsingham's wife, killed in the Blitz, a striking-looking woman, whose purple-blue eyes seemed to follow my every thought and move. Must run in the family, I said to myself. Beneath the painting, on a shelf, stood a single, pale pink rose in a narrow-stemmed vase. The rose, no doubt, a constant reminder to Walsingham that although beauty may be fleeting, any love worth its salt never is.

"I cultivated it myself. It's a 'Common blush China,' crossed with a climbing 'Noisette,' which perhaps helps explain its colouring and intense fragrance. I call it the 'Shanghai Lily,' a name I shall happily retain despite the recent Communist takeover of Shanghai; things of beauty are ever recurrent."

It was Walsingham, returned to the room, but I'm not sure I managed to catch all he'd said, as my Whisky had suddenly gone down the wrong hole and I was doubled up, coughing and spluttering. He'd called it the 'Shanghai Lily'? A coincidence? I should cocoa. There was no such thing where he was concerned.

Simon handed me a tumbler of water and I tried desperately to stop myself from hiccupping. "Eye-eye," I said to myself, "as usual, there's even more to this than meets the eye."

Walsingham sat down, waved a hand in the direction of the plate of cheese and crackers. "Please help yourself," he said. Then he reached for his glass of malt Whisky. "To continue, then. Firstly, Jethro, let me say how very grateful I am that you chose to bring the matter directly to Simon's attention. If news of what's occurred were to leak out, the resultant erosion in public confidence in the institutions of law and order would be considerable, which in turn would seriously jeopardise the internal security of the Realm. A situation I'm determined to avoid." He paused. "To that end, even though I once promised you, Jethro, that I wouldn't call on your skills again, I needs must ask for your help, and what I have in mind is this."

Colonel Walsingham laid out his plans for "Monkey" Jim and me, and I suppose I should've guessed what he had hidden up his sleeve. He always did have this knack of asking for the bloody impossible. Thing was, he also had this way of explaining things that made them seem all too reasonable, and before I even knew what I'd done, I'd reached forward, stuck a big piece of cheese on a crème-cracker, and swallowed the lot whole.

All of which is to say, I didn't feel the trap snapping shut on the back of my neck.

But, then, you never really do, do you?

TAKING ON PROVISIONS

Our revels ended, Colonel Walsingham went off to a formal dinner in the City, the main purpose of which was for the well connected to have yet another opportunity to connect with people of kind. Deputy Assistant Commissioner Watts was scheduled to be there, so it gave Walsingham the perfect opportunity to get a close look at his quarry.

'*Quis custodiet ipsos custodes?*'

Someone who's a member of the same club, that's for sure.

Simon drove me back to the safe house. Neither of us said much. I stared out the windscreen, watching the headlight beams push back the darkness, wondering at all the moves that still needed to be played out before our journey's end. As usual, food had been laid on for us, a cold collation, together with bread and cheese and pickles, the just desserts for anyone foolish enough to miss the regular mealtime. I ate everything off my plate, feeling very hungry for some reason, and when we'd finished I told Simon I'd leave off talking to Jimmy about the necessaries until morning.

"I need a walk before bed," I said, "help clear my head."

This time they took no chances. I counted at least two of them trailing me, but there may have been more, so I didn't take any chances either and went on past the telephone-box by the church and headed in the direction of the Tube station, knowing I was bound to come across another kiosk sooner or later. I didn't mind the extra walk. The minders were just doing their job. I knew it was more about them not allowing anything to disrupt Walsingham's well-laid plans than it was about me. I wasn't offended. Anyway, it gave me more time to think. The most pressing matter being, of course, how to get Walsingham what he wanted, because just like the rest of London, Walsingham wanted "Monkey" Jim.

"I need a statement from Mr Mooney," he'd said, as always, the very voice of reason when at his most unreasonable. "I need him to formally identify Watts and Messima as the two men heard in conversation on the recording, and to confirm date, time, and place. The legalities of submitting the wire spool in evidence are currently being dealt with, and I expect no difficulties on that score. Next, I need Mr Mooney to formally identify Watts in person. I also need him to retrace his movements at Scotland Yard and identify which rooms he was given access to. Lastly, I need him to confirm that he was indeed at Meridian Mansions on the night of Fox's death."

Not too much of a tall order; just get "Monkey" Jim to testify against himself in open court and get himself banged up for the rest of his natural. Not that he'd have much chance of even surviving that. The kingpins of the Smoke could order someone topped in prison as easy as they could have someone lifted from off the streets. And despite Walsingham's promise that any testimony given would be deemed King's Evidence and Jimmy would be given immunity from prosecution, he'd still have to survive afterwards, and the fate of a known 'grass' was never pleasant; death was the least of it. And even though Colonel Walsingham meant a whole lot to me, Jimmy didn't know him from a hole in the ground, so what grounds did he have to trust him?

But Walsingham brushed aside my concerns. "Mr Mooney's evidence can be given in camera, Jethro. There's no need for him to appear in open court. He needn't even appear under his own name. I promise, I'll ensure that he's kept safe. The key to it all now is that you find some way to convince Mr Mooney that it's in his best interests to go back into Scotland Yard."

"Let me try and get this straight, Mr Walsingham, sir," I said. "You want Jimmy Mooney to march into Scotland Yard, as bold as brass, and you want me to march in there with him? I'd say you had to be joking, only from past experience I know you're not. What I think you need to understand, sir, is that as far as 'Monkey' Jim's concerned, the 'Bladder,' by which I mean Scotland Yard, is his worst nightmare, writ large and made flesh. It's much more than a building to him; it's been a dark shadow that's been hanging over him since birth. Like all the rest of London's criminal fraternity, he hates the bloody place. Wild horses couldn't drag him back to there again. He'd very likely top himself, first."

Walsingham nodded, I thought in sympathy, but he leaned forward in his chair and steepled his fingers and gazed at me from over the top of them. I knew the look of old: Walsingham wanted what Walsingham wanted and it was my job to do or die. We all had our given parts to play in his grand scheme of things, a realisation that prompted a sudden thought.

"Can I ask you a question, Mr Walsingham, sir? Only, it's been on my mind ever since Simon mentioned it."

He nodded, not taking his eyes off me for a second.

"May I ask you how you first came to hear of my supposed demise? Was it perchance during one of those little chats on émigrés and politics you occasionally have with my old mate, Raymond Karmin?"

There wasn't a moment's hesitation or evasion. "No. As a matter of fact, Jethro, I heard it from one of my many other private sources. Why do you ask?"

"Er, no reason. Just wondering."

Whoever said that knowledge is power didn't know the half of it; it's having the power to get hold of the knowledge in the first place that truly sorts out the men from the boys. And the truth of it was, Walsingham always did seem to know a little too much about me than was good for me.

I blinked alert. There was a telephone-box lit up in the distance, as welcome a sight as seeing the right-route-numbered double-decker bus trundling towards you out of the distant gloom. I glanced at my wristwatch and picked up my pace. I had a few things on my mind that were best addressed by Ray Karmin—as ever, in times of trouble, my North Star.

I tossed up a coin in my mind and it came down tails and I stuck two pennies in the slot and dialled the telephone number for "Buggy" Billy's house. The receiver at the other end was picked up after the third ring and I pressed button 'A' and waited for the pennies drop.

"Yerse," a voice growled. "This better be something I wanna hear."

"Is that Ealing 8463?" I said. "Is Father Fabrikant in?"

"What was it you said? Ealing 8463? Nah, wrong number."

The phone went dead. I pressed down on the hook and kept the handset pressed to my ear and waited for the telephone to ring. Sure enough, within half a minute Ray called back. "How can I help?"

No messing. "Got some news concerning Mr W, thought you should hear it hot off the press," I said. And I told him all about Walsingham's plan of action and my concern over Jimmy Mooney's role in the proceedings. "Our Jimmy's changed; he really has. He's just a shadow of his former self. And you know how stubborn he can be sometimes when he has a mind. I suppose what I'm trying to say is I'm very worried he'll just stick his heels in and won't see reason." The line went dead for a moment. "Er, Father Fabrikant?"

"Still here, old son, still here," Ray said. "One thing I do know is that 'Monkey' Jim's a pragmatist at heart and always has been. You have to be in the creeping game, as you well know. So don't you worry yourself about our little chum. He may well surprise you with how quickly he gets the picture. Still, it might not be a bad idea if you also tell Jimmy that "Buggy" Billy says it's kosher." He paused again. "As for you, just you remember, you've been right through the mangle and then some, so it's only natural you're going to see the worst of things. You should go a bit easier on yourself, old son," he said. And then he chuckled. "You know, if you weren't supposed to be dead, I'd say you were in desperate need of a good night out on the town."

"From your lips to God's ears," I said. "This 'doomed to walk the night' business has got me right browned off."

"Understandably so, understandably so, but all things considered, you're doing very well. Just remember to take it one step at a time. Other than that, I suggest you and Jimmy do exactly what Mr W wants. He's the only one with enough clout to fix it all. He's your 'Get Out Of Jail Free' and 'Collect Two-hundred Quid' cards all rolled into one. Not to mention your very own personal 'Resurrection' card, as well. Anything else troubling you?"

"No. I mean, yes. Er, let me ask you, how are we fixed?

"Financially, you mean?"

"Yes."

"Well, let's jut say you could retire to the Scilly Islands for the rest of your natural and not have to worry about the price of beef, bread, or beer, or about having a substantial roof over your head. Why, what's on your mind?"

I told him what I had in mind.

"What you do with the tom is up to you. It was your caper from the very start. There'll always be blood on the stones, whatever we do, so all things considered it could be a good solution, all round. You've always been one to pay off your debts, the good as well as the bad. So have at it and with my blessings. That it?"

"How's Joanie doing?"

"Still pretty devastated about it all, but muddling through. The Victory Cafe's open again. People have mobbed the place in support. Never seen it so busy, though everyone's careful not to mention your name. As busy as it gets, though, she keeps your favourite table at the back all set up for you. Knife, fork, spoon, 'Reserved' sign, the lot; off limits to all, even to me, 'Buggy' Billy. I only wish I could tell her you're still alive. She'll play bloody hell with me if she ever finds out I knew. That's something else you're going to have to sort out when you come back from the dead."

"It's enough to make a ghost weep, all this," I said.

We agreed on when I'd try to call again. I said my cheerios and Ray said his and I replaced the receiver and turned to go. On a whim I turned round again and dropped another couple of coppers in the slot and called one of the many numbers I had for Tommy. And wouldn't you know it, but I got him first time. He picked up on the third ring.

"T for temperance," he said.

"J for Jonah," I said. "Fancy a drink tomorrow lunchtime?"

"Got trouble?"

" No, I'm dealing with that. It's something Spottsy was asking about."

"I'm over the far end of Knightsbridge in the morning, visiting a club Spottsy's got a new interest in, place called the Karanda. That's over towards your way, isn't it? Will you be coming on that little pop-pop bike of yours?"

"Yes. I was thinking maybe somewhere around Fulham."

"Alright, make it the far end of the King's Road. World's End. How does that suit you?"

"Very appropriate," I said. "I'll be there at twelve on the dot."

"Well you get them in, then, because I won't be there till twelve-thirty at the earliest. You be in mufti, will you?"

"No, uniform of some sort. Nothing too pukka. One of the utility boards probably—gas, water or electric."

"Fair enough. I'll bring some shillings for the meter. I'll also be in old hat and coat so as not to shame you. You alright for money?"

"Yes, thanks. I've hardly had to touch the wad Spottsy gave me."

"See you," he said. "Be lucky." Then he rang off.

SHADOWS IN THE SMOKE — 343 —

And I turned and pushed open the door of the telephone-box and stepped out into a cold world still slowly turning towards morning.

I tackled 'Monkey' Jim over breakfast.

"'Buggy' Billy sends his regards, Jimmy," I said. "Says he hopes you're keeping fit and says for me to tell you that what I'm about to tell you is kosher."

Jimmy nodded, smiled, but said nothing.

"So, here's the strength of it. Our Mr Bosanquet, who you've met on and off this past week, works for a certain VIP gentleman who just happens to have a great deal of pull in the string-pulling department, by which I mean to say he can get hooks into all sorts of very important people." I paused and tapped the side of my nose. "Works on the QT. In the shadows. Goes by the moniker 'W', and if there's one man in all of London who can help sort out all the shit we're in, it's him. Thing is...er...this Mr 'W' wants us to do our bit in the coming caper." And with that I tiptoed my way through what I knew of Walsingham's plan.

Jimmy listened intently and said nary a word till I'd finished.

Given all the times down through the years he'd told me how much he hated the 'Bladder', I fully expected Jimmy to reject Walsingham's idea out of hand, but he didn't. He nodded his head, scratched his chin, and then looked me straight. "Seems fair enough, Jeffro," he said, in a voice barely above a whisper. "I'm no nark, no 'grass.' Never have been, never will be. But I reckon this business is different. Has to be, really, given who and what's involved. So if this 'W' bloke is really as good as 'Buggy' Billy and you say he is, then no problem, I'll go down the bleedin' 'Bladder', again, and with a good heart. We'll both go, and we'll do what we have to, so we can both get out from under and get back on with our lives. Okay?"

There was my old teacher, teaching me again, reminding me of something my old mum used to tell me: If you ever couldn't get out of something, you got stuck right into it instead. If need be, you stuck your arm all the way into the pickle-jar, right up to the elbow. You grabbed hold of the pickle and you took it and you swallowed it. You did whatever you had to do and then you put it behind you and you moved on, end of story.

I bit my tongue and nodded my agreement.

And that was the exact moment I came over with a very bad case of the itches, which is never a good sign.

TURNING THE CORNER

Tommy was as good as his word. The big hand on the clock on the wall had barely clipped the number six when in he came. He looked a mile uneasy.

"Didn't see your little motorbike anywhere outside," he said quietly, as he sipped the pint of beer I'd just handed him.

"Left it parked up beyond Fulham Road and walked down so I could have a little look-see before I came in."

"Yes, I suppose you've got to think of things like that when you're supposed to dead. I hardly recognised you."

"I'll just keep working on it then," I said, "until such time as I can disappear before your very eyes."

"Very Arthur Askey," he said, "but you might need to disappear. And dead sharpish, too. I just bumped into two of the King's Cross mob at the Karanda club: Jimmy Pottle, the big bald one, and Bobby Boyle, the other knife merchant, the one with the coal black hair, looks like a diddikye. You wouldn't normally see them this far up West, but now with Ronnie White and Spottsy having third shares in the club with Messima, it likely won't be the last. Fuckers acted like they owned the place, showing off those NORTO tattoos of theirs like they were George Medals or something."

"The Karanda was old Rene Sempke's place, wasn't it? When did that change hands?"

"A couple of weeks back. Messima pulled in Rene's marker

and brought in Spottsy and Ronnie White as partners to try and bring the two mobs closer together. The way Messima reckons it, it'll help cut down on friction, especially with old man White and his brothers each doing a seventeen stretch for manslaughter and Ronnie left in charge. I can't see it myself, not with the nasty little sod throwing his weight around everywhere, trying to prove himself. Always been the same, though. Never trust a White—the fuckers are always looking for nasty ways to stick one up you."

"Clever of Messima, though, forging alliances like that. This rate, it won't be too long before he'll have all of London sewed up. I need another drink. What you having? The same?" Tommy nodded and I got them in.

"What's on your mind," he said, "them missing diamonds?"

I nodded. "Yes, there's this middle-man may be able to help." I paused. "Some Canadian bloke, so I understand. So I should see Spottsy, soon as."

So there I was drifting like smoke through the backstreets of Fulham, the afternoon shoppers oblivious to the fact a dead man walked amongst them, and I'd just reached the Fulham Road and was about to cross over when a big black motor slowed down and I thought, "Eye-eye, watch it." And I turned away as if suddenly caught by something on display in a shop window and stared at the reflection of the motor in the plate glass as it fractured and flowed past. I took a deep breath, got myself ready to run, then slowly exhaled when I realised the motor was simply slowing down to turn into the hospital.

Out the corner of my eye, I saw the indicator sticking out and the red brake lights winking off as the motor turned and disappeared from view. "Nit that then," I said to myself and turned round and walked smack into two blokes hurrying along the street, heads down, hats on, deep in conversation. One of them, the biggest, bumped into me and all but knocked me flying. "Mind your manners," he growled.

I didn't say anything, just kept on walking, but it seemed the bloke was in no mood to let things pass.

"Oi, you," he yelled after me. "I told you to mind your fuckin' manners."

"Why don't you mind them for me," I yelled over my shoulder and just kept on walking. Not of course the cleverest thing to have done in the circumstances, as in any street or pub in London it was really only asking for trouble. But then again, maybe I really wanted an opportunity to hit out at something solid, feel my fist hit home against flesh and bone, perhaps even spill a little blood, something to tell me I was still alive. So I rolled my neck and shoulders in preparation, easing the muscles I might have to use, and flexed my hands and got myself prepared to smack someone very hard.

That roll of my shoulders might've been what set them off, because the bloke yelled out, "Oi, you, tosser, come back here and say that again to my face." Which of course quickly brought me to my senses and, rethinking the situation, I took it on my toes. Thing was, I knew the voice and it was as bad a dose of worm-powder as ever could be imagined, because the two tearaways in hot pursuit of me had to be either Messrs. Pitcher and Bumaree or Messrs. Pitcher and Shipman. How about that for odds, in a city of eight million and more people? I ask you, of all the corners, at the ends of all the streets, in all the Postal Districts, in all of London, why in hell did they have to bump into me at that one?

I dashed up the street and careened round the first corner I came to, but not before chancing a quick butcher's at what was happening behind me— always essential when assessing angles and speeds. Somewhat surprisingly, it was Pitcher leading the charge with Bumaree bringing up the rear. I was just very glad that only one of them was fast off the mark, had the two of them come at me together, things might've turned out very differently.

I found myself in Park Walk, with a lamp-post to my left and decorative iron railings to my right; all in all, a nice orderly little street with two-storey houses, plus attic and basement, in the Georgian style. Not as genteel perhaps as those in Chelsea proper, but pleasant enough, and not exactly your usual setting for cold-blooded murder. I ran full-tilt at the lamp-post, stuck out an arm, just as I'd done when I was a kid, grabbed hold of it and swung round, so as to launch myself, like a sling shot, back in the direction of the corner, hoping against hope that my timing was dead on.

It wasn't exactly what someone following me in hot pursuit would've been expecting as they themselves turned the corner. And what is it they say, 'The bigger they are the harder they fall'? Well, Pitcher certainly went arse over tit and down like a ton of bricks smack onto his ugly face when I slid and skidded into his legs like I was tackling him on a football pitch. I was up and off my own arse in an instant and I turned to see him, ex-prize fighter that he was, balanced on his knuckledusters, trying to push himself back up onto his knees, and very helpful of him, as he'd positioned himself nicely for me to get in two really good kicks to the side of his head. Down he went again.

He rolled onto his back and I stepped in fast and stomped down on his testicles, then did it a second time for good measure. As his head came up off the pavement again, I kicked him smack under the chin and it was lights fully out. I grabbed hold of the scruff of the neck, dragged him across the pavement, and pushed him head first down the basement steps of the nearest house. Then I pulled my scarf from around my neck and wrapped it tightly around my left hand.

Seconds out. Round two.

Bumaree already had his knife out as he rounded the corner. Funny thing was I'm sure neither he nor Pitcher had the faintest idea it was me they were chasing, they just wanted to beat someone up to keep their hands in. Blood will always out with some people. Difference being though, since Bumaree had last had a go at me, I was leaner, a good deal fitter, and even though I'd just enjoyed a couple of pints, I wasn't anything like drugged up to the eyeballs. More importantly, perhaps, I'd been trained in hand-to-hand knife fighting by a certain Mr. Carter, who even I had to admit had proved a most excellent teacher.

I didn't plan for it to be a fight to the death, but there was really no other way out for either of us once it all went off. I feinted right as Bumaree came at me knife in hand. I think he was rather surprised when I revealed I had a proper fighting knife to his switchblade. My new Fairbairn-Sykes was by far the stronger blade and was double-edged to his one. Not exactly the sort of weapon he'd normally come up against, even though both had come out of the War—his from the soldiers returning from the Italian campaign, mine from British Commando forces whose job it was to inflict maximum damage on the enemy and quickly disappear back into the shadows.

He thrust and I parried and I could see in his eyes that the shock of steel against steel sobered him up rather sharpish. It'd all too swiftly turned from a bullying lark to a dance of death, both of us making a thrust here, a thrust there, with me just waiting for him to overextend himself. To force the issue, I went on the back step, eased off my fighting stance just enough to invite him in, and sure enough he lunged at where he thought my belly would be. But I was already swivelling around to trap his arm, twisting my whole body to force his arm to turn with me or risk it breaking, the crushed nerves in his arm causing him to open his hand and drop his knife. I forced him to the ground and followed him down, kneeing him hard in the kidneys. I slashed down the entire length of his knife arm, just like gutting a fish, cutting through flesh and tendon till I felt the scrape of steel against bone. He cried out and howled something awful and I stepped back and leaned down to pick up his stiletto from off the pavement.

Out the blue, someone hit my arm and sent the knife flying.

I spun round, my Commando knife ready to do some more very serious damage and only just managed to pull back in time.

"Stop that, you hooligan, or I shall call for a policeman from the nearest police box." The old lady who'd hit at me with her umbrella looked both startled and appalled, then she froze rigid and her face went from flushed anger to deathly white.

"You do that, love," I yelled at her, "and you better call for an ambulance, too, while you're at it. Otherwise, just be nice and sod off."

It was only momentary distraction, but it was enough for Bumaree to get to his feet and scarper.

Worse, the old lady seemed to recover just as quickly and she started hitting at me again. I thought, "Fuck this for a game of soldiers," and shook her off, threatening to clout her one, and she landed arse first on the pavement. I turned, picked up the switchblade, closed it, pocketed it, and set off after my fast disappearing former assailant.

The only mistake Bumaree made was forgetting his Highway Code, and that after Clement Atlee's government had gone to all the trouble of producing a new edition not three years before, where it instructed you in no uncertain terms to "*stop, look right, left, and right again*" before crossing the road at right angles and keeping a careful look out at all times. It even went so far as to advise that if your view of traffic was obscured by a stationary vehicle you should take particular care, and that if you didn't, you could be knocked down.

Wise words.

The No. 14 bus that hit Bumaree, though not going at full speed, was travelling fast enough to knock him flying. It was the big Humber motorcar going in the opposite direction that probably killed him. Much later, I wondered whether it was the same big black motorcar I'd seen earlier, and who knows, it could well have been—funnier things have happened. By the time I reached him, my own knife back in its sheath and out of sight under my coat, his body and limbs were all at odd angles, his head a gratifyingly bloody mess of crushed brain and bone. And as all the traffic slowed to a stop, as if by order, the conductor got off the bus and went to join the driver who was already bent over the inert body of Bumaree. The bus conductor took a close look, then stood up and shook his head and said with an air of solemn authority, "I was an ARP warden during the war and I had to deal with lots of dead 'uns in the Blitz, and I can tell you this one's definitely past saving."

On the far side of the crowd, the old lady was screaming her head off again, this time gesticulating with her umbrella at something down in the basement of a nearby house, but as no one in the assembled throng could see Pitcher's body, they just assumed she was some hysterical old biddy and told her to shush it. Someone cared enough to yell out that the accident had already been reported and the ambulance was on its way. And, as if on cue, its blue light flashing, its alarm bell a-ringing, the ambulance drove out of the hospital gates, not two hundred yards away, and entered Down Stage Left.

I slowly drifted away from the crowd and lost myself in a side-street, and began heading back to where I'd parked the Bantam. Along the way I dropped Bobby Boyle's switchblade down a drain. He certainly had no more need of it, and suddenly out of the clear blue again I found myself thinking about Harry "Rabbit" and "Tosh" Collis. Boyle had definitely had a hand in each of their deaths and I was glad I'd had a chance to square that circle.

I hadn't gone but a hundred yards, though, when the itches came over me again. "Just where in hell was the third hard-man, Eddie Maytum—alias Mr. Shipman?"

PLAYING THE 'BLADDER'

I didn't say anything about what'd happened when I got back to the safe house. Simon Bosanquet would've played merry hell with me for jeopardising everything so late in the game, and it didn't bear thinking about what Walsingham would've done to me had he found out.

Bumaree had gone to meet his maker, Pitcher was out for the count, but that still left the nagging question of whether the other knife-merchant Shipman had been in the crowd somewhere. If he was and I'd been recognised and got myself fingered, it'd really put the cat amongst London's pigeons. And this time I had no one to blame for my nasty itches but me.

I did my best to cover up my disquiet and, if nothing else, when Simon greeted me with news that D-Day was scheduled for three days hence and that he'd brief Jimmy and me on the detailed plan of action sometime later that evening, I at least had something more solid to worry about.

We dressed for dinner, Jimmy and me in newly cleaned second-hand clothing that'd appeared in our rooms as if by magic. It all fit, so somebody must've sized us up pretty well. Along with the suits, we were each given a new pair of shoes—good ones, too, from Jermyn Street—as well as new white shirts and silk ties with little crests on them. Jimmy, resplendent as he was in striped trousers and black jacket, was almost unrecognisable when he finally emerged. While I did my best to do justice to a single-breasted dark blue number. It was like being fitted-out with a 'demob' suit again, but as we were to learn, it was our first introduction to the disguises we were expected to wear when we stormed the ramparts of Scotland Yard.

Dinner over and the evening's other conversations set aside, Simon passed the port and got down to business. "We wanted something that'd pass muster and yet not attract too much undue attention, as anything other than a policeman's uniform stands out like a sore thumb."

I threw a look at Jimmy and he threw one back at me, the whole mad idea suddenly all too real.

"So we rather thought that you could both be inspectors from the Ministry of Works on a visit to assess the current state of the long overdue repairs. It'll provide the perfect cover for wandering the corridors on all floors without fear of approach. Colonel Walsingham spoke to the Commissioner personally, and he's on board with it. Added to which, I'll be in attendance at all times, in police uniform, so you'll be quite safe."

So that was it. We had seventy-two hours to turn ourselves into pukka civil servants, to which end Simon arranged for someone to come give us a crash course on the more arcane aspects of the MOW. Simon knocked me for a bit of a six at the end of the meal when he quietly pulled me aside and asked me please to be sure to stay within the confines of the safe house for the immediate future. He said it'd cut down on the chances of me running into any more of the sort of people I should still be trying to avoid.

I grinned—what else could I do?—and nodded. I should've known better. The clever untrusting sod had known me for who and what I was and had had me followed. God knows what the minders must've made of the mess I'd left in my wake. I didn't put it past Walsingham using it as blackmail against me at some future date, but as you do with dark thoughts like that, I left it to slither and slide into the shadowy recesses in the back of my mind.

The following morning we were each handed our official MOW passes, complete with all necessary seals, stamps, signatures, and numbers, including our respective civil service grades. I was an Executive Officer named 'B. Ritz, Esq.' and Jimmy was a Senior Executive Officer named 'G. Duckworth, Esq.'

I wondered where they'd dug those names up from.

A big maroon-coloured motorcar—another Humber, of all things—came to take us to Scotland Yard. The driver turned out to be one of our regular minders now dressed in an official-looking blue-serge uniform and peaked-cap. And there we were, the men from the Ministry.

Funny thing, but it was on that drive to Scotland Yard that the scales finally fell away from my eyes regarding "Monkey" Jim. You can be that close to people sometimes you lose sight of who they really are. It'd been staring me in the face. Jimmy was no longer the harried and haunted old lag of yesterday, he was more the sleek, debonair 'fox' of yesteryear. And even I had to admit that with the black overcoats and Homburg hats we'd been issued that morning, we not only looked the part, we looked like we'd been thus attired for years. The horn-rimmed spectacles and neat little moustaches we each sported—my touch, that—only added to the effect, and even the hair on our heads had been cut in the appropriate style by a bloke specially brought in from Trumper's. His pretty young assistant had manicured our nails as well. All it took then was a dash of Geo. F. Trumpers' 'Extract of Lime' and we even smelled the part. Jimmy looking every inch the senior civil servant and me the dutiful underling with promise.

We turned off Parliament Street, down into Derby Gate, entered through the 'IN' gate, went under the fabled granite and redbrick archway, and pulled in to a parking space reserved for visiting VIPs. The driver opened the rear passenger door and we alighted, doing our best to look dignified. In the cold light of morning Scotland Yard looked as forbidding and as foreboding as ever, and I don't know about Jimmy, but I had to swallow hard before I could even take the first step. Our driver retrieved our official MOW monogrammed briefcases from the boot of the Humber. And then he escorted us across the roadway to where Simon Bosanquet was waiting at the foot of the steps leading up to the big oak and iron-studded door of the Norman Shaw building.

They saluted each other smartly.

Then Simon, resplendent in the full dress uniform of a Metropolitan Police Commander—shiny buttons, black-and-white-chequered peaked-cap, swagger stick, brown leather gloves and all—escorted us into the bowels of the 'Bladder.' It wasn't lost on me that despite the confidence Walsingham had shown in us, neither he nor Simon wanted either Jimmy or me to be out of their sight for a single moment. And knowing how we normally operated, I suppose I couldn't really blame them.

Me, I'd have made damn sure everything portable was nailed down very securely.

We spent the first half hour getting used to the place and letting the place and its people get used to the sight of us or until such time as we disappeared into the green and cream-coloured walls. It was still a bit touch and go to start with and in truth what confidence we had in those early moments was due to the amount of silver braid on Simon Bosanquet's peaked cap and the silver crossed tipstaves within silver bay-leaf wreath insignia on his shoulderboards.

The idea was that Jimmy would retrace his movements from his earlier visit, completely unaided. He'd identify the offices he'd gone into and give a detailed statement as to what'd occurred inside each one. Bosanquet and me would duly note down everything in our official-looking little black books, both of which would later be used as evidence. So once we'd made our gimlet-eyed assessments of the very impressive marble hall and corridors of the ground floor, we marched up the equally impressive marble steps to the mezzanine, had a look round, then made our way up to the first floor, the Yard's acknowledged "corridor of power," and did the business. I wouldn't say Simon hurried us, exactly, but he kept a sharp eye on his wristwatch at all times. We were on a tight schedule.

There were no top brass to be seen anywhere along those seemingly endless corridors, just support staff and other functionaries, but it didn't merit too much comment as again it was all part of the plan. Everyone above the level of Commander was attending a special meeting called by the Police Commissioner—a meeting of such supposed importance that each attendee had been asked to wear his "number one" dress uniform. And such was the number of attendees, rather than it taking place in the Commissioner's office, it was being conducted in a large high-ceilinged room on the ground floor normally employed as the main briefing room for the CID. The usual raised platform and row-upon-row of hard-backed chairs having been removed to make way for a long glass-covered conference table set with the requisite number of leather chairs, notepads, water jugs, and ashtrays.

Once we'd completed our tasks, Simon escorted Jimmy and me back downstairs to the ground floor. And after ensuring the coast was clear, he ushered us through an unmarked door situated just along the corridor from the big meeting room. The small, cramped room we found ourselves in was a hive of quiet activity, orchestrated as well as conducted by none other than Colonel Walsingham.

The immediate impression was more of a map-room directing movements in the midst of a battle rather than an office administering to the daily duties of the Metropolitan Police. What hit you immediately was that everyone was wearing headphones. Centre Stage was a large table covered by a plan of the main meeting-room, complete with little wooden blocks, displaying the name and current position of each of the senior police officers in attendance, the whole business being constantly monitored by two stern-looking women. A bloke in the far corner was fiddling with what looked to be a radio receiver-cum-switchboard. In the other corner, a couple of stenographers silently tapped away on their machines, while next to them, two other women were transposing everything they were hearing into shorthand. There were two cameras on tripods facing a curtained wall. And two portable Webster 180 recording machines standing side-by-side on a trestle table, their wire spools turning. It was very clear nothing was being left to chance or allowed to fail and, other than for 'Monkey' Jim, there was a backup plan for everything. My job was to help Jimmy stay focussed. Not that he looked like he needed much help in that department.

Walsingham removed his headphones, nodded a welcome, and pointed to where we each should sit. Jimmy was immediately directed around to the far side of the table so he was unable to see the little counters that would've told him who was who and who was sitting where. There was a set of headphones next to our respective places and when we put them on we were immediately transported to the meeting-room just along the corridor.

"Thank you, gentlemen, for adjusting your busy schedules to accommodate me, but I think this morning's meeting will prove of great significance to the future success of the Metropolitan Police Force. Of late, there have been many harsh criticisms by politicians, the public, and the nation's newspapers alike about the rising tide of crime in the capital. And even though it's widely understood that an increase in crime is the inevitable aftermath of every "great war," and even though I acknowledge that we still suffer a dire shortage of men in uniform, I offer no excuses. I will say, however, that in my opinion, a seriously depleted Metropolitan Police Force has, in the face of an almost insuperable task, discharged its duties with extraordinary courage and ingenuity, and I am justly proud of them and of each of you. I am under no illusions about the severity of the problems we face, and my only response is that we must now seek to redouble our efforts in both solving crime and in securing our streets from those who would seek to destroy the good order of the Realm.

We must ably demonstrate to one and all that the business of policing our capital is in good and capable hands. And to that end I intend to renew my commitment to the task ahead and make a statement to that effect in the presence of all now assembled. I would then ask you each do the same, in respect of yourselves, the Force, and the good people of London."

It was the voice of the Police Commissioner himself, Sir Harold Scott— the only man in the entire room who knew what was actually going on behind the scenes and the reasons for it. Though, as I later learned, he didn't want to know which of his senior officers Walsingham was trying to ensnare. He said he wasn't a good enough actor and he'd give the game away immediately by the look of utter disappointment that would be sure to cloud his face.

In comparison, Jimmy Mooney's task was simplicity itself. All he had to do was listen in and pick out Watts' voice from all the others in the meeting-room, unaided and sight unseen, and once he'd properly identified the man, to make a statement to that fact. Watts' actual words and the time he uttered them would then be correlated and confirmed by the stenographers and the women taking shorthand. After which, of course, came the second acid test: Jimmy was to be confronted with the assembled throng and had to pick out Deputy Assistant Commissioner Ernest H. P. Watts by sight from all those around him, again unprompted and unaided.

Did I say simplicity itself? Pick out a man he'd seen in the distance, stepping in and out of his chauffer-driven motorcar, a man he'd followed through all weathers on his little Bantam motorbike, again from a distance, a man whose house he'd burgled and seen all too briefly as a shadow on the stairs. A man he'd once heard speaking in another room. I tell you, knowing what was riding on it, my hands started to sweat, I don't know about his. And there were no three tries to get it right, either. When Jimmy Mooney pointed the finger, it had to be definitive. No second guesses allowed.

As each officer stood up to speak, the bloke in the charge of the microphones dialled down the sound so that Jimmy couldn't hear him give his name and rank. We, however, could hear everything. It was only when the officer concerned was making his statement that Jimmy was permitted to hear his voice. And even though he was the eleventh person in a row to get up and make a speech, Jimmy nailed Watts by the end of his very first sentence. Even so, Walsingham made him sit and listen to everyone else, just to be sure. But Jimmy didn't falter once or have second thoughts about his decision.

Then it was time for the Second Act.

Jimmy was asked to turn round and face the wall and the curtains were drawn back to reveal one of Walsingham's favourite spying devices: a two-way mirror. It was evident now what the Ministry of Works had been up to for the last few days: secreting a forest of microphones around the meeting-room and fitting a two-way mirror between the anteroom and the tiny room we were in.

Directly in front of us, on the other side of the looking-glass, there was a table covered with bone-china cups and saucers, all arranged in close-set ranks. Beyond that, there were the double doors to the main meeting-room. On the right was the door leading to the corridor outside. On the left, several coat-stands were doing sterling duty under the weight of an ungodly number of official-issue dark blue mackintoshes. Adjacent to these, a long trestle table all but groaned under the weight of three dozen or more upturned dark-blue peaked caps, displaying the black-and-white-chequered band that signified Metropolitan Police VIP. Each cap graced by its attendant silver-tipped swagger stick and pair of brown leather gloves.

As a stage setting it wasn't up to much, but it more than did the job. You could definitely feel the tension rising in our little room. Then, as if on cue, an expectant hush settled upon all in the audience as the curtain went up.

ACROSS THE FOOTLIGHTS

The lights in our room dimmed, and the sound in our earphones was turned off. The very first people we saw enter the anteroom were a couple of tea-ladies whose job it was to ensure the tea and coffee urns were hot and that the milk jugs, sugar bowls, and biscuit tins were full. So when the door to the meeting-room opened and the first wave of silver braid and medal-encrusted uniforms burst into the anteroom, it seemed for one awful moment as if we were about to be engulfed by a sea of dark blue serge—a sight guaranteed to make any honest-to-goodness villain immediately turn very queasy.

"Now that's what I call a bleedin' police line-up," Jimmy said, his voice hoarse with emotion. I wasn't the only one to chuckle, but we'd have laughed at anything at that point.

The way the Yard's most senior police officers hit the refreshments tables you'd have thought they were storming the Normandy beaches, and at first it was hard to tell one from the other. Then Jimmy stiffened and I followed the line of his gaze and saw the man his eyes had alighted upon, and I all but stood to attention myself. For standing in front of us, seemingly not more than three feet away, was Deputy Assistant Commissioner (Legal), Ernest Harold Percival Watts himself, and if not preening exactly, he certainly wasn't letting a perfectly good mirror go to waste. And for a moment, with the sound off and everyone standing in silence, it was like a dumb show within a play, with Jimmy staring in fascination on one side of the two-way mirror and Watts doing the same on the other.

I felt the bile rising inside me at the sight of Watts and he was lucky there was an invisible wall between us, because I'd have throttled him with my bare hands, if I could've reached him. And time slowed down around me as it does sometimes on a creep and I thought of all Jimmy and I had been forced to go through because of him. We'd been cast as unwitting shadows upon the walls of whatever castle in the clouds he'd dreamed of building. Whatever his motives it'd almost cost Jimmy and me our lives and had certainly cost Harry "Rabbit" and "Tosh" Collis theirs, and young Bob Miller his, and the five nameless members of Shadow Mob as well.

And there he was, the bastard, resplendent in his uniform, looking as dapper as Claude Rains ever did playing Captain Renault in *Casablanca*. He looked to be about the same height as the famous British actor, too, as he was unquestionably the smallest man there—certainly on the wrong side of the Met's regulation minimal height of five feet eight inches. To counter it, though, he'd adopted a ramrod-straight military posture and supported it with excellent tailoring. He also wore his hair brushed back and brilliantined into submission, with just enough grey showing at the temples to make him appear distinguished, and this taken together with his perfectly trimmed moustache made him look not so much like the arch villain of the piece, but a matinee idol playing the role of a clever and conscientious policeman. That's always the trouble though with appearances: they can be so very deceptive.

But Jimmy was in no doubt about which of the assembled policemen was Watts, and he pointed him out and then formally identified him a second time for Walsingham's benefit. And as if to punctuate the moment, the clicks of the shutter planes of both cameras opening and closing echoed around the room and I couldn't help but be put in mind of the sound of a guillotine blade falling, which tells you where my head was. At which point, the sound was turned back up in all our headphones and I heard for real the man I'd only ever heard as a disembodied voice coming out of a machine or as a muffled voice in a hallway when I'd been hiding in the footwell of his desk.

And when he spoke, even I recognised it as the voice on the wire recording, a voice so fussily precise in its articulation as to suggest an overly educated foreigner and yet so mannered as to seem pretentious. He oozed self-importance, and he struck me as being yet another little man whose ambitions far outstretched his abilities. Small men with big ideas—history was full of them. Emperor Nero, Napoleon, Little Caesar, Darby Messima and now Ernest H. P. Watts, the man who would be Commissioner of Crime. And I almost laughed out loud, because as hard as I tried I still couldn't put Watts and Messima together; chalk and cheese wasn't in it—they were complete bloody opposites. Then the second shoe dropped. They weren't opposites at all; they were like two fucking peas in a pod. They were both small in stature, overly dapper, and fussily precise in all they did. They were both driven to succeed to the point of obsession. And as they'd both amply demonstrated in the pursuit of their aims, the ends justified the use of any and all means, however despicable, destructive, or deadly the consequences.

Then two things happened.

A police sergeant entered into the anteroom, saluted, and handed Watts a message. Watts put down his coffee cup and read whatever was written on the piece of paper. He seemed a little puzzled by it, but nodded his head in affirmation anyway. Then he reached for his cap, gloves, and swagger stick, and left the room, accompanied by the sergeant.

At which point Walsingham signalled that that part of the day's undertaking was concluded and that he and Simon Bosanquet had to leave immediately to attend to the next phase of the operation. He asked that everyone continue writing up their reports and thanked Jimmy and me for our assistance and asked that we all please remain inside the room until the Commissioner's meeting had concluded and the Yard's top brass had all departed. Then he and Bosanquet slipped out quietly and once again we were left in the all-too-capable hands of our minders.

Trouble is, working any caper in daylight stretches the nerves like catgut on a fiddle and the whole business in the 'Bladder' took that to new lengths. Not to mention all the cups of water I'd had since I'd been in the room. And, as nature will, it all took its course. Suddenly, I desperately needed to pee. So I put my hand up like I'd done when I was a kid at school to ask if I could be excused to go to the lavatory. And as by that time it seemed that most everything was over, bar for the shouting, at least for Jimmy and me, I think the minder in charge felt confident enough for me to go relieve myself unescorted. Anyway, one of the other minders took me to the door and gave me directions—turn right, the first corridor I came to, then third door on my left—and off I went.

I turned the corner, got a fix on the requisite door and I don't know whether it was the fact I rolled my shoulders to help relieve some of the tension that'd built up over the course of the morning or that I took my spectacles off to rub the bridge of my nose, but something must've broken the spell. I pushed open the door, got that immediate whiff of disinfectant that presages lavatories, both public and private, in London, and went in to do my business. And even before I could get my fly buttons open the door from the corridor banged shut behind me and a gruff voice from out of my nightmares drowned out the sound of water flushing in the urinals.

"Fuck me, if it isn't you, you scumbag, newly risen from the grave. I heard you were dead, but it'd be just like you to eel your way out of even that. What the fuck you doing here on hallowed ground, you piece of shit?"

Detective Chief Inspector Browno—for it was he—didn't wait on an answer. He just lunged forward, punched me in the kidney, and I all but peed over the wall as my spectacles went flying across the floor and I fell to my knees on the hard, cold wet tiles. He reached in, grabbed a handful of hair, pulled my head up and was just about to belt me a wicked backhander across the face, when he stopped dead and stared at me, really hard.

"Wait a minute, wait a bloody minute. What a brassbound, blind, fucking excuse for a fool I've been. It's got to be you, hasn't it? What with Mr. W being here, sorting out something that needs sorting. You're here with him, aren't you? I remember seeing your face looking like that once before, only I didn't recognise it then—there was too much dried blood, mud, and shit all over it. Was that you, tied to the fucking chair, that time at that house in Berkeley Square, the one owned by that posh bastard, Lord Belfold, the one that topped himself?"

It was a lot for me to follow and I desperately needed to pee, so I just nodded blankly and said, "I really need to pee," and it was as if the world tilted again, for he pulled me up and turned me round to face the urinal and held me up by my shoulders until I completed my by now very urgent task.

The deed done, he asked, "Can you stand by yourself?"

I coughed and said, "I think I can manage, thank you."

He went over to the hand-basins and washed his hands and dried them on the roller-towel, then went over and stood, arms crossed, his back firmly against the door to the corridor. "Beg pardon for bashing you, just then," he said. "Force of habit."

I stumbled over to the line of hand-basins, noticed my glasses had been placed on the side of one of them, and I turned on the hot tap and washed my hands and face.

"So it's you Mr Walsingham's been calling on this last year or so when he needed a bit of creeping done?" I looked at him in the mirror and nodded; there was no point in denying it. "I should've fucking known when I kept coming up against those bloody red cards on you," he said. "God, I can be as blind as a fucking bat sometimes. I have no fucking idea why it was so important Messima be brought in this morning. I work on a fucking need-to-know basis, I do, but I do know it's got to be something big if it's got the Old Man and all the other top brass all sitting round in dress uniform, in the same room, wagging their little pinkies over cups of tea and coffee."

I didn't say anything, I just wiped my hands, tried to brush myself down as best I could, combed my hair with my fingers, and put my glasses back on.

I looked at him in the mirror and he'd gone so still he seemed to be part of the wall. And as I stood there not making a sound, his big round doughy face suddenly revealed itself as a complex interplay of edges, angles, and planes, with almost as many facets to it as a round brilliant, and as he ground his teeth back and forth, the shadowplay of him thinking it all through flitted back and forth across his face. There was a push against the door from outside, but it didn't budge an inch.

"Cleaning," he yelled. "Come back in five minutes, I'll be finished then." There was a murmur from the other side of the door, followed by a sudden flicker in Browno's process of thought, because his eyes lit up and he did something I'd not heard before—he laughed. Or I think it was a laugh; it was more a grunt followed by a loud expulsion of air. He'd cracked the riddle. "Fuck my old brown boots, it's something to do with this NORTO business, isn't it?"

This time I thought it best to equivocate. I waggled my hands in front of me. "I can't really say," I said.

He looked at me, his eyes narrowed—shrewd, calculating— as he struggled to re-establish some sort of balance in the new world order of 'thief-takers' and villains newly revealed to him. "Okay, then," he said, "a fucking nod's as good as a wink to a blind man. I can fill in the missing bits of the puzzle myself." He scratched his chin with a big sausage-sized finger. "This incident in here never happened. Got it? From what I've heard about what was done for Mr. W in the past, you've already earned any remission coming to you, ten times over, even before all this malarkey that's going on. So, as much as it fucking pains me to say it, I'll be watching your back from now on. If you ever do make it back out into the land of the living, that is."

I nodded, but said not a word, as it still hurt to stand, let alone speak. Then a light bulb went on over my head. "I need to ask a favour," I said. "Concerning one of your own."

His eyes narrowed again. "Who? Some copper already got the bite into you, has he?"

"Nothing like that," I said. "That goes with the territory. No, it's one of the Ghost Squad that's in danger. Only I recently had this run-in with a couple of hit-men that thought I was good and dead. I did for one, the other's probably in hospital, but they always operated as a gang of three, and it's the third bloke that worries me. The three of them were about to torture and kill me when this Ghost Squad copper steps in, takes over, and says that topping me was down to him. Only, as you can see, he didn't go through with it, and he as good as saved my hide. Out in the real world, his name is 'Gus,' Augustus Coulton— tall, thickset; dark haired bloke; ex-Military Police, Army of the Rhine. Don't ask me how I know that, just get word to him that his undercover identity is likely blown, and if he gets the hell out the Smoke, he might well live to see another Christmas."

Browno gave me a very odd look and then nodded. "Consider it done," he said, standing away from the door. "And you better take your own fucking advice, too, and just disappear off back into the shadows. And fast."

Then he turned and was gone and all I was left with was the sound of the outer door closing and the echo of water flushing in the urinals.

NONE SO BLIND

Later that evening, back at the safe house, Simon Bosanquet pulled me aside. He looked like he'd had a long day. I suppose we all had in one way and another. He didn't say anything about what'd gone on with Watts at the Yard. And I didn't say anything about the strange coincidence of Messima having been brought in for questioning, same day, same time. What he did say was that enquiries were ongoing and we should remain at the safe house for the time being.

"That's only wise and proper," I said, "but I do need to ask a favour." He nodded. "I need you to kill off Jimmy Mooney," I said. "And fast."

To say he gave me an odd look would be an understatement.

"Whatever happens to Messima," I said, "Jimmy's life isn't going to be worth tuppence out on the street. The 'notice' on him may well get cancelled, but there'll always be some idiot that won't have got the message who'll try and make his fortune by taking it out of 'Monkey' Jim's hide."

"What about you?" said Simon. "Aren't you in danger, too?"

"I'll take my chances," I said. "The 'notice' on me was nothing like the money put on Jimmy's head. That was an unheard-of amount, as big as a win on the football pools. If it ever got out how much he'd helped Scotland Yard with their enquiries into Messima, he'd end up as cat's-meat, no question."

"What can I do to help?" he asked, catching on fast.

"He'll need a new identity. A new name, new passport, and papers."

"That can all be arranged," he said amiably, as if he did that sort of thing every day. "A week should do it."

"And once he's officially dead," I said, "you'll need to sort out any and all issues to do with probate. You've also got to get the powers that be to waive the currency export restrictions so he can get whatever money he's got hidden away out of the country."

"Easy enough to do," he said.

And that's when I thought, "It really is a different world on this side of the looking-glass. And no messing."

I often asked myself why I hadn't recognised "Monkey" Jim, my old teacher, at the very beginning of the caper. There was the climbing belt, yes, but there were a number of creepers who used them and used them well, though none as expertly as Jimmy. What very few people knew, though, was that he usually used two belts at once, clipping and unclipping as he went, whether going up the stack-pipe or down, making mincemeat of any supports securing it to the wall, somehow always managing to maintain his unhurried slow, slow, quick, quick, slow movement. Thing was, though, he'd only been using one belt that fateful night back at the Mansions. Still, you'd think that of all people I would've recognised him. I was blind to it because I was so sure he was still doing porridge in the Scrubs and wasn't due out for another year yet. But then there are none so blind as those who will not see. If I'd actually seen him using a second climbing belt, the scales might've fallen from my eyes. As it was, I'd been in a hurry to climb back up to the roof of the Mansions and get off and out of it, proud, gleeful even, that I'd bested whoever it was I'd seen climbing up from the murky gloom below. Funny what you can't see for looking, sometimes, even when it's your own history that's staring you in the face.

"I've been meaning to ask you, Jimmy, how are you fixed for money?"

"Can't grumble. Harry seems to have left me a tidy bit. I got a couple of nice stones I put by for a rainy day." He patted his tummy. "Got the old money-belt out of hock—gave it a good going over with dubbin, just in case."

"You have been thinking ahead," I said.

We were sitting in the common room at the safe house, me drinking the hair of the dog to try and get over the effects of the little celebration we'd had the night before for a job well done. Jimmy, of course, was stone cold sober and drinking the teapot dry.

"Thanks again, Jeffro," he said, raising his teacup in salute. "Thanks for all you did to get it sorted. I'm just so very glad this whole nasty business with Watts is all done with." A shadow flittered across his face. "All I've got to friggin' worry about now is Messima. You, too, me old china."

"I reckon Messima is going to have far too much on his plate to be worrying about the likes of you and me," I said, trying to look sober myself.

"But Messima's got a memory like a bleedin' elephant," Jimmy said. "Even if he did get put inside, which you know as well as I do is highly unlikely, he could still pull strings and have someone topped, especially if he thought they'd double-crossed him. More than that, with such a huge bleedin' price on me head, I'll always be looking over my shoulder, waiting for a sudden cosh on the back of me head or a chiv in me ribs."

"Not if people think you're good and dead, you won't," I said.

He stopped dead—his teacup halfway to his mouth, his eyes staring into space—then he blinked himself alive again. "This Mr. W and Mr. B, they could arrange that sort of thing, could they?"

"How do you fancy another little boat trip on something a little bit bigger than the old *Phoenix*? Ever thought of going to Australia and maybe staying a while?"

He blinked again, the wheels turning and turning behind his eyes, and the idea of an undreamt of future slowly opened up before him. And he stood on the threshold and gazed out at the very possibility of a life "down under." I could tell by the look on his face he immediately saw the merits of the idea—a new name, new country, new start, the slate wiped clean—but then another shadow flittered across his face.

He looked at me. "I...I..."

"No worries on that score," I said, for once seemingly having Ray's ability to read minds. "I'll look after the ladies for you, and Harry, too. I'll find out where he was buried and have them all interred together in a little plot of ground at Kensal Green, all just as you originally wanted. That's the least I can do for you... and Harry...considering."

He went deep inside, into that private place we all of us have, and after about a million years he looked back at me, his eyes glassy bright with the sudden sheen of dammed-up tears. "I still miss them all something chronic, Jeffro," he whispered.

"They'll each one of them always be with you, deep down inside. They're part of you, and there's nothing ever going to come take that away."

"You'd do that for them, would you?" he said, softly. "A little bit of London all their own, with a proper gravestone and everything?"

"My word on it, Jimmy," I said. "All set up in perpetuity. Fresh flowers, the lot. I'll even send you photos, care of the General Post Office in Sydney."

And like he always did, he just nodded the once and in less than a fortnight he was gone—aboard a ship, out of the Pool of London—and that was one of the last times I ever saw him.

Simon Bosanquet was as good as his word. A small piece ran in the local *Ealing Gazette* about an unknown man who'd been knocked down and killed while walking on the A406,

Gunnersbury Avenue, close to the Common. It reported that
the man appeared to have been dead for several days since
the supposed time of the accident. The following week, a two-
paragraph piece said that a recently unidentified hit-and-run
victim had been positively identified as one James Matthew
Mooney, and that his body, which was in an advanced state of
decay, had since been cremated at public expense at the West
London Crematorium, Kensal Green. Simon also untangled
whatever red tape there was in getting Harry Mooney's body
disinterred and transported to pastures new. Then after
sufficient funds were deposited, and a number of visits made to
the wizards at J.S. Farely, monumental masons on the Harrow
Road, Kensal Green Cemetery did the Mooney family proud.
There was a little plot overlooking the canal, close enough to
the ornamental iron railings for the sun to throw a daily fan
of shadows across the large slab of Portland stone that marks
the Mooneys' little bit of England. On top of the bare slab
were the names and relevant dates of all the Mooneys and, at
the centre, two little animals, carved in stone, sat together in
quiet contemplation of the trees and allotments over by Little
Wormwood Scrubs.

My first thought had been to get the people at Farely's to
sculpt Romulus and Remus, with or without the she-wolf, but
I abandoned the idea as being a bit too much like all the other
monuments in the cemetery. And if nothing else, the Mooney
brothers were a pair of honest-to-goodness originals, full of
humour and whimsy, so in the end I settled on the unlikely
pairing of a rabbit and a monkey. They're still there, lost now
amongst all the seraphim, cherubim and angels, elephants,
horses and unicorns, and all the other fantastic animals and
figures that populate Kensal Green Cemetery. I try and visit
on the anniversary of the Jerry bombing that took the Mooney
women. And once or twice over the years I've almost thought
I caught sight again of "Monkey" Jim around town, but I've
never pursued whoever it was; the little bouquet of bright blue

flowers left on the slab of Portland stone were witness enough to him having passed that way.

One other little incident while we're at it.

Not long after he left for a life 'down under', I got a parcel in the mail, sent 'care of' the Victory Cafe and postmarked 'Southampton.' I knew immediately it was from Jimmy, and when I opened it, there was a cigar box inside, with the keys to his lock-up in Ealing Broadway, as well as sets of keys for his BSA Bantam runabout and Reliant three-wheeler. In a separate cardboard box I found his pair of Kriegsmarine night-glasses, the ones he'd bought down Loot Alley, and all but identical to the ones that'd been smashed when I got lifted off the street by that band of NORTO gorillas. There was a picture postcard inside the parcel, showing one of the monkeys from the monkey house down Regents Park Zoo. On the back were scribbled the words: *'J., Just in case you ever need to get back out on the tiles again. Be lucky'.*

I had to laugh.

He'd signed it, 'Kangaroo' Jim.

BY WAY OF KENSAL GREEN

"Cemeteries give me the willies, Jethro. Odd fuckin' place to meet in the dead of night." Cold breath steamed from the corners of Spottsy's mouth.

"Not if you're supposed to be dead," I said.

He stamped his feet, I think to keep warm, rather than in annoyance. "This being dead business must get old very quickly," he said. "Coming back to the land of living soon, are you?"

"I certainly hope so, Jack," I said. "From what I hear, this NORTO business has gone right off the boil. So, maybe, with a bit of luck, it won't be long before I can be re-born again."

Jack nodded his head and had another go at stamping his feet. "True. Since a couple of them King's Cross tossers got theirs in spades, things have definitely quieted down. Almost back to normal, I'd say, though with Messima in the game you can never be too sure. That little Maltese ponce could survive the seven plagues of Egypt and still come up smelling of Rose's Lime Juice. Still, I have to say I'm very pleased to hear you've come up trumps for me in regards them missing diamonds. Tommy said you mentioned something about it being a foreigner what did it?"

"Sheer chance on my part, Jack," I said, slipping into a little spiel I'd put together based on how Ray had originally intended to fence off Mrs Fox's jewellery. "Nosed round the Garden and just happened to bump into this old geezer I did deals with before the War—his sons run his business now, but he still has his ear to the ground. Only, he heard whisper about this collector in Chicago who turned down an offer on the stones from a dealer in Toronto, on account of the VIP bloodstains on them. He put Jew and Jew together, called a relative of his in Rotterdam, came up with a name. For a price, of course."

"There always is," Spottsy muttered.

I advanced my pawn to King 4.

"Word was the Meridian Mansions job was set up by some big-shot Canadian businessman who was in town and saw the sparklers in a picture-spread in one of the magazines, who then got on the transatlantic blower and brought over some top-class creeper from Toronto to do the business."

"A foreigner, eh?"

"It had to be, if you think about it, Jack. Couldn't have been a London 'face.' Given the size of the purse Messima put up, everybody and his brother's uncle was out looking. Somebody somewhere would've put the finger on someone sooner or later if it was a local talent that'd done it."

"Yes," agreed Spottsy. "Had to be a fuckin' foreigner. No one in the Smoke could've escaped Messima's dragnet for that long. So, you reckon you can get it all sorted, do you?"

I brought my queen out and moved it diagonally across the board.

If Spottsy had swallowed that little lot, it was already checkmate.

"Wheels already well in motion," I said.

Spottsy scratched his chin. "This Canadian bloke—play ball, will he?"

"Believe so. What with blood still on the jewellery, and blue blood at that, and his top buyer turning him down, it'd be a sure case of fast-diminishing returns. So once he got word the insurance payout had been doubled, he does his sums, sees he can still be in profit. He not only gets the lion's share of the reward money, it all but caps the caper, leaving him free and clear. Very smart of him, really."

"Very smart," said Spottsy, counting on his fingers. "So let's see who's in on it then. The Canadian gentleman. Bloke in Rotterdam. The old geezer in the Garden. You, of course. And me. That's five pots to piss in. Am I correct?"

"That's it," I said. "From what I understand, the, er, Canadian gentleman wants forty per cent off the top; the middleman, the usual fifteen per cent; which leaves the remaining forty-five per cent, divided three ways."

"I can do the fuckin' sums," said Spottsy, irritably. "Equal fuckin' shares then, is it?"

"Seems only fair," I said. "Everyone gets the standard taste. Plus, of course, you do get to deliver the bacon. On top of which, word gets out on the street that you can still get difficult business done when others can't. Do your reputation a world of good."

"Yes, there is that," Spottsy mused. "There is that."

I could hear the wheels grinding away in his head. "So little, from so much"—the reward money might well be six figures, but it whittled down to almost nothing when there were five snouts at the teats and you were last in line.

My queen had had his king in check with nowhere for it to go for the last five minutes. All it needed was for me to proclaim, "check mate."

"Er, I was thinking," I said. "It could be whittled down to only four bites of the cherry." Spottsy slid his eyes in my direction. "Only, there's this something you've got that I've rather taken a shine to."

"And what would that be?" Spottsy asked very, very quietly.

"Your narrowboat, the *Phoenix*," I said, jumping right in. "Without that old girl, I don't know how I'd have survived being dead," I said. "That No. 7 turned out to be real lucky for me, as is witnessed by the fact I'm still here."

"The *Phoenix*, eh? You could buy a whole fleet of fuckin' lorries, a warehouse, and a motorboat with your share of the money."

"Too true, Jack. But as I said, Lady Luck definitely smiled on me while I was on the *Phoenix*, and that counts for an awful lot." I couldn't push it too hard; I didn't want Jack to think me a steamer. But then again, there're few occupations more larded with superstition than thieving for a living, and Jack knew that as well as me. "And when it comes down to something as important as luck, it's never just about the money, is it, Jack?"

He nodded, as he did the sums again in his head. It'd make his take thirty per cent of the reward money—more than the bloody Rotterdammer, more than the old *schnorrer* in the Garden, and almost as much money as the crafty sod who'd put up the job in the first place. Not too shabby, considering.

"And you'll be the middleman for me? Sort out all the arrangements? Make sure it all goes hunky-dory?"

"No one's likely to welsh on the deal, are they, Jack, not once word gets round you're involved."

"All right then, Jethro," he said. "It's a deal. You keep the *Phoenix*, I'll keep your share of the payout." He took his leather glove from off his right hand, spit on his palm, and held out his hand. I did the same. We shook on it and the deal was struck. "*Mazel und broche.*" And with 'good luck and blessings', the good ship, *Phoenix*, lucky No. 7, was now all mine.

No, I hadn't gone 'Dolally'.

Simple truth was, I owed Jack Spot for helping save my life; Tommy Nutkins, too. And even though neither of them would ever use it to call in a favour—well, Spottsy would—in my book, the credit and debit columns always need to be kept in balance.

Not forgetting that, when all was said and done, I'd still end up with some serious cash in my pocket, split fifty-fifty with Ray, of course.

FINDING TRUE NORTH

And just where on God's green would I have been without Ray Karmin to guide me? I'd been that worked up about Darby bloody Messima and all his dark deeds, literally seething with anger, seeing nothing but blood red, I was in dire danger of losing my head for real. Ready, set, and raring to go challenge Messima and all the other bastards in NORTO to a fight to the death on any stretch of cobbles they cared to choose. Not that Messima or any of the other gang bosses would've gone toe-to-toe with me, not when they had whole armies of hard men ready and waiting to do their fighting for them. So whichever way you looked at it, there could've only ever been one ending: I'd have been beaten to a bloody pulp, cut into little pieces with carving knives and choppers, stuffed in a bag, and thrown in the river.

And how had Ray dealt with it all, dealt with me? He'd seen me coming apart at the seams and steered me back into the shadows so I'd have a better chance of coming through it all alive and still in one piece. He'd had me hide away with Glover for a couple of weeks—out of sight and out of mind— until all the blind hot rage had had time to dampen down, and had even had me thinking it'd been my idea from the very start. But the plain truth was he'd stage-managed all the exits and the entrances and I'd played the many parts as written—I'd played dead, I'd played the ghost, I'd played the bastard, I'd even played the fool—and here I was still very much alive and kicking, and a lot of it down to Ray. Family aside, hands down, my very best 'old china.'

Talking of which, Joanie played merry hell with me when I called to tell her I was really alive. But I'm no steamer; I got to Church Street late enough at night for it to be all but deserted and telephoned her from one of the Apostles. That way she had a few minutes to compose herself. I did too. The front door was on the latch and as I closed the door behind me and turned to climb the stairs the light in the stairwell went on and I looked up and saw Joanie standing on the landing outside her flat. She peered down at me, in the dim yellow light, as if to prove to herself that it really was me, but she didn't say a word. Neither did I. I just continued to climb my way back up to the land of the living.

Then there we were, face to face, and the tongue-lashing when it came was like a volcano erupting and she rained blow after blow after blow against my chest with her tiny fists and, between sobs, called me every despicable name under the sun. Then she shook her head from side to side as if to dismiss me and turned and went back into the flat. I gave it a few moments and followed her. I heard a noise and saw Bubs, Joanie's old man, standing in the shadows in the living room, waiting for the storm to subside. He smiled and nodded a greeting and pointed in the direction of the kitchen, and I smiled back and nodded and went on through.

Joanie was standing over by the sink, facing the window, still sobbing. Then, bit-by-bit, relief slowly overcoming grief and anger, her sobs finally subsided and she sighed a huge sigh and wiped her eyes on the sleeves of her dressing gown and silently began making a pot of tea. She turned and just stared at me, blankly, still not saying a word, and we both waited in silence for the tea to mash—a few of the very longest moments of my life—then she served up three cups, called for Barry to come in from the other room, and we all sat down at the kitchen table.

"You better tell me what happened," she said, her voice dull and flat and dangerous. "And if you tell me a single lie, Jethro, I swear to you, I'll murder you again, myself."

So I told her.

She didn't like it when I told her why I had no choice but to play dead and why I had no choice at all in not telling her the truth of it at the time.

"If there was any chance at all I was really alive, Messima, the whole lot of them, would've reckoned that you'd know the truth of it and they would've had eyes watching you and the Victory from morning until night, just on the off chance that you or someone let something slip. And if for one instant they thought me alive, they'd have taken you hostage and just waited for me to come get you. Your grim visage was the only real protection I had."

"He's right, Joanie," Bubs said, softly. "Even you mentioned a good few times as how there always seemed to be a lot of new faces in the cafe."

"Did 'Buggy' Billy know you were alive?" she asked, ignoring Barry.

"Never spoke a word to him," I said. "I know he's a hell of an actor and might've covered it well, but again, I didn't want to put someone I love in any more danger than they already were."

It seemed to mollify her. And after all, it was only a white lie.

It was Ray Karmin I'd told, not "Buggy" Billy. Thing being, to all intents and purposes Ray was someone else entirely and someone entirely unknown to her.

When I finally went upstairs again to my own little flat—at last back in my own skin, as it were—the letter from Joanie I'd dared not open, let alone leave a thumb or fingerprint on, was still there on the kitchen table, undisturbed, unopened, and unread.

During the War, every single time I'd gone away again to sea, Joanie had posted a letter urging me to come home safe and sound, and somehow even with the millions of tons of merchant ships being sunk around me, right, left and centre, and sometimes even from under me, I'd always managed to return. It was as if her very prayers for my safe passage were given form and each letter became a totem of the never-to-be-taken-for-granted, wished-for good luck and good fortune. So when she'd heard the rumours I'd been lost to the river, she'd again written down her plea for my eventual safe return and sent it to me—via the Victory, this time—for delivery to the flat, the only place in all the world she knew I'd always return to if there was still breath in my body.

I all but choked as I read her words.

Jethro, my dear, dear brother, come back to me, to us, we all need you to be alive and in our lives. Know that you're always in our hearts. Keep you safe 'til next, wherever you are. Your loving sister, Joanie. x x x x x

I still have Joanie's letter in a little silver frame standing on my desk, next to an old brass pocket-compass I used when up on the lids. In my life, I've found that true north can be found by the most surprising of means.

Word of my resurrection soon made the rounds, along with all the usual references to me and my nine lives. "Buggy" Billy and his boys helped get the word out that Messima had simply wanted to put the frighteners on me because he suspected I'd helped Jack Spot on the Heath Row job, and that me not being a steamer, I'd got out of town as fast as my little legs could carry me and gone North, to Leeds or thereabouts. It seemed to fit with most people's rather dismal view of me: that I really had lost my bottle for all things creeping and criminal. And that suited my needs perfectly.

Me taking a well-deserved holiday was out the question, as Joanie and all the rest of them would only start worrying again that I'd gone missing. So for the next couple of weeks or so, I made the rounds of the markets, the billiard halls, the spielers and the pubs, then I did the theatres and the coffee shops and

Gambas and the all the rest of it, knowing all eyes would be on me. The more happy-go-lucky I appeared, the more people seemed to accept me, pleased that at least something or someone was back to normal.

Even 'Binnsy' seemed pleased to see me. And when he spotted me walking down the street, that first day back, he whipped off his glasses and wiped them over and over again with his dirty handkerchief, as if he couldn't believe his eyes. He got such a laugh from the usual bunch of layabouts holding up the walls of the Tube station, he repeated the pantomime for weeks until it wore as thin as his skin.

"Hat-trick of aperpays, is it, Jeffro?" he said.

I nodded. "Ta, Binnsy," I said, "I need to catch up on events."

"Then it's off for a cuppa over the Bridge, is it?" he said, to remind me again that he never missed a thing.

"Yeh, I could murder a cup of tea," I said.

"Nice to have you back among me regulars," he said.

"You can say that again, Binnsy," I said.

"Nah, wot I meant was, I missed yer money," he said, coughing a huge gob of phlegm and spitting it into the gutter. "See yer, Jeffro," he said.

"Not if I sees you first," I replied.

"Gertcher!" he wheezed. And I waved the linens over my shoulder, like a battle flag, pleased as 'Punch' to be finally out of the shadows and back in the land of the living, or at least what passed for it around Church Street.

IN CAMERA

Live and let live? Not always. It's a different world on the other side of the looking-glass. The guilty are dealt with differently there. One presumes for the public good, but the rest of us back in the real world rarely seem to be the better for it. There's 'the letter of the Law' and then there are those who, in purported Defence of the Realm, read between the lines and make annotations in ink invisible to the likes of you and me. And should a servant of the people ever prove untrustworthy or become an embarrassment to any of the noble institutions of Law and Order, wiser heads and colder hearts prevail. More often than not the problem is then dealt with behind closed doors, *in camera*—as those in the know would have it—where people or things are very quickly and quietly swept under the carpet. Or they're confined between the covers of some obscure report and hidden away at the back of the file cupboards of State, along with all the rest of the skeletons.

Such was the case, it seems, with Ernest H. P. Watts, former Deputy Assistant Commissioner ('L' Division) of Scotland Yard, despite Simon having given me his word things wouldn't be hushed up. To be fair to Simon, though, the final decision wouldn't have been his. If you learn anything at all from your time in the shadow world, you learn you have little or no influence on events and you're never ever privy to anything you don't need to know.

What I do know is that both Watts and Messima were at the
Yard on the same stretch of corridor, at the same time, on the
same day, and that it was no accident. It's an old police trick.
Two suspects, each unaware the other's been brought in for
questioning, both then given a quick sight of the other and
led to believe their erstwhile partner-in-crime has already
implicated them in some way. Nothing too specific at first,
everything left to the imagination, which not unnaturally soon
runs riot, with inevitable results. Later, it's a simple matter of
filling in the blanks on the official reports as to who said what,
when, about whom, so that everything matches up.

I can well imagine how it happened, and with Walsingham
directing the action it would've all been timed down to the
second. The police sergeant enters—Down Stage Left—and
hands Watts the message. Watts reads it and smartly exits the
anteroom, accompanied by the sergeant, and off they march up
the corridor, Watts believing he's been summoned to an urgent
meeting with the Home Office permanent under-secretary or
some such luminary. Meanwhile, Detective Chief Inspector
Robert Browno and his detective-sergeant enter—Up Stage
Right—and escort Darby Messima and his brief along the same
corridor, from the opposite direction—Messima, not under
arrest, but under the impression he's been brought in to help
the police with enquiries into some incident or other at one of
his many Soho nightclubs.

And thus the two unsuspecting parties bump into each
other as they round the corner—Up Stage Left. It's hard to say
whether it's Watts or Messima who reacts the most as they're
suddenly brought face-to-face, but I see the two men being so
startled that not a single word passes between them, the frowns
and puzzled looks exchanged more than enough for the poison
to do its work. After which Watts is escorted off in one direction
while Messima and his solicitor are led away in the other and
then taken into an interview room, which marks the next scene.

It's all total conjecture on my part, of course, but I think it highly likely that an interview did take place that day. And I suspect DCI Browno and his detective-sergeant would've stayed with Messima and his brief only until such time as a uniformed senior police officer accompanied by a tall, distinguished-looking, grey-haired gentleman in civvies entered the interview room. I'm sure Messima and his solicitor would've been not a little surprised to then see both Browno and his sergeant exit, never to return.

I can hear Simon Bosanquet conducting the interview in his trademark flat, monotone delivery, devoid of all emotion. He'd have only done it for effect, but I know from personal experience just how devastatingly effective it could be—the slow, relentless assembly of tinder dry facts that left you in no doubt at all the authorities were in possession of evidence that could see you burn at the stake, if not in hell. After all, the facts were plain enough. That one Darby Alphonse Solano Messima had been a prime mover in the setting up of NORTO, an illegal confederation of London gangs. An unholy criminal alliance that sought to operate in parallel with an illegitimate court system—the so-called Shadow Court—the sole purpose of which was to establish NORTO's authority and maintain it by the meting out of extreme and unusual punishment upon accused wrongdoers.

I suspect Simon wouldn't have given Messima too much time to ponder before also informing him that by undertaking such acts, he, Darby Messima, and others as yet unnamed, had wilfully and maliciously perverted and obstructed the course of justice. And that any and all actions conceived and carried out under the aegis of said criminal organisations—NORTO and Shadow Court—constituted serious offenses against the public peace and the good order of the Realm, and that all such offenses were indictable under both Sections One and Two of the Defence of the Realm Act.

Messima, when cornered, was as dangerous as a rat with rabies. So I not only see him denying everything, but going hard on the attack, denouncing the whole affair as a clear case of entrapment and that if it ever came to court he was sure he'd be both acquitted and exonerated. At which point he'd sue the Metropolitan Police for every penny they possessed.

That would've probably been the moment Simon Bosanquet asked Messima to confirm or deny his presence at the death of the late Nigel Fox MP, or even perhaps asked him to clarify his relationship with a man called Earnest H. P. Watts—two things Messima would've wanted kept under wraps at all costs. At which point, Messima likely told his brief to "go fuckin' wait outside." Then with Messima, to all effects, *in camera*, all Simon had to do was play the all-incriminating wire-recording.

I don't know how long it would've been before it dawned on Messima that he'd more than met his match in Walsingham and Bosanquet, but I'm sure that after a few moments' sober reflection, seeing that his little outburst had had absolutely no effect, he'd have realised that his usual 'Plan B' of bribery had even less chance of working. So he'd have then resorted to the only possible way-out left him. Something, say, along the lines of: "It's become very clear to me that Watts has lost his bottle and turned 'nose' to save his own skin. And such being the case, I have a few things to say in my own defence, and if you're interested, I'm willing to make a statement."

Granted, I may have adopted a little bit of poetic license in all that, but I reckon that if the interview happened, it was something along those lines. Had to have been.

I have no idea when or where Colonel Walsingham had his little heart-to-heart with Watts, but it probably took place around that time or very soon after. I'm sure the powers-that-be were all extremely concerned about the potential damage to the good standing of Scotland Yard should the real facts ever surface. There's little doubt though the result would've been much the same whoever it was pulled the strings—Walsingham or some exalted person even higher up the greasy pole of State—but pull them they did.

E.H.P. Watts, Esq., erstwhile DAC-'L' of Scotland Yard, having apparently suffered an acute nervous breakdown, was quietly removed from office and sequestered in an exclusive private sanatorium that specialised in the treatment of unfortunates afflicted with advanced delusions of grandeur.

Why did Watts enter into his pact with the devil? Who ever really knows why they do what they do? Ray and me discussed it a good few times over the ensuing weeks, during our Monday night games of chess, our thoughts and reflections probably as valid as anyone else's.

Ray—ever the student of human behaviour—reckoned Watts obviously felt his true worth was never fully appreciated or properly acknowledged. So when the job of Police Commissioner of the Metropolis went to Harold Scott, a man whose credentials were in no way a match for his own, who also received a knighthood on taking office, Watts became deeply embittered and resentful. A situation then made worse by the initial success of the Ghost Squad and the subsequent accolades awarded the Deputy Assistant Commissioner (Crime), whose idea it'd been.

Watts then of course set out to prove his genius by building a better mousetrap to control crime in London. As DAC-'L' it was easy enough for Watts to get hold of the CID files on Messima, soon after which he sought him out as a potential partner in crime. The price Messima extracted was a copy of the secret list of Ghost Squad officers so he could prove to all of London's villains he could do what no one else could and was thus worthy of the title 'Boss of the Underworld.' Only, then, having thought himself on the very verge of success, Watts had been entrapped by the very device he'd dreamt up. Nigel Fox—the one man in all London who could help turn his dream into a reality—had died in such a way as to shackle Watts to Messima forever. After Messima had dealt with Fox's body, cleaned up the mess, and set his false trails, he began to blackmail Watts. And the abyss had opened up and Watts had fallen into the ninth circle of hell—the realm of ultimate treachery—only to find Messima icily indifferent to his plight.

Simon Bosanquet—still very much wearing his copper's hat—later surmised that Watts had felt stifled in his job as an administrator of legal matters in the Metropolis. That he'd craved action and danger in equal measure and at the very least had wanted to be head of the CID and the Special Branch. More than anything, though, it appeared he wanted to be the Assistant Commissioner 'Crime', the head of all of London's detectives.

Watts' story doesn't end there, though; there's many a slip between this life and whatever comes next. A trip, a fall, a single misstep or a loss of balance can all serve as unexpected precursors to death. At least that's what apparently happened to Watts the following year. He slipped, hit his head against the side of the bath and, falling to the floor, hit his head again on the metal surround of a set of bathroom scales, and cracked his skull and died. An almost exact replay of the death of Nigel Fox MP. Funny that.

I'm pretty sure it was an accident. Has to have been.

I do admit, though, there are times, in the dead of night, when the world narrows down to just me and a bottle of Scotch, when I can't get the idea out of my head that Simon Bosanquet had a hand in it somewhere. And I don't know why I should think such thoughts, but I do.

Still waters run very deep in Simon, as does his inbred sense of justice.

Of course, when I see I've managed to get way down below the label, my thoughts run even deeper—and darker. That's when I think I see someone moving in and out of the shadows and in and out of the bathroom window who looks an awful lot like Jimmy Mooney.

That's when I know it's time for me to put my Whisky glass way, way out of my reach.

OLD ENDINGS REVISITED

Given the way an awful lot of things turned out, I don't find it too fanciful to imagine Walsingham having a word in Messima's shell-like ear when he had him in for questioning. Something, say, along the lines that unless the self-styled 'Boss of the Underworld' agreed to become a reliable conduit of information, Walsingham would ensure word got out in the Smoke that he, Darby Alphonse Solano Messima, was a 'grass' of long standing, and that it was his secret relationship with Scotland Yard that'd been the real foundation of NORTO and Shadow Court. Messima would've known all too well he wouldn't last ten minutes on the street if even a hint of that got out. All that would've been required was for Messima to give a deposition under oath, *in camera*, again, and 'Bob's yer uncle', the grass could be cut on a regular basis. But then as I've said before, Colonel Walsingham was nothing if not practical. He was certainly never one to waste a useful asset that could be quietly tucked away inside his box of tricks. It was just Walsingham putting into practice his very own "austerity measures"—doing his bit to follow the government's mandates that people 'Waste Not Want Not' and 'Make Do And Mend.'

And I only say all this because it appeared to Ray and me— purely as interested bystanders, of course—that for a good few years afterwards, Scotland Yard seemed to have its finger very firmly on the pulse of London's underworld. It was almost as if someone was still hiding in the shadows with their eyes and ears on all that was happening in the Smoke. Impossible, of course, as the Ghost Squad was completely shut down not long after Watts was removed from office. The official reason being that the authorities were overly fearful that London's streets and alleyways, clubs, pubs, spielers, and dens of vice offered far too much temptation for undercover detectives to resist, and that widespread corruption was therefore inevitable.

It might've all been just a bunch of coincidences.

And yet, and yet...

The inquest into the death of Nigel Fox MP was re-opened, the previous verdict of murder quashed, and a new finding of "death by misadventure" entered into the record. The now undisputed facts being that Fox had attended a private dinner in the Soho district of London and at some point during the evening had slipped and hit his head and died. No one else was to blame. Given the deceased's social standing and political celebrity, his dinner companions had, in a blind panic, committed a gross and foolish act by trying to cover up what was plainly an accident. That Fox's Meridian Mansions flat had been burgled and his safe robbed of valuables that same night was an unfortunate coincidence. It was this single event that had led the Metropolitan Police to surmise that far darker motives were at play. And this in turn had given rise to the widespread press and public speculation regarding the case.

All of which had only served to further obscure the true facts of the matter.

The words 'cover up' appeared nowhere in the Coroner's report, but it did tie things up very neatly. Its one saving grace, in my opinion, was that it also officially cleared the late Nigel Fox of any and all questions regarding misdeed or misconduct. In response, Mrs Fox issued a statement saying how very relieved she was that her husband's good name had been restored and that the whole sorry story could at last be put to rest. The linens then had another field day, whitewashing over the blacking they'd previously given her husband's reputation. The moral of the tale of course being that if you want to hide a grave, just dig another one on top.

One quick final note about Mrs Fox: She was as good as her word and paid the full additional reward for her missing jewellery, which I'm sure she found far more comforting than the memories of her husband's affair with his personal secretary.

Then right out the blue, the press, in urgent need of fresh blood, alighted upon a new villain, one Ronald White, scion of the infamous North London crime family. And onto his narrow shoulders they heaped the blame for all the recent gangland violence. The general consensus, backed by a veritable army of eyewitnesses, was that the young head of the King's Cross mob had sought to control all of the crime in London and it was only when older, more sober heads within London's criminal fraternity had sought to resist his audacious plan that the usual balance between law and disorder had broken down. It was White and his notorious henchmen Jimmy Pottle, Eddie Maytum, and Bobby Boyle who were solely responsible for all the carnage and death. And thus it was that the young gentlemen from King's Cross suddenly found himself arrested and charged for his and everyone else's sins.

In the end, the event the linens all touted as being "the trial of the century" never took place on account of the sudden death of said Ronald White. How it happened is still unclear; suffice to say, early press reports said that rather than stand trial, a man charged in connection with eight, possibly nine, murders of persons as yet un-named had himself died as a result of jumping from an unsecured upstairs window of an East End police station.

Pitcher, Shipman and Bumaree, of course, played only very minor roles in the ongoing proceedings, given one was already dead (on account of me), one still in a coma (ditto), and one still in hospital recovering from a burst appendix. Funny thing about that being it was Shipman, alias Eddie Maytum, Pitcher and Bumaree had been going to visit at Chelsea and Westminster Hospital that time I'd bumped into them on the Fulham Road. How's that for odds?

Anyway, in lieu of Ronnie White, both Pottle and Maytum were arrested and formally charged and transferred to a hospital ward in Brixton Prison to await trial. While on remand there it seems inmate Pottle had his feeding tube accidentally disconnected, while inmate Maytum got himself knifed to death in the exercise yard. It's still anyone's guess who put out the 'notices' on the them, but it's an old saw that stilled tongues stay stumm, as no one's left alive then to contradict the given version of events.

Messima did stand trial, although he was never charged with murder, as no one had actually seen him kill anyone with his own hands. No witnesses meant there was no case to answer for. In the end, Messima was charged with contributing to riotous assembly, causing a public affray, and committing a breach of the peace—all very serious charges, but nothing that'd see him hanging from the end of a rope. Only, with justice being neither blind, nor averse to silken entreaties, what occurred then was a replay of the old legal two-step.

To wit: first have the accused admit to a lesser charge. Then get a very expensive barrister to get it reduced on appeal to a simple matter of assault. All of which is but a very short step to the payment of a large fine or full acquittal.

After all, justice—or what passes for it—is all too often only ever a question of money, and Messima always had plenty of that.

Not surprisingly, over time, the Shadow Court lost whatever grip it'd once had on crime in the Smoke, and all the old rivalries resurfaced again. The King's Cross mob was certainly never as powerful again as it'd been before and during the War. Harry McShane and the Upton Park mob grew in influence and formed an alliance with none other than Jack Spot.

Retribution was still handed out to thieves who proved a little too dishonest and to bent coppers who hadn't straightened things as efficiently as they'd promised, but it was nothing like it was before. Good smackings were still dished out, money in brown envelopes continued to change hands, various coppers' wives still drove Jags or enjoyed lavish holidays, innocent people were put away to protect the guilty, there was the odd fight on the cobbles to determine which villain ran what racket—be it gambling, vice, racetrack betting, the dogs, dirty books, the photo-tout trade in Trafalgar Square, and much later, of course, drugs. But self-interest, mutual distrust, and the eternal lusting after whatever it was another gang had led to previous associations breaking apart, and everything went back to normal, as it were.

A motorcar backfired and the massed ranks of pigeons wheeled indignantly round and round the forecourt of the British Museum. I followed the display of aeronautics and the world turned again and, not surprisingly, took me with it. Me, I was just dead pleased I hadn't ducked for cover at the sound.

I'd treated myself to a quiet stroll through the Egyptian Galleries. A place I'd found utterly fascinating ever since Ray had first introduced me to its mysteries, back before the War. A place of secrets beyond fathoming; with giant statuary staring off into a world beyond imagining, alongside tiny delicate gold figurines and jewellery as exquisite as anything the world's best jewellery houses could ever offer. It was a completely different world that always offered tons of food for thought.

And what with a whole morning of that, followed by a lunchtime pie and pint with Ray across the road at the Museum Tavern, I have to say I felt really truly alive again. All past shadows fully faded from mind.

I had a sudden lovely thought that had me tacking to starboard, picking up my pace, and heading for a new port of call. I could telephone the ever-lovely Natalie. If, that was, she was back from her latest round of modelling at Mr Dior's couture house in Paris. She and one of her friends, Barbara, something or other, another real beauty, were coining it over there— posh photographers and women's magazines were falling over themselves to throw work at the two of them. Another lovely thing about seeing Natalie was that she probably wouldn't have heard anything about my supposed death, or any of the horrors I'd gone through. And that'd be a very nice change all by itself.

I'd had enough of living and dying in the shadows to last me several lifetimes.

As it was, what with a seemingly never-ending stream of concerned family and friends, I'd about had it up to here, going over all the ins and outs and ups and downs of the caper; all renditions of course suitably edited for public consumption. Not that I was complaining, mind. I knew full well I wouldn't even be alive if it hadn't been for one old china after another sticking out a helping hand when I had need—a circle of friends, each one a pearl beyond price.

Simple truth was, I wanted to be left alone to fade back into the foreground, so I could get on with doing what I do best: a nice bit of burglary involving singularly tasty pieces of jewellery. Though, as I well knew, there was fat chance of that happening for the next few weeks, even months. As it was, Joanie would hardly let me out of her sight. And, if ever I was, I then had Bubs following my every move, insisting that he drive me in his taxicab to wherever it was I wanted to go, which was very nice of him, but also very limiting to my movements, if you get my drift.

Where was I? Oh yes, the ever lovely Natalie and whether she was even in London or not. So, of course, straightaway, I started thinking about 'Plan B.' I could also try telephoning this other very lovely girl who worked the chorus line at the Prince of Wales. I'd almost got around to putting down some sand with her that time I'd helped out on *Harvey*. Christine, her name was. Another dark-haired smasher. I could definitely see myself making some sandcastles in the sky with her. We could maybe have a day out in Brighton together. Ride the donkeys. Bite on a stick of rock.

And so there I was, in Montague Place, round the back of the British Museum, and there on the corner of Malet Street was the line of telephone-boxes I'd often had occasion to use, and every single one of them good and empty, almost as if they'd all been patiently awaiting me. I chose trap number four, for luck. It was a good choice, too. No one had used to it to have a quick pee in since its last scrubbing out with disinfectant.

I dug into my pocket and felt around for some loose change.

A couple copper pennies of the Realm coming right up. George V's head, Edward VII's head, or George VI's head—shiny or dull—it mattered not one wit. But not a single penny did I find. I had nothing but a threepenny-bit, a six-penny piece, a shilling, a couple of two-bob pieces, and a half-crown. The only other ready money I had on me was a fat fold of fivers, all primed and ready to start burning holes in my pocket, but no earthly good at all for making a telephone call with, even if I'd wanted to call the King himself.

I stared mournfully at the black handset. I ask you, why are there never enough coppers around when you need them?

A LONDON LEXICON

'aper-pays:	(back slang) newspapers
Apples and pears.	'apples'; stairs
Argy-bargy:	argument, confusion
B 'n' E:	breaking and entering
Banged up:	locked in a cell
Bangers and mash:	cash
Barnet (Fair):	hair
Beak:	magistrate
Bees and honey:	money
Bent:	crooked
Berk:	idiot, or worse (rhymes w. Berkeley Hunt)
Binns:	spectacles
Bladder:	('bladder of lard') Scotland Yard
Blag:	robbery with violence
Blitz: the Blitz.	Period of Nazi bombing of London during WW II
Blow:	blow open a safe with explosives
Blower:	telephone
Boat:	'boat race'; face
Bob's your uncle:	everything will be absolutely fine
Bones:	form of skeleton key
Bottle:	(bottle and glass = arse) nerve

Brass:	prostitute; or money
Brass hat:	senior officer (Forces)
Brassard:	a taxi-driver's licence disc
Bunny:	rabbit and pork; to talk
Butcher's:	to look (butcher's hook)
Case:	to survey, or check out premises prior to burglary
China:	'old china'; (old china plate) a really good friend; a mate,
Chiv:	a knife or razor for cutting and slashing, not for stabbing
Climb/er:	usually refers to the act of cat-burgling; or a cat burglar
Clock:	clocked; to take a look-see
Cocoa:	rhymes w. 'say so'
Collar:	traditionally, when a policeman arrested a criminal by taking hold of him by the collar ie. 'to have one's collar felt'
Copper:	a policeman; a penny coin
Cosh:	a club made of lead, or iron, or wood, or hardened leather
Cowson:	pejorative; cf. 'whoreson'
Cozzer:	policeman
Crack:	to open a safe
Creep:	entering a dwelling by night, quietly and without noise
Creeper:	cat burglar
Daisy roots:	boots
Dickey-bird:	word
Diddikye:	gypsy

Doddle:	anything easy to achieve
Dog and bone:	telephone
Drag:	motorcar; to draw on a cigarette
Drinks:	'big drinks'; money, bribes
Drum:	a house or an apartment
Dubbin:	grease used for softening and waterproofing leather
Earner:	a bribe paid to the police
Face:	a crook of some repute
Fag:	cigarette
Fence:	receiver of and/or trader in stolen property
Fiver:	five quid; £5
Germans:	(German bands) hands
Gertcher!:	an exclamation of dismissal; be off!
Ginger:	('ginger beer') queer
Glim:	a torch
Grand:	a thousand pounds Sterling
Grass:	an informer; to inform
Gob, gobbed:	to spit out whatever is scoured from one's throat
Gone Dolally:	gone mad; der. boredom felt by British Army troops stationed at Deolali transit camp, in India
Gone for a Burton:	broken, smashed
Guv'nor:	gang boss or senior policeman
Gyppy tummy:	stomach troubles, diarrhoea
Half-inch:	to pinch; to steal
Harry Rag:	fag; cigarette
Hat-trick:	three in number

Hatty:	policeman in helmet, uniform
How's-yer-father:	nonsense; rubbish
Iron:	(iron hoof = poof) homosexual
Jack :	alone; "on my Jack Jones"
Joanna:	piano
Khazi, karsey:	(p) toilet
King Lears:	ears
Kip:	sleep
Lallies:	(p) legs
Latty:	(p) flat, room, house
Lills:	(p) 'lilly whites', hands
Linens:	newspapers (linen drapers)
Mack:	mackintosh, coat
Mangarie:	(p) food
Manor:	the territory of a particular policeman or criminal
Mazel und broche:	Yiddish: 'luck and blessing'; words that bind and seal a deal
Mince pies:	'minces'; eyes
Minder:	bodyguard, trouble-shooter
Mutt and jeff:	deaf
Naff:	(p) not very good, below par
Nancy:	effeminate man; or homosexual
Nark:	an informer
Narked:	to be very irritated
Nobble:	to interfere
Nod:	"land of nod"; to be asleep
Nosh:	Yiddish: food
Oglefakes:	(p) spectacles, glasses
Old Bill:	the police; policeman
Onk:	(p) nose

Petercane:	small crowbar
Peterman:	safe-breaker
Polari:	(p) an intimate chat, a talk
Polone:	(p) woman; (derogatory) man
Ponce:	pimp
Porridge:	time spent in prison
Prile:	three; a hand of three cards
Queer:	'to queer'; to spoil, put out of order
Rabbit:	to rabbit on; talk a lot; 'rabbit and pork' rhymes w. talk
Sarky:	sarcastic
Screwsman:	burglar or safe-breaker
Shufty:	to take a quick look
Shyker:	(p) a woman's wig
Skels:	type of skeleton key
Skint:	without money
Slap:	(p) make-up
Smoke:	London ("the Smoke")
Snout:	informer; or tobacco
Spieler:	drinking club
Spiv:	(back slang; VIPs; 'very important persons') black market street trader
Spuds:	potatoes
Starting price:	amount of bribe needed to straighten a bent copper
Steamer:	'steam tug' rhymes w. mug
Stoppo:	an escape; a getaway
Stumm:	to stay silent
Swallow:	to accept a situation without protest

Tealeaf:	thief
Team:	a gang of people that regularly work together
Tearaway:	small-time criminal, known to be reckless and violent
Titfer:	hat; rhymes w. 'tit for tat'
Tod:	on one's own; alone (Tod Sloane)
Tomfoolery:	jewellery
Top:	to kill
Tosspot; tosser:	a worthless person
Trade:	(p) sex
Troll:	(p) to walk about (esp. looking for trade)
Turtledoves, turtles:	gloves
Trouble and strife:	wife
Twigged:	to understand something
Twirl:	key, skeleton key
Vada:	(p) to see
Villain:	a crook of some standing
Whistle:	whistle and flute: suit
Wide:	"wide boy"; street wise
Yonks:	a very long time

(p) = Polari – denotes slang used by homosexuals, also theatricals

A MAP OF JETHRO'S LONDON